Gathering Pearls

Bedside Books
An imprint of American Book Publishing
American Book Publishing
P.O. Box 65624
Salt Lake City, UT 84165
www.american-book.com
Printed in the United States of America on acid-free paper.

Gathering Pearls

Designed by Melissa Montoya, design@american-book.com

Publisher's Note: *This is a work of fiction. Names, characters, places, and incidents either are the product of the author's imagination, or are used fictitiously, and any resemblance to actual persons, living or dead, events, or locales is entirely coincidental.*

ISBN 1-58982-189-0

Schuh, William, Gathering Pearls

Special Sales

These books are available at special discounts for bulk purchases. Special editions, including personalized covers, excerpts of existing books, and corporate imprints, can be created in large quantities for special needs. For more information e-mail orders@american-book.com, 801-486-8639.

Gathering Pearls

William Schuh

For Goomba, Buddy, Yummy, and Pumkin

But God chose the foolish things of the world to shame the wise; God chose the weak things of the world to shame the strong.

I Cor. 1:27

Prologue

The four friends sat in their corner booth at O'Malley's. The eatery—famous for its three-dollar pitchers of beer, freshly made hot potato chips, and the biggest cheeseburgers on the south side of Chicago—was a popular spot with the twenty-something crowd, many of whom attended the nearby University of Chicago medical school. Michael Hamilton and Lori Lange were wedged together on one side of the booth, with Greg Jameson and Linda Miller in their usual spots across from them.

"I'm really going to miss you two after tomorrow," said Linda as she wiped a spot of ketchup from her mouth and motioned to Greg that he had a similar spot on his chin.

"It's not like we'll never see each other again," Michael said. "We'll be at your wedding in two weeks."

Lori nodded her agreement. "I don't have to be in Birmingham until the end of June. And I'm going to be calling you at your mom's house every day to get all the wedding details lined up. What kind of maid of honor do you think I am?"

"I know," Linda said. "We'll see each other at the wedding and probably on vacations and stuff. But it'll never be like it is now. We won't be roommates anymore."

Lori and Linda had lived together all four years of Lori's medical education. At first, Lori didn't have much luck finding a fellow med student to room with when she first came to Chicago. Her southern accent quickly distinguished her as being from Alabama, and although the guys fell for her soft voice and curves, her female peers couldn't decide if she was a hick or a daddy's girl, hiding behind her fancy clothes and family money. They compromised and hated her for both.

Then, behind the cosmetics counter on one of her frequent trips to Marshall Field's, Lori found Linda. Linda had a knack for making her customers feel special. She would pamper each client as if she were the only person in the world. And that was just the kind of attention Lori needed after feeling snubbed by most of the student body.

In between talking about color palettes and smelling cologne samples, the conversations would drift to a more pertinent topic: men and what was wrong with them.

In the course of their conversations, Lori discovered that Linda was looking for a roommate. Lori decided the offer for a room—and the chance to spend some time with a woman who wasn't out to make her mark in the world of medicine—was something she couldn't pass up.

Linda was a refreshing break from the females Lori had encountered on campus—she was easy to talk to and she liked Lori just because she was a girl, not a doctor-to-be. And Linda discovered Lori wasn't shallow like so many of her other friends.

Linda had moved from the small-town scene in tiny Monroe, Wisconsin, where she had had enough of farms and boys with no ambition beyond graduating from high school and working at the local tire manufacturing plant. She wanted more. She wanted the good life. Meeting the right one of Lori's fellow students might just get her into that life.

Greg swallowed another bite. "Honey, we have to grow up sometime. We can't stay in school forever."

"You almost did, Greg," Michael teased. "If it hadn't been for Lori's help with microbiology, you'd still be a second year."

"Oh, shut up," Greg said good-naturedly. "Like you did any better with your interpretation of pathology slides. Besides, like I'm going to need micro when I'm a surgeon."

"That's right. All they're going to teach you is how to golf and whittle," joked Michael.

Michael and Greg had enjoyed ribbing each other ever since the first day they had met—during orientation week during their first year at med school—and their friendship had grown from a friendly rivalry over baseball teams. Greg talked about the Chicago Cubs and whether they'd be able to make the baseball playoffs. Michael was a White Sox fan who didn't hold back his feelings about the Northsiders and their poor history of pennant race performances.

Greg called the White Sox "minor leaguers," so he and Michael would argue and rib each other for what seemed like hours.

Before the end of orientation meetings they already were planning a day of skipping school to catch a game. The only argument was whether to go to Wrigley Field—home to the Cubs—or Comiskey Park, the home field of the Sox.

Michael and Greg soon moved in together, sharing a two-bedroom apartment three blocks from the University of Chicago College of Medicine. Posters of the Cubs and Sox alternated on their wall, one team's poster put up by one roommate and pulled down by the other. The poster wars continued until they finally agreed on displaying posters of the Bears and the Bulls and rooting for Chicago football and basketball.

Linda broke in. "Come on, you guys, I'm serious. This is our last night together like this. After you three graduate tomorrow our lives are going to be heading in different directions. It'll never be the same." Linda seemed more sentimental than the rest of the group. She was the one who'd pull out the camera at nearly every event and paste together the scrapbooks of their lives together.

"I think it's rather fitting. Tonight's almost like our first night out together," joked Michael.

"It doesn't look like much has changed," said Greg.

Lori and Michael were the first to become a couple, although on Lori's part, it was more of an "I'll go out with you if you'll stop bothering me" evening than a real date. For Michael, it was so much more. Lori had enchanted him since the first time he saw her, and on that first date he treated Lori like a princess.

Before the end of the first semester, Michael and Lori were an unexpected "item" on campus.

At the urging of Greg and Linda, who wanted their respective roommates to set them up with someone nice, Michael and Lori arranged a blind date. Michael and Lori introduced Linda and Greg; the four went on a double date to a movie. Afterward, Linda suggested stopping by a spot she liked—a neighborhood tavern that served great burgers and had booths for intimate conversations. O'Malley's quickly became "their" spot. They celebrated birthdays, finals weeks, Linda's promotion at the store, and any other special occasion by tipping back a few at O'Malley's.

Linda and Greg's relationship took off like a prairie fire and resulted in an engagement before the end of their third year. The four became inseparable and spent most of their free time together. Although she tended to feel left out when the other three discussed medical issues, being engaged to Greg was enough for Linda. Becoming a doctor's wife was as close to science as she ever wanted to get.

Michael and Lori planned to marry, too, even though they hadn't made it official yet. Tuition, books, rent, and traveling for residency interviews seemed to chew up all the money that could have otherwise gone for a brilliant- or marquis-cut diamond in a solitaire setting. It didn't matter much to them that they couldn't afford an engagement ring. They had each other, which is all they wanted anyway.

"I just want you all to know how special you have been to me," Linda said. She turned to Lori and said sincerely, "You've been like a sister."

Lori reached over and held Linda's hand. "We know, sweetie. I'm going to miss this too. Our all being together helped me make it through these last four years. It's like we're family."

Michael and Greg rolled their eyes at each other.

"I'm going to miss you too, schmoopy pie," said Greg with mock emotion.

"Give us a hug, snoogly bear," cried Michael.

The men laughed at their attacks on the ladies' sentiment, but Lori and Linda just rolled their eyes and ignored them; the two girls had grown accustomed to such behavior from the boys.

"Then I want you both to promise that we'll always stay close." Linda sat up straight for her statement. "That we'll stick together. That our families will do things together, and we'll always stay in touch."

"We will," said Michael, wrapping his arm around Lori's shoulders.

"Then promise," Linda persisted. "I want to hear you all say it." Linda wanted something tangible that she could sear into her latest scrapbook. "Or better yet. Here, sign this." Linda grabbed a napkin and wrote "Best Friends" on it; then passed it around the table. "This is going into my scrapbook."

Michael and Greg signed the small napkin, and then raised their right hands in the way they would the following morning for the Hippocratic oath. They mumbled without much enthusiasm, "We promise." Lori continued to hold Linda's hand.

Greg lowered his hand, picked up his glass of beer and raised it in the air. "To friends."

Michael and the ladies followed. "To best friends."

They were the best of friends. They felt their relationship would stay that way forever. They had no reason to think otherwise.

1

"Okay, let's see if any of you have learned anything from me in these last three weeks," Dr. Michael Hamilton quipped. He began placing X-ray films onto the lighted viewing box that filled the back wall of the radiology department viewing room in the basement of St. John's Hospital. The crowd of medical students huddled around their mentor in the ritualistic dance of wanting to be close enough to see what "the attending" was showing, but not so close as to cause them to be called on to read the film.

Michael finished displaying the poster-sized exposures and stood off to one side of the group. He ran his fingers through his graying hair, then took on the stance of a football coach on the sidelines. "Come on. This is the last day of class. Don't get lazy on me now. I'll give you all a hint. It's a CAT scan of the head."

The group chuckled at the blatantly obvious clue. Dr. Hamilton had always defied the attending's code of conduct by being pleasant and downright friendly to his students—a change of pace to which they had not been quite accustomed when they had first arrived at the Rockford campus of the University of Illinois College of Medicine. His bedside manner and seemingly endless stream of jokes led some of the students to believe that Michael had given up a career on stage to become an oncologist.

"I see we have no volunteers." He paced back and forth like Penn State's legendary football coach Joe Paterno. "That's the attitude I like to see in future doctors—indecisiveness mixed with cowardice." Michael changed his voice to sound like Gomer Pyle. "Gol-lee! I'm sorry, Mrs.

Jones, but I don't know what's wrong with your husband. He has some illness, but I'm afraid to look for it."

The students laughed. The ice had been broken. Tensions had eased.

"Come on, now. Harris, you try. Step on into the hot seat and see if you can get one answer right before the end of the year."

No longer afraid of making a wrong guess, Sean Harris stepped up to the films. He was a mediocre student, but at least he hadn't caught the virus of arrogance that seemed to have infected the other students.

"Well," he said, pointing to the images of the patient's brain. The brain was displayed in a series of slices going from the top of the skull down through the eyes, the sinuses, and ending with the base of the skull. "There's an abnormal signal here. Looks like a mass."

Sean's finger pointed to a large, gray, misshapen area in the left cerebral cortex.

"Very good, Mr. Harris. I'm glad you saw that. If that mass were any bigger it would have jumped off the film. Is that all you see?"

Sean checked the films again, looking disappointed. He had found the mass and had hoped that he would have been able to pass off his turn to the next victim. Dr. Hamilton was not about to let him off so easily.

"What else do you see? What is your patient trying to tell you?"

"It's an inanimate object, Dr. Hamilton. It can't tell me anything."

"You're partly right. One-half point for Mr. Harris." Michael made the sound of a bell. "One more point and you qualify for our lightning round worth up to seven dollars and a lifetime supply of Rice-A-Roni."

Sean smiled at the game show reference but knew that Michael was still expecting an answer. After staring at the film for a moment more, all he could come up with was a weak, "I don't know."

"Never has a more correct answer come from your lips." Michael turned to his young pupil. "It's perfectly all right to say that you don't know something. In fact, the further along you get in your training you will find yourself saying those words more often than not. Even the great William Osler, that giant of medical practice and education, felt that saying 'I don't know' was the finest thing a true physician could ever utter. But don't be satisfied with just saying that. Be sure to finish your 'I don't know' with a 'but I'm going to find out.'

"That's enough for you, Sean. I've picked on you enough."

Sean took a deep breath and stepped back into the lineup as Michael looked for another victim.

"Rowan. You look like you could use something to get your mind off of your upcoming board exams. How far away are those now?"

The entire class answered in unison, as if rehearsed. "Three weeks."

"Ah. Not enough time to get any real studying done, but just long enough to allow a true anxiety disorder to develop."

The class laughed, partly because of the humorous statement; mostly to ease their own tensions about the upcoming, career-determining exams.

"Look, guys," Michael began. "And gals," he continued, pointing to Leslie Howard, who always made it a point to make sure the group knew a woman was among them (although with her shape, any breathing male could tell she was a woman). "I know that none of what I've taught you in this last semester will be on your first board exams."

Medical licensing exams are giving in a series of three separate tests. The first takes place after the second year of medical school and covers only the basic medical sciences—anatomy, biochemistry, physiology, and the like—but before the end of the second year, future doctors take courses to prepare themselves for their years on the hospital wards. Such was the class taught by Michael.

"But medicine is much more than the basic sciences that you've had crammed down your throats over the last two years. So much more. Once those tests are over, you've got the rest of your careers to focus on what doctors really do. You aren't going to be scientists working in a lab. You will see and treat people. Take that scientific knowledge and apply it to affect people's lives. Hopefully, in a positive way, right, Harris?" A touch of wisdom, a touch of humor—that was Dr. Hamilton.

"So you're saying we should blow off studying for the next few weeks? I'm all for that," remarked Rowan.

"On the contrary, Mr. Rowan. I want you to bust yourselves open for this test. I would feel awful if any of you didn't pass your boards. I want you back here for the next two years so that I can really torture you during your oncology rotations. No more Dr. Nice Guy. But I must commend you all for your attempt at distracting me from the task at hand in order to avoid having to answer my questions. Rowan, I believe I was picking on you."

Rowan stepped forward to view the film. The large, gray mass had already been identified, so he knew that Michael wanted to hear something more than that in his attempt.

"What else do you see?"

Rowan remained silent.

"What does the surrounding tissue look like? What else is happening to the brain where the tumor is located—where it's not located?"

Rowan could see that the brain tissue on the side with the tumor did not appear the same as its mirror image in the other cerebral hemisphere. But saying that the brain "looks different" didn't seem like a scholarly statement. "There's some abnormal contours to the surface," said Rowan, pointing to the film.

"Or better yet, a lack of contours. In layman's terms, the brain is getting smushed. Very good, son." Michael let the young student off the hook. "As your colleague pointed out, the tumor is affecting the normal structure of the brain. See how the mass is putting pressure on the rest of the brain, forcing everything out of its normal position?" Michael acted like a weatherman in front of a map showing a cold front moving across the plains. "This sort of picture is usually seen in tumors that have grown rather rapidly. The brain didn't have a chance to make room for the invader, and, as a result, the entire left side of this poor man's head is affected."

"So how did this guy present himself?" asked Leslie.

"Good question, Miss Howard. Suppose you answer it."

Like every great teacher, Michael turned the question back on the presenter. It was an admirable technique—unless you were the one he was doing it to. Leslie let out a small sigh. "Um, he could have had a headache, I suppose."

"Too general. Anyone else?"

"Seizures?" contributed one.

"Paralysis?" said another.

"Both very good possibilities," answered Michael. "And all of those could be the presenting sign of a brain tumor. In fact, this poor man was seen in the emergency room last night because of difficulty speaking. His wife couldn't understand him. An affliction suffered by most husbands, based on my personal observation. Myself included. But in this fellow's case he slurred his words. Some speech was completely unintelligible. Thinking that he had suffered a stroke, the admitting physician ordered a CAT scan. The tumor was found, and that's how I got involved in the case."

"How'd he take the news?" asked one of the students. "About having a brain tumor."

"Haven't told him yet. I met with him this morning. Talked with him as best as he was able and examined him. He has some interesting physical findings that my fourth-year student better be able to pick up on when he sees him this afternoon. But I told the man and his wife that I was going to review all his films and get back up to his room later today."

"You knew he had a tumor when you met him this morning?" asked Rowan.

"Yes, of course I did."

"I thought doctors were supposed to tell their patients everything. Why didn't you tell him the news?"

Michael knew when a golden teaching opportunity presented itself. He could usually see them coming. "Good question. Why would I keep information like that to myself?"

The students all backed away from Rowan, isolating him and making him more likely to be called on to answer his own question.

"Step up here, Mr. Rowan." Michael pulled a deck of playing cards out from the side pocket of his lab coat. "I usually keep these here to perform card tricks for my younger patients, but I think you'll qualify for today."

Michael began to shuffle the deck like a Las Vegas dealer. His quick hands and ability to fan out the deck led the students to believe the stories they'd heard about Michael; how he would perform magic tricks and sometimes put on small shows for the hospitalized children at St. John's. A smile and a laugh could take their young minds off their terrible illnesses. "A simple demonstration," began Michael, as he counted out twenty-one cards, "but one, I think, will make my point." He fanned out the twenty-one cards and held them out to Rowan. "Pick a card, any card."

Rowan looked around the room, as if he'd get some sense as to which card to pick or avoid. Selecting a card, Rowan pulled it close to his chest, guaranteeing that Michael would not be able to see it.

"Take a good look at it. Show it to the others if you wish. I like to have witnesses to my greatness." Michael turned away, giving Rowan the opportunity to reveal the six of hearts to his fellow students. "As medical students, I'm sure you have the powers of memorization necessary to remember what card you've selected. Now put the card back into the deck for me." Michael took the restored deck and began to shuffle. "What I didn't tell you is that these are not ordinary cards. I picked them up on a trip to central Africa."

"Is that why they have a picture of Florida on them?" asked Rowan, eliciting a chuckle from the class.

"Quiet. No critics allowed here. Just go along with the illusion. Now as I was saying, these cards had a spell placed on them that would allow them to speak to whoever had touched them. That means both you and me." Michael dealt the cards out, face down, and added a mystical quality to his voice. "These cards will talk to you and to me, and thus will reveal the identity of the card you have selected." Michael finished dealing the cards into seven piles of three cards each. "Now, let's see what the cards have to say. Rowan, pick three piles of cards, please."

Rowan looked over the assortment, as if trying to figure out the trick. The stacks all looked the same. The cards all seemed to be facing the same direction. No pattern on the cards indicated that Michael was working with a marked deck. Things were on the up and up. At least as far as he could tell, knowing Dr. Hamilton. "Fine. These three," he said, pointing to sets nearest to Michael.

Michael pulled those stacks away. "The cards tell me that those you've selected can be discarded." Michael put those piles off to one side. "Pick another two stacks."

Rowan pointed to the outside pairs.

Michael removed the other two sets. "The cards seem to feel that you wanted to keep your selections." Michael moved the remaining piles next to each other. "Pick one more."

Rowan did as he was told, and Michael removed the pile not selected. The one remaining set of three cards was spread out in a line. "Pick one," he told his victim.

Rowan selected a card, which Michael then removed. "The cards have narrowed themselves down to these two. Your job is to listen to them and select one final card."

Rowan pointed to one in a very offhanded fashion, unimpressed with the trick. Michael removed the opposing card.

"The cards have spoken," said Michael as he turned over the remaining card revealing the six of hearts.

"How'd you do that?" asked the usually silent Harris.

"It's a trick. The cards must have been rigged someway," retorted Rowan, not wanting to reveal that he didn't quite catch the secret or any of Michael's sleight of hand.

"Magicians never reveal their secrets," Michael responded, raising his eyebrows as he returned all the cards into one stack and began shuffling them. "But amazing you with my talents was not my intention. Who can tell me why I did this?"

Leslie loved the opportunity to show up her male counterparts. Her higher grades and test scores (as well as being the star of their fantasies) weren't always enough to satisfy her desire to prove herself to the group. "It's obvious that you knew which card it was the whole time."

"Very good, Miss Howard. Continue if you will."

"Knowing where the card was, you just slowly removed all the other cards. If Rowan picked the stack with it, you kept that pile. If he selected stacks without it, you pulled them off."

"A+ for the lady. Good powers of deduction. That should carry you far, as if it hasn't already."

Leslie smiled and looked around the room, making sure all the others knew *she* was right—and they were not.

"But as for the secret behind how I knew where the card was, I'll keep that to myself for now. So how does this apply to our poor patient?"

"Are you going to cure him with a card trick?" asked Glen Brown. His was a voice seldom heard, and for good reason.

"Nice guess, Glen. Have you thought about truck-driving school? No. No magic trick is going to help this poor gentleman. And no, I'm not going to have the diagnosis written on a card and have him select it from the deck." Michael returned to his game-show host voice. "Too bad! You picked brain tumor with a future of radiation and chemotherapy. You *just missed* the card with 'Trip to Hawaii with a bikini model.' Better luck next time on Select Your Fate."

As quickly as he could turn on his humor mode, Michael returned to his role as medical educator. "The point here is that, yes, I knew where the card was the whole time. I could have just as easily pointed it out right at the beginning. You would have seen me find the card, and that would have been that. But instead, I set you up to follow a different scenario. Of course, cards cannot talk to us. I don't have any true magical powers. But if you're honest with yourself, you'll admit that for a brief moment you believed I was having that card find its way into the one remaining place."

The class all nodded in agreement.

"That's the point. It's all in your presentation. Right now I know the diagnosis of our patient. I could walk right up and tell him. He'd know the truth, and the information would have been exchanged. Is that how it should be done? Should I say, 'Mr. Jones, I'm Dr. Hamilton. You have a brain tumor. You might want to send out your Christmas cards a little early this year'? No. That's not doing him any favors, and news presented like that may cause him to get depressed, give up on himself, and may even affect whether or not he picks certain treatment options that could bring him some benefit."

"So you lie to him," said Rowan.

"No, Mr. Rowan, never lie to your patients. Just give them the truth in a way that will not hurt them. Like in this case. No one wants to get bad news from a stranger. That's what I was when I met this gentleman this morning. Instead, I talked with him. Held his hand. Told him the possible things he and his wife were facing. Then I promised to be back.

"Right now they are having time alone with each other to think about what I've told them. When I come back later as I promised, they will see that I'm a man of my word; that I can be trusted. Then I'll tell them what we truly know—that there's a brain tumor in his head. We don't know what kind it is; if it's malignant or not. We don't know whether or not it will respond to treatments. But I'll tell them that whatever it is, we will find out together. That they won't go through this alone. I'll be with them each step of the way. I'll tell them whatever I find out as I discover it, and I'll include them in all decisions. I won't be the guy who brought them bad news; they'll see me as the one who's going to help them during this difficult time. I'm their friend, their advocate, their doctor.

"That, my pupils, is how you talk to patients. That's how you gain their trust. Without that you may as well take all of your knowledge and go work in a lab somewhere. Let this lesson be your clinical pearl for the day. Take that information and store it away like the treasure it is. You'll need it someday."

The class was impressed. How a man who joked around more than any other professor could hold the keys to their future still fell beyond their understanding.

Michael looked at his watch. "I'll get off my soapbox now. I think we've run over our time."

The class let out a disappointed groan, partly due to their desire to learn more from Michael, partly due to their realization that after class, only books and studying were waiting for them back in their apartments.

"Go on now. I've got work to do. I really have had fun teaching you these last few weeks. Enjoy your exams and the rest of your summer break. I hope to see all of you next fall as you begin your third year. Bring some of what I taught back with you. You'll need it."

The class all lined up to shake Michael's hand as they slowly filtered out into the hallway. Michael pulled the films off the wall and slid them into the protective jacket before handing the file back to the file room staff for storage.

Michael walked out into the hallway behind his class. Their cheerful voices overshadowed his own thoughts as he pondered the job he had before himself. He had delivered bad news to countless people. He had even gotten pretty good at it over the years. But that didn't make it any easier.

Each family conference and discussion over the probable diagnosis always brought him back to the most difficult one he had ever faced—the time he had to tell his own father that he was dying of pancreatic cancer. His father's fears and anxiety built with each passing day of awaiting the results of his tests. Michael grew angry at the fact that his father's doctor hadn't even broken the news. How could Dr. Schwartz have been so callous; so heartless? Let the man sit in pain for three days wondering what was wrong with him.

Michael often relived that day he sat down on his father's hospital bed. He was only a medical student at the time. No one had taught him how to approach patients. Michael hadn't heard any talks from his teachers like the one he had just given to his own students. All he knew was that his father was going to die. And soon. And no one had bothered to tell Dad yet. The word "cancer" fell from Michael's parched mouth as if it were a bomb. Michael never forgot the look on his father's face. The change of expression. The way the life drained out of it with the news. Being a doctor himself, Michael's father knew what the diagnosis meant. His father suspected the diagnosis all along. But Michael was the one who said the words. The words that now he repeated on a daily basis. And each time he did, when he looked into the eyes of his new patients, he'd see his father.

As if the situation with his father hadn't been bad enough, Michael had caught hell for breaking protocol and reading his father's chart without written consent. But he didn't care about proper procedure. He cared about his dad. Besides, his dad wanted to know what was wrong. He *needed* to know. He deserved the truth, and was grateful to Michael for getting it.

Maybe that's why Michael was so good at telling patients about their medical conditions. Because he not only hated the state of cancer, he hated that each person to whom he told bad news was someone's father. Or mother. He'd vowed never to let someone find out in a cold, uncaring way. Never. But that professional excellence had come with a price.

Michael turned down a hallway, leaving his class behind. As an oncologist who needed to be near the cancer center and radiation treatment facility, Michael had been given an office in the hospital. Sure, it had been part of his list of demands for transferring up to Rockford from his research position at the University of Alabama at Birmingham, but he needed an office in the hospital so he wouldn't have to commute from a clinic each day for rounds. He also "needed" (and received) a country club membership, full professorship with the University of Illinois, and a company car, along with a salary never before seen by other hospital staff members. He still wasn't sure if the move was worth it.

"You have some messages," said Sally, his nurse, as Michael entered his office.

"Any important ones?"

"I've handled most of them. But I'm going to let you take care of the ones from your mother."

Michael let out his breath in a way that sounded more like a bear growling. A disgusted bear. "Fine. What did she want?"

"Which time? She called five times. I think she fell again last night."

"I wouldn't be surprised."

"You know, you've got to do something with her or she's going to wear you out."

Michael gave Sally a "thanks for your concern but butt out" look, grabbed the message slips from her hand, and leafed through them. Mom. Mom. Mom. Prescription refill request. Mom. Mom.

Michael put the five slips from his mother into his coat pocket and handed the refill request back to Sally. "Give Gladys one month's worth. No more after that. I'm not going to supply codeine to that woman any longer."

Michael went into his office and sat down at his desk. Stacks of papers, books, and student evaluation forms left only a few square inches of workspace. Michael tossed his mother's messages onto the desk to cover the remaining walnut laminate. He knew he could only put off calling her for a short while, but he planned to stretch that time out as long as he could.

He reached for his coffee pot on the corner table of his office. It had taken several weeks of driving around town after he first arrived in Rockford before he found a Logli supermarket that stocked coffee flavored with chicory. He had grown accustomed to the southern taste during his glory years in Birmingham. In Alabama, Michael had enjoyed a full professor status that came with his three research grants and a lab with seven graduate students. Four published articles a year. He was the envy of his field. He had it good. He had it no longer.

Mom had done pretty well for the first five years after Dad had gone. They had bought their home before Michael was born, and lived there for close to fifty years. She didn't want to move out, even though it was too much for her. Still, she had managed. She was getting close to eighty now. Michael had hired local people to mow the lawn, clean the house, and even check on her from time to time. All from the comforts of his hillside home in Vestavia Hills, Alabama. But that had eventually become too far away. She needed more care. And Michael had promised his father that he would look after his favorite girl. Deathbed promises can be hard to go back on.

So with the final straw being dropped on Michael's camel's back—a kitchen fire that left $15,000 damage—Michael agreed to move back home. Well, almost home. Marengo, Michael's small hometown, was fifteen miles from his present Rockford location. He lived close enough to stop by his mother's nearly every day; Rockford was the town closest to his mother where he could find work with a medical school and still have a practice that would fit his area of expertise.

It wasn't what he wanted or what his wife, Lori, wanted. But it was the best he could come up with. The arrangement would keep his mother in her home, and Michael running back and forth all day long. And all it cost him was a major disruption in his career.

He resented her for it.

The best part about his new job was the teaching. That was the one criterion he demanded in order to make the move north. Michael wanted to interact with students, mold their minds, and watch the physician in them bubble to the surface. But the academic year was over now. The students had completed their year, and all he had to face was several months of diseased patients until the students returned in the fall. The best part of his job had been taken away for three months.

Sometimes he just wanted to stick his mother in a nursing home and be done with it. Dump her off with a packed suitcase and keep on driving south until the dirt turned orange. But he would always see his father's picture on his shelf in the office, and guilt would set in. As much as he resented his mother for all the years she failed to support his career choices and for messing up his professional life, Michael just couldn't do that to her, and he wouldn't do it to his dad's memory. He often felt that the wrong parent had died. Being between a rock and a hard place seemed like a better place to be than where he was right now.

Michael thought about the call he'd have to make. The concern he'd have to put into his voice. The compassion he'd have to feign. He put the messages down. He'd put the call off for a little while longer. He had a patient upstairs he needed to talk to. Telling a man that he had an incurable brain tumor seemed like an easier task to handle. And one he'd rather face right now.

2

Will Jameson climbed out of his mother's car pulling his swim bag after himself. The large, nylon bag was stuffed with all the essentials the ten-year-old would need for his morning swim meet. The towels, goggles, and sunscreen that filled the compartment were kept company by boxes of snacks to feed Will and his younger brother, Paul.

"Help Paul out of the car, sweetie," said Linda from the comfort of the front seat.

"I will."

Paul worked his way across the suede seats and got out on the same side of the car as Will.

"Where's my drink?" asked Paul, handing his towel to Will.

"Oh, I forgot about the cooler." Linda climbed out of the car and opened the trunk to remove the cooler. "Here, I'll bring this for you."

Linda left the car running in the drive-up lane of the Alpine Valley Swim Club and helped her children make their way into the clubhouse.

The Alpine Valley Swim Club, home of the Dolphin swim team, was a private club founded for and run by families not interested enough in golf to join a country club. Lawyers, doctors, software designers filled the roster. They had big money and a need to spend it. The Alpine Valley Swim Club gave them that chance.

The club boasted five pools: a kiddie pool completely fenced in, a two-foot-deep pool for younger swimmers, a lap pool, a general swimming pool, and a diving pool with three- and ten-meter boards. Large deck areas with lounge chairs surrounded all the pools for the women who wanted to be seen in their swimsuits but didn't want to get wet. The clubhouse had spacious, carpeted locker rooms; a video arcade; snack bar and formal restaurant; and a lounge with a wide-screen television equipped with a DVD player and a full bar. On weekend evenings, valet parking completed the picture. Having a swim team gave many parents the opportunity to have someone else watch their kids for three hours a day. The swim meets helped satisfy the competitive nature of the parents; the kids just had fun.

Linda and her children made their way out onto the pool deck. Will walked behind his mother while Paul tagged behind Will, dragging his towel along the wet pavement. Other swimmers had already arrived for the meet and had begun to set up their camp area for the day.

Will's coach, Don Thurston, was walking alongside the deck. "Good morning, guys," he said to Will and Paul. Linda walked past him without saying a word.

"And good morning to you, too, Mrs. Jameson," Don called out. "Go sit down for a while, guys. I'll be calling you for warm-ups soon."

Paul and Will followed their mother to a shady spot on the deck.

"You kids stay here. Mommy has a headache. I'm going to go lie down for a while in the clubhouse." Linda pulled her sunglasses over her bloodshot eyes and left her children for the quiet confines of the air-conditioned lounge.

Don, who coached the kids during his summers off from college, went back to work setting up the pool for the meet along with his part-time assistant and full-time girlfriend, Rachel.

"How did wonderful kids like that end up with such shits for parents?" asked Rachel as she watched the scene between Linda and the boys.

"Beats me," replied Don. "I guess that's why I like to keep an eye on them all the time."

"Well, you better not ever treat our kids the way their parents treat them or I'll have to pound on you."

Don gave Rachel a surprised look. "So you've got us married and having kids, do you?"

"Oh, please. You know you want to."

"Sure, I'll have kids with you, but I never said anything about marrying you." Don knew that his statement would cost him. He quickly jumped away, but not in time to escape the towel Rachel snapped at him.

Rachel and Don finished readying the pool. They put in the lane lines, starting blocks, timing pads, bullpen benches, and the judge's table. They were finishing as the rest of the swimmers arrived in their baggy sweats, carrying their bags and coolers with them.

An all-day swim meet required as much packing as a camping trip. Sleeping bags for resting. Game Boys for entertainment during the hours that may pass between events for some swimmers. Trading cards. Cans of Pringles and bags of chips. The healthy snacks—carrots, apples—tended to stay in the coolers. The meets were just as much a social gathering for the kids as they were for the parents.

Don got the team into the water for warm-ups. Will and Paul did their laps together, circling up and down the lane performing freestyle, breast, back, and butterfly strokes. After finishing, they got out and toweled off. Will took Paul over to their towels, which they had laid out to catch the sun. Will opened up a small box of cereal and a juice box for his little brother. He knew that Paul would need some breakfast before the meet. Will sat down next to him and opened up a box of granola bars. Breakfast out of a box wasn't the best way to begin the day, but it was all Will knew how to fix. He rarely got any help in the morning. Mom would only fix coffee, and Will didn't like to drink that.

"Hi, Will," said a soft voice. "Can I sit with you?"

Will looked up to see Erin Block standing next to him. He had to squint to block the sun that shone past her.

"Hey, Ariel!" Paul said. Erin had long red hair that reached down to the small of her back. That, along with being the fastest girl on the team, earned her a team nickname—that of the Little Mermaid.

"Hi, squirt," said Erin.

"Yeah, we've got room. Move over, Paul." Will liked Erin. She showed him attention. She liked him for no particular reason. Sometimes that's the best way. Will shared his granola bars with her, and she brought out some sliced oranges from her own bag. The three sat together amid the din of activity from other swimmers as if the rest of the world didn't exist. To them, it didn't.

"Can you come over after the meet?" Erin asked. "My mom and dad will take us to the movies."

"I'll have to ask my mom," replied Will. "I don't think we're doing anything this afternoon at my house." Will knew that he'd have the whole house to himself all day. It got very lonely having wealthy parents.

"Is she here yet?" asked Erin, looking around the crowd.

"Yeah," replied Will. "She's taking a nap inside."

Don's booming voice interrupted everyone's conversations. "Let's go, swimmers. I need you all right now. Line up and give me your attention."

Game Boys were dropped. Sports drink bottles were closed and left behind. The kids all gathered around their coach for the last-minute pep talk and the team cheer. Don realized many years ago that no matter what he said to inspire their best effort, nothing got his team more revved up for the meet than the opportunity to yell their little heads off. And the "Dolphins Rock" cheer let them do just that. The kids all started chanting in their loudest voices:

> Give a yell,
> Give a shout,
> Let me tell you what it's all about!
> Give a scream,
> Give a cheer,
> Who's the team of the year?
> Look out now,
> Get out of our way!
> The Dolphins are here to stay!
> Dolphins swim,
> Dolphins win,
> The Dolphins rock!

Following their burst of energy, all the kids went back to their places and waited for the meet to start.

The poolside filled with parents and the air filled with the scent of sunscreen and lattes. Morning newspapers and paperback novels were in various stages of completion by those who realized they might have to wait hours between their children's events during the five- to six-hour meet. Cell phones were not banned at poolside, which greatly improved adult attendance.

Following the cheers by the respective teams and the singing of the national anthem, the events began. Parents who had volunteered to time the events were given stopwatches and clipboards. Small cards with each swimmer's name and the event being run were stacked on the judges' table. Prior to each race, the coaches picked up the cards. The participants for that event were brought to the bull pen area and lined up in the order they would appear on the blocks. The cards were passed to the timers, who then would record each swimmer's time for that event. Don's hours of preparation the night before made the whole scene work smoothly. Organized chaos, he liked to call it.

Because of the sheer number of swimmers in Paul's age bracket, there were usually five or six heats of each event. But through it all, Will kept an eye on his little brother and knew when Paul would be standing on the blocks. Paul's little skinny body was poised on the platform, waiting for the starting horn to release him. Will made sure Paul could see him before the start. And when Paul dove into the water for his attempt at swimming twenty-five meters, Will shouted out for him as he swam the entire length of the pool. Will knew that he would be the only family member cheering for the little boy, and he wanted Paul to hear him.

Paul finished third in his heat. His time was not good enough to land him a ribbon, and Will knew it. But Will wrapped his arms around Paul and congratulated him as if he just had swum the Channel. Paul was all smiles. He had finished. That's all he really cared about.

Will's first event came later: the fifty-meter freestyle. Paul watched his brother walk from the bull pen to the blocks. He was proud of his brother; so was the crowd. The coach and the team all chanted Will's name. Even some of the high-school swimmers cheered. Will held the team record in three events for his age group. Will's consistency added valuable points to the team's score at each meet, and that had helped the Dolphins win four meets so far this season.

Will climbed up onto the blocks as he scanned the crowd for his mom's face. Linda had risen from her nap long enough to pull out her video recorder. Will couldn't find his dad. He pulled his swim goggles down. The goggles did an excellent job of keeping the pool water out of his eyes. But they couldn't do anything about the water his eyes produced on their own. Just once, he thought. Just once, why couldn't he come to see me?

The horn sounded, and Will hit the water. He broke the surface of the pool and went into his freestyle stroke. Pulling steadily through the water he quickly came out in front of the other swimmers. He pulled and kicked his way down the lane before flipping at the wall to return. Will held the lead for the whole fifty meters and finished three body lengths ahead of the second-place swimmer. Will had done it again, and the team loved it. So did the crowd.

The team greeted Will with cheers and slaps on the back as he pulled himself out of the water. Linda ran up to him. "Honey, you did great. I got the whole thing on tape so we can show your father."

"Thanks, Mom."

"Go get something to drink and rest up. I'll be back to see your next event." Linda walked off to her resting place.

Erin stood at the end of the pool. "Here's your towel," she said, handing it to Will. "Good race."

"Thanks." The two went back to their blankets. Paul ran off to play with some of his friends on the playground, leaving the two alone.

The pair sat, talked, and played cards while taking turns waiting for their events. The morning drifted by, alternating between times of silence and uproar. Will finished second in three of his events, which was something new for him. He didn't take much notice of it, but Don did.

"All right, guys. Last event." Don brought together his freestyle relay team. "You guys have been doing great today. I hope you saved enough of your strength for this last one."

"Will used his up smooching," said Randy, one of the other swimmers.

"Shut up, Randy. I could beat you any day."

"That's enough, both of you," Don scolded. "Save that energy for the pool. I want clean exchanges. No one leaves the blocks early. We've had one disqualification already today, and we need these points if we're going to win today. All right?"

The boys nodded in unison. Don dismissed them to get into their positions, but he held Will back. Don had an odd feeling and needed to address it. "I have noticed that you have been slowing down today, Will. You doing okay?"

Will nodded. "Yeah. I think I'm just a little tired."

"Okay, if that's all. You let me know if there's anything else."

Will hurried to catch up with his teammates. Watching him walk away, Don noticed a slight limp to Will's gait that had never been there before.

Being the anchor swimmer, Will lined up last in line. The other teams took their positions, and Will took one last look around the crowd before placing his goggles on. He let out a sigh of disappointment.

The horn sounded and Randy hit the water. The crowd roared as the swimmers slid through the water. Randy reached the far end of the pool first. A flip turn, and he was on his way back. Tom, the next swimmer in line, stood in position, waiting for Randy to touch the wall. A quick exchange and Tom was away. Randy climbed out of the water. "I got us the lead. Don't blow it, Jameson."

Will glared at Randy. "Don't worry about me. I can handle it."

Tom completed his lap, handing the race over to Brian. Tom had lost a little time, but the Dolphins were still in front. Brian was definitely the weakest of the four swimmers, but did his best. Will's team was neck-and-neck with the visiting Belvidere Marlins. Will knew what he needed to do, but his right leg was sore, and more so than it had been all day. Just a muscle cramp, he told himself as he shook his leg.

Will watched his teammate touch the wall, and Will dove in.

Kicking furiously, Will started to pull with his arms. He felt good and strong. The water flowed past him as he raced down the lane. Out of the corner of his eye, Will saw the swimmer in the lane next to his. Usually, Will was out in front by now. Instead, he could see the top of his opponent's head slightly ahead of his own. Will pulled with all his might, but instead of taking four strokes per breath he now was taking two. The wind had fallen from his sails; Will was tiring.

He did his flip turn to head for home. Will had dropped to third place as he kicked with all the energy he had. He was less concerned about winning now than he was about finishing. Will's arms cramped up and his legs went tight. He could hear the crowd yelling for him to pick it up. He was trying, but his body wasn't cooperating.

Now Will was breathing with each stroke, something beginners do. He put the strength he had left into the final ten meters. When he finally touched the wall his arms gave out, and Will sank to the bottom of the pool in pure exhaustion. Will placed his feet on the bottom of the pool and stood up. He had come in fourth, and the rest of the team let him hear their disappointment.

Something was wrong. Will knew that now. He had never before become so tired while swimming. Sure, on some mornings when Don pushed the team and he swam five hundred meters at a time, Will would get a little burned out. But not like this. Will waited for one of the timers to reach a hand down and take Will's hand to help him out of the water.

Will limped past his teammates and the jeers they tossed at him. He sat down on his towel and took a moment to catch his breath.

"You all right, buddy?" Don had arrived to check out his favorite swimmer. "I've never seen you dogging it like you just did."

Between breaths Will gasped, "I just got really tired, that's all. I think I'm going to be okay."

Don rubbed Will's head. "Okay. But you just sit here and rest a bit. I'll check back on you later."

Will's events were done and he was glad of it. He didn't want to watch any more of the meet. He'd have to miss Erin's race. He hoped that she'd understand.

Will was sitting in a shady spot by the time Paul found his way back from the swings.

"Did we win?" he asked, not really caring about the outcome.

"I think so. They haven't announced the final results yet."

The meet was ending, and the other swimmers were packing up their stuff. Parents were carrying bags of gear and pushing strollers as their children walked empty-handed toward the clubhouse. Will was not going to get that kind of help.

"Hey, Paul. Would you mind getting our stuff? I want to sit for a minute longer."

Paul scampered off and returned a few minutes later, dragging the bags. He'd obviously pulled them through every puddle on the deck on his way back to Will's spot. Will was too tired to care, though he had at least caught his breath.

"Thanks, man. I'll carry things from here."

The boys walked into the clubhouse and found Linda, who was still sleeping.

"Mom, wake up." Paul shook his mother's arm until Linda opened her eyes.

"Is the meet over already?" Linda looked around the room trying to get reoriented.

"Yeah. We're hungry. Can we go out to lunch?" asked Will.

"Sure, sweetie. I don't know what your father's doing for lunch, so we'll just go without him." Linda checked her cell phone to see if she had any messages from Greg. There weren't any. "Grab your stuff and let's go." Linda rose from the chair and helped Paul gather up his gear, which seemed to continually drop from his arms.

The three walked out to Linda's car and loaded the gear into the trunk of the green Mercedes. As they climbed into their seats, Don approached the vehicle and tapped on Linda's window until she rolled it down—just far enough so she could hear him. The cold air from the car's interior hit him in the face as he bent down to speak to the boys' mother.

"You know," Don said, as if she weren't ignoring him, "I am a little concerned about Will. He was really tired today."

"He just had an off day."

"It's not just that. He seemed to have a sore leg, too. Is everything okay?"

"He'll be fine. I'll have his father take a look at him later. But thanks for noticing." She cut Don off. "I'll see you on Monday for their practice."

As Don watched her drive away, he was overcome with sadness for the Jameson boys. Will and Paul were such great kids, something their mother clearly didn't see. She had loaded them into the backseat of her car like so many packages.

Don shook his head as he watched the car pull out onto the road.

3

Greg liked to play The Doors in the O.R. He played the music loud. The heavy bass and long solos kept his head bobbing during otherwise routine hernia repairs. He especially liked to drum with retractors on his patients during "L.A. Woman." His own boom box system with four speakers lined the far side of the tile-lined room. CDs were stacked alongside— Aerosmith's *Toys in the Attic*, The Who's *Who's Next*, and Led Zeppelin's *BBC Sessions*. He didn't much care for the crap from the '80s, although he did occasionally enjoy some Green Day. Greg's desk was covered in electronic equipment that could rival any found in a fraternity house. He still lived in those days. Graying hair can't stop a man from acting juvenile, and Greg Jameson proved that fact daily.

Maybe he was trying to hold onto his youth. Maybe he wanted to show off to the young nursing staff that he was still a stud. Or maybe he just liked the music. The St. John's rumor mill had many theories. Gossip at the hospital had been raised to an art form. And Greg had never been excluded from its clutches.

But to those who thought they knew him best, Greg was just a big kid hiding behind a surgical mask. The Greg they knew was fun-loving and always joking around, although usually not at the most appropriate time or place. But at least he wasn't a stuffed shirt. Rules were for other people. The O.R. was laid back. He never wore a tie. Everyone called him by his first name. He'd do anything to get the nuns' panties in a bunch, even though he was known to say that they probably all wore thongs anyway.

A mediocre surgeon would have been dismissed by the nuns who served on the hospital board, but Greg was well above mediocre. The problem was, he knew it. No one else had his level of production. In the years since joining the St. John's group, Greg had racked up the highest level of income of any of the general surgeons. He never turned down a case. He'd be at the hospital whenever he was needed—at two o'clock in the morning, whether it was a weekend, holiday, or his sons' birthdays; whether or not he was on call. His patients loved him. The accountants loved him. His family barely knew him.

"Pull that back a little. I can't see," Greg directed his assistant. The retractor pulled on the incision and exposed the underlying abdominal cavity. Greg poked his finger into the opening of his nineteen-year-old patient in order to widen an area large enough to find the inflamed appendix. "Doubt this is the first time she's been poked," Greg joked to his male assistant. Julie McMahon, his scrub nurse, just rolled her eyes.

Greg had made a few crude remarks earlier about his patient. Of course, while she was awake Greg had been the poster child for caring and compassionate physicians everywhere. He held his patient's hand and spoke calmly to her and her mother. Greg explained the nature of appendicitis and the risks of not proceeding with surgery. The potential complications that can arise during the procedure and post-op were minimized as Greg sang of his success rate. He was good at talking smoothly. Silver-tongued, he liked to call it. "My mouth can do amazing things," he'd say. Julie knew he wasn't just talking about his bedside manner.

The young cheerleader from Rock Valley College had come down with nausea and belly cramps that her school medical center initially called a touch of the flu. But after one full day of vomiting and the development of lower abdominal pain, she was referred to St. John's emergency room. Greg had just completed his rounds when he got the page to stop by the E.R. before leaving for the morning.

Shelly was a simple, textbook case. She had no previous health problems, no allergies, and her pregnancy test was negative. He could have her in and out of surgery in twenty minutes. Greg was going to be late for Will's swim meet anyway, so why not get in a little overtime production?

The smooth talk stopped once the patient was prepped and sedated. Unconscious patients can't hear what goes on in the O.R. and, for the most part, they wouldn't want to. Greg could revert to his baser nature. The music would be turned up. The language would devolve. The silver tongue would become tarnished. The O.R. would begin to resemble a fraternity house bar. At least no one was drunk.

Greg often would take the opportunity of having an unclothed patient lying before him to get in a few comments and off-color jokes. Julie once walked in on a breast biopsy case where Greg was speaking in a high voice, holding each of the patient's breasts, having them talk like puppets to the rest of the staff, describing their anguish with the upcoming surgery. Julie cleared her throat just as Greg had one breast shriek, "Oh, no, get that scalpel away from me." She knew that her anatomy was often the topic of discussion, and she left no room for conjecture as to her disapproval.

"So I was pulling my last call as a medical student. Forceps, please," Greg spoke to his assistant as he conducted his surgery. He loved to hear himself talk. His hands and mouth would move as if in their own separate worlds—like a man talking to his neighbor while fixing a crack in the driveway or grilling chicken in the backyard. "When good old John Walker came in. His name fit him. Both black and red. Come to think of it, I'm not so sure that was his real name. But that's what we called him." Greg began clamping off bleeding vessels and probing deeper into Shelly's belly. "I must have admitted that drunk fifty times during that year, all for acute alcohol intoxication. Seeing as we were a VA hospital and the slob had been honorably discharged, we couldn't send him away. The only times we didn't deal with that waste of skin was when the cops picked him up and he'd take a swing at one of them. Either on the medical ward or in the police station, that man would sleep it off at the taxpayer's expense. Suction here." Greg pointed to a bleeding vein.

"Well, I was sick of him, as was the rest of the nursing staff. He was a belligerent cuss. He was always shouting at the nurses and demanding anything he wanted. Like the world owed him for his serving in WWII as a cook in Guam. The resident refused to see the guy. So did the intern, if that tells you anything more you need to know. Not to be outdone—scissors please—I vowed to get rid of the guy too."

"What'd you do?" asked Rob, his assistant.

"I figured anyone who would drink himself that sick must have a desire to end his life. Why else would any sane person drink that much? Cut." Greg finished tying off a bleeding vessel and wanted the ends of the sutures trimmed. "So I get the intern doing the psych rotation on the phone. I explained that I had a guy who continued to ingest lethal doses of various substances despite numerous admissions. We didn't know what else to do with the guy, so perhaps a visit on the locked psych ward might help get to the bottom of his mental health problem. I mentioned that the patient also had a little to drink, which was the truth. Well, the sap bought my story. We loaded up ol' Johnny boy and took him over to the locked ward. Buff 'em and turf 'em." Greg laughed with pride. "I got to finish my call with some sleep and never had to deal with the son of a bitch again.

"And to make things even better, I heard that John ended up causing more problems on that ward than ever. Once he woke up and figured out where he was, he took a swing at the intern and busted up some furniture. They ended up sedating the guy, and the intern who accepted him got reprimanded for accepting an unsuitable candidate without consulting the attending."

The rest of the room laughed along with Greg. He usually regaled the crowd with stories of his past. They were never sure which ones were true, if any, but the stories at least passed the time.

"Found it," proclaimed Greg, as he pulled up the swollen appendix. "Mother, look at. Another two hours and this sucker would've popped." Greg clamped off the appendix at the base near the colon. A second clamp was placed on the wall of the colon in normal, healthy tissue. "Scissors."

Greg cut across the base and removed the diseased finger-like stick of tissue. Pulling it from Shelly's abdomen, Greg looked for his specimen tray to place the appendix. "Julie, where's my tray?"

"Oh, it's over on the prep table. I'll get it."

Greg sighed in disgust that a moment of his precious time had been stolen from him. "Come on, sweetie. Move that cute little ass of yours."

Julie paused for a moment, gritted her teeth, and proceeded to fetch the tray like the good, obedient servant she was.

Greg dropped the appendix into the metal tray, and then turned his attention back to his patient. Dissolvable gut sutures closed the incision made in the colon where the appendix had been attached. Pouring saline into the open incision, he irrigated the wound several times, each time removing the fluid with his suction wand. When he was sure that all of the possible contaminants from the nearly ruptured appendix had been expunged, Greg closed the incision.

Another set of dissolvable sutures closed the deep tissue layers of fascia and muscle. Four sutures brought the subcutaneous layer together; then he finished by placing five stainless steel staples across the skin. Nice and neat and it only took twenty-three minutes, as Greg looked at the clock. As

Shelly was young and fully insured, Greg would see a proper reimbursement for his fees. Not a bad morning.

Greg popped off his gloves and gown, wadded them into a large ball, and shot them across the room into the waste bin standing next to the door. "He shoots!" His aim was short. The gown fell to the ground where it would remain until housekeeping came by later and properly disposed of it. "Oh, he was fouled," Greg announced, trying to justify missing his shot.

Greg sat down at the dictation desk, opened Shelly's thin chart, and jotted down a few lines of text indicating that he had performed an appendectomy, and dictated his note. Next, he picked up the phone and dialed into the dictation line. Rattling off the patient's name and clinic number, Greg then described in detail the entire procedure as quickly as he could, and with as much emotion as a disinterested Catholic rattles off the rosary.

He finished his dictation, closed the chart, and headed out the door of the O.R. before the nurses had Shelly's incision covered and dressed. Greg walked out to the waiting room and found Shelly's mother. Cute, he thought, but her worried look signaled to Greg that he'd better give a good performance. He sat down next to her and held her hand. "She did just fine," he began in his Marcus Welby voice. "The appendix was inflamed, but we got it out before it could rupture. She was a real trouper. No complications. She's going to be sore for a little while, but I think Shelly will get back to her old self in no time." Always throw in the patient's name. It makes the family think you care.

Shelly's mom's face lit up at the good prognosis. She praised Greg, and he ate it up. After all, he deserved it. He was wonderful. He was his own best fan.

As they stood, she put her arms around him and gave him a hug. Greg felt her breasts pressing against him. He didn't understand the emotions of parental concern that this mother was displaying.

Shelly was his last case for the day. Greg looked at his Rolex. One o'clock. He had missed lunch. Not uncommon. Will's swim meet would be over by now. No sense rushing home. Linda would probably be in one of her moods anyway. "Where were you?" "Why are you so late?" "Don't you know what missing family things means to us?" She just didn't get it. He worked hard for them. Did she think their big house and vacation home was handed to them? That her Mercedes was placed on their doorstep by some benefactor? Everything he did was for them. The late hours. Days away. Midnight calls. He was a good provider. That's the man's job. The least she could do was appreciate his hard efforts instead of criticizing him for missing a few birthday parties and anniversaries.

As a surgeon, Greg knew he only had a few more years to really rake in the money. His hands already had signs of arthritis. How much longer could he continue to cut? Ten years? Fifteen? He had to make his big money now. Lord knows Linda wasn't helping him hold on to much of it. A few more years at this pace and then he could slow down. They'd have the funds by then. He'd be able to devote more time to family.

He believed the lie. It gave him the comfort he needed. It justified his career. Greg walked down to the cafeteria. A peaceful lunch here beat a loud conversation at home. He selected the deep-fried entrée of the day and added a salad, as if one would cancel out the other. Two Diet Cokes rounded out his tray.

The doctors' dining room was empty. Most of his colleagues had rounded on their patients and headed home. That was okay. He had the television to keep him company. He'd grown used to the solitude. On occasion, an on-call physician would wander through to get coffee or snacks. Greg sat facing the door. He liked to be noticed when someone walked by. Get noticed. Be seen. Let the others think that he was the busiest guy on staff. His enlarged ego needed continuous feeding.

His cell phone rang. Greg put down his fork and swallowed his bite of chicken-fried steak. "Dr. Jameson."

"Did you forget where you live?"

Greg sighed. "Oh, hi, Linda."

"Are you almost finished? The kids are done and want to go to a movie today."

"I only have a few more things to do. I had an emergency case crop up." Generic to-do lists can never be argued with. "How'd the swim meet go?"

"Great. The boys swam really well. I think they won the meet." She was also adept at lying. She never let on that she missed the whole thing herself. But if Greg chose to think that she was a devoted mother and wife, then so be it. "By the way, you could have dropped them off at the pool this morning on your way to the hospital." Her voice had grown icy.

"I'm sorry. Did you have to get out of bed before noon today?"

"Don't start with me, Greg."

As a doctor, Greg found it medically amazing that a woman could continuously be on the rag. "You know, I did have to get in here early." Greg looked around the room where he had sat a mere seven hours earlier enjoying a western omelet and hash browns. "I can't be a taxi on my days on duty."

"Fine." Linda didn't need an argument right now. Her head still ached from the vodka on the rocks she'd poured down her throat the night before. "So, will we see you this afternoon?"

"I doubt it. But tell the kids they did a good job for me."

"You could tell them yourself once in a while."

"Don't you start with me now. Give them a pat on the head for me. I'll hurry home as soon as I can. If you want to go to a show, don't wait for me. Who knows when I'll get away?"

"Whenever I damn well please" didn't sound like the kind of answer he should give.

"Okay. We'll see you for supper then. When you get home, the lawn needs mowing."

"Fine." He'd be glad when the boys were old enough to do that job. "Good-bye, Linda." Greg went back to his lunch. He had just bought himself a few hours. A few peaceful hours. He'd find something to do. The afternoon was his now. Stay here at the hospital where he was a god, or go home and be a mere mortal husband. It wasn't a difficult decision for him to make.

Greg finished his lunch and left his dirty tray on the table. Someone would be along to clean it up. He walked up to his office. The deserted waiting room and empty reception desk indicated how medical offices seem to think that health care is a nine-to-five, Monday-through-Friday operation. He walked past his overflowing mail slot and down the soft, carpeted hall to one of his three offices.

St. John's had provided Greg with a personal office and two exam rooms. He was supposed to use his office as a third exam room, but he had placed a couch where the exam table should have been. He had replaced his standard-issue desk with his own oak Thomasville, complete with a computer terminal and keyboard drawer.

Greg sat at his desk and pulled a soda from his compact refrigerator. He turned on his PC, placed his icon on his files for the U of I, and double-clicked it open. He had been working on a proposal for the last six months. With some free time today, he hoped to finish it.

"Let's see if we can get control back next year," Greg said to himself. He opened his file for his proposal:

ASSIGNMENT OF THE SURGICAL CLERKSHIP TO THE ST. JOHN'S SITE

Greg had been after the surgical teaching assignment for the third- and fourth-year medical students ever since losing that plush position to the competing Rockford General Hospital and Clinic. With three major hospitals in the Rockford area, the dean and trustees of the U. of I. College of Medicine had been able to carefully select who got the teaching assignments. The trustees considered the quality of the physicians at each hospital, along with the patient mix. Many factors were put together, along with who owed whom favors. The results of these decisions had medical students spending their student-loan money on gas to drive all over town to different sites for their last two years.

Greg wanted to get the surgical rotation brought back to St. John's and under his control. "Professor Gregory Jameson." Greg smiled. "That has a nice ring to it." Gaining the recognition and status of a professor was a long, unfulfilled dream. A physician's résumé always seemed empty without a reference to a teaching position. Greg had never had one of those. And it bugged him.

When all your friends have just as much money as you do, as much power, and a trophy wife—whether it's number one or three—you need to have something to up the bragging rights. Pissing contests were routinely held in the doctors' lounges and at national conferences. Colleagues constantly dropped names of publications. Who's earned a Ph.D.? Who's the new director of clinical improvement? Greg hated them all. He wanted to be one of them. Jealousy made him hate who he wanted to be.

"Guess I'm going to have to earn it, unlike some people." Greg looked at his graduation class photo that hung on his office wall. Standing one row in front of a much-younger Greg Jameson stood a similarly eager-faced Michael Hamilton. "Just waltz into town and have the whole thing handed to you on a silver platter. Hell, make it 24-karat gold."

Greg began typing. He had already listed the number of surgical cases he and his colleagues had performed over the past year. The success rates and the complications, malpractice claims (both filed and settled) were necessary information the board considered. He stressed the mix of cases that the students would be exposed to, and how St. John's was superior in both its general surgery as well as cardiovascular surgery. He added the strengths of the facility, including subspecialty backup and the quality of the call rooms.

Chapter Three

He included everything he could think of. He was not just on a quest for academic advancement. This was a vendetta.

Greg had grown to hate Mike Hamilton. Michael seemed to fall into success, while Greg felt he had struggled to gain his own. Granted, Michael had come into medical school with a Ph.D. in biochemistry under his belt. He had published four articles during medical school alone; two in the *Journal of the American Medical Association*.

"Thought I'd never have to see you again," he muttered to the photo. "I sure as hell didn't invite you to come into my clinic." Dogs don't like any other four-legged creatures sniffing around in their own backyard. The memories stirred in Greg's head. Thoughts that he had tucked away for fourteen years came bubbling to the surface as if no time had passed.

They had all been friends once. They worked in the same study groups. Mike helped Greg get through the basic sciences, and Greg helped Mike during cadaver lab. Greg smiled involuntarily as he reflected on those early days. The fun times. The times before Mike had broken Greg's jaw.

Beep beep, beep beep, beep beep. Greg's pager snapped him back to the present. The number flashing on the tiny screen indicated it was Nancy from the surgical floor in the hospital. Greg picked up the phone and dialed.

"Dr. Jameson, hi. Mrs. Tepper's blood pressure is falling, and she's a little short of breath."

Incarcerated hernia, Greg thought. Patients were much easier to remember by medical problem than by name. "What are her vitals?"

"BP is eighty over thirty-five. Pulse one-twenty. She's puffing pretty badly. Her oxygen level has dropped into the eighties."

"Bump her up to 100 percent oxygen by mask and open her IV fluids up. I'm on my way." Greg put down the receiver and closed his computer files. "Guess you'll have to wait," he said to his computer. "Mrs. Tepper might take a while."

With any luck, Mrs. Tepper would take him long enough for him to eat supper here. Missing family dinners was something he was willing to sacrifice in his quest for surgical sainthood. Besides, he didn't like Linda's cooking. He liked her penchant for carryout food even less.

Greg put on his white coat and closed his office door. He wasn't in a hurry to get to the floor. He was sure that he'd fix up Mrs. Tepper just fine. Look good in front of the nurses, like a hero riding into town and saving the day. He loved it. He lived for it. It was a good day. He got to spend it with his favorite person.

4

Will stood up on his bed, even though he knew he wasn't supposed to. For a while, he'd thought his name was "Stop all that damn jumping." But he wasn't standing on his bed to jump. He held his ribbons in his hand. Don had handed out the ribbons from the last swim meet after practice tonight, partially as reward for a job well done, but mostly out of recognition for trying their hardest.

Will had taken first in only one event. The blue ribbon would go on the top of his bulletin board hanging over the head of his bed. The three second-place ribbons would go underneath their counterparts. Medals and certificates of achievement hung on different corners, along with patches from the pools he'd swim at during away meets. Will liked to fill up his board each summer. He liked to see that he was able to accomplish things, even if no one else seemed to notice.

He carefully pinned each ribbon onto the cork with a thumbtack. The neat rows of blues, reds, and whites were beginning their march across the board. Looking down, Will saw the remaining yellow ribbon that was the reminder of his failure in the relay. When Don handed out the ribbons to the relay team, the other members ceremonially tossed theirs into the trash in the locker room, but not before filling Will's ears with their sentiments of disappointment. The first place spot to which they felt entitled was denied them by Will's shortcoming.

For a moment, Will wanted to discard that ribbon as well. Even his father knew what the color yellow meant—failure. That was not allowed. The only time Dr. Greg Jameson seemed to notice his son was when Will did something wrong

Will thought about hiding the ribbon, but he had nothing to be ashamed of. He had done his best. He remembered how exhausted he'd been when he'd climbed out of the pool. No, someone had to help him out, he remembered. But he hadn't held back. He didn't wimp out, even though his team seemed to remind him that he had every chance they could. No, he had given it his all. And if his best effort gave him a fourth place, then he was willing to accept that. It was who he was.

"You can't win every time you try," Don had said as he handed out the ribbon. "Then the victories would have no meaning." Don's words of encouragement echoed in Will's mind.

So with his tongue sticking out of the side of his mouth, Will took his yellow ribbon and placed it up next to the other blue ones across the top of the bulletin board. A symbol of victory over his self-doubt certainly deserved to be proudly displayed. He would just have to keep the door to his bedroom closed so his father wouldn't notice the ribbon.

"Will, come see my room," Paul called out. "Come see! Come see!" He waved his arms to emphasize his urgency.

Will jumped down off of his bed and smoothed the covers to erase any evidence of his violation of a house rule. Paul was hopping up and down as he waited for Will. When Will arrived, Paul proudly pointed to his achievement. He had pinned his two purple participation ribbons onto his bedroom wall at his eye level.

"That's great, Paul. It looks just like the trophy case at school."

Paul beamed with pride at the sight of his ribbons. Will just didn't have the heart to tell Paul what a whipping he was going to get for putting holes in his wall. "Did you show Mom yet?"

"Not yet. Come on, let's go get her!"

Will reached out to grab Paul's arm. "Hold on a minute," he said. "Let's make it even better before we show Mom and Dad." Paul seemed to like the idea. He liked any idea Will had.

Will walked back into his room and looked around for something to use. His dresser was nearly cleaned off. Only a lamp, a tray with a comb and brush, and a small mahogany box that he had bought with his vacation money on a trip through the Smoky Mountains last year were on top. The room had to be neat. Junk had to find a place or it would be thrown out.

A plain blue chair stood in the corner by the window to the backyard. A bookshelf was stocked full of books. Will moved to the closet. All the good junk would be in there anyway. Behind the suits hanging on the lower rod was a stash known only to Will. Will pulled out an old baseball glove that had barely been broken in. Still fit, though. Will slid it on and pounded his right fist into the pocket. Will remembered when he got his mitt. His father told him to go outside and they'd play catch. He promised Will that he'd only be a minute. He'd be out after he got off the phone. His dad never came outside. The words were still fresh in Will's mind. The promises never kept.

Will tossed the glove back into its hiding place. He moved his soccer cleats out of the way. They were still muddied from two seasons of play. Will recalled being dropped off three nights a week for practice and games on Saturdays. After the games he'd be waiting by the equipment shed for his ride home long after the other kids had left.

Will found board games that had been rarely played. *Mad* magazines tucked away where Mom's disapproving eyes would never find them. Old folders from previous school years. A ten-year-old's treasures are like anyone else's: memories

Will found what he was looking for at the bottom of the heap. He had received a certificate for completing a summer reading program when he was only seven. Mom framed everything back then, and a photocopied award was not to be excluded. First it hung on the wall in the kitchen before moving to Will's bedroom. Later, it was ignored like most things around here. The paper inside meant nothing to Will. He read to find adventure and to go to places where the heroes could be believed in. He received that from his books. The certificate had no value.

The frame, however, could do so much more. Will slipped the back off of the frame. A piece of cardboard held the certificate in place. Being careful not to smudge the glass or cut himself, Will turned the paper over and replaced the certificate with the blank back now showing. He replaced the cardboard and the backing and admired his creation, a framed blank piece of paper.

"Here we go, Paul." Will walked back into his brother's room. "This is just what you need." Will took the pins out of the wall and let the ribbons fall to the floor. He rubbed the marks left by the pins in an attempt to cover their presence. He'd have to come back later with his water paints and do a better job. "Those ribbons of yours deserve to be displayed, buddy." Will set the frame up on Paul's dresser. Then he put the ribbons over the face of the frame and attached them to the top with the pins. It was a makeshift award case, but Paul got the idea. "How's that look?"

"Wow. That's great. Where'd you get that?"

"Oh, I made that special for you. You earned those ribbons. They should be put out here with style."

Paul's beaming face told Will he had done well. Will knew that the ribbons were worthless. Just show up and you get one. But sometimes in life, just showing up is enough. And they made Paul feel like a winner. Being told that was important for anybody. But especially for his little brother, who most likely would only be told that by strangers.

Paul began to rub his stomach. "I'm hungry now. Can you make me something to eat? I think Mom's sleeping again."

Paul raced out of the room, but Will took his time. He was surprised at how short of breath he had become with such a small amount of activity. But he had swum hard today at practice. It was okay to get a little tired. Besides, he didn't have time to rest or take a nap on the couch. Paul was hungry. And Mom was no help on some of these nights.

The two made their way down the staircase. The dark oak handrails made a more than adequate slide for Paul, but Will walked slowly down the stairs. At the bottom, Will saw his mom sitting in the formal living room. Head tilted back on the sofa, her bottle of vodka sat on the table. At least she hadn't spilled it on the carpet this time. Her left hand still held her glass, even though her snoring indicated the sedative properties of the alcohol had done its job.

The entryway into the living room had sliding French doors. Will closed them as quietly as he could. He didn't want Paul to see her passed out, and Will didn't want to wake her. She could be mean sometimes, or worse, overly emotional. She'd start crying or apologizing for being drunk. Will didn't want to deal with either one right now.

Paul climbed up onto one of the tall barstools at the kitchen's breakfast bar. He switched the small television set on, and gave his undivided attention to *Dexter's Laboratory*. Will opened and closed cabinets and pored through the fridge looking for something he could fix for the two of them to eat. "How about some chicken nuggets?"

"Yeah. That'd be fine. And some corn too." Paul was easy. His young tastes could easily be satisfied by Will's limited cooking ability.

Will nuked the processed chicken and corn. He set out plates and poured milk into two cups. Over the years he had grown to be short-order cook. The two sat in the kitchen by themselves and ate their supper. No sitting around a table with the whole family. No "How was your day?" This was their routine. But they were together. They had each other. That's more than most people have. They were happy.

After dinner, the boys finished off a box of cupcakes. Will cleaned up their table. Loading a dishwasher with two plates, two bowls, two cups, and a microwave dish or two doesn't take very long.

"Come on. Let's go play some checkers," Will offered.

"I get to be red," Paul insisted. "And I get to go first. And I get to win." Paul liked to set the stage before the game began.

The brothers went to Paul's room and played some games. Will was careful to win only once. They read stories, talked about swimming, watched TV, and passed the night.

"Think Dad will be home tonight?" asked Paul.

"I reckon. But he might get in too late for you. So you better start getting ready for bed." Will helped Paul put on his pj's, brush his teeth, and wash his face. Paul never put up much of a struggle.

Paul bounded into his room, all set for bed. He grabbed his picture frame of ribbons and took it into bed with him. His latest prized possession.

"Goodnight, Willie."

"Goodnight, Paul. I'll come check on you later. You can keep your light on."

Paul rolled out of bed and turned on his water-filled aquarium night-light. He liked to watch the plastic fish bob up and down with the bubbles.

Will walked back downstairs. Opening the doors to the living room he found his mother right where she had been. The vodka bottle was a little emptier than it had been when he had checked on her earlier. "Great. She drinks in her sleep." He walked over to the table. He picked up the bottle and replaced the cap. Will carried the bottle back to the liquor cabinet that disguised itself as a bookshelf. She had left the door open, but Will knew where the key was hidden for those nights when she hadn't. He brought her glass into the kitchen, dumped the remains and the half-melted ice into the sink, and placed it into the top rack of the dishwasher.

Now for the hard part.

"Come on, Mom. It's time to go to bed."

"Hey, Willie. I'm sorry. Can I fix you something to eat?" Linda struggled to get up, but she fell back into her chair.

"No, I'm not hungry." Will helped her to her feet. His shoulders only came up to her mid-abdomen, but he still worked quite well as a crutch.

"Is Paul okay?"

"Yeah, he's in bed."

"I'm sorry, sweetie. Mommy is just a little unhappy tonight," she said, as if tonight was any different. She stroked his hair. "You're such a good little boy." Her words spilled out of her mouth as easily as her vodka had poured into it. "You deserve a better mom than me."

Will found it hard to argue with her at that particular moment, especially as she tripped over her own feet. Will had worked out a system of getting her up the stairs. He'd place one of her arms on his shoulder, the other on the handrail, and then climb one step at a time.

The routine was the same each time he helped her. She'd ramble on about one thing or another as they walked. She mumbled about being alone at night. She'd complain that the best years of her life were slipping away. And she'd say she gave up her career for a family. That one hurt Will the most every time he heard it. Will learned just to agree with her. It led to fewer tears.

Once in her bedroom, Linda would find her way into bed by herself before falling onto the sheets. Pulling the blankets up to her chin, she drifted back to sleep still mumbling to herself. Will closed her door, but not before placing a wastebasket beside her bed, just in case she decided to bring her vodka back up during the night.

With his mother and brother in bed, Will went into his own room. The house was quiet. Dad was not home yet. He had the whole house to himself. And that was the last thing that he wanted. Being alone wasn't on his list of goals in life. Will picked up his phone. He wanted someone to talk to. Erin was the one person who came to mind. "Hello, Mrs. Block. Is Erin there?"

"Yes, Will. Hold on a sec," came the cheerful voice. Will heard the sounds of the Blocks' kitchen as the phone was handed from mother to daughter. Will heard voices, laughter, and music. The sounds of a home. In his own house, Will heard only silence.

"Hi, Will. What's up?"

"Oh, nothing. I just wanted to say hi." He just wanted to hear her voice.

"All alone again?"

"Yeah."

Erin knew she needed to change that subject. "What was Don talking to you about today after practice? You're not in trouble, are you?"

"Nah. He wanted to know if I was okay. My times have been off the last few days of practice."

"I noticed that too. I didn't want to say anything, but you didn't seem like yourself last Saturday at the meet. Usually when I cheer for you, you at least finish first or second. I was even doing my double good-luck chant," she said, as if her childhood superstitions were based on scientific fact.

"I've just lost some speed. Don said that he'd work with me some more so that I can be ready for districts at the end of summer. They're having them at our pool this year."

"No duh. I was at the meeting too. That's an all-day meet. You want to sit together?"

"All day with you? I don't want your cooties."

The two kids continued to throw small insults back and forth, along with hefty doses of teasing. By the end of their twenty-minute conversation, Will once again wore his trademark smile. And Erin had thoroughly twisted her long, red hair around each of her fingers.

Will didn't want to hang up, but Erin's mother pointed out that the two of them had spoken long enough. Will and Erin said goodnight.

"You two sure like to gab, don't you?" Erin's mother said to her young daughter after the receiver had been replaced.

"Yeah. I think he needs to have someone to talk to." Erin knew most of what Will went home to each night after practice. What would be there and what wouldn't. That's part of what drew her to him. Erin had a nurturing quality about her. "Mom, can you help me? I want to bake some cookies for Will and bring them to him tomorrow."

"Sure, hon. I think we have some of those frozen chocolate chip ones." The two went back into the kitchen. Erin's father also liked his cookies. The women decided to bake for their men.

Will sat with the phone on his lap. The room was once again quiet. But he didn't feel alone anymore. He picked up the TV remote and clicked on his television, trying to fill his room with sound. But the TV couldn't fill it with the sounds that Will heard at Erin's house.

He channel surfed. Infomercials. Talk shows that were more like shout shows. Old movies. Will found a station that played old reruns. *The Brady*

Bunch was on. A happy family. Laughter. Jokes. Love. He clicked the TV off. He found that show too depressing.

5

"So you're going into fifth grade in the fall, eh, Will?"

"Yup." Will hopped up onto the exam table of Dr. Roberts' office. The cold paper sheet on the table scratched the back of his bare legs as he sat down. His thin gown covered him, but he still felt a little embarrassed about sitting in a room wearing only his underwear with his mother standing right there. But Dr. Jeff Roberts always made him feel better.

"You know, Linda, you were lucky to get this guy's school physical scheduled. I've been booked up since March."

"I know. I guess I forgot to make the appointment when his teacher sent out the notices at semester break. Life gets so hectic."

"Couldn't agree with you more."

Will just rolled his eyes and kept his mouth shut. He had hoped that he wouldn't need any shots this year, but his dad noticed that Will's physical needed to get addressed. Dad at least noticed that aspect of Will's life. Will snorted. Maybe he should have taped a message on a bottle of gin. Then his mother would have noticed.

"But when Greg called, I figured I'd just work you in. That's the least I could do for one of my partners." Jeff Roberts had been Will's doctor since birth. As one of the last few family practitioners who hadn't been driven away from obstetrics by the malpractice risks, Jeff felt that the only way to truly know his patients was to meet them on day one, literally. He had joined St. John's group right out of residency and never looked at another job.

A short man, he was balding on top but had the dignity to avoid a comb-over. He was content with his practice—no hidden agendas, no desire to reach into the heights of administration. He was a family man. The three loves in his life were his patients, his wife, and snowmobiling. Will sensed that Dr. Jeff was someone who could be trusted. He always had been.

Jeff wrote in Will's chart. It was a rather thin document so far. Documentation included birth records, immunizations, well-baby visits, and ear infections. The chart was fairly boring, from a medical point of view.

"Going out for any sports this year?" Dr. Jeff asked, knowing that sports physicals required further documentation.

"Nope. They don't have any for fifth graders," Will said, a little disappointed. "But I'm swimming this summer."

"That's good for you. I was never much of a swimmer myself. They never let me use my swim fins and air tank." Jeff tried to coax a smile from his young patient. "But you know what's the best thing about swimming, don't you?"

"Uh, the exercise?" Will offered, not sure of what answer Jeff was looking for

"No." Jeff wiggled his eyebrows up and down. "The girls in swimming suits."

Paul, who had been occupied with the bucket of toys and books along the wall of the office, popped his head up. "He just likes Erin. Don't you, Will?"

Will blushed. He knew the code of honor among boys his age. Girls were taboo. Admitting to liking one sealed a certain and horrible fate.

"Oh, got a little sweetheart, do you, Will?"

"Shut up, Paul." Will was angry that his secret had been revealed, even though it was a well-known secret.

Paul giggled. "Yeah. He likes her. They talk all the time at the pool and at home on the phone."

"When do you use the phone, Will?" asked Linda, who was somewhat surprised that her son was interested in girls.

"At night. When you're asleep." Will glared at his mother. His voice indicated that he wanted the topic to be dropped. Linda realized that her son witnessed her drunken spells and decided to change the subject.

"But that's normal for boys his age, isn't it, Doctor?"

"Yes. I think it's healthy to develop relationships at any age." Jeff turned to Will. "Don't let anyone tease you, son. It's okay to like girls. I like them myself. One in particular." Jeff gave a wink and a nod to Will.

Will smiled. He knew that he wasn't going to be teased by Dr. Roberts. He wished that his own father would behave that way.

"So how is swim season going this year?" Jeff put down his pen and approached his young patient for his exam.

"Pretty good."

Jeff looked into Will's throat, then shined his penlight into Will's eyes and watched the normal constrictive response. He palpated Will's thin neck. "Did you have a cold lately? Sore throat or anything?"

"No."

"What is it?" Linda asked.

"Oh, nothing. He has a couple enlarged lymph nodes. Could just be a reaction from something." Jeff stepped to Will's side and took his stethoscope from around his neck. After warming the diaphragm with his hands, Jeff placed it on Will's back. "Give me a deep breath."

Will complied. Air rushed in and out without any obstructions. Jeff nodded to Linda indicating things were fine. Jeff next placed the diaphragm on Will's sternum. Will's heartbeat was regular. No murmurs that could foretell of problems that might occur during strenuous physical activity.

Jeff patted the table where he wanted Will to lay his head. "Go ahead and lie down." Jeff placed his hands on Will's abdomen. Will giggled and squirmed at his touch

"Try to hold still," Jeff instructed. Jeff pressed on Will's abdomen, pushing in all areas. "Does any of this hurt?"

"Nope."

Jeff pressed under Will's left ribs. "Does that feel okay?"

"Yep."

Jeff felt again. This time he told Will to take a deep breath and hold it. "Have you been tired a lot lately?"

Will didn't have to think about that question. "Yeah. Sort of."

"He has been complaining of that," Linda said, trying to become the caring mother. "What is it?"

"His spleen is a little bit enlarged." Jeff pressed around on Will's belly a little more, looking for anything else that might be amiss. He found nothing. "Do you have anything else out of the ordinary, like a rash or fevers?"

Will shook his head. Aside from being tired he had felt about the same.

"What do you think it is?" asked Linda.

"Could be anything or nothing." He felt along Will's groin for any lymph nodes. His search turned up empty. "Might be mono." He turned to Will. "Been kissing that girl of yours lately?"

Now Will was embarrassed. He and Erin had kissed once during a swim meet. Will had been walking to the snack bar. Erin was hiding in the maintenance room. As Will walked by she had jumped out, grabbed him, and pulled him into the room with her. Before he knew what was happening, Erin had placed her lips right against his. To say he was surprised would have been putting it mildly. To say he was pleased would have been an understatement. The whole kiss lasted only five seconds. Will kept his eyes open the whole time, mostly out of shock at what was happening to him. But he saw that Erin's eyes were closed.

Afterward, they both swore an oath to never tell anyone. They never did, although Will did have a difficult time explaining his perpetual smile for the rest of that day. But now that day was coming back to haunt him. Will had heard of people getting diseases from each other through kissing and stuff. But he never thought he'd catch something. Great. What did Erin give him?

"No," he lied. "Why? What's mono?"

"It's a virus that causes an illness like a cold or flu. It can get serious in some cases, but that's pretty unusual." Jeff turned to Linda. "That would explain his fatigue and the swollen glands in his neck. But in his case, the problem might come from the spleen. Being enlarged like this could put him at risk for rupture if he gets injured in his side." He turned to Will. "You might be out of swimming for a few weeks, young man. You can't be involved in sports until your spleen comes back down to normal size," Jeff explained.

"No swimming?" Will wailed. "That's not fair!"

"I never said that it'd be fair. That's just the way it goes sometimes. You don't want to get really hurt, do you? Or give this to anyone else?" Jeff reasoned with Will.

Will thought about some of the members of his team that he wouldn't mind getting sick. But he didn't want that. Nor did he want to have to sit on the deck and watch for the rest of the summer.

"I'll have to get some blood work for documentation. The school will need to know." Jeff returned to his desk to write down his findings in Will's chart. He released Will to go get dressed behind a curtain in the corner of the room.

"How long will this take?" asked Linda, who was adding up all the other errands she still had to do.

"Not long. About two hours. If you like, you can leave his school form with me. I'll get the results later today, fill in the rest of the info, and drop it off at Greg's office this afternoon."

"That'd be fine. We don't need it until registration."

"That's this week, Mom," Will reminded her as he came out from behind the curtain. "That's why we had to come today, remember?"

"Oh, that's right," she bluffed. "Yeah, just give it to Greg. He can bring it home tonight."

"I'll check a blood count while we're at it," Jeff said. "Sometimes these mono tests are off, and I can pick up the diagnosis from his white cell count." Jeff turned his attention from Linda to his young patient. "Don't worry, Will. It will all be from one needle stick."

Needles. Will hated needles. He'd just have to look the other way, squeeze his eyes shut, and try his best not to cry.

Linda took the lab slip from Jeff and told Paul to put the toys back into their box. Herding her children toward the door, Linda thanked Jeff for working them in so quickly.

Jeff smiled. "You're welcome."

Linda and the boys walked down the hallway to the reception area. Anne, Jeff's nurse, smiled at them as she carried a stack of charts back to Jeff's office. She dropped them loudly on his desk. "You're now a half hour behind schedule, you know."

"Yeah, I know." Jeff didn't care. He was going to give each patient the time needed. His full waiting room indicated that Jeff's patients didn't mind the extra wait to receive that kind of service. Anne, however, liked schedules. You could set your watch by her. Punctual. Jeff wondered if her next five orgasms were already scheduled on the monthly calendar on her ever-present Palm Pilot.

His afternoon went smoothly—as smoothly as an office that fulfilled the law of entropy could run. Patients who were in better shape than Jeff were asking for disabled parking stickers and patients with colds were in search of an unnecessary antibiotic. Pap smears. Jeff hated Pap smears. A daily grind is a grind no matter what profession one practices. At least he got to be home at night. He'd put up with any kind of day to have that to go home to.

"Lab results are back from this morning." Anne knocked and entered Jeff's office. "Normal results here and abnormals in there." She had sorted the lab test results into two piles for Jeff. Anything to speed up Jeff's pace.

"Okay, I'll get to them."

Anne stood in the doorway with her arms crossed and foot tapping.

Jeff dropped his pen on the chart before him. "Fine. I'll do them now." He picked up the stack with the normal results and thumbed through them, initialing each page as he went. "Just send out a 'normal result' card to these."

"Okay." Anne took the stack back, and pointed to the other half of her work. "And those?"

"I'll check them and let you know."

Anne nodded and closed the door behind her.

Jeff picked up the remaining sheets and looked them over. Each abnormal test would require an additional test. That meant a phone call or letter. Jeff picked up his pocket tape recorder and dictated letters to his patients with the lab results that needed follow-up.

Then he came to Will's results: infectious mononucleosis serology—negative.

Jeff stared at the sheet of paper. He had been so sure. "Well, let's see the blood counts." Jeff knew that early mono could give false test results, but that the white blood cell morphology could give an indication of the infection. He turned to the next lab slip. His eyes widened. "Oh, damn it." Jeff dropped the paper on his desk and leaned back in his chair. A lump grew in his throat as he thought about Will. Jeff's job came with many intangible benefits. Now he was facing one of the tangible realities.

He needed to talk to someone. He needed some advice. He knew whom to call.

"Communications; Jean," came the voice on the other end of the phone.

"Hi, Jean. It's Dr. Roberts."

"Good afternoon. What can I do for you?"

"I need you to page Dr. Hamilton for me. To my office, okay?"

"Yes, sir. Will that be all?"

"Yes, Jean." Jeff hung up the phone. He'd wait for Mike to call before he'd let his mind run off in all directions. At least that's what he told himself.

In St. John's pediatric ward, Michael's pager vibrated in his pocket. He let it finish its vibrating dance without finding the button to silence it. Michael was finishing a magic trick and his hands were currently locked together with steel chains. During his magic shows he kept his pager on silent mode. He didn't want anything to upset his rhythm. The children on the pediatric ward were a captive audience, and he liked to return the compliment.

Michael had already completed several tricks for the group of children who were gathered in the visitor's lounge. He left his chain escape trick for last.

"Now make sure that the chains are tight against my wrists," Michael instructed his young assistant. Roger, a boy who'd had intestinal bleeding but was nearing the end of his stay on the floor, was helping Michael. The apprentice had wrapped a metal chain around Michael's wrists and began to lock the ends together."

"Ow. You don't have to try to make me into a patient." The kids laughed. It was a sound the nurses and parents loved to hear.

"Okay, thank you very much, Roger." Michael stood back up and showed the crowd that his hands were now securely locked together. "As you can see, my young assistant has locked me up pretty good." Michael showed his wrists to the group and made an unsuccessful attempt to separate his hands. "Now we will see if I truly am the greatest escape artist in the land. Roger, if you'd place that handkerchief over my arms for me, we'll begin."

Roger lifted a large, red square of cloth and placed it over Michael's outstretched arms. Within seconds, Michael had his left hand out and placed it on Roger's shoulder.

"Now, I'm going to need plenty of room to do this trick properly, so please step back just a little bit for me." Michael escorted Roger a few feet away, then place his hand back under the cloth. Now with both hands under the handkerchief, Michael moved his arms back and forth as he grunted and groaned to show how hard he was working to free his hands. He moved his arms up and down until the cloth flew off and landed on the floor, revealing that his hands were again locked in the chains.

"Agh! This is harder than I thought. You really locked me up good. Do you practice this at home? Do you lock up your sisters and brothers?" Michael looked out in the audience to the couple who had identified themselves as Roger's parents. They shook their heads. "All right. Cover me back up again."

Roger picked up the cloth and again placed it over Michael's bound hands. Almost immediately, Michael pulled his hand back out from under the cloth.

"Now, this time, Roger. I'm going to need a little more room, okay?" Michael moved Roger away from him. Clearly showing his freed hand, Michael patted Roger on the head, pointed his finger at him, and then waved to the crowd. "Let's try this again." He placed his hand under the cloth. A second effort of struggles, grunts, and swaying of the arms yielded no success. The handkerchief fell to the floor again showing Michael's hands securely fastened. "I just don't get it. I can't get out of these locks." He turned to Roger. "Did you do something to these chains? Are you a magician too? Did you place a spell on these locks to keep me from escaping?"

Roger just smiled. The other kids were all laughing that Michael didn't seem to notice that he had already escaped twice. All the kids seemed to forget where they were.

"All right, young man. Let's do this again. Only this time you are going to help me. Pick up the handkerchief and place it over my hands." Roger complied. "Now put your hands under here with mine."

Roger looked around the room. He was somewhat skeptical, but the other patients urged him on.

Michael held Roger's hands. "Now, on the count of three you're going to help me get out of these." Michael lifted and lowered their hands as he counted. "One. Two. Three." Michael threw the handkerchief into the air and revealed both his hands, now with the chains removed, and Roger's hands were now securely bound with the locked chains. "Thank you. Thank you." Michael bowed to the audience. Looking down, Roger saw that now his hands were securely locked together. Partly stunned by the turn of his circumstances, Roger just stood there. Not knowing if the trick was over, he just began to laugh. The whole crowd burst into applause before Michael released the chains from his assistant. "That's all for today. We all have to get back to work, and you need to get some rest."

"Can't you do just one more?" Roger asked.

"I'd love to, but the nurses need to get back to their duties. If they don't do twelve hours of drudgery per shift, the union gets very angry." Michael made sure that his words were loud enough to be overheard by the staff. The nurses just rolled their eyes.

Parents and kids came up to Michael as he packed his tricks back up into his little black box. Worn from years of use, the case had seen hundreds of shows over the years, each one just as effective as the last. The number of magic tricks grew over the years to the point where Michael only stored those tricks he planned to use that day into the case. The overflow of magic cards, boxes, scarves, and wands filled several boxes in his basement.

"That was just great," exclaimed one parent. "I haven't seen my son laugh in weeks."

"That's what this is all about," Michael said, smiling. "Kids don't seem to be afraid of a doctor who makes them laugh."

Michael's pager buzzed against his leg again, signaling that he had ignored its first beckoning. He politely said his good-byes to the group, picked up his box, and walked over to the nurses' station.

"Nice show, Dr. Hamilton," said one nurse.

"Thanks," Michael said, as he dialed the number flashing across the digital screen.

The phone rang.

"Finally," Jeff said. "Hello."

"This is Michael Hamilton."

"Hi, Michael. This is Jeff Roberts from Family Practice."

"Yes, I remember you. What's up?"

"I'm going to need some help here. I have a patient who's going to need to see you. But I wanted to call you first to see what you think." Jeff read the lab report to Michael. He went over Will's exam and discussed all the findings. "So, do you think that's what he has?"

"Most likely. I'll need to see him before I'll say anything definite."

"Poor kid."

"Yeah," Michael agreed. "Give me his name and clinic number. I'll have my nurse call his parents to schedule a visit."

Jeff agreed to call Linda and tell her what the findings showed.

"Got those labs finished yet?" Anne popped her head in the door.

Jeff sighed heavily as he turned toward Anne. "Yeah. All but one."

Anne narrowed her eyes. "What's wrong?"

"Oh, I'm still not very good at breaking bad news."

"Who has something wrong?" Anne asked, no longer in a hurry to finish her day.

"You remember Will Jameson?"

"Dr. Jameson's son? Yeah."

Jeff turned from Anne to gaze out the window. He shook his head, wishing the news were different. "He has leukemia."

6

"Where did you get these?" asked Michael as he examined Alan's inner left arm. The portly sixty-four-year-old sat on the exam table covered only with a small cloth smock.

"What?"

"These bruises. You've got about ten of them on this arm." Michael picked up Alan's right arm and gave it a thorough look over. "There's nothing on this side. And I know that you aren't on any aspirin or blood thinners."

"Oh, those." Alan shrugged, as if they weren't important. "I got those in church."

"Church? What kind of church do you go to?" Michael sat back in his chair and waited to hear stories about human sacrifice and rituals of self-flagellation. "Or do you belong to some sort of cult?"

"Oh, no, it's Gloria Dei. Over off Alpine."

"Yeah, I know where that is. They beat you there?"

Alan shook his head. "I guess it's my own fault," he said sheepishly. "I'm not much of a morning person. I tend to nod off halfway through a sermon. I've tried everything I know. Coffee. Soda. There's just something about Pastor Richard's monotone voice that could have lulled Sam Kinnison to sleep. So as I start to nod off, my wife leans over and gives me a pinch. Some of them are pretty hard, as you can see."

"Why only the left arm?"

"'Cause that's the side she sits on. I don't want her hurting my right arm. I need that for my bowling."

Michael shook his head at the simple acceptance Alan had of his situation. "So you just let her do this to you week after week?"

"It's not so bad. I've only had one three-pinch sermon. What's a guy supposed to do? Besides," Alan winked at Michael, "it gives me an excuse for elbowing her in the ribs at night when she snores." Michael made a mental note to have an extra cup of coffee the next Sunday morning, just in case Lori had the notion to keep him awake in a similar fashion.

"Well, getting back to your case. Bruises excluded, I think you're doing quite well. Your prostate cancer seems to be in check. I think we can just put you onto recall for a follow-up visit in six months. Sound good?"

"Yeah." Alan was putting his shirt back on. "Want to know some real good news?"

"I'm always ready for some of that."

"I still haven't gotten any of that, you know, limp-dick syndrome."

"You mean impotence?"

"Yeah, that. My soldier still salutes when the parade marches by."

An image of Alan and his wife flashed through Michael's mind. Her pinching him, his elbow hitting her ribs, then the two of them falling into bed together. "Please don't talk like that," he chided Alan good-naturedly. "I haven't eaten lunch yet."

Alan laughed as if he were a high school boy sitting in the locker room, bragging to his friends about a recent conquest.

"With that, I think we can bring this session to a close. You get dressed—that is, if you're able to get your pants back up. And stop out at Sally's desk to set up your next visit."

"See you later, Doc."

Michael walked up to Sally's desk near the reception area. A stack of charts to the left of her phone needed Michael's attention. Labs. Test results. Those to the right were hers. She was busy writing on her notepad with her phone headset on as Michael approached.

"I need to see Alan back in six months," he said as he handed the chart to Sally.

She covered her phone mouthpiece with her hand. "Don't mind me, I'm only on the phone." Michael walked away. He knew that he was on her turf. It was best not to anger her. Wives may come and go, but a good nurse like Sally was a rare find.

"I'll tell reception then." Michael retreated. But Sally didn't let him get too far.

"You got a callback from Meadowbrook Nursing Home. You got a patient that you're thinking of placing there?"

"So to speak." Michael picked up the message slip that Sally was holding out with her left hand as she continued to write with her right.

"I'll bring your next patient back when I'm finished getting my voice mail messages."

"No rush. I'm going to call these people back."

"Oh, you got a call from Dr. Cooper's office," Sally called out as Michael walked away. "He's called an urgent department-head council meeting tonight. He wanted to make sure that you'd be there."

"Great. That can never be a good thing."

Michael handed Alan's chart to the receptionist and walked back to his office. Closing the door, he sat at his desk and looked at the message slip from Sally. Meadowbrook Nursing Home. He had sent many patients to nursing homes over the years. They had been frail, elderly people who were unable to care for themselves. Most had been in hospice. He sent them there to die. Few disappointed his predictions.

The top left drawer of Michael's desk held brochures from the major nursing homes in the area. Valley View, Riverside, Boone County. Michael had been looking as far east as the Lutheran Home in Arlington Heights. They were all basically the same. They all had double rooms, vinyl floors, activity planners, and dining halls. The homes had all the finest luxuries that Illinois public aid could buy. Brochures paint one picture. Michael saw another.

Nursing homes were filled with the smell of urine in the air, which was only interrupted occasionally by the pungent scent of feces. Demented souls lying in their beds, crying out at all hours of the day and night. Call lights going unanswered for hours. The blank stares on the faces of the residents haunting the hallways. Once strong, independent people now only looked forward to a rare family visit and a game of bingo. Those images never made it into the advertisements.

Michael looked over his stack of pamphlets for the one center that would have the feature he most desired. But none of them offered absolution. No one would remove the guilt felt at the prospect of sending a family member out of her home and into a land of the walking dead. No. He couldn't find that.

The message from Meadowbrook told Michael that the admissions co-ordinator had bed space available. If Michael wanted to secure a bed for his mother, he'd need to drop off a deposit of three thousand dollars by the end of the day. Holding the message in his hand, Michael looked at the picture on his desk. It was a picture of his father and Michael on graduation day. His father's arm was around Michael's shoulder. His dad's smile clearly showed his pride in his son.

Michael tossed the message into the drawer and slammed it shut. He'd put it off for now. He'd have to at least discuss the plan with his mother. He knew what she'd say. Maybe that's why he hadn't brought it up before. He wished for an answer.

He picked up the magic wand that he kept on his desk. The same one he'd used for years. Waving it over his desk, Michael mumbled to himself. Tapping the wand on the desk signaling the end of the spell, he opened the drawer. But the contents were as before. No one brochure was standing up with sparking stars swirling around it. No music. No bells. "Damn. Gotta work on that trick."

"Patient's ready." Sally's voice, calling from the doorway, brought Michael back to his present list of duties.

Michael tossed his magic wand onto his desktop and stood up. Putting off a tough decision wasn't one of his characteristics. But this one was getting easier to do. He walked to the hall. "What've we got?"

"Dr. Jameson's son Will."

Michael remembered his conversation with Dr. Roberts of only five days before and the likelihood of seeing another child with leukemia. The idea of seeing another young face go through chemo flitted through Michael's mind. He returned to his desk and put his magic wand into his coat pocket. "Just might need this."

He pulled the young boy's chart from the clear plastic slot hanging by the door and knocked.

"Hello, young man. I'm Dr. Hamilton," he greeted Will as he entered the office. Seeing Will, Michael was surprised at how much he looked like his father.

"Hello." Will seemed upbeat.

Michael turned to Will's mom who was sitting on a small couch placed below all of Michael's diplomas. "Hello, Linda. Nice to see you again."

"Hi, Michael." She offered her hand. "It's been a while, hasn't it?"

"Yeah. What is it now? Fifteen years?"

"Something like that. How's Lori?" she asked uncomfortably.

"She's fine. Getting along really well. She's still getting used to living up north. You know how she hates the winters."

"She never was one for snow." Linda chuckled as she remembered the sight of her former roommate falling into snowdrifts on Michigan Avenue on their first night out together.

"How've you been?" Michael asked.

"Fine," she lied. "That is," she said, pointing to Will, "until this happened." Then she leaned in toward Michael and whispered. "I still haven't told him yet."

"What about Greg?" Michael asked. "Is he coming today?"

"No," she looked down at her feet. "He's got a meeting. Said he couldn't get out of it."

"I see he hasn't changed much." Michael dropped the chart onto the desk and sat down. The labs from Will's last visit had been inserted for Michael's review. He looked them over as he quietly spoke to Linda while Will sat at a corner table reading a book. "Does Greg know what we're planning to do? Or do I need to call him later?"

Linda sat upright and shook her head. "Oh, no. You don't need to call him. He said for me to just talk to him when we get home."

Michael bit his lower lip and looked at his old friend. "He doesn't know you're here, does he?"

Linda had a tough time lying to Michael. She dropped her eyes so that she wouldn't have to see his face. She didn't want to see the look of disappointment in his eyes that she had seen before. "No. No, he doesn't know. And I don't want you to tell him either."

"Linda, this is his son. No matter what I think of the guy, he still has the right to know."

"I know. But just not right now. Let's find out some more about Will first. I'll tell him, I promise."

"Tell Dad what?" The silent Will had decided to speak up when he heard his name mentioned.

"Oh, honey. We need to talk with Dr. Hamilton and have him look at you today to find out why you've been so tired lately. Then we'll let Daddy know so he can help take care of you."

"You said I had an infection that would just run its course and that I'd be okay in a few weeks. I've got a conference swim meet in about a month.

Was that another lie?" He turned to Michael. "What kind of a doctor are you?"

Michael smiled. "I'm a blood doctor. I treat problems that happen in people's blood."

"So I have something wrong with my blood?"

"That's what we're here to find out," Michael said. Michael turned his attention back to Linda. "His labs do point toward what Dr. Roberts suggested. He's anemic. Blood count is about seventy percent of where it should be. His platelets are low. White cell count is about three times the upper normal limit. I hear he has an enlarged spleen and some lymph nodes as well. Has he been complaining of any strange pains at all?"

"You can ask me, you know," Will piped in before his mother could speak. "I am right here, after all."

Michael smiled. He liked to see kids have a little self-confidence. "You're right." Michael turned to Will. "Sometimes I ask the parents these questions when their child isn't as old as you are. Have you had any aches or pains lately?"

"Yeah. My legs have been sore a lot, and my hips right here." He pointed to his upper thighs on both sides.

"Let me see." Michael felt along Will's hips. There was nothing to feel, but Michael took this as his opportunity to start an exam on his young patient. "Hmm. I don't feel anything." Michael began to look in Will's ears. "Anything else out of the ordinary? Things like a rash, nose bleeds, or stomach cramps?"

"No."

Michael looked in Will's mouth, eyes, and started to examine the rest of his patient. "How about sweats at night or a loss of appetite?"

Will's face showed his concentration on the questions being asked. "Not that I can think of."

"That's good." Michael listened to Will's heart, pushed on his stomach, and felt all along Will's skin for any masses or swellings. Michael noticed an enlarged spleen, lymph nodes in Will's neck, groin, and armpits. Overall, Will seemed otherwise to be in pretty good shape. There were no signs of neurological involvement or any organ damage. Plus, the kid had defined deltoids and pecs.

"He checks out pretty good," Michael said as he dropped back into his chair. "You can tell he swims. He has good muscle definition." He turned to Will. "That means you're ripped."

Will smiled.

"However, we still have to explain his lab results." Michael paused, then dove in. "I'm going to have to perform a bone marrow biopsy."

"What's that?" asked Will.

Michael pointed to the small of his own back. "I have to stick a needle into your hip bone right about here," he explained. "Then I draw out some fluid. That's where your blood is made. It's like a blood factory. You see, Will, some of your blood cells aren't forming quite right. They start out okay, but then along the way they turn into something else. These cells are preventing your normal cells from growing like they should."

"It's like they're crowding out the good cells," said Linda.

"What would be causing that?" asked Will.

Michael hedged a bit. "I'm not sure exactly. That's what I need to find out. I need to look for those cells so that I can see what's making them do that and find out the best way to treat it."

Will looked puzzled. "But I don't feel sick."

"I know. Not right now, you don't. But if we don't do this and get you the right medicine you might get sick later on."

"Oh." Will thought for a moment before he spoke. "Kind of like telling someone to stop drinking so much before they get liver problems." He stared pointedly at his mother. Linda ducked her head. If she had thought she'd hidden her drinking from Will, she now knew she hadn't.

"How'd you know about drinking and liver troubles?" Michael asked.

"I read a lot," Will told him. "And watch science shows on television." He turned to look at his mother. "I learn a lot that way."

Michael nodded. "Well, good for you. It's important to learn things. I'm a fan of science myself. Maybe someday you'll grow up to be a doctor like your dad."

"Will this bone test hurt?" Will asked.

"Yes," Michael said honestly, "it's going to hurt a little. But I'll give you some medicine to make it not so bad."

"When should we do this?" Linda asked.

"Now. I don't see any reason to put it off." Michael reached into his desk. "I'll need you to sign this consent form," he said.

Linda quickly scanned the paper. "What's all this stuff?"

"Lawyer stuff, mostly," Michael said. "Basically, it says that you're letting me do the procedure, and that there is a risk of some complications like bleeding and infection. But don't worry, I've done hundreds of these without any problems."

Linda signed the form and Michael placed it in Will's chart. Then he motioned toward the door. "Let's go on down to my procedure room." Michael led his young patient and mother down to the end of the corridor. Will smelled the antiseptic in the air and began to worry about what was going to happen to him.

Will walked into the room and noticed the large electronic table in the center. Michael stepped on the separate control buttons for the foot and head platforms raising and lowering the parts of the table to get into the right position for Will. Will looked up at the large, swiveling, surgical light that was overhead. Two steel cabinets that stood against the far wall held supplies for IV tubing, fluids, gauze pads, and antiseptic scrubs. Will saw Michael rummaging through the kits for placing IV lines into chests, abdomens, and spinal canals while the doctor was looking for the things he'd need.

Michael finally located the kit and supplies that he was looking for. "Have a seat right up here," he said, motioning for Will to hop up onto the table. Michael called down the hall for Sally to join them. Then he drew up a small amount of morphine into a syringe and placed it on his tray.

"What are we going to do?" asked Sally arriving in the door.

"Bone marrow. Will you set up for the smears?"

"Sure." Sally began her process of setting out fifteen glass microscope slides onto a separate tray. She and Michael moved about in silence getting their equipment ready. They'd done hundreds of these tests, and they had developed their own routine. Will didn't notice their efficiency. All he saw was the needles and scalpels. He knew whose hip they were aiming for.

"Don't you worry none about this, fella," Sally said with a smile. "Dr. Hamilton is real good at this. Why, I'll bet you won't feel a thing."

"Then let's do this on you," Will grumbled.

"I've already had one," Sally said, ruffling Will's hair. "Two years ago."

"What was it like?" he asked.

"Not too bad," she assured him. "Bet you'll do better than I did."

Will smiled at that comment.

"Lie on your left side here, Will," Michael instructed. "I'm going to give you a little shot in your hip to numb you up. It might make you sleepy." Michael lowered Will's pants enough to expose his backside. Will felt a little embarrassed at having his backside exposed in front of his mother. Will shut his eyes, gritted his teeth and took a deep breath as the needle broke his skin. He could feel a warm sensation as the morphine flowed into his muscle.

"There, that ought to do it." Michael removed the needle and wiped away the small drop of blood that formed at the injection site.

Sally opened up the bone marrow kit as Michael washed his hands and pulled on his sterile gloves. Once they were snug, Michael reached into the kit and pulled out a paper drape. He placed it under Will's left hip. Then using iodine soap, Michael scrubbed Will's right hip area several times. "This is just some soap to get the area clean. We don't want any infections cropping up." Finishing, Michael took a second paper drape and placed it over Will, creating a sterile field from which he could work.

Michael drew up another syringe with some lidocaine, which would act as a local anesthetic. Pushing with his thumb, Michael was able to locate the exact spot on Will's hip that he wanted to biopsy. "Okay, I'm going to numb up your skin a little now. You'll feel a poke and a burn. The medicine stings a little. Kind of like a bee sting." Michael stuck the needle into Will's back and injected. Thanks to the morphine, Will didn't pull back or grimace as much as he had with the first injection. Michael pushed the needle in further until he could feel the tip hit Will's pelvic bone. The soft periosteum gave way to the syringe and allowed the lidocaine to numb up the sensitive tissue.

"Are you okay watching this?" Michael asked Linda. "There's going to be some blood. You can wait in the waiting room like the rest of the parents do if you'd like."

"No, I'll stay. I'd like to be here for this." Linda never was much for the sight of blood. She always had Greg take care of the kids' cuts and scrapes. He had once even stitched up a cut on Paul's leg in their kitchen, which was one of the few good things about having a surgeon around the house. But maternal emotions can be a powerful force. Something that even the purest of Russian vodkas cannot dull.

Linda looked at her son. Her firstborn. Facing a cancer diagnosis and holding up with a bravery that she wished she had. "I'll be fine. I'll be fine." She walked around to the front of the table so as to avoid having to actually watch the procedure. Pulling up a stool, Linda sat down putting her face on the same level as Will's. She reached out her hand and held his. His hand seemed small in hers. He seemed like such a grown-up little man the way he handled himself. The way he watched over Paul. Sometimes Linda forgot that he was still just a little ten-year-old boy. She stroked his hand and touched his hair. And felt every pain that he was now experiencing.

"Okay, Will. I'm going to put a little pressure on your hip now." Michael made a small incision with a scalpel and pushed a large bore needle into Will's skin. The local anesthetic numbed the sharpness of the pain, but Will gritted his teeth when he still felt some discomfort.

Michael pushed and twisted the needle through Will's flesh until the tip of steel struck bone. Michael had been generous with the local anesthetic in this part of Will's hip, and the needle barely made the boy jump. "Here comes a little pressure." Michael placed his left hand on top of Will's hip for leverage, and began boring the needle into the bone. Back and forth, Michael twisted the handle of his instrument until he was sure that he had reached a depth sufficient to obtain his desired quarry. Removing a stylet from the center of the needle, Michael prepared to aspirate out the bone marrow. He placed a 10 cc syringe onto the end of the needle.

"Here comes some pressure. This may hurt a bit." Michael pulled on the plunger of the syringe with enough force to pull the viscous marrow from its home. The intense pressure caused Will to cry out in the worst pain he had ever felt. "I'm sorry, buddy. I know it hurts. We're almost done." Michael patted Will on his back, then turned to Sally. "Go ahead and give him another two milligrams of morphine." Sally complied.

Will's tears were matched by Linda's. Michael hurriedly pulled out enough of the red fluid to fulfill his needs. He removed the syringe from the needle and handed the sample to Sally. Before giving the marrow time to clot, Sally pushed the marrow out onto several glass slides. With the quickness and dexterity of a Japanese chef cooking a dinner in front of his customers, Sally took small droplets of marrow and smeared them out onto all of the remaining slides. The small spicules of bone in the exact center of the smear showed that she had made perfect specimens.

"Just one more thing to do, then we'll be done."

"I hope so," came Will's small voice. Linda's mascara had begun to run.

Michael repositioned the needle onto another piece of bone to be a biopsy specimen. A quick, sharp twist snapped the piece of bone off into the center of the needle. Then with gentle ease, he removed the needle from Will's back.

"That's it. You're all done. And you did quite well, I might say." Michael removed the small cylinder of bone from the needle and dropped it into a specimen cup filled with preservative. Then he placed a small piece of gauze over the wound and taped it into place. He then removed the paper drapes and pushed them into the wastebasket that was near his feet. "You can roll over onto your back, buddy," Michael said. He helped Will shift his position.

"How did it look?" asked Linda.

"Won't know for a day or so. But I'll get in touch with you when I get the results. Let's let him get some rest. I like my patients to stay on their backs for thirty minutes. That puts pressure on the site and prevents excess bleeding."

"Okay. I'll stay with him here, if that's all right."

Michael smiled. "Of course it is. You know, Linda, he made a comment about drinking earlier. Now that he's asleep you can level with me. Are you back on the sauce?"

She dropped her eyes. "I'm not as bad as you think."

"And what am I thinking?"

"That I'm home all day by myself for the most part. Greg's never there. I get lonely. So I have a drink or two to calm me down."

"One or two?"

"Okay, so it's a few more. What's it to you? I don't have to answer to you."

Fifteen years can be a long time between conversations, but sometimes it can seem like no time has passed at all.

"You can do what you want to yourself. Drink yourself blind. Get into a fight with Greg over it. I guarantee I won't be losing any sleep over it. But this little guy is my patient now. And most likely he's facing a pretty rough road. I don't want him to be facing it alone. He's going to need some support. Hell, he's going to need a lot of it. He's not going to need a drunken mother to deal with. When he's throwing up from chemo I don't want him to have to see his mother in the stall next to him bringing up a bottle of Bacardi."

Linda glared at Michael. "I'm not a bad mother. I've tried to stop."

"I know it isn't easy. But you've got to think about him now. He's got to be your priority." Michael pulled up a stool and sat down next to Linda. "Are you still chasing away your guilt?"

Linda sat in silence.

"You know, I never blamed you for what happened between Greg and us. It wasn't your fault. We've been able to deal with it and move on. You've got to do the same. Forgiveness isn't in a bottle."

"I know. But sometimes I just feel that I could have done something to stop it."

"Let it go. Just worry about your own children." A ringing sounded from Linda's purse. She dropped Will's hand and fumbled around in her bag for her cell phone. Wiping the tears from her eyes as if the caller would be able to tell that she had been crying, she flipped open the phone and pressed the caller button. "Hello."

"What did you want?" asked an irritated Greg.

Linda sighed. "I needed to talk to you, but it can wait until you get home.

"No," Greg snapped. "You've got me. What did you need?"

Linda turned away from Michael and held her hand over the phone. She didn't want Greg to know that she was with Michael. "I'm here with Will. We had an appointment."

"An appointment? With whom? What's wrong?"

"I've got it under control. I'll tell you about everything when you get home tonight."

"Is he okay?"

"Right now he is."

"Where are you? At Roberts' office? I'll be there in a few minutes."

"No, we're not at Dr. Roberts' office. We had to see a specialist."

"Okay, now you've got to level with me. Where are you?"

Linda hesitated. She knew how Greg would react. She didn't need that right now. She never did. What she wouldn't have given for a vodka gimlet right then. "I'm here with Michael."

Greg was quiet for two of Linda's deep breaths. Then Greg finally spoke. "Hamilton?"

"Yeah." Greg had spoken Michael's name through grinding teeth. Linda did her best to hold her ground. "Dr. Roberts called with some of Will's test results. He insisted that we get Will in to see a specialist and made special arrangements for today."

"Why didn't you call me? I can get anything around here I want."

"I tried. I paged you, but you didn't call me back until now. Maybe you should respond to my pages faster."

Michael couldn't help but overhear the conversation. It seemed that Greg hadn't changed much. He tried to have pity on Linda for having to put up with Greg all these years, but she didn't seem too motivated to change herself, let alone her husband. Michael turned his attention to Will, who thankfully was still asleep and missing out on his parents' conversations, though he probably had endured many like it.

Michael looked at Will's sleeping face. He was innocently asleep, and oblivious to the condition that his body harbored. How could his parents argue about whose fault it was, accusing each other of wrongdoings, while their son was ill? They should be thankful to have such a wonderful kid. Thankful they were able to have kids at all. They were luckier than Michael and Lori would ever be. Michael looked at the young boy. A son. A son that he could never have. Michael took a deep breath and blocked out the sounds of Linda and Greg. He stroked Will's soft blond hair. "Don't worry, little guy. I'll take care of you. I know what kind of man your father is. I'm not going to let that man hurt you. He's hurt enough people already."

7

Greg's pager went off again. Four times in the last three minutes. "Am I the only one working here today?" yelled Greg looking at his pager.

"Were you talking to me?" asked Linda.

"No. Look. I gotta go. We can talk about this when I get home."

"Of course. Your job comes before the rest of us, doesn't it?"

Greg had grown accustomed to her sarcasm after years of listening to it. Linda's tongue had begun to lose its sting. "Don't start with me. I'm not in the mood." Greg looked at the numbers flashing across the digital screen of his pager and thought about the amount of work that each number was sure to inflict.

"Where have I heard those words before?"

"Just cut the crap and get Will out of that man's office. I don't want him touching my son."

"Will is my son too. I want to find out what's going on with him. I think Michael is the right guy for him to see."

"Go ahead. Take his side again."

"I'm not taking his side. I'm taking Will's side. I just wish that you'd be on his side too."

"Oh, that was a good one. Did you rehearse that in the car on the way over?"

Linda shut her eyes and rubbed her temples. Her headache was starting up again. It could have been from arguing with Greg, or it could be that her hangover hadn't completely lifted. Greg and Jack Daniels. Both men in her life were equally skilled at causing a migraine. "Will's waking up now. I'm going to take him home. We can talk about this later."

"Waking up? What did that man do to him?"

"Michael did a bone marrow biopsy."

"You let that butcher stick a needle into my son's hip? Are you trying to piss me off on purpose? 'Cause I have to tell you, you're doing a pretty good job of it."

"It's what he needed to do, Greg." Linda jabbed her finger at the phone as if Greg could somehow see the gesture. "You weren't around and wouldn't return my page. Maybe next time you could act like a father and show up for part of Will's life." She flipped her phone closed and ended the conversation. She clutched her hands and let out a groan that seemed to follow most conversations that she had with that man. Reopening the phone, Linda punched the power button and eliminated any chance that Greg could call her back.

"I see you two are still on the honeymoon," Michael said.

Linda grinned tightly and pushed the cell phone back into her purse.

Greg heard the dial tone mocking him. He slammed down the receiver and stood up, swearing under his breath. He looked around the room for something to throw. Greg's pager went off again and quickly became the object he desired. The small plastic casing shattered on the wall as the door to Greg's office opened.

"Hey, I hope you weren't aiming that at me."

"Oh, hi, Chuck," Greg said, somewhat sheepishly. "If you want to talk to me, you'll have to take a number. I have several pages to return."

Chuck pointed to the debris that now lay on the floor. "I think you just erased them. So…how many pagers have you gone through this year?"

"Get the clinic to stop buying defective products. Those things should be able to withstand the impact of a five-story drop."

Chuck pulled his own pager from his belt. "Same one for seven years," he said smugly. "I'll get you another one issued. Of course, your next paycheck will be docked $300 to cover the cost."

"Fine." Greg was still fuming about Linda and not in the mood to deal with another nagging wife. Greg went back to the work on his desk. To himself he muttered, "Chuck's pager probably lasted so long because it only goes off twice a year."

"You know, as your medical director, you should at least act like you're listening to me when I am speaking to you."

Greg lifted his head and stared directly at Chuck. Chuck Cooper was the medical director for the St. John's medical group. An honorary title bestowed upon the biggest kiss-ass the nuns could get their hands on. And they loved their choice. He wasn't a bad doctor. He had a pretty good practice for about ten years. He never excelled, but didn't cause any trouble either, which was the perfect combination for an administrator. Good enough to do the job, but not so good that he'd be missed from the practice as he transitioned into administration.

Administrative life suited Chuck. He fit well behind a desk—the solid oak covered his expanding waistline brought about by his sedentary position. His managerial style was more like trying to make all the kids in the sandbox play nicely with each other. Greg liked to kick sand in the other kids' faces.

The two doctors didn't mix well, but one of the advantages, from Greg's perspective, was that a touchy-feely administrator tended to shy away from confrontation. And Chuck could never make a hard, firm decision on his own. He preferred decision by committee in order to make everyone happy. Get all the sides to agree then have everyone shake hands. It was a perfect job for someone with no innate opinions.

"To what do I owe the honor of this visit? Did you get your foot stuck in your mouth and you need me to remove it?"

"Good one." Chuck pretended to laugh. "No. I need to speak to you about something." Chuck stepped all the way into Greg's office and shut the door.

"Sounds serious. Is it budget-cut time?"

"I wish. This morning our clinic was served with legal papers. We're being named in a lawsuit."

Greg was never impressed with lawsuits. He had been sued several times. Most of them had been frivolous suits from unhappy patients. The clinic settled them all before they ever went to trial. Greg liked those. He never had to admit to any wrongdoing. "I take it that I'm involved in this one?"

"Indirectly. You aren't named in the suit, but it does pertain to you."

"Well, what is it? Is it a case of mine?"

"Not exactly. We're being sued for creating a hostile work environment by allowing certain behaviors to go unchecked. Apparently some employee has taken offense to your behavior."

Greg's eyes opened wider than usual and his jaw dropped. "What'd I do? I don't yell at anyone. If anything I make this stuffed-shirt place more fun to work at."

"I'm not denying that you have fun here, Greg. That's not what this suit is about."

"Then what is it about?"

"St. John's Clinic and Hospital is being sued for sexual harassment." Greg sat in silence for a moment before Chuck filled him in on the details. "The papers named the clinic and hospital as the defendants against the claim of propagating an environment that allowed for sexual harassment of one of our female employees," said Chuck. "It seems you have apparently exhibited tendencies that offended someone. The plaintiff claims we knew about your behavior and never intervened. The papers cited several issues that we're going to have to look into. Crude jokes and comments were mostly listed, but also they claim you've made more than one reference toward female anatomy."

"I've never touched anyone, Chuck."

"No one's claiming that you groped them in the linen closet, Greg—although Lord knows that that accusation would be hard for you to deny. They just claim you've made a lot of comments that some people have found offensive enough to affect their work. I must admit, when I read some of the things that you've allegedly done, I just bust a gut laughing. "

"If I'm so bad, then why haven't I been named in the suit?"

"It's economics really. The hospital and clinic have deeper pockets. The plaintiff stands to make more money in a suit against us. But don't go getting all comfortable. I'm sure that you will be served papers sooner or later." Chuck hopped off the table. "Needless to say, this has a few of us concerned, the sisters especially. Sex scandals involving the church seem to find their way into the newspapers. And we never come out looking good in those articles. I hope you don't have any plans for after clinic today."

"Well, actually, I—"

"Good. I knew you'd be free. The hospital and clinic come first. The sisters have called an urgent department-head council meeting for tonight at half past five. We want you to be there. It's in the board room." Chuck turned at the door. "Don't be late. You don't need any more black marks put into your file."

Greg slumped in his chair. "Why does this stuff happen to me?" He was less worried about being named in a suit than he was pissed that someone would dare to accuse him of doing something inappropriate. He was too narcissistic to see his own faults.

Greg finished out his afternoon clinic without much enthusiasm. He only pretended to listen to his patients' concerns during visits. As he looked over healing incisions and palpated benign abdomens, his mind raced with names of people, nurses, and secretaries. Who would do this to him? Who could he have possibly offended? Time moved slowly for Greg as he waited for the meeting like a boy waits for his father to come home from work so the punishment could be handed out. At first you feel dread. Then you just want him to walk through the front door so you can get it over with.

"How nice of you to clear your busy schedule for the evening, Dr. Jameson," Sister Margaret said. Her voice, much like a young Katharine Hepburn, seemed to welcome Greg into the boardroom. But she was as wise as she was old. And during her tenure as chief administrator of St. John's, she learned sarcasm as well as the scriptures. "I trust you didn't have to leave some young nurse in a compromising state of undress in order to be with us this evening."

Greg realized that any quick response to that question would only dig his grave deeper. But he held no love for the sisters, so what the hell? "Just the one. But it's okay. I left her with a vibrator."

"That's quite enough, Greg." Chuck interjected. "Just take a seat and we can get started."

The long oak table sat in the center of the boardroom. Nine chairs fit along each side with one at each end. The walls were paneled with mahogany and decorated with large oil paintings of the administrators who had graced this room with their presence over the years. Medical directors hung along the south wall, and mother superiors on the north. Greg couldn't wait to see Sister Margaret's sour puss immortalized and hanging on that wall. Greg's assigned seat was conveniently placed opposite of the rest of the faculty.

"I believe you know everyone here," began Chuck. "Sisters Margaret and Elyse." Chuck motioned to the two nuns who sat on the board. They nodded cordially. "Drs. Wilson from radiology, Kaplan from internal medicine, Birnbaum from O.B., McMichaels from your own department of surgery, Krannert from family practice, and Hamilton from oncology. We also have with us our attorney, Mr. Mark Brannon, from risk management." All the doctors nodded a small welcome to Greg. Even Michael.

"Causing more problems, Greg?" asked Michael. Greg didn't answer his old friend. His cold stare did that for him. Instead, he turned his attention to Chuck, who began:

"Alrighty then. I'd like to thank you all for coming at such short notice, but obviously we've had an incident today that will require our immediate attention, along with utmost discretion. Mr. Brannon, would you like to summarize the case that has been handed to us?"

"Certainly." Mark Brannon stood at his seat as if he were standing in a courtroom. "I'll just read the important facts. June 17, in the county of Winnebago in the state of Illinois, a lawsuit has been filed against the Hospital of St. John's by the plaintiff, Ms. Julia McMahon."

Greg flinched at hearing the name of his own scrub nurse. Mark continued to read from the document and translate the legal terms into English. The papers alleged that Greg had, on numerous occasions, made sexual remarks and innuendoes toward Ms. McMahon and other staff members. They claimed that several complaints against Dr. Jameson had been filed with the head of nursing, and that those complaints had not been followed through. By allowing Dr. Jameson to make his remarks and to be allowed to continue to practice without any intervention on behalf of the nurses, the suit had been filed against the hospital.

Mark finished reading the paper and took his seat. Then he handed out an itemized list of comments and actions that the plaintiff accused Greg of having committed. The list was two pages long, single-spaced on both sides. The group looked over the accusations line by line in silence. The nuns made the only sounds, overly accentuating their exhales after reading a particularly offensive phrase.

"Are these allegations true, Dr. Jameson?" Sister Margaret asked as she looked over the top of her wire-rimmed glasses. Her furrowed brow indicated her displeasure with the man. "And mind you, I expect the truth here."

Greg looked over at Mark. "Should I answer that?"

"This isn't a deposition. Nothing said here is being written down. We're just trying to see what kind of liability the hospital is under."

Greg tapped a pencil that had been set in front of him. "No. No, I didn't do anything inappropriate."

"You never said any of those things that have been spelled out in the suit?" asked Blake McMichaels. Blake was a surgeon. He knew what went on behind the closed doors of the O.R. He himself was guilty of most of the points described in the papers, but he wasn't a peer in this room. He had a department to run.

Greg hesitated. "What do you want me to say? No one in this room is a Boy Scout. The sisters included. Maybe I said some things once in a while. I mean, who doesn't? But I never did anything that would warrant a suit like this."

"Dr. Jameson," the young Sister Elyse piped in, "the fact remains that not everyone's name is listed in the suit. Just yours. But as a consequence, your actions will affect a great many people in this room and this community. A large settlement against this hospital could greatly impact many programs for the underserved in this community. In order for us to respond correctly to this legal action, we need to know the truth in this matter. Did you or did you not..." She flipped through her copy of the papers. "...make reference to this nurse's posterior?" She placed the papers down and adjusted her glasses so as to look directly into Greg's eyes.

"It was her ass," he spoke. "Say it with me. Ass. And yes, I made a comment about it. She has a nice one."

The gasps from the two sisters signaled their displeasure and shock with Greg's response.

"Those are not exactly the words we need to hear from you, Greg," Chuck said. "And that's definitely not the way I want you to handle this if it comes to a deposition."

"Oh, come off it, Chuck. Can't you see my point? They're just words, harmless sayings. If you're going to get all hot and bothered about a harmless comment here and there, then you're going to have to attack more physicians than just me."

"What may be harmless to you is an entirely different matter to another," Sister Margaret pointed out.

"But talk like that is how it is in the O.R.," Greg said defensively. "That's what we do. Those are things we say. In my opinion, sexual slurs and references are one of the few fringe benefits that we still have around here. Hell, the nuns have taken away all the other fun."

"Dr. Jameson, I have held my tongue long enough on this matter," said Sister Margaret. "If it's 'fringe benefits' and 'fun' that you wish to discuss, then let's bring up the fringe benefits of having a highly skilled and motivated nursing staff. Men and women who love their jobs and do it well and, I might add, make it possible for you to do yours. Would you like to have nothing but unseasoned nurses fresh out of school? Nurses who would require extensive training to get to the level of expertise that our current staff exhibits? How much 'fun' would that be? Please remember what a tight labor market we are currently in. And what about the fun of being awakened each and every night by the floor staff when even the slightest problem arises? What if you had nurses who can't start IVs, couldn't control delirious patients, or calm upset families? These are things that a trusted and loyal nurse could handle easily so that you'd never get called about it. These sorts of things come from having staff who love their jobs enough to put up with the sort of grime that you leave in a wake behind you.

"But nurses like that will not stay in a hospital if they knew that we'd allow behavior like yours to go unchecked. There's a nursing shortage, Dr. Jameson. Fine nurses like you're used to could pack up and go to any of the other facilities in the area. The only way to keep them is to make sure this environment is the finest in the area. And a doctor who makes his nurses uncomfortable about even coming to work does not lend credence to that issue."

Greg listened to Sister Margaret but could only absorb the fact that she had quite a mouth on her. The other members of the panel agreed with the sister. If not for the nurses, their jobs would be miserable as well. And the thought of a hefty lawsuit verdict could spell financial shortage at the end of the year for each of them. Money was their motivating factor.

"With that said, I take it that you are not denying these allegations. Is that true, Dr. Jameson?" Mark Brannon wanted to get back to his area of expertise.

"I may have said those things and done some of the stuff that she listed. But that doesn't make me some sort of predator."

"That's not why we're here, Dr. Jameson," continued Mark. "But I do think that your answers have given us the information that we need." Mark looked to the rest of the panel. "There's no way we can let this thing go to trial. If he talks like this on the stand, the jury would award the plaintiff anything she wants."

"Is your advice, then, that we move to settle this matter out of court?" asked Sister Elyse.

"Without a doubt."

"What was the amount listed on the suit?"

"Five million dollars. Plus, they want an educational program on sexual harassment in the workplace put into place for the physicians, as well as a counseling and support group for any nurse or employee who feels he or she has become a victim."

"How much would a program like that run us?" Blake asked.

"Not much really," said Chuck. "A full-time counselor with benefits is less than eighty grand a year. We could always find extra duties for that person." Chuck was nothing if not plugged in to the personnel issues of the staff.

"How much would our insurer cover on this suit?" asked Sister Margaret.

"Two million," Mark said.

"Well, we certainly do not want to encourage such large amounts by making such an offer to the plaintiff," the sister argued. "Mr. Brannon, as our attorney, Sister Elyse and I feel that you should make an appropriate offer of settlement in this issue. The counselors and educational programs would be easy to implement and could come out as a popular move on our part." Sister Margaret's tone said she wanted to bring the matter to a close.

"That's not all," continued Mark. "The final demand named in the suit is to have the offending physician removed from the staff. That's you, Greg."

"What? They want me fired?"

"That's what's listed in the suit," Mark stated matter-of-factly. Michael Hamilton just smiled as his old friend squirmed in his seat. Sister Margaret also smiled.

"We can't let that happen," piped in Blake. "Greg's far too valuable to this hospital and to our staff. He's an excellent surgeon who is greatly needed." Blake saw the figures flashing past him. Greg was one of the busiest surgeons on staff. He billed well over two million dollars a year. His surgical schedule was filled for the next three months. Replacing Greg would be a nightmare that he didn't want to have to face. So he'd have to defend Greg instead.

"We can't go to the plaintiffs with just a dollar figure and the promise to set up some counselors," continued Mark. "They'd throw the offer right back in my face. They want some punitive action taken against Dr. Jameson."

"Well, I'm not willing to let him go," countered Blake.

"I have a thought." Michael decided to let his voice be heard. "If it's some punitive action that they want, why not give them something that will suffice but let Greg keep his job?"

"Such as, Dr. Hamilton?" asked Sister Elyse.

"There's a sensitivity class offered at Rock Valley College. It focuses on issues common today including sexuality, race, and alternative lifestyles. Perhaps Dr. Jameson should be required to enroll in that course and have to get a passing grade. Gaining that type of experience may enlighten him, as well as satisfy the plaintiff's demands."

"Sensitivity training? You want me to take sensitivity training?" barked Greg.

Michael looked straight at Greg as if to spark an old memory. "I think it's long overdue, don't you?"

"That sort of thing just might work," commented Chuck.

"It's something I can bring to the negotiating table," answered Mark. "I assume that the hospital will cover the cost of the tuition."

"Of course. Excellent idea, Dr. Hamilton," said Sister Margaret. "Once again you've proven that our hiring you was one of our better decisions. Gentlemen, I think our business here is concluded. Again, I thank you for coming. Mr. Brannon, do let me know how the negotiations pan out."

"Will do."

The members of the committee began to file out of the room. They had been kept from their families for an extra hour tonight and wanted to keep that time from expanding.

"Wait a minute," protested Greg. "I don't want to take some stupid class. Don't I have a say in this?"

"No, Greg, you don't," Michael said. The emptying room left the two of them still seated alone at the table. "Once again, your behavior has come back to haunt you."

"Oh, don't go getting all high and mighty on me."

"I'm not. I'm just not surprised that you've gotten yourself into this mess. You never were good at controlling your actions, and look what it's caused this time. But true to form, you're only concerned about how this will affect your free time."

"I don't have to sit here and listen to you." Greg got up from his chair and put on his sport coat.

"Don't run away on me. I want to talk to you."

"I've got nothing to say to you, Mike."

"It's not about this. You know I think you're a pig. But I want to talk about your son. I saw him today."

Greg turned and pointed his finger at Michael like it was a weapon. "You keep your hands off my son. I don't want you doing anything to him. The last thing my family wants is to have the likes of you doing Lord knows what to my child."

"I'm able to remain professional and keep personal things out of my practice, Greg."

"Maybe you didn't hear me." Greg lowered his voice and spoke through clenched teeth. "I said I don't want you touching my son. You are not his doctor. I'll get someone I trust."

"You don't even know what's going on with him."

"Well, I certainly don't respect *your* opinion." Greg turned and walked out the door. He never looked back at Michael.

"Enjoy your sensitivity class," Michael called after him. "It's about time you took one."

8

Her hair was auburn, not brown. She hated being called a brunette. No proper lady from Birmingham would have "brown" hair. She wore it shoulder-length, which gave her the ability to brush back a few locks behind her ear. And when she tilted her head a certain way, she could cause a passing gentleman to walk into a signpost.

The few strands of gray that had the audacity to invade her head were promptly plucked out—or colored with the utmost discretion. It was her hair that first caused Michael's heart to beat with a different timbre—her beautiful, auburn hair flowing over the top of her white lab coat. That, and her hazel eyes. Granted, that was all he could see of Lori that first day, not that he didn't try to see more of her. But the long white coat, rubber gloves, and face mask was the standard fashion statement of first-year medical students working in the cadaver lab. And the cut of a lab coat rendered the wearer genderless.

But her eyes and hair were enough for him. It would have been enough for anyone. In fact, Michael paid forty dollars and a week's worth of lecture notes to another student to swap places with him so he could be in Lori's dissecting group. And to do that, Michael had outbid three other infatuated males. She had mesmerized him from day one. And she knew it.

His obnoxious behavior and stunts, such as throwing his voice to make the cadaver speak, initially wore heavily on Lori. She was a serious student during a time when women were just becoming accepted by the traditionally male medical profession. And Michael's stunts seemed more like the pranks of an adolescent than a medical prodigy.

But opposites do have a way of attracting each other. He had conned her into coming to the lab for a late-night dissection review the night before an anatomy exam. With the promise of his being serious, she agreed. And for the most part, Michael was. They reviewed the abdominal cavity and pelvis. All the arteries, major nerves, liver, pancreas, bile ducts, kidneys, and musculature were meticulously identified and isolated.

Just when Lori was convinced that she had been wrong about Michael, just when she was surprised to see that he was as committed to his work as she was, he reverted.

"I've got a magic trick for you."

Lori sighed. "Gonna make yourself disappear? That's a trick I'd like to see."

"Come on. I'm serious. Now watch this." Michael rolled up the sleeves of his coat to reveal his unusually hairy arms. "Nothing up my sleeves."

What a gorilla, thought Lori.

"Now, you think you've seen everything in this man's belly, right? You've seen it all."

"Yes," she said flatly. "We've covered it all."

"Well, watch this." Michael reached his hand into the cadaver's abdomen and stirred around under the small intestines. "I'll bet you didn't know that this man's abdomen also contains a human heart."

"You've got a lot of anatomy to learn," she said.

Michael pulled out a small, plastic-wrapped package. "I believe that this is for you."

Lori was certain she had not seen that package during their recent review, and so was startled by Michael's sleight of hand. "That's not a human heart," she said, studying him through narrowed eyes.

"Yes, it is," he said, his eyes unwavering. "It's mine."

Lori felt a lump in her throat, the kind that wouldn't go away no matter how many times she swallowed.

"Open it. Please."

Lori's usually calm hands trembled slightly as she took the package from Michael. Caught off guard, she had lowered her defenses and for the moment, she wasn't a serious professional; she was simply a woman.

"Just open it," Michael repeated.

The sealed plastic bag and cloth lining kept the formaldehyde from soaking into the cardboard box and envelope that were enclosed. Lori removed her gloves and pulled the envelope from the bag. Michael had written a card that described his feelings for her, how long he had felt that way, and how he would never let those feelings change. An honest-to-goodness love letter. Lori was speechless.

"Now open the box," Michael instructed.

Lori wiped a tear from her eye and then lifted the lid of the velvet-lined box. She saw a gold pendant in the shape of a caduceus, the symbol of a physician.

"It seems like that's the only thing you've ever wanted," Michael said softly. "To be a physician, I mean. So I figured that if you could have that, then you might be willing to let something else into your life. Or someone."

Thoughts raced through Lori's mind. How dare he? She didn't need a man. Did he think he could buy her with a piece of jewelry? But when she spoke, all that came out was "It's beautiful."

"Do you like it?"

"You shouldn't have. You probably can't afford this any more than I could."

"That's not the point. I'm not trying to buy you with expensive things. I just want to be a part of your life. Whatever you do, wherever you go, I want to be there. There are a lot of things in this world that I can do without. Unfortunately, you are not one of them."

Lori had had suitors before, though she never let them get too close. She never wanted to have a serious relationship. It didn't figure into her life's plan. Work hard, study hard, and become your own person. And if anyone gets too serious, just cut 'em out. But that was exactly how Michael was able to get there. He was never too serious to pose an actual threat to her. He was always joking around and being more of a class clown than the other guys—womanizers, really—in their class. He had snuck up on her and caught her off guard. But catch her he did.

Before she could respond to his last statement, Michael leaned over their object of study and kissed Lori. They kissed long, and she gave no resistance. And from that moment on, the two were inseparable. From late-night study sessions to long walks after classes, their lives together had begun.

Later on, Michael teased her about their meeting. A cadaver lab is a little offbeat. Other couples can tell their grandchildren stories about meeting over a cup of coffee or at a dance. Very few can claim they fell in love over a seventy-five-year-old victim of prostate cancer.

Lori still wore her pendant. When it wasn't hanging from her delicate neck, it stayed safely in the marble jewelry box Michael had given her on their tenth wedding anniversary. Tucked away in the lid of that box was Michael's first love letter to her. Unlike most love letters, this one didn't carry the scent of a man's cologne or aftershave. It smelled of formaldehyde, and if that was a bit unconventional, it was just another example of their less-than-typical life together.

It was that pendant Lori was removing as Michael walked into their bedroom.

"You're home late," she said. "What kept you?"

"I had a department-head meeting. Then I had to make evening rounds late. I'm so glad I got roped into being the head of this department."

"You could have turned them down, you know."

"Nah. I had to rebuild my career once we moved up here." He loosened his tie and walked into their closet to undress.

"You didn't want to be a plain old practitioner like me?"

"Tell you what—I'll let you be *my* department head. You could call emergency meetings for just the two of us in my office." He walked up behind Lori, who was still standing in front of her dresser. He put his arms around her, pulling her close to him. "We could lock the door and tell my nurse that we were not to be disturbed for an hour or so."

"Who'd take the minutes of our meeting?"

"Oh, I'd install a video camera for us to catch all the action."

Pulling away from him, she said in mock anger, "You're disgusting." The idea of an office interlude had crossed her mind once or twice in the past as well. She swung her hand in a poor attempt to slap his behind as he walked away. "Besides, I don't think they'd let a neurologist be the department head of oncology."

"I wouldn't put anything past this administration." Michael walked into the bathroom and began to brush his teeth.

Lori joined him. "Why? What happened tonight?"

Michael spit the blue paste into the sink, but a rim of foam was around his mouth. "Oh, we got slapped with a lawsuit today. Not too unusual. But I just don't like the way they're handling it." He told Lori about the situation with Greg, and how the hospital chose to try to settle the case. Granted, a trial tended to be messy, and the group certainly didn't need the negative press. But Michael got the impression that Greg was going to get off relatively easy. "If it were me, I'd have fired him on the spot."

"Well, there's definitely no love lost between the two of you."

"And there isn't with you. Don't tell me you've forgotten about what he did."

"No, Mike. I haven't." Lori slipped into a long nightshirt with a face of a teddy bear on the front. "Don't forget that I was the one he did that to. I'm just saying that I've gotten past it. I realized long ago that he wouldn't change. You either move on or get stuck with your hate."

Michael crawled into bed wearing only his pajama bottoms. He pulled the sheet up to his waist. "I'm enjoying my hate, thank you very much."

Lori crawled into bed next to her husband. "That's not like you."

"I know. But at least I did help get him sentenced to a sensitivity training class."

"Greg? In a sensitivity class?" Lori's laughter filled the room. "Oh, to be a fly on the wall in that class."

"It just seems like he squirms his way out of every situation he gets himself into," Michael said. "Except now I think he's facing one that he never thought he would."

"I'm sure that he's been the subject of a lawsuit before."

"I'm not talking about that." Michael's expression turned from one of vindictiveness to sorrow. "I saw his son today."

"At work?"

"Yeah. Linda brought him in. Cute little guy. Looks uncannily like his dad, poor sap."

"How is Linda?"

"She's fine, at least for now. When I tell her the news, she's probably going to lose it."

Lori raised her eyebrows. "Oh?"

Michael nodded. "I ran tests on Will—Greg and Linda's son—and I'm relatively certain he has leukemia. He seems pretty healthy for the moment. And the numbers of his cell counts, along with the types of cells present, give him a pretty good shot at a cure. But I know how Linda handles conflict. It's not going to be pretty." Michael sighed heavily. "And the thing that gets to me," he went on, "is that this is a nice kid."

"You know that cancer can hit anyone, nice or not."

"That's not what I meant. Will's really a sweet kid. Part of me feels sorry for him just because of who his dad is. I mean, I'm going to do right by him. I'd never let the fact that Greg is his dad get in the way of what I do." Michael's face broke into a grin. "Granted, knowing how much it's going to bother Greg that I'm his son's doctor is going to be worth it. I may even waive my fees."

Lori curled up onto Michael's shoulder and rubbed her hand on his belly. "What's really getting to you? You don't get personal with your cases."

Michael took a deep breath. He felt strangely empty inside. "It's just hard." He stroked and smelled her hair. That auburn hair. "It's just not right that a guy like Greg gets to have a kid like that when…"

"When we can't," Lori finished.

"Yeah."

"You knew about that when we got married, honey."

"I know. Still doesn't make it any easier."

She stopped rubbing Michael's belly and pulled herself up to look into his eyes. "Are you okay with this? I mean, do you ever regret having married me? Do you ever wish you were with someone who could give you kids?"

"No," Michael answered without hesitation. "Not for a second. I'm in love with you and only you. If you can't have children, then I can't have them either. We're in this together. I just think that we would have made great parents, that's all."

Lori nodded in silent agreement.

Michael grinned. "At least, *I* would have made a great parent. I can't speak for you."

She pulled on a hair on Michael's belly. "Behave yourself. You weren't the only one I could have married, you know."

"Yes, I know," Michael assured her. "Half the med school was after you. But none of them were as cute as me. Hey, watch this. I've got another magic trick for you. Keep rubbing my tummy like that for a minute." Michael leered at her and wiggled his eyebrows.

"Stop it," Lori scolded. "I'm not interested in seeing your 'levitating bed sheet' trick."

"Come on," he cajoled her. "You can help. Dress up in that little outfit of yours made out of string and oxygen and be my lovely assistant."

"Is that all you think about? Sex?"

Michael pointedly took his own pulse. "Yep. Still alive."

"Well, I can throw a bucket of cold water on that," Lori said with a smirk. "Your mother called again tonight."

Michael groaned and sat up on the edge of the bed. "You sure know how to spoil a mood."

Lori reached for his hand. "Mike," she said softly, "you've got to do something about her. She's a dear woman, but you've got to figure out what you're going to do." Then Lori's eyes widened and she affected a crazed look. "Figure it out," she said, "before I kill her."

Michael laughed but it was mirthless. "I know."

"We did move to this place just to help her out, you know."

"The thing she needs," Michael insisted, "is to move to a nursing home. I just can't bring myself to do it. You know that I promised my dad I'd watch over her."

"She needs more than watching over. I think she's just lonely. But I don't have the time to be her social life."

"I'll call her tomorrow to find out what the latest phone calls were about. And I'll get her to stop calling *you* every time she takes a step."

"Thanks. I knew you'd handle it." Lori leaned back over to him. "Now then…" She kissed his ear and began to rub his belly. "If you're done rambling, I think you were about to show me a little magic trick."

9

"Where are you going?" Paul asked, as he stood at the end of Will's bed, hanging on the footboard.

"Mom says I have to go to the hospital for a while," Will said as he placed underwear, socks, and shirts into his suitcase. "I won't be able to come home for a few weeks."

"What's wrong?" Paul asked. "You don't look sick."

Will had heard the word "cancer" used around the house a lot in the past three days. He knew the meaning of the word, and he knew it was serious. And hearing his mother cry at the mention of the word only gave it emphasis. Still, Will saw no reason to frighten his little brother. "I'm not sure what's wrong. I don't feel any different than I did before. Except for being tired a lot." He folded up a pair of his favorite sweat pants and placed them into his case on top of his socks. "But I guess something must be wrong or else they wouldn't make me stay there for so long."

"Can I stay with you?"

"No. I have to stay in a room by myself." Will saw Paul's face grow longer. "But I want you to come see me a lot, every day in fact."

Paul climbed up on top of the bed and began to bounce up and down. "What would we do?"

Will thought about what he had been told. He'd be staying in an isolation room. Everyone entering the room would need to wash their hands and put on hospital gowns. And he wouldn't be able to leave the room. It sounded a lot like a prison cell. "I've got that covered." Will pulled back the clothes in his suitcase to reveal a stack of comic books and Game Boy cartridges.

"You almost ready, honey?" Linda called from the bottom of the stairs. Paul immediately jumped off the bed. Will covered up his secret stash.

"Yeah," replied Will, closing his bag. Paul tried unsuccessfully to lift the suitcase off the bed. "Thanks, Paul," Will said. "I can get it." The boys took the stairs in a series of three jumps and landed on the kitchen floor with a loud crash.

"Please be careful," Linda admonished them. "I don't want you to get hurt."

"But, Mom," Will said, "we're going to the hospital anyway."

Linda studied her son. He suddenly seemed older than his ten years. She wondered how she'd not noticed the pale complexion, the sunken eyes, and the fatigue. Any mother who loved her child would have noticed such things sooner, when a better chance for a cure would have been possible. But not her. She was a terrible mother. The honking from the garage broke her reverie. "Never mind that, young man," she scolded gently. "You don't want to have a broken leg as well. Now come on. Your father's waiting in the car for us."

Greg honked the car horn repeatedly, unable to keep his impatience in check. Will and Paul each grabbed a granola bar and a juice box from the fridge. Will shut off the coffee maker as if it was part of his morning ritual; then he carried his suitcase out to the car. Linda lifted the case into the trunk and pressed the lid closed.

"Hop on in, boys. Keep your feet off the seats." Greg already had turned the ignition over and the Mercedes hummed with life.

"Michael told us to be there by eight o'clock," Linda said. "He wants to run some tests before he starts the treatments."

Greg placed his sunglasses over his eyes without acknowledging her comment. Then he backed the car out of the garage. Will and Paul played in the backseat, seemingly oblivious to the events that were to unfold later in the day. Greg placed a CD in the stereo to drown out their young voices.

"I'm glad that you seem to have come to terms with Michael taking care of Will," Linda said, breaking the silence. "I know he isn't too popular with you right now."

Greg kept his eyes straight ahead as he exhaled heavily. Linda shifted in her seat to look out her window. "Fine," she said tersely. It was going to be a quiet ride. Greg wielded the silent treatment like a fencer his foil. Linda covered her eyes with her sunglasses and, like her husband, covered the window to her soul.

Weaving down Perryville Road and past CherryVale Mall, Greg found his way to Interstate 90.

"Where are you going?" Linda asked, somewhat alarmed. "The hospital is the other direction."

"We're not going to St. John's this morning."

"What are you talking about? They're expecting us." Linda looked at her watch. "In fifteen minutes."

"Guess they'll have to be disappointed."

Linda's mouth dropped open. "What the hell are you doing?" she demanded. "You agreed to follow Michael's advice and start Will's treatments today."

"I never said such a thing," he said calmly. "I agreed to get Will the treatment he needs. That's all. I never said that he'd get it from Hamilton."

Linda threw her arms up in amazement and shook her head. "So where are you taking us?"

Greg stared at the road ahead as if he hadn't heard her. He was in control. He was the decision maker and he enjoyed his place on that throne. He looked in the rearview mirror and caught Will's eye. "Hey, buddy. Daddy's got a surprise for you."

"Are we at the hospital?"

"No, not yet. I'm not taking you to Daddy's hospital today. We're going to see one of my old friends." Greg turned his attention to Linda. "I'm getting a second opinion at Northwestern."

"We're not going to see Dr. Mike?" Will asked.

"No. I want you to see someone else. Someone who is even better than Dr. Hamilton."

"But I like Dr. Mike. He's funny. And he treats me like I have a brain in my head."

"You'll like Dr. Morgan, too," Greg insisted. "You can trust me, can't you?"

Will knew when a conversation with his father was over. Even Paul tapped Will on the leg and gave him a look that said to shut up.

"Yeah, Dad. Of course I can." Will slumped back into his seat and stared out the window. What was going to happen to him?

Linda glared at Greg and said through clenched teeth, "So you just took it upon yourself to change our plans and not tell me anything about it?"

"Pretty much," Greg answered smugly. "Sort of like how you took Will to see Mike without telling *me.*" He shot Linda a scathing glance. "Don't accuse me of being underhanded, Linda. You're a master at it. "

Greg wove the black Mercedes in and out of the increasingly heavy and slower-moving traffic as they neared the Chicago suburbs. A small Geo Metro with a bumper sticker reading "Chicks dig me" seemed to be crawling along in the passing lane and refused to let Greg pass, despite the number of times Greg flashed his lights and leaned on his horn. Greg's blood pressure climbed. After a few moments of riding the smaller car's tail, Greg finally managed to swerve around and in front of his prey, coming dangerously close to clipping the bumper. Stomping on the gas pedal, Greg flew past the small car so fast he barely had enough time to flip off the bearded driver.

"I have to go to the bathroom," Paul announced.

"You can hold it," Greg dictated. "It's not that much farther."

"Dad, we're only at Schaumburg," Will said. "We have at least a half hour to go." Will had been to Chicago several times before. Traveling to swim meets usually meant going to the more affluent suburbs, especially for state competitions and junior Olympics. He knew his way around. And looking out for his brother meant that he was willing to take the risk of confronting his father.

"I'll get us there in time," Greg assured him.

Linda stared coldly at Greg.

"What? I don't want to stop now. The traffic is getting heavy, and I don't want to lose time."

She shook her head knowing that if Greg himself needed to stop, he'd accept no arguments. But he just didn't get it.

The Chicago skyline appeared, along with the orange construction barriers. "Typical," Greg muttered. It seemed there were two seasons in Chicago: road construction and winter. The four lanes trimmed down to two as the traffic slowed to a snail's pace. Greg turned off the CD and listened to the radio for the traffic report. I-90 and I-95 were backed up all the way to Congress Avenue, the main thoroughfare to downtown Chicago. Fortunately, their Ohio Street exit was before the traffic jam and allowed them to avoid Chicago's heavily congested Loop.

On Michigan Avenue, Greg took every opportunity to blow his horn at the taxicabs and commuters cars that filled the busy streets. Linda looked out her window at the shops that lined both sides of the wealthy shopping and dining area of the Gold Coast. She turned her thoughts to what expensive items she could buy to get even with Greg.

They pulled into the parking garage across the street from the main entrance to Northwestern Memorial Hospital. Greg got out of the car, set the car alarm with his key chain, and began walking ahead of the family. Linda held the hands of her two boys and tried to keep up with her husband. Paul walked with the unmistakable dance of a child in search of a restroom. The large, glassed entryway to the hospital opened up into a marble-walled atrium. Pillars of stone and plaques of brass spoke of the opulent years before Medicare and managed care trimmed the fat from the medical system. Will looked up at the ceiling and was impressed with the sight of the old building. Paul just wanted a restroom.

Greg stepped to the head of the line at the information desk. "Dr. Morgan's office," he said imperiously.

The smiling receptionist spoke calmly to Greg. "Sir, there are other people in line. You'll have to wait your turn."

"I'm Dr. Jameson from St. John's Hospital in Rockford. Dr. Morgan is expecting me."

The receptionist held her smile. "I'm sorry, Doctor," she said pleasantly. She was familiar with physicians and their occasional lack of proper etiquette. "Of course. Dr. Morgan is on the fifth floor. You can take the elevators right around this corner." She pointed toward the bank of elevators at the top of a small flight of steps to her left.

"Is there a bathroom nearby?" Linda asked as Greg walked away from the desk.

"Yes, ma'am. Up the steps and to the left."

Linda thanked her as she took Paul's hand and walked in the direction she had been given. Greg looked at his watch, clearly irritated with the delay. After using the facilities, Paul, Will, and Linda returned to the atrium. Greg was standing by the elevators, having pushed the button as he saw them approach. "All set now?" he asked with just a hint of irritation.

Paul nodded his head. "Yup."

Linda glared at her husband. "Was that too difficult for you?" she asked through clenched teeth. "We didn't throw your timetable off?"

The elevator arrived. "Just get in."

"I get to push the button," Paul announced as he ran into the open car.

"The lady said it's number five," said Will. Paul reached up and pressed the round brass-plated button. The elevator stopped on each floor, which angered the impatient Greg. Finally reaching the fifth floor, Greg grabbed Will's hand, marched out of the elevator and made his way to the reception desk.

"Will Jameson to see Dr. Morgan," Greg said to the receptionist as he looked down the top of her blouse. "We have an appointment for quarter past nine."

The receptionist looked at her computer screen, moved her mouse, and clicked a few times until she found what she was looking for. "Yes, here you are." She looked over the counter at the two boys. "Which one of you is Will?"

"I am."

"Have you been here before?"

"No, ma'am. Not at this hospital."

She smiled. "You'll like Dr. Morgan. He's really nice." Her smile brought a similar one to Will's face. She handed Will and Paul some stickers of cartoon characters and then turned her attention to Greg. "I'll need you to fill out these forms." She handed a clipboard and pen to Greg, who promptly passed the duty on to Linda. "You can get these back to me any time this morning. Dr. Morgan asked that you be brought back to his office as soon as you arrived."

Greg shot Linda an imperious look as the four were escorted to Dr. Morgan's office.

"Dr. Morgan will be with you in a minute," the receptionist said. Then she turned to Paul. "There are some books on that little table in the corner. And there are magazines, building blocks, and other toys too."

Paul quickly grabbed one of the *Highlights* magazines and settled himself in a chair as Will sat up on the exam table. The receptionist turned to close the door. Greg watched her out of the corner of his eye to catch a view of her backside. Linda pretended not to notice. What was the point? Greg's behavior wasn't going to change.

"She seemed nice," Greg remarked once they were alone.

Linda nodded. She wouldn't allow him to bait her.

Dr. Morgan's office gave a snapshot of the man himself—diplomas on the walls next to pictures of fishing trips, coffee mugs filled with pens, a personal touch designed to add a sense of comfort. "You'll like Dr. Morgan, Will," Greg said. "He's an old friend of mine."

Will nodded. He didn't like being so far away from home to see a doctor, but he didn't want to argue with his father.

Daniel Morgan knocked on the door and entered the room. "Good morning." His gray hair and rounded face indicated an age that was far greater than Greg's. "I'm Dr. Morgan. You must be Will." He walked forward and shook Will's hand.

"How come you have to knock on your own office door?" asked Will.

Daniel stopped for a moment to ponder the question. "You know, I've never been asked that before. Good question. I guess it's just to be polite when I walk into a room." He turned to Greg. "Good to see you, Greg. This must be your wife."

Linda shook Daniel's hand and the three took their seats. Daniel sat at his desk and Greg took the chair closest to Daniel's. They exchanged the necessary pleasantries about the trip in from Rockford before settling in on their discussion of the matters at hand. Greg and Daniel were more acquaintances than old friends. They had met at a conference for chief residents at San Diego back when they both were completing their training. As the only two attendees from the Chicago area that had a propensity toward golf and drinking imported beer, they spent most of their free time together. They had kept in touch over the years. Occasionally, Greg would take a day off from work and drive in to play a round of golf at Daniel's club in Hoffman Estates.

"So you want me to take a look at your son, do you, Greg?"

"Yeah. We'd like to get the opinion of an expert in this matter." Greg opened his briefcase and took out copies of Will's chart. He had photocopied all of Michael's notes, the lab work, and the bone marrow biopsy report. Greg handed the stack over to Daniel.

"Looks to me like someone's done a lot of work." Daniel took the papers and turned to Will. "How're you doing, son? Feeling all right? Hurting anywhere?"

"I feel a little tired most of the time," Will said for what seemed like the hundredth time. "And my hips are a little sore." He rubbed his lower back as he spoke. "You're not going to put a needle into my back, are you?"

Daniel picked up on Will's reference to the biopsy. "No, I just want to talk today." Daniel looked through Michael's handwritten notes. "He's being seen by Dr. Hamilton?"

"Yes," Linda said. "Have you heard of him?"

"I don't think there's anyone in my field who hasn't."

"I know that he's fairly well known," injected Greg. "But I really want Will to be seen by people who are experts in this field." *As long as it isn't Michael.*

"Oh, it's an expert you want?" Daniel reached for a book on his shelf. "Here, take this." He pulled off a thick, red-covered book titled *Hematological Malignancies.* "Open up to the chapter on leukemias." Greg began flipping through the pages as Daniel removed another book. "When you've found it, do the same to this book." The book *Hematology and Oncology* was set down on the desk. "And this one." Daniel pulled a total of five books off of his shelf. *Care of the Pediatric Patient, Current Oncology Practices* and *Diagnosis and Treatments in Modern Oncology.* "Look in all of them."

Greg opened up the first book to the chapter on leukemia. He saw the name of the author: Michael Hamilton, M.D. He repeated the process for the other books that had formed a fairly good-sized stack on the corner of Daniel's desk. With each book, Greg found similar results. "Edited by Michael Hamilton, M.D." "Written by Michael Hamilton." "Chief author, Michael Hamilton." Linda picked up one of the books and smiled. This was all the validation she needed. Greg, however, grew increasingly frustrated.

"You already are seeing the expert in the field," Daniel said. "Most of what we do here is based on his work." Daniel leaned back in his chair and rubbed his chin. "You guys are actually pretty lucky to have him out at St. John's. When we heard that he was going to leave Birmingham we made a play to get him to join us here. We thought for sure that St. Jude's in Memphis was going to get him. Kind of shocked us all that Rockford would win the bidding war."

Greg saw his plans falling apart before him. "Well, it depends on how you define winning."

"Are you unhappy with him?"

Will looked up. "I like him."

Daniel spun his chair over toward Will. "I hear he's quite a magician as well."

"Yeah. I saw him do some tricks once."

Greg fumed. The only magic he felt Michael could do was to fool people into liking him. "He may be nice and all, but I'd really like Will to get his care here, if that's okay."

"I don't see why. Your insurance is with an HMO in Rockford, isn't it?"

"Yes, but—"

"So you'd have to pay out of pocket to come here. We're talking eighty, ninety grand for the whole induction therapy alone."

"That's okay." Greg was willing to go broke just to prove his point.

"That's actually beside the point. I don't know if there is something personal between you and Dr. Hamilton, but you had better put that behind you. I know that if my own son had this disease that I'd want that man to take care of him. To be quite literal, Dr. Hamilton wrote the book on this." Daniel replaced the books neatly on his shelf. "You came here for a second opinion. My advice is to take that little boy of yours back to Rockford and let Dr. Hamilton treat him. It's the best thing you could do for Will."

10

"All right, someone give me the name of another animal." Michael stood at the front of the visitors' lounge area. The entire pediatric ward population formed a semicircle in front of him. Most of the nursing staff stood at the back of the room as well. They didn't like to miss out on Dr. Hamilton's magic shows. The nursing manager of the floor didn't seem to mind if the on-duty nurses watched the shows; all their patients were sitting in the room with them.

Michael stood in front of a small table draped with a red cloth that hung all the way to the floor. A formal top hat was sitting upside down in the center of the table, ready to receive the items that Michael would toss into it. Beside the table, an easel held a large picture frame that bordered a black background. Behind Michael was a large open trunk that held the contents of tricks previously performed—water pitchers, magic boxes, silk handkerchiefs.

"Tiger," blurted out Anna from her wheelchair, momentarily forgetting about her broken leg.

"A tiger. Excellent choice." Michael wrote down her suggestion on a slip of paper, then folded it neatly in half and dropped the paper into the top hat. "Who else has one?"

Hands shot up all over the room. Amid the IV poles and bandages Michael recognized the faces of disease. But for now, they were just kids—kids who could take their minds off their illnesses for a while as they watched Michael perform magic. Michael made sure that none of his tricks were scary. No swords or anything that would give the perception of pain. The final trick, the magic picture frame, gave Michael a chance to involve everyone. Shouts of "Elephant!", "Zebra!", and "Bear!" filled the room. The suggestion of "snake" brought a unison response of "Eewww!" from all of the girls. Michael wrote down the name of every animal on slips of paper and dropped them into the hat.

"Has everyone given me an animal name?" Michael looked around the room. No more hands went up. "I think we have enough names. Now I need a volunteer." Hands again shot into the air. Michael looked over the crowd of faces, each one begging to be chosen. Then he saw the door to the unit open as Will came through the door. Michael was relieved to see Will. He'd been worried he might have to delay Will's treatments. But his smile faded when Will's father walked in behind his son. Greg and Michael's eyes met briefly, and neither was happy to see the other. Michael wished he actually had the power to make someone disappear.

"Ah, there's our volunteer now," Michael said, pointing at Will. "Come on up here, Will. I need you to help me out."

Will looked at his mother, who assured him it was all right. He put his suitcase down and waded through the sea of envious kids until he reached Michael's side.

"Everyone, this is Will. He's going to be here in the hospital for a while."

The other children all let out a "Hi, Will," welcoming him to their private world. Will nodded and waved. Then he turned to Michael. "Sorry we're late."

"That's okay. I'm just glad you're here. I'll show you to your room later, after we've finished in here. But for now, will you be my assistant for this feat?"

Will shrugged his shoulders. "Sure. What do I have to do?"

"Just reach into the hat and pull out a piece of paper. It's part of a trick. But don't show it to me."

Will bent over the top hat and saw a number of slips of paper. He reached his hand inside and swirled it around for a moment. Then his hand emerged with his selection, and he held it high in the air.

"Now I'll turn around and cover my ears. Show the paper to the audience, but don't let me hear anyone shout out what the animal is." Michael plugged his ears and turned around, and Will, realizing that now he was center stage, was a bit nervous. A morning of traveling and thinking about tests didn't exactly set him in the frame of mind to star in a magic show. But Will had been before crowds at his swim meets, and he decided to just go with the situation. Will took the square of paper and unfolded it. "Lion" was written in bold letters. Will pressed his extended index finger against his lips to hush the crowd as he walked around the area making sure that everyone saw what name had been selected. Then he returned to his spot by the table and placed the now refolded paper beside the hat. "Oh, great Hamiltini! The audience is ready."

Michael turned around to stare at Will. He hadn't been addressed by his stage name in years. Not since he first started magic in the seventh grade. Not that coming up with "Hamiltini" was a stretch of the imagination, by any means. After all, old Bill Collins, who had taught Michael his first magic trick back in his shop, was able to come up with it. "Fine. Now I am going to need all of you to concentrate on the animal that you've selected. Think about it hard, because I'm going to have to pick up on those thoughts."

The children all pressed their hands against their foreheads and temples as the word "lion" occupied their brains.

"And now, I will make your thoughts come together and cause the image of that animal to appear in this frame." Michael approached the picture frame with its empty background. He pulled a large black cloth from his case and fluffed it out in front of the audience to show that there was nothing hidden in its folds. After a final shaking, the cloth was draped over the picture frame covering up the entire surface. "And now, ladies and gentlemen, I present to you—your animal." Michael pulled the cloth off of the frame in one quick movement. The frame now contained a large, color photograph of a lion.

Throughout the audience, eyes opened wide and mouths dropped open, and not just the children's. "I've never figured that one out," said the head nurse to her colleague.

"Is it always a lion?"

"No. That's the part I don't get. It's always something different."

The silence soon was taken over by an eruption of applause and shouts.

"How did you do that?" Will asked softly, as if he and Michael were the only two in the room.

"Ah, a magician never reveals his secrets. That's the first and foremost code of honor." Michael smiled at his young friend and ruffled his hair before turning his attention back to the applauding patients. "Thank you, thank you," said Michael as he took a final bow. "That concludes the show for today." Disappointed cries rose from the group. "Sorry, but some of you have treatments still scheduled. Plus, I can't keep these nurses away from their jobs any longer without getting them into trouble." Now the nurses stationed in the back of the room voiced their disappointment. "Off you go now. Back to your rooms."

Michael turned to find Will looking into the trunk and picking up a plastic pitcher. "Just what do you think you're doing, young man?"

Startled, Will quickly hid the pitcher behind his back as if Michael was of slow wit. "Just looking at your stuff. Quite a lot of things you have."

"Yes, I do," responded Michael, who reclaimed his pitcher from Will's hands. "And the key point there is that it's mine." Michael set the pitcher on the table and began placing the other magical pieces into the trunk for storage.

"Sorry. I didn't mean to."

"That's okay. I'm not upset with you." Michael folded his table draping and placed it on top of the top hat that now sat in the trunk. "I just don't want you poking around in there. You see, Will, there's something you need to know about magic. It doesn't really exist."

"Then how'd you make that lion appear?" asked Will with a quizzical look on his face.

"Ah. That's my secret. But that's all magic is: secrets. Knowing what to do, where to hide things, how to make something seem like something it's not. That isn't very mysterious, is it?"

"Not when you put it like that."

"Exactly my point." Michael closed the lid to the trunk and set his left foot on the lid. "If you knew the secret to all of the tricks, well, that wouldn't be very entertaining, would it?"

Will thought for a moment before he answered. "No, I guess not."

"That's why I don't want you looking in there. You just might find out something that you'd rather not know." Michael's answer seemed to satisfy Will, yet left the boy wondering just what might be in that trunk.

"Very impressive, Michael," said Linda as she approached. "I don't recall your having such talent in the old days."

Greg wasn't too far behind. "Sure you do, Linda. He was an expert on illusions. Making things seem not as they really are."

"I think you're mistaken, Greg. I seem to recall someone else as the authority on smoke screen and deception." Michael wanted to say more, but Will was present, so Michael held his tongue.

"You'd like to think that, wouldn't you?"

"I did witness one illusion today that I'd like to find an explanation for." Michael looked pointedly at Greg. "What exactly caused you to disappear today and not show up until three o'clock?"

Will began to stammer about oversleeping and not having an alarm clock, but Linda broke in to defend him. And take the blame. "Sorry, Mike. It was my fault. I guess I'm just not really dealing with his condition very well. He's my baby." Will rolled his eyes at the thought of his mother still considering him to be a little child. "The idea of his having to be admitted and given all of this medicine. How sick he might get. Well, I guess it was too much for me. I kind of panicked and went into a small case of denial."

Will was taken aback by his mother's words. Sure, he had seen her cover up for his father's actions more than once. She'd minimize his missing dinner parties and being gone for a weekend. Mom was never too happy with Dad's lack of consideration for others. But she tolerated it just the same. But today seemed different somehow. The ride back from Chicago was a colorful one. From the backseat, Will heard the conversation between his mom and dad and the unpleasant words that were exchanged. Typically, when his parents started arguing, Will hid in his room, but he couldn't do that on the interstate. His mom berated Dad for undermining Dr. Mike's work. Dad accused Mom of disloyalty at taking Dr. Mike's side. Will could tell his father didn't like Dr. Mike.

For her part, Linda had presented herself as a loving and caring mother, and Will was taken aback by this never-before-seen outpouring of attention by his mother. It was almost as if she were putting on an act, like she often did when their schoolteachers would make a home visit, or when Grandma came over. Maybe this was just an act, too, to get on Dr. Hamilton's good side. Or maybe she was doing it to get under Dad's skin. Or maybe, he hoped, it was because she hadn't taken a drink from her liquor cabinet in a week.

"If you must know the truth, Mike," interjected Greg, "I kept him with me."

"Practicing oncology now, are you, Greg?"

Michael's cool response irritated Greg. "Not that I couldn't. It doesn't seem to require any real skill. Not like a surgeon's anyway. No, I took him for a second opinion with an old buddy of mine at Northwestern."

"Who'd you see?" Michael asked. "Daniel Morgan?"

Greg seemed deflated. "Yeah. How'd you know?"

"You'll find that there are very few people in this field that I don't know or haven't worked with in the past. Dan often calls me for advice on his more difficult cases. In fact, he called this morning to let me know that you'd stopped by."

Greg's attempt to sidestep Michael had been foiled and it left him speechless, which was a rare occurrence.

"I trust your visit with him answered any remaining questions that you might have had."

"He wasn't as helpful as I would have liked."

"Then I guess it's a good thing," Michael said dismissively, "that you're here with me." Michael turned his attention to Will. "Better late than never, I suppose. Did you pack your stuff?"

"Yes, sir." Will pointed to his suitcase.

"Good. You're going to be here for a few weeks. Hope you're ready for that."

"Not really."

"He's worried about missing swim practice," Linda explained. "He has a few more meets coming up that he had hoped would get him ready for districts at the end of summer."

"Around here, we take things one day at a time," Michael said, not unkindly. "We'll have to see how you are after your treatments before I make any promises about attending swim meets."

Will's face fell. Summer was an awful time to be sick. A cold or a stomachache would have been bad enough, but to be stuck in the hospital for several weeks would be torture.

"Come on." Michael decided to be Will's personal escort. "I'll show you to your room. Grab your bag."

Will followed Michael from the lounge area through a set of double doors into the main pediatric ward. A central nurses' station with three worktables was positioned in the middle of the room. Each table had a central portion cut out to hold patient charts. A secretary's desk was situated at the front of the other tables and a bank of cabinets and countertops along the back surrounded a sink and four computer terminals.

The whole area was clean, and decorated for and by children. Hand-drawn pictures hung on the wall. Wagons filled with stuffed animals were placed at convenient locations around the floor. Puzzles and games were within easy reach. The patients' rooms were along the perimeter in a circular fashion so that all the rooms were visible from the nurses' station. The walls facing the nurses' station were made mostly of glass. It allowed the most visibility for the nurses to see the patients, but offered the least amount of privacy. Each patient's room had an outside window with a view of the park. Will wasn't going to get one of these rooms.

"You'll be over here," said Michael as they rounded the corner from the secretary's desk and entered a short hallway that had only one door. They approached the glass door and entered a small room. The room barely had enough space for the five of them. A sink with several soap dispensers stood near the entrance. A large cupboard with stacks of neatly folded cloth gowns stood next to a hamper filled with gowns that had already been worn. A refrigerator and a cabinet filled with snacks occupied another wall. Two other doors led to the patients' rooms.

"This is the reverse isolation area," Michael explained. "These rooms have been especially designed to prevent infections from getting into the patients' rooms. Will, you'll be staying in this one." Michael pointed to the one on the left. "The only entrance into these rooms is through this prep area. Once your treatments begin, your immune system is going to be weakened. The medicines we give to fight your leukemia will also wipe out your own normal infection-fighting cells. Until your body is able to regenerate these cells, you will be at risk of catching an infection. Any infection. That's why we use these precautions and keep you here. All your visitors will need to wash their hands with this special soap, put on one of these lovely gowns, and cover their faces with a mask. You, of course, will have to stay in your room at all times, unless you want to wear a mask and gloves to leave for a few minutes. The air in your room, the water you drink, all of it is filtered to keep germs out. Even your food is specially prepared to keep germs away."

"Sounds like solitary confinement," said Will.

"Do you know about that?"

"I watched that movie *Papillion* once."

"You'll find this cell a little cleaner than those on Devil's Island. Plus, we have both PlayStation and GameCube to keep you company."

Will entered his room. A single hospital bed sat near the window. A private bathroom with a shower was near the doorway. A television was suspended from the ceiling. Two end tables completed the décor.

"You can unpack your things into the drawers along that wall. There's also a closet behind those doors."

Will sat down on the bed and tested the springs. "Kind of like the dorms at summer camp," he announced. "Only without the lake or camp-fires."

"Or the mosquitoes," interjected Greg, who wanted to make sure his voice was heard.

"I'll leave you all to get situated," Michael said. "I have some arrangements to make for you, Will. We've lost some time today, but I'd still like to get you ready and give you your first round of treatment tonight." Michael shook hands with Linda and made the attempt with Greg. Greg didn't comply. Michael left the room and went to the nurses' station to fill out Will's admission orders and instructions for the first round of chemo.

Greg and Linda helped Will unpack his things; then hugged their son. Linda did her best to hold back her tears, but failed at the attempt. Greg gave Will a pat on the arm and told him to be brave. Paul bounced on the bed. The family said their good-byes and promised Will they'd be back after supper to stay with him for a while. Will liked that idea.

Michael waited until Greg and Linda left before returning to the room. "I thought I'd tell you what to expect tonight," he said, sitting on the bed next to Will. "First, I'm going to have to get a catheter put into your shoulder just about there." Michael pointed just below Will's collarbone. "It might hurt a bit, but that will give us a way to give you your medicine. And we can draw blood for lab tests without having to stick you in your arm as often. The medicine I give you likely will make you sick. Throw up, that sort of thing. Think you can handle that?"

"I had to swim a mile once," Will said. "I don't think this could be any worse than that."

"Good man."

"Dr. Hamilton?" Will said timidly. "When you asked me today why we were late, you knew the answer already, didn't you?"

Michael paused, then said, "Yes. I did."

"If you knew, then why did you ask?"

Michael was impressed with Will's question. "You sound a lot like my students. They ask me questions like that. That proves that you know how to think. You will find you can learn a lot about someone in how they act when confronted. I knew why your dad took you to Northwestern today. But I got to see how you responded to that. Today you defended your parents. You stuck up for them, and your mother protected you. I'd say that that tells me a lot about you. What did you learn today?"

Will reran the conversations that he had witnessed in the lounge and the room. "I learned that you are a pretty good magician."

"Thank you."

"That you and my father don't get along very well. And that it's best that I tell you the truth. You don't seem to be the sort who likes to be lied to."

Michael looked at Will as if the boy had the mind of one much older. Someone who, perhaps, could teach something to Michael. "No, Will," he said. "I'm not."

11

The county road curved and sloped as Michael drove through the small hills on the east side of Rockford. The rolling landscape reminded him somewhat of his former subdivision south of Birmingham. The hills in northern Alabama would easily dwarf those in Illinois, but Michael had learned to appreciate the scenery nonetheless. The sloping hills brought back happy memories of driving home from the hospital along a winding road; of passing through the tree-covered hills and spying the occasional ranch home. His favorite memory was of Lori, wearing a halter top, meeting him at the door. And even though he was now driving to his home, his destination on this evening would not hold such a pleasurable sight. For he wasn't heading toward the home he shared with Lori. He was going to his childhood home, the home where now only his mother lived.

The sun had nearly set as Michael glanced at his watch—quarter past seven. He'd be late and likely would be told so several times. Not his fault, he'd say. That's the life of a doctor, always on call. But she wouldn't listen. As the wife of a doctor herself, Cheryl Hamilton had spent many days and nights wondering when her husband would come home; many nights reheating suppers and sleeping alone. It was no kind of life for a weak-willed spouse.

"Maybe if you spent less time at the hospital and more time at home you could have given me grandchildren by now." How many times would Michael have to hear that line? How often would she remind him how his life constantly disappointed her? "I told you that you shouldn't become a doctor. I knew what lifestyle was heading your way. But no, you had to go and be like your father." Her words made Michael wonder what kind of marriage his parents truly had.

He'd try to explain. That he had to stay late to take care of a little boy. He had to do a spinal tap to look for evidence of spread of the leukemia to the brain and spinal cord. It was time-consuming caring for someone. Not that she'd know. She only seemed to care about herself. Cheryl would hear the whole story and only hear that her son put the needs of a stranger ahead of her own. The widow's thoughts often focused on herself after many days and nights in an empty house.

The whole evening was rehearsed and played out in Michael's mind. From their conversations on the front porch down to the supper he was bringing that wouldn't measure up. He needn't even show up for the conversation if it weren't for the guilt trip that she'd send him on if he no-showed. The cornfields along Route 14 streamed by his car window. The tops of the plants were breaking through the topsoil and reaching for the sky. Less than two feet high, the cornstalks would be over Michael's head by the end of July. The stalks would reach more than seven feet tall before the detasselers would come by and pluck off the tops to ensure proper fertilization of the plants. Michael remembered his summer job. Getting up at the crack of dawn and riding tractors until midday, pulling off the tassels of the fall harvest. Not bad money for a kid. He earned enough to buy a bike and a set of snow skis. A smile grew on Michael's face as he thought about his younger days.

Then he thought about Will and his illness and how his childhood would contain memories far less pleasant than Michael's. That is, if Will made it to adulthood and was able to reflect back. It was nearly seven o'clock before Michael had written the chemo orders. Will was probably getting his first doses of the agents as Michael was driving. Michael and Will were definitely having different evenings, though Michael felt both would prove to be equally nauseating. Michael thought about his mother and how Will's delayed therapies would seem like an inconvenience to her. Other's lives were affected by Michael's practice. These people had real-life problems. His was not a job filled with housekeeping duties. She just didn't get it. But Lori did. She understood what Michael's life was all about. She lived it. She spoke the medical language. She'd listen to Michael talk about his day. Hear the horror stories while rubbing his temples and kissing the top of his head. How a brain like hers ended up in a body like that was beyond him. But as long as that body ended up in Michael's arms and in his bed, he didn't care.

The outskirts of Marengo appeared, with Henderson's car dealership coming into view. Henderson's always advertised the lowest prices in town, which wasn't difficult for the only dealer in town. When Michael was growing up, Marengo was a small town with only seven thousand people. But that was many years ago. Now the population had exploded to well over 7,500. Michael chuckled to himself. Some things in small towns never changed, although he wished, as he drove toward his mother's house, that sometimes things would. He drove into town, past older homes and the fire station, and pulled up to the crossroads near the center of town. He stopped at the traffic light—the only one Marengo had when Michael was growing up—and as he waited for the light to turn green, he looked straight ahead in the direction of his old house.

To his left was the main business district; the area where he'd had a paper route as a boy. He'd enjoyed that route, running up and down the busy sidewalk, delivering the *Daily Herald* as he dodged pedestrians and shoppers coming in and out of stores. This area of town was popular for after-school fun too. He'd stop for candy at the old bike shop, then go sit on all the sofas in Beckman's Furniture store before getting chased out by old lady Beckman. "Don't go getting stains all over our furniture," she'd yell as he tore out of the store. "I'll make your father pay for anything you ruin," she'd call out as the screen door banged shut behind him.

A car horn honking behind him let Michael know the light had turned green. He pulled into the intersection. Then, on a whim, he decided to turn left. He wondered if Bill's old shop was where he remembered it. Could he find it again? Did he have time to try? He checked his watch. He was already late. What would five more minutes cost him? He didn't care. Michael drove slowly down Main Street, past pharmacies, a hardware store, eateries, and a bank. Awnings covered the sidewalks in front of the more prestigious businesses. He saw groups of men sitting on benches outside the barbershop, all drinking bottles of Dr. Pepper. No scene like this existed in Rockford or Birmingham. It only was played out in tiny villages and old Norman Rockwell paintings. But Bill's store wasn't on the main drag.

Michael turned down Calhoun Street, a narrow roadway that was more of an alley. Two cars could barely fit side by side on it. The main features here were the rears of shops and a collection of Dumpsters. A garage and storage facilities were the only other businesses. Then, at the end of the street, near the railroad tracks, Michael saw the building. He pulled off to the side of the narrow street and parked his car. The shop front looked the same, although aged, much like an old man still resembles his high school photograph. The building was made of white brick with a black doorframe. The face was square and the roof was flat. The large sidewalk out in front now had grass springing up in the cracked pavement, the result of years of neglect. The small bike rack was still out front, the one that had held Michael's golden Stingray with the banana seat and Bill's three-wheeler.

Michael walked up to the front of the store. The brick facing only came up to Michael's knees. A large, plate-glass window filled the front of the store. Painted letters stretched across the top of the glass in three lines. The lettering was faded, and there was a hole in the glass over the last word. But Michael could still read it: The What-Not Shop. The place was abandoned now. The shop had closed after Bill Collins died. Michael always had been surprised that the place managed to stay open as long as it had. It was off the beaten path and was hard to find, even for those intentionally looking for it. Michael was sure he had been Bill's only customer.

He stepped up to the window and pressed his face on the glass, covering his eyes with his hand to block the glare. The floor was dirty with dust and debris. The shelves that had occupied the center of the shop and formed a small aisle were gone, along with their contents. Bill had stocked the finest merchandise a dime could buy. The stock was mostly small plastic gifts and gadgets, things like snow globes, back scratchers, plastic jewelry boxes, small games, oversized sunglasses, funny wigs, and practical jokes like onion-flavored toffee. The back of the shop had a large counter with a glass case for gum and candy bars. A metal antique cash register had stood on the corner of the counter. But Bill never used it. It had too many buttons. He had kept what little cash and coins that were exchanged in a small metal box hidden on a bottom shelf. Michael knew this because he often had to help Bill count out the change to pay Michael for the newspaper every Saturday morning, often fumbling with coins that seemed too small for his uncoordinated fingers.

Michael turned his eyes to the front left corner of the shop. A large glass case with glass shelves stood alone. Michael smiled at the sight of his favorite spot. Bill's magic corner. All the tricks that Michael first learned to perform had once been in that cabinet. Books on card tricks, handcuffs, disappearing balls, wands, canes, handkerchiefs, and assorted tricks had filled the shelves. Bill loved to demonstrate these tricks to Michael, especially any new tricks that had just arrived in a recent shipment. But Bill's hands were slow and not very coordinated. So Michael could easily see how the trick was done. But each time, Michael acted astonished as Bill pulled off the big finish—or tried to. His Saturday mornings at the shop had become Michael's favorite time.

Michael walked to the door. He put his hand on the tarnished brass handle, pushed on the thumb lever and pulled. It was locked. He tried the door a second time, but got the same result. He stood in the doorway, disappointed. It was the doorway that he had so often walked through with a smile on his face. It was also the doorway where he had earned his first black eye. That day had been so long ago, yet it remained so vivid in his mind. He had just started his paper route. A fast bike and a job that provided spending money brought an independence that he had never felt before or since. Michael was riding his bike down Calhoun Street with his red canvas sack full of neatly folded and rubber-banded editions of the *Daily Herald*. As he approached the What-Not Shop, he noticed four other bikes parked out front.

Sounds of breaking glass and shouts came from inside the store. Michael hopped off his bike and dropped his bag of papers. Four all-too-familiar faces were busting up the place. Bill was trying to stop the vandals, but a fifty-year-old man with cerebral palsy wasn't too fast and couldn't put up much defense. People had picked on Bill for as long as Michael could remember. Taunts were hurled at him as he rode his special three-wheeled bike down the streets. Apples and snowballs were thrown at him, depending on the season, all because he had a handicap. But that was all some morons needed. Bill was shouting at the teenagers to get out. But his drawled speech that, as usual, was accompanied by a stream of drool from the corner of his mouth only brought more jeers from his attackers.

Michael knew the boys, as did most people in town. The Hunt brothers, Randy and Butch, and their two accomplices, Bobby Hastings and Glen Schultz, did most of the petty crimes in the community. They all were two years ahead of Michael in school—when they went to school—and usually were up to no good. Randy, the younger Hunt brother, had curly black hair, freckles across his extra-wide nose, and a pair of eyes that didn't line up correctly. He tended to keep his mouth closed to hide his large, misaligned teeth. He was trying to open the decorative cash register and not having much luck. Bobby and Glen, whose bellies continually stuck out from under their T-shirts, were helping themselves to candy bars and gum, stuffing their pockets with one hand and their faces with the other. Empty wrappers littered the floor, along with the candy from which they'd taken one bite and then tossed away.

Butch, the older Hunt boy, liked to break things (mostly the law). Busted porch lights and car windows all over the town had been blamed on him at one time or another. Right now he was settling for a collection of seashell ashtrays. Michael was outraged at what he saw, but the gang was too engrossed in their crime spree to notice the young paperboy. Michael rushed into the shop and knocked Butch over. The thug fell backward, striking his head against the corner of a metal shelf and opening up a gash that spilled blood on the floor. His screams caught the attention of the other three. Randy came to his brother's defense while hurling profanities and threatening to end Michael's short life.

Bill kept a broom in the front corner of the shop by the door. He was always sweeping the sidewalk in front, like any other proud shopkeeper. Michael had another use for it. He picked up the broom and thrust the broomstick like a staff into Randy's oncoming gut. Randy let out a groan as he doubled over, the wind knocked out of him. Michael took the broom and swung it over his head, hitting Randy on the back of his skull. The delinquent dropped to the floor like the sack of excrement that he was. Bobby and Glen looked up from their feast. These two boys were pretty much cowards without the Hunt brothers to back them up. Seeing their two tough friends on the floor was all they needed to decide to clear out. They ran out the front door, never looking back, but hollering that they'd get back at Michael for what he had done. "Retard lover," they shouted without turning back.

Butch had pulled the tail of his striped shirt up to his particularly large forehead to cover the bleeding wound. "You creep! I'm gonna kill you, Hamilton."

Michael held the broom high like a sword over his head. His heart was pounding like it was going to jump out of his throat. His mouth was dry as cotton as his nerves solidified. Butch didn't take any extra time exiting the shop after his threat. Obviously, he meant to put off killing Michael for another day, a day that still hadn't arrived. Randy, however, was not about to stand down from the challenge that Michael had declared. Randy was smaller than his brother but full of spit and fire. He charged Michael and tackled him to the floor while punching ribs and giving shots to the face. Michael countered by wrapping his arm around Randy's neck and squeezing the air out of Randy's lungs. The two rolled on the floor, kicking and punching, knocking knickknacks off shelves, and cussing at each other.

It wasn't until Sheriff Wilson walked in and pulled Randy off Michael that the fighting stopped. Bill had managed to set off the alarm when the boys had started to wreck the place. Michael and Randy hadn't noticed the flashing lights on the squad car as it pulled up outside the store. It wouldn't have mattered much if they had. Neither was willing to hold back a punch.

A hefty man of strong stock, Sheriff Wilson held the attention of anyone who happened to be locked in his grip. "What the hell's going on here, boys?" His words echoed in Michael's head. Butch, Bobby, and Glen had all disappeared, riding home to spread lies and create alibis supporting their side of the story.

"He started it," Randy insisted.

Michael gave his version of the confrontation. Sheriff Wilson seemed to already know who was involved. Randy denied even being in the store and said that Michael pulled him in and started beating on him. But Michael had a witness. Bill stepped in and told the story in a quivering voice. Sheriff Wilson had to calm Bill down, as he was quite agitated about the violence he had seen and the condition of his shop.

"Who are you going to believe? Me or some retard?" Randy demanded.

In the end, Wilson pulled Randy out of the shop by his collar and tossed him into the backseat of the squad car. As he passed by, Randy called Michael a retard lover and spat on Michael's bike. As Sheriff Wilson drove off with one-fourth of Marengo's version of the Hole in the Wall Gang, Bill patted Michael on the shoulder. "Thank you," he slurred.

Michael shrugged. "Here's your paper." He relived that moment for weeks, wishing he had said something more compassionate, like, "Sorry that this happened." Or "Too bad I didn't kill the bums." But he didn't have to. Bill knew that Michael acted as a friend that day. Michael only hoped that his actions would make up for what he himself had done to Bill in the past. Michael remembered watching Bill turn in silence and walk slowly to the back of the store, dragging his good leg behind his bad one. Bill quietly started cleaning up the shop and never said a word; never got angry with his attackers or voiced a hateful thought. It was as if he was incapable of uttering a negative thing against another of God's children. Either that or he was used to being treated like his life didn't matter to others.

As Bill silently moved about the store, the look of despair never left his triangular face. His shoulders hunched in his oversized black jacket as he tried to pick up the remains of his possessions. Bill's gentleness touched Michael, who picked up the broom, only this time to be used as intended. Michael stayed in the shop that afternoon to help Bill—sweeping, cleaning, picking up broken items and placing the undamaged ones back on the shelves. The two had done the best they could to get the place back in shape. But no good deed goes unpunished. By the time Michael finished at the shop and then completed the rest of his route he was late for supper. Walking in the front door, late, covered in dirt, with a black eye and a torn shirt (a good Sunday shirt, no less) made his mother hit the roof.

Mother.

Michael came back to the present. He remembered why he'd driven to Marengo tonight. She'd be waiting. Michael looked in the window. The shop was empty again and the figures gone. He stood alone on the street. Michael looked at his watch. He'd be late again. He'd have a car to take him home tonight instead of a bike. But regardless, he was sure that, once again, when he walked through the front door his mother would read him the riot act.

12

The old neighborhood looked the same, as if these past twenty years had passed overnight. Michael recognized the houses, but not many of the owners. Kids were playing in their yards in much the same way he had done years ago. Michael slowed his speed as he drove down the tree-lined Anderson Avenue, just in case an errant ball or nonhelmeted child crossed his path. The Hamilton house—a two-story English Tudor with front hedges that desperately needed trimming—occupied a corner lot. The large oak in the front corner of the yard was clearly visible from the side streets, but Michael's tree swing, once almost part of the tree itself, had long since been taken down. Funny, Michael thought as he pulled into the driveway, how the place seemed smaller than he remembered it.

A green four-door Chevy sedan sat in the driveway. Michael nodded appreciatively. That would be Maggie's car, bless her. He pulled up next to it and got out, taking a large, brown paper bag from the backseat. "Hi, Maggie," Michael called out to the buxom woman exiting the front door. "Thanks for hanging around until I got here."

"That's okay, Doc. You know I don't mind."

"How's she today?"

"Her old self," Maggie responded with a shake of her head. "Trying to do too much on her own, as usual. I caught her trying to rearrange the furniture in the family room when I came back from the store. I swear that woman is going to break a leg or something one of these days." Maggie rummaged through her oversized blue purse for her car keys. When she found them, she held them up in the air in her right hand with a satisfied grin. "And when she does break something," Maggie went on, "I'm sure she'll find a way to put the blame on me."

Michael nodded. "She is cantankerous."

"I have another name for it," Maggie said. "But Pastor Belcher don't like me using those words." Maggie squeezed into the front seat of her car and turned the engine over. Calling out, "See you tomorrow," she backed out of the driveway.

"Thanks, Maggie," Michael called after her. "You're a gem." As much as she complained about his mother, Michael knew the two women got along. And he was grateful for that. Prior to Maggie, Mom had gone through more caregivers than James Bond had gone through women. Michael took a deep breath and trudged up the front steps. He pushed open the screen door and stepped into the house, calling out, "Hi, Mom."

"You're late!" Cheryl Hamilton was a small woman but her voice was strong enough to chastise Michael from two rooms away. She was sitting in a wheelchair in the kitchen, a walker by her side. Her wisps of white hair were partially combed across her scalp, and a small blanket covered her shoulders, even though the night was warm.

"I know," Michael agreed. "I'm a rotten son."

"Don't joke about that," Cheryl said petulantly. "You leave me here all day with that woman."

"Maggie's a good person, Mom. She looks out for you." Michael would defend anyone willing to put up with his mother. Setting the brown bag on the kitchen counter, he leaned over to give his mother a peck on the cheek. Her bottles of medicine stood in a line on the counter as if waiting their turn to be called into action.

"Did you take your pills today?" he asked, picking up the bottles and shaking them.

"No. I don't think that woman is giving them to me right. She's trying to give three blue ones in the morning and only one red one at noon. I swear, son, I think that Maggie is trying to kill me."

"I know. I'm paying her extra to make it look like an accident."

Cheryl continued as if she hadn't heard him. "One of these days you're going to walk in here and find me face down on the floor—dead. And where'll she be? Probably watching TV or carrying my good silver out to that jalopy she drives."

Michael shook his head as he unpacked the brown bag, laying out the Styrofoam containers of food he'd brought from the hospital. "I hope you don't insult her like this to her face." Michael reached for a switch near the ceiling, one that intentionally was out of his mother's reach, and flipped the circuit breaker to bring power to the stove. It was a safety feature—installed after the kitchen fire—that kept Cheryl from cooking when she was home alone. He then turned on the oven.

"That's broken, you know," his mother informed him. She still hadn't caught on.

"I'll get it started," Michael assured her. He transferred the contents of the containers to his mother's pots and pans. "I brought you some good stuff for dinner tonight."

"I don't like that hospital food," Cheryl groused.

"You know you're on a restricted diet, Mom. And this is a lot easier than my cooking for you. It'll be ready in just a minute." He wheeled her to the dining table, and then began looking through her cabinets. "Where's your kit? You didn't move it again, did you?"

"You know I hate that thing. It hurts."

"Mother, I need to check your blood sugar before you eat. If you keep hiding your glucose monitor, I'll just bring another one from work."

She pursed her lips. "It's in the bathroom under the sink."

Michael shook his head as he walked out of the kitchen. "Was that so hard?" He had never experienced raising a child, but somehow felt he knew what it must be like.

The downstairs bathroom had been converted to fit Cheryl's needs. Guardrails along the tub and an elevated toilet seat were now the standard décor. Under the sink, behind a stack of towels, Michael found Cheryl's glucose monitor kit.

The aroma of the chicken was filling the kitchen as Michael returned. "You've got to find a better hiding place than that, Mom."

"I didn't hide it. Maggie did. I think she doesn't want me to get well."

Michael sighed. "That's not true, and you know it." This was the same argument that they played out nearly every day. He knew his mother was angry that she was old and alone. He knew she was upset that she had lost control of her life. Logically, he knew these things, yet Michael hated that he was forced to spend time taking care of a woman who didn't have "thank you" in her vocabulary. She wasn't where she wanted to be—hell, neither was he—but she wanted to share her misery. He took his mother's hand

and wiped the tip of her pinkie with an alcohol pad, then fanned it dry before sticking a small lancet into her skin to draw blood. Cheryl's whimper came out at the same time as the drop of blood. Michael placed the red drop onto a test strip, and then wiped his mother's finger clean. Walking to the stove, he dished up his mother's supper while the monitor measured the level of glucose in Cheryl's blood. A small beep signaled the completion of the test. "One-forty-five. You have been taking your medicine."

"I think she puts it in my food," Cheryl complained.

"Smart Maggie," Michael said with a smirk.

Cheryl snorted. "Not really. I used to find my pills in pudding and mashed potatoes. That made it easy to spit them out." She turned her head away and looked out the window. "Now I think she crushes them up. I don't like her. She's sneaky."

"Maggie's just what you need," Michael said, setting his mother's dinner in front of her. "But if you'd rather, I'm sure I could find a nice place for you to live with people your own age and a little nursing supervision thrown in."

"You're talking about a nursing home, aren't you?"

"Well, yes."

"Over my dead body. Those places are where you go to die."

"Not anymore, Mom. There are some that are set up for people who are more independent. They provide a nice place to live and some good people to watch over you."

"So that you wouldn't have to, right?"

"That's not it at all."

"Yes it is, Son. Yes it is." Cheryl looked down at her plate, but wasn't looking at the food.

Michael couldn't argue with her. She was right. He was tired of making the commute every day, tired of listening to her complain about the food, the temperature of the room, the axis of the earth. And he was tired of missing dinners with Lori. Lori was getting tired of it, too, though she'd never complain. For her part, Cheryl may have been the most tired of all of them. She was tired of being a burden; tired of not being able to walk up a flight of stairs or cook a meal. She hated needing help to wipe her own bottom, and hated losing her independence along with her youth.

"I'm doing all right here by myself," she insisted. Then she added grudgingly, "I suppose Maggie makes things go pretty smoothly while she's here."

"Fine. We don't have to talk about that now. It was just a thought." Michael had left his briefcase full of nursing home brochures in his car. They'd just have to stay there for another time; a time that he hoped would come soon.

"Aren't you going to eat anything?" Cheryl asked. "You know I hate to eat alone."

"Nah. I'll wait until I get home. Lori's waiting for me."

"That's nice. I guess that's one good thing about not having a house full of kids. You don't have to have dinner on the table at a certain time."

"Don't go there, Mom." He was tired of her meddling into his and Lori's reproductive life.

"What? I didn't imply anything. I said that it must be a nice thing." Her tone inflected a sincerity that was not there.

"I know what you meant."

Cheryl had stated repeatedly how her life just wouldn't be complete without grandchildren. She wanted a slew of them—kids she could spoil and send presents to. Kids she could sit on her lap while she told funny stories about their father. Kids to take away the silence and emptiness that now filled her life. Was that too much to ask? She didn't think so. And she never missed a chance to let her feelings be known. "You act as if I'm a bad person for wanting grandchildren."

Michael sighed heavily, exasperated by the conversation that had taken place over hundreds of miles and over many years. "You're not bad, Mom. It's just not something that's going to happen."

"Fine." Cheryl went back to her dinner. "I just wish you could tell me why."

Michael shook his head. Instead of offering an explanation, he simply walked into the next room, leaving his mother alone with her dinner. He couldn't have this discussion with her now. Why should he have to explain himself in any case? It was none of her business, but she couldn't understand that. Michael thought of Will and what a sweet boy he was. His face and blond hair were etched in Michael's mind. Michael longed to have a boy like Will. Cheryl wasn't alone in her feelings about his having children. He just covered his feelings better.

After dinner Cheryl wanted to sit in the family room, so Michael helped her get settled. She eased herself into her lift chair, then reached for the evening paper. "Remember when you delivered the paper, Michael?"

"Yes."

"You were so proud to have your own job. Very serious about your work, you were. You had a lot of your father in you."

"Thanks, Mom."

Cheryl shifted herself slightly in her chair. "I'll be fine, honey, if you want to go. I can see myself to bed."

"Got your lifeline?"

"Right here." She held up her small electronic device that allowed her to call for help in an emergency. "Now go on."

"Okay." Michael leaned over and gave her a kiss. "I love you."

"I love you too," she responded without looking up. "Not much in this paper these days."

Michael kissed the top of his mother's head and left her to her paper. By the time Michael pulled out of the driveway the sun had set. The sky was a deep red; it would be black before he got home. The trip was automatic now. He'd drive down the same streets and take the same turns. Michael glanced at his briefcase. Seven nursing homes and independent living facilities had met with his approval. He had narrowed it down from a field of thirty-five. It was time to choose a home for his mother. Now all he needed was to discuss it with her. He had tried to bring up the subject tonight. But he couldn't do it. *Maybe tomorrow*, he thought. *Maybe tomorrow.*

13

Will retched again, filling the gray plastic basin with vomit. He hadn't been able to keep down any of his breakfast. But this was not food. There was none of that left. He had heaved his stomach acid and was now down to the bitter bile. It wasn't that he hadn't been sick before. One time he had the stomach flu so bad he had missed a week of school. But this was worse. The chemotherapeutic agents had filled Will's veins and now were working their deadly magic on his body. His innocent cells were dying off along with the harmful ones. The chemotherapy agents were poisons that brought the body's sense of self-preservation back to life. Vomiting was the body's only way of ridding itself of any harmful substances. The nausea came in large tsunami-like waves. Will had been given a shot for the nausea, but now he was beginning to wonder if it was meant to get rid of the nausea or cause it.

He wiped the sweat and spit from his face, only to vomit again. He rubbed his now sore stomach muscles and decided this was not going to be on his list of fun things he got to do over the summer. All in all, he'd rather have been at swim practice.

"Sucks, don't it?"

Will lifted his head from his bucket and looked around the room. He hadn't heard anyone come in, and that was definitely not the voice of his nurse. Where was the voice coming from?

"Over here."

Will spit into the basin once more as he tried to rid the foul taste from his mouth. He turned toward the window on his far wall and saw a boy about his own age looking back at him. "Who are you?"

"I'm Eddy."

Will saw the boy speak but his voice seemed odd. Then Will realized Eddy's voice was coming through a speaker just below the window. Eddy was a small boy with a large bald head. A big grin covered his freckled face, and his waving arm let Will know that Eddy was very eager to say hi.

"What's your name?" Eddy asked.

"Will." He spat in the bucket again.

"Puking sucks, don't it?"

"Doesn't it," corrected Will. "It certainly isn't what I wanted to do today, if you must know." Will noticed Eddy's puffy face and remembered that Dr. Hamilton said the steroids might cause that.

"Don't worry," Eddy said. "You'll get used to it. Just puke your guts out, brush your teeth, and try to get some sleep. That's what I did my first time."

Eddy motioned for Will to come over to the large window that separated the two rooms. It had been built to allow the patients in both rooms to visit with each other while still maintaining their independently sterile environments. Curtains on either side of the window allowed the occupants to have privacy, if they so desired.

"C'mere. I can't hear you too good from there. You have to push your button on the intercom." Eddy pointed down to the speaker box. "These were put in last year when I was here for my second round of chemo. Now we can have someone to talk to when we're not allowed to have anyone in our rooms. They don't want us passing germs and stuff like that."

Will fought off another wave of nausea. He didn't want to throw up in front of a new kid. He took a deep breath and swallowed hard. "So we can talk back and forth to each other?"

"Yeah. And that's not all. Watch this." Eddy pushed another button. "Hi, Cynthia," he said in a syrupy voice. "I miss you."

"What do you want, Eddy?" came the response from the intercom.

"I just want to hear your sweet voice," Eddy cooed, trying hard not to laugh. Adolescence had come early for Eddy. He was only eleven years old, but he'd grown up fast in the last three years as he coped with his illness.

"Who's Cynthia?" asked Will.

"My nurse," Eddy answered. "She's cute." He wiggled what would have been his eyebrows if his chemo hadn't caused him to lose his hair. "She's got big boobs too."

"I heard that, Eddy." Cynthia scolded. "Don't make me come in there and knock you around. Don't forget, I can take your temperature any way I want."

"Oh, crap!" Eddy covered his rear end with one hand and his mouth with the other. Will laughed. It was a much-needed change in his mood.

"Now, don't you corrupt Will, Eddy. I don't want to have to deal with two troublemakers."

"I'm not corrupting him," Eddy said sweetly. "Honest."

"Uh-huh, I'm sure," Cynthia responded. Then she turned her attention to Will. "Will, how are you doing? Feeling any better?"

Will searched for the button on the intercom.

"You don't have to push nothing," Eddy said. "She can control the intercom from her station." Eddy chuckled. "She threatened to turn it off on me one night 'cause I was bothering her too much. But she didn't. She always keeps an eye on me."

Will nodded an acknowledgement to Eddy, then said, "I'm a little better, thanks."

"I'll bring you some Sprite and crackers," Cynthia offered. Will heard her walk away from the station before the speaker went silent.

"So, what do you have?" Eddy asked.

"Leukemia."

"No duh. Everybody who lands in these rooms has leukemia. I mean what kind?"

Will wanted to say that he had a rotten kind. The kind that makes your stomach turn inside out. "It's something with initials. I think it was A-L-L."

"Ah, lymphocytic," Eddy said knowingly. "That's the good kind. At least you've got a shot at a cure."

Will gulped. Eddy said what he thought, that was for sure. Dr. Hamilton had told him that the chemotherapy might help slow down the cancer, but no one had mentioned his chance of survival. He was glad to hear the words spoken by another kid.

"Me," Eddy went on, "I'm screwed. I've got AML. That stands for myelogenous. It's a different kind of white blood cell. My cells have a funky chromosome or something in them that makes them harder to kill or something. Anyway, it practically takes a miracle to kill off my bad stuff and keep it away. I've gone through three rounds of chemo already."

"Has it helped at all?" Will asked.

"Nah," Eddy said matter-of-factly. "Oh, sure, for a little while. It knocks out my bone marrow pretty good, and I'm not too bad for a little while. One time I got to stay home for a whole month before I had to come back. But those bastard cells keep coming back. This is my last shot."

Will felt light-headed. He hadn't eaten much in the past twenty-four hours and what little he did was now in the toilet. He pulled up a chair next to the window and sat down. "What do you mean?" A "last shot" sounded too final for his young ears.

Eddy shrugged. "I've had all the stuff they can give me. My cancer cells just keep coming back. Wish my hair would." He rubbed his smooth scalp. "Anyway, they're going to try to completely wipe out all my bone marrow cells. Then they'll give me new bone marrow. It's called a transplant. Out with the old and in with the new."

"Will it work?"

"Hope so. I can't stand to see my mom cry anymore." Eddy plopped himself onto his bed. "She does that a lot nowadays. What about your mom? Does she cry a lot?"

"Sometimes," Will admitted. "Yeah, I guess so." Mostly, Will remembered, his mom cried at night when she thought Will was asleep.

"I mean, I know I'm sick and all," Eddy said. "And sometimes I think about what would happen if I didn't get better, you know? But when I see how sad my mom gets, I just want to get better for her. So I'm hoping this bone marrow transplant thing works."

"What do they have to do to you?"

"I just go through the same chemo as before. They nuke me a bit too. Try to get rid of all my bone marrow cells."

"Sounds rough."

"Yeah. But once all the tests show my cells are gone, they just put new ones back through this." Eddy pointed to the catheter that ran into the left side of his chest and entered his major vein. "But it's roughest on my dad."

"Why on your dad?" Will asked.

"'Cause he's giving me his bone marrow."

Will's eyes widened. "How does he do that?"

"He has to have an operation," Eddy explained. "They take a bunch of his normal cells from his bones. It's like what we get done to us, only they do it, like, fifty times."

Will winced as he remembered his one bone marrow biopsy. He couldn't fathom what it would be like to have that done fifty times. But Eddy's father was going to do it.

"Ouch," Will said succinctly.

Eddy grinned. "My dad's pretty cool about it. Both my parents were tested, but my dad had a better match for the donation. He's always said that he'd do anything for me. Guess he was right."

Will wondered if his own father would give his bone marrow if Will needed it. Would he go through the pain if Will's life depended on it? Suddenly, Will felt very envious of a boy he barely knew with a disease far worse than his own. He felt the nausea coming back.

"Feeling sick again?"

Will nodded, unwilling to speak.

"I'll call Cynthia," Eddy said, seemingly happy for an excuse to talk to his nurse.

Will held up his hand. "No," he said weakly. "You don't have to. I'll be all right in a second." Will lifted his head and inhaled deeply, fighting to keep from throwing up. He looked at Eddy through tired eyes. "Does it always feel like this?"

"Nah," Eddy said with an air of authority. "You only get sick for the first day or two after each treatment. You stop puking after that."

Will nodded and smiled. So there *was* a light at the end of the tunnel.

"Then you just sit back and enjoy your room for a few weeks," Eddy went on. "Your cancer cells start to die off and that means your blood counts are checked every day. And hey, watch out for Angie. She's a lab person who draws your blood. She couldn't hit a vein if it was as big as your arm. Look." Eddy rolled up his sleeve and showed Will the bruises up and down both his arms.

"Don't they draw blood through my catheter?" Will asked. "That's what Dr. Mike told me."

"Yeah, but sometimes it doesn't work and they have to use the needle method."

Will looked at his arms and imagined what they would look like after being jabbed with needles. His mom would probably freak. Paul would think it was cool in a gross sort of way. Would Erin still like him if he looked like that, or if he were bald?

"But then there's Melissa," Eddy said. "She's really cute."

"Like Cynthia?"

"No. Well, sort of, only different. She has a really cute face and smile. Plus, she always smells nice."

"You're really into girls, aren't you?"

"Not as often as I'd like to be," Eddy said with a laugh.

"What's that supposed to mean?" asked Will.

Eddy stopped laughing and looked slightly confused. "I don't know. But I heard my older brother say it once, and my mom slapped him. So I figure it must be something good." Both boys chuckled. "I don't see him much now, though. Most of my days, I'm here on the ward."

"I have a brother too," Will said. "I guess I won't be seeing much of him either."

Eddie shrugged. "It's not like we're prisoners here or anything. Your brother can come and visit. We just have to stay in here until our normal cells come back."

"Do you think they will?" Will asked.

"They should. And if they don't, there are some medicines that'll help to boost them along. The normal cells die off just like the cancer ones do. Then the hope is that some of our normal cells survived the chemo and that they can grow back. Until they do, we could catch just about any germ and not be able to fight it off. So every day the vampires come in and draw our blood to see where we are. Until then, we're stuck in these isolation rooms."

"How long does it take?" Will wanted to know.

"I spent three weeks here one time," Eddy said, "before it was safe for me to go outside. I got bored out of my head. I played all the video games they had here at the hospital, and my dad even went out and got me my own system with new cartridges."

"That's pretty cool."

"Yeah. My dad forgot to bring it this time. My mom said she'd get it for me tomorrow."

Will wondered when he'd get a visitor. Where was his mom? His dad even worked in the building. Why hadn't he stopped by?

"Nintendo GameCube," Eddy said, as if the words were sacred. "All they have here is a SuperNintendo. It's a piece of crap, if you ask me. My parents said they got me my GameCube to keep me company, but I think it was 'cause they were just glad I was alive."

"After your treatments?"

"Yeah, I got pretty sick. I had a fever of 104 degrees. My cell counts were bupkis. The doctors didn't know where the infection was, or if I even had one. Man, they took X-rays and blood tests. I had a CAT scan. Did you ever have one of those?"

"No."

"They're not too bad. But the dye they shot in my arm sure did burn. I was kind of out of it for a couple days before the fever finally broke. Turns out I only had a sinus infection, if you can believe that. Dr. Hamilton said I could have died. It's hard to think that you could die from something so simple."

Eddy, Will realized, was way more accustomed to the notions of death and dying than Will was. It was if he were talking about going for a walk or playing a game. Will didn't like thinking about death. He abruptly changed the subject. "You have Dr. Hamilton too?"

"Yup. Just this past year though. We had some other guy before him. I didn't like him as much. He had oily hair and his pants were too short. But I like Dr. Hamilton, even if he does stab me with that big needle."

"Yeah, I like him too," Will agreed. "He treats me like I'm a person and not just a stupid kid."

"Right. And he tells jokes and kids around."

Will nodded. "Yeah, he's funny. But have you seen his magic tricks? I like that most of all."

Eddy's smile broadened as he recalled the number of times he'd seen Michael's shows throughout his many stays in the hospital. "I've seen hundreds of his tricks," Eddy boasted. "There's the disappearing balls, the jumping match sticks—hey, once he even burned up a dollar and made it reappear in a sealed envelope."

"Wow!" Will said. "No fooling?"

Eddy nodded. "No fooling. Of course, I know they're just tricks, but I can't figure out how Dr. Hamilton does them. And he wouldn't tell me either, no matter how hard I begged!"

Will leaned back in his chair, content to listen to Eddy's conversation jump from one subject to another—sports, girls, video games. It was like surfing the Web with a person instead of a computer. And Eddy's words were soothing and kept Will's mind off his nausea or wondering about his fate. He already missed his swimming and his friends at the pool. But Eddy helped to take away some of the loneliness. In a strange place, in a strange way, Will had found a friend, and it felt good.

"So I figure that next summer I'll get a new bike," Eddy was saying. "Either I'll have grown out of my old one, or I'll be sick and they'll get me one."

Cynthia's voice broke in on the conversation. "Hey, chatterbox, how are you feeling now?"

"Better now," answered Will.

"Okay, I'll bring you a snack."

Will took his plastic basin into his bathroom and poured the contents into the toilet. As it flushed away he felt the last remnants of his nausea go with it. He brushed his teeth to get the remaining sour taste from his mouth, and then went back to his bed.

Cynthia was outside the door washing her hands and putting on rubber gloves. Will's cell counts were still in the normal range and he didn't need the strict isolation yet, but putting on gloves had become a habit for her, and Cynthia wasn't about to break out of her routine.

"Here you go, little man," she said. She carried a cup of soda and a plate with saltine crackers—a veritable feast in Will's hungry eyes.

Will sat on the edge of his bed Cynthia set up his tray table and placed the snack in front of him. She leaned over in front of him and straightened up Will's gown in a motherly fashion.

"Anything else I can do for you right now?" she asked.

"No, thank you. This'll be fine."

"Just call if you need me."

When she was gone, Will turned to Eddy, who was standing at the window with an inquisitive look on his face. "Well?"

"You were right," Will said with a smile. "They are big."

14

The nausea was still strong. The retching had slowed its pace but she still had dry heaves. Her stomach was empty, yet her body was still trying to expel the remnants of whatever contents it once held. There was a bitter taste in her mouth and a burning in her throat. And her abdominal muscles ached—a feeling that had become all too familiar. Linda sat up slowly and moved her face away from the toilet. The bathroom walls hadn't stopped spinning yet. She brushed back her hair from her face and pulled the wet strands that were sticking to her neck. Another glamorous beginning to a beautiful day, Linda thought ruefully. Alone in her spacious Martha Stewart-decorated bathroom, her arm around the toilet bowl, Linda wallowed in regret and self-pity. But that was why she drank in the first place.

How could she ever have chosen to marry a man like Greg Jameson? Why hadn't she left him when she had the chance? Why was she drinking her life away just to get back at him, only to find that he rarely noticed, and she was only punishing herself?

"Oh, I'd kill for a Bloody Mary right now," her brain screamed as if on autopilot. But she couldn't get off the floor. "No," she told herself. "No, you don't want another drink. That's what got you like this in the first place, Linda." She rubbed her temples and took a deep breath. This time she didn't trigger a coughing fit. "Never again," she muttered. "I've had it. I'm going to quit." Her words echoed in her head. She had said those words before, hundreds of times. She even had begun to believe her own lies.

But her mirror didn't lie. Oh, how she wished it would, at least once in a while. There were dark rings under her bloodshot eyes and dried saliva in the corners of her mouth. She looked older than her thirty-seven years. Sunglasses and a private estate were her saving graces; they kept the eyes of the world off her.

She was glad no one could see what she had become. Linda had fallen a long way from her days on the dean's list at the University of Chicago. Not that a degree in English literature was a sure bet for fame and fortune, but it should have gotten her farther than where she was now.

She'd been popular in college. No, more than that. She'd been hot stuff—on the pompon squad, a sister in Phi Kappa Theta. She'd even been a member of King's Court for homecoming her junior year. No wonder she had Greg chasing after her—Greg and a few dozen others. He was a bit crude, but he'd charmed the pants off her, frequently.

Was it the prestige of dating a medical student or the prospects of the financial security as a doctor's wife that finally won her over? She couldn't remember anymore. The engagement party her friends at Marshall Field's threw for her after she got engaged sure was a status symbol. "How lucky you are." "Girl, you're set for life." "I wish I had a man like that." Her friends' words still rang in her ears.

If only they knew what Greg was really like. If only they could see him now, the way she did. Sure, the signs were there when she was dating him. She just couldn't see them. Or wouldn't. Or maybe she saw a glimmer of what Greg was really like, but chose not to believe it. Power and status convinced her to put up with anything.

Linda splashed cold water on her face. It stung a bit, but she was falling into her self-punishment phase of her recovery. She needed to wake up, and the coffee pot was downstairs, and probably empty. He never left her much in the bottom of the pot.

She should have known what Greg would become when she saw what he did to her best friend, Lori. He ripped her life apart and got away with it. Linda knew that when he wormed his way out of that situation that she'd never be able to get the best of him. He knew it too, and had told her so.

"Don't cross me, Linda," he warned her when she'd indicated she was going to testify against him at his hearing. "You need me. You're nothing without me. And if you testify against me, then I can't trust you anymore. I sure don't want a future with someone I can't trust."

Little by little, over the years, Greg had done a beautiful job of whittling away her self-confidence. Her wedding had been the day of her dreams but the marriage quickly had become a nightmare of continually covering for Greg. She had gone from a self-confident woman to a budding codependent. She stopped seeing her friends. She stopped going to church. She passed up job interviews that would have sent her across the country. He didn't want any competition for her devotion.

So she kept her mouth shut the way Greg had told her to. She betrayed a friend. She had sold out her integrity for the love of a man—if you can call that love. She let her life drain away until she became the shell she now saw standing in front of the mirror. She had even grown to recognize her new identity as if it was a statement of fact or an ugly truth. Thank God for Will and Paul. Not that she was the best mother in the world. But at least by giving birth to two wonderful kids she had done something right with her life.

Will. Her thoughts finally turned from herself. She had been drinking so long to forget about her own sorry situation that she had forgotten about her little boy. Despite her questionable child-rearing capabilities, Will had grown up to be a fine young man. He was polite, considerate, and well-mannered. But now, she thought as she began to sob, she could add "dying" to the list of his qualities.

It wasn't fair. What little boy deserves to get cancer? Why couldn't it have been her? Hell, why couldn't it have been Greg? She smiled. That would relieve a lot of problems. He had good life insurance. They'd do just fine without him. No, she told herself. That's not right. No matter what Greg was, Linda knew that her present state was just as much her own doing as Greg's. Her upbringing forbade her to wish evil upon another person. Greg had enough trouble of his own with his lawsuit. She didn't need to heap any more misfortune on him.

Linda sighed. Now a sexual harassment suit. It wasn't a big surprise. Linda made her way unsteadily into the bedroom and sat on the unmade bed. Greg's clothes from the night before were strewn on the floor, as if waiting for Linda to pick them up. The shades were pulled down. She didn't want any sunlight coming in and hurting her eyes. Nine thirty in the morning. The sounds of Paul's morning cartoons emanated from the downstairs living room. Bless him. He was doing so well without his big brother around to help him. Will had taken over Paul's morning care while she spent her time upstairs falling deeper into her depression. Her children were growing up without her, she realized. And that thought just fed her depression.

Well, no more. She would change that, starting right now. Linda squared her shoulders and walked into the hallway, pulling on a bathrobe to cover the vomit stains on her T-shirt. She could see Will's room from the top of the stairs. The door stood open; Linda had left it that way. Closing a bedroom door was the way her parents had indicated that Grandpa or Grandma had died. She didn't want to think about that with Will.

The room beckoned her. She half-expected to see her son asleep in his bed. Instead, she saw a neatly straightened bedspread, books sitting in a line on the shelves, trophies aligned on the dresser, and ribbons hanging along a bulletin board. She sat on Will's bed, feeling like an intruder in her son's world. Not so far off, she told herself. At times she seemed like a stranger who only showed up for holidays and birthdays. Birthdays, she thought. He only had celebrated ten so far. Would he get to have an eleventh?

Linda reached for Will's photo album, a gift from her mother who was far better at cataloging the important things in life than Linda now was. The first page had pictures of her in the hospital after Will was born. She looked so young. She was sober then. She had stayed dry for the entire pregnancy, except for an occasional glass of wine. Will was so small. It was hard for her to believe that her little boy was so big now. She slowly turned the pages. There were pictures of birthday parties, Will's first bike, and vacations at the family's condo in Breckenridge. Those were happy times, or so it seemed at the time.

Will's birthday party pictures showed him blowing out the candles on his cake, children laughing and playing games, and eating cake and opening presents. Linda remembered the moms enjoyed drinking her screwdrivers. Linda looked at pictures of Will as he learned to ride his bike. There was a young Greg, taking off the training wheels and running alongside Will as he wobbled down the driveway and into the street. She found the pictures of the time when the whole family was getting ready for a ride. All she remembered of that day, though, was making an excuse of having a headache to cover her inability to operate a bike after drinking four Bloody Marys that morning.

There were pictures of vacations to Colorado. Linda remembered the flights. The stewardess brought small bottles of Smirnoff and orange juice even before the plane left the ground. Linda was grateful that altitude sickness from being in the mountains had the same symptoms as a hangover. It gave her the perfect cover for how she felt every day. She missed out on skiing in the winter and biking in the summer, but she always seemed to have plenty of time for Irish coffee in the lodge.

Linda closed the album. The pictures were too depressing. She had missed out on some of the best times of her life. And for what? To numb herself from what she had become? To get even with Greg for what he had done to her? Or as an excuse to avoid standing up for herself? She wasn't sure anymore. Up until now her choices had affected only her. Or so she thought. But now, looking around her son's room, Linda wondered if running from her troubles was a tendency she was inadvertently teaching her children.

Paul never came to find her in the morning. Will stayed away from her most of the time. No one asked her to join in on a game around the kitchen table. Confronting a person with a problem was one way to show love for them. No one confronted Linda.

Now Will was facing a bigger problem. And he couldn't run away from it. He was going to have to face this disease head on. Be strong. Have courage and faith. Linda started to weep again. But he was so little. His ten years couldn't have prepared him for this enormous challenge. Who would Will have to lean on? His father still hadn't visited. His younger brother was scared. All Will had left was his lush of a mother. Some choice. Linda's maternal instinct had been beaten up. Trampled on, was more like it. Linda had drowned it in alcohol. But somewhere inside of her was a voice that reminded Linda of the day Will was born. How she had once sworn protection to her little boy in that hospital delivery room—the same hospital that Will was sleeping in. Linda needed to fight for him. If she couldn't straighten out her life for herself, she needed to do it for him.

Linda did something that she hadn't done in years, something that she was not sure she still knew how to do. She prayed. She prayed for strength to fight the illness that plagued her and for her son to recover. She prayed for forgiveness for the way she had all but abandoned her own children by simply walking out of their lives.

When she was done, she wiped the tears from her eyes and stood up. She was more scared now than she was ever before in her life. What if she couldn't do it? If she fell flat on her face in attempts to dry out and become a mom, would she go right back to the bottle? Fear of failure had been her strongest deterrent in the past. And that feeling was just as strong as it ever was. But now, at least, she was willing to try. Linda walked back into her bathroom and washed her face and brushed her teeth. She combed her hair and sprayed down the strands that seemed to have a mind of their own. She made the bed and got dressed. No sweat pants. She found a nice pair of summer shorts. A flowery blouse slipped over her black lace bra. "Start with the outside and work your way in, girl."

Downstairs, she found Paul sitting in front of the TV with an open box of Lucky Charms spilled out in front of him. The marshmallow pieces were the only items being consumed.

"Morning, honey," she said in a light, cheery voice.

"Hi, Mom," came the small voice. Paul never took his eyes off the set.

This wasn't going to be easy. "Hey, do you want me to make breakfast for you?"

"Nah. I've got some."

"Marshmallows aren't exactly a good breakfast." Right, Linda, she chided herself. As if you know about healthy habits. "How about pancakes? Do you want some of those?"

"I don't want to go out to a restaurant. I'm watching my show."

"We don't have to go out for them. I'll make them for you."

Paul turned his attention away from *SpongeBob* for a moment. His eyes opened wide. "You'll make them for me?" he asked in a voice that seemed a cross between disbelief and gratitude.

"Sure, honey," her voice cracked. "I'll make them for you." Linda hoped she would remember how. She found an all-purpose baking mix in the cupboard and read the instructions on the side panel. Linda mixed, measured, and poured out the pancake batter. The batter sizzled as it hit the griddle. She flipped and stacked up twelve pancakes before calling Paul to the table.

The two sat together at the kitchen table, eating pancakes and talking amiably. Paul was having fun and only spilled syrup on the table twice. They laughed as they ate through the stack. Linda looked at her son, at the way his face lit up with the excitement of being the center of attention. She was amazed at how much he looked like his father. But there was one difference between the two, she thought ruefully. Unlike his father, Paul was happy to be with her.

She excused him from the table to go play while she did the dishes. They'd go for a walk later, she told him. Paul brought his plate and cup to the sink before he left. Will had raised him well. Linda cleaned the kitchen—another attempt at cleaning up her life by polishing the counter-tops. The plates were stacked in the dishwasher and the pans set in the dry-ing rack. The kitchen had sparkling countertops when she was finished. She walked into the family room. She had more cleaning to do. The liquor cabinet behind the wet bar was locked. It was intended to be a deterrent for the children, but it would have been better if there had been a lock there for her. She opened up the doors and saw the smorgasbord that was her life. Twelve-year-old bottles of Chivas, Russian vodka, Kahlua for after dinner, and three varieties of Bacardi all seemed to stare at her, inviting Linda to join them. All that was missing was gin. She had run out of that.

She opened up the bottles and began to pour them out into the sink. The empty bottles fell into the trashcan with a loud thud that reminded her that she still had a hangover. But that didn't deter her from her mission. She poured and softly said good-bye. She finished with a bottle of Greg's favorite scotch. He'd be pissed when he found out that she had poured it out. Tough. Greg's feelings weren't exactly foremost on her mind.

The trashcan was full. The recycling collector was sure to think the Jamesons had had a wild night. Linda was proud of herself. She had done it without taking one last sip out of the bottles. But she had one more thing to do. She went into the den. She wanted to be out of earshot of Paul who had resumed his place on the floor in front of the TV. She sat behind the desk and pulled the phone book from the center drawer. St. John's was a large facility and had an entire page of the phone book dedicated to its numerous departments. She found the one she was looking for, picked up the phone, and dialed.

"Hello. St. John's Recovery Center. I'm Rhonda. How may I help you?"

"Hi," began Linda. This was harder than she thought it would be. "I'm Linda Jameson. Dr. Jameson's wife." As if that fact would gain her extra attention. It would. "I need your help." Linda paused and summoned her courage. She thought of Paul and of Will. They were going to need her, and now she was not going to let them down. She was tired of the lies, and ashamed of whom she had become. Having that in her heart, she brought up the words she thought she'd never hear herself say: "I'm an alcoholic."

15

Julie McMahon rolled over in bed and found she was alone. The satin sheets were smooth and a little moist, but not as warm as they would have been had her partner been there. Waking up by herself made Julie feel a little used and cheap, not the way she pictured her romance would have turned out. Nearing thirty years old, her dreams of finding and marrying Mr. Right seemed to be slipping farther and farther away. She imagined herself being a doctor's wife by now. Not his mistress.

She could still smell his cologne. Its light scent clung to the pillowcase and Julie pressed it to her nose while inhaling deeply. She closed her eyes and pretended her lover was still in bed with her, touching and caressing her. She imagined his hand running down her spine to the small of her back. She preferred that image to knowing where his hands actually were at that moment—most likely being stuck into sterile rubber gloves before grabbing a scalpel.

Morning O.R. time was precious. Surgeons fought over it. But then, they'd fight over anything, Julie had found. Who has the bigger car, the bigger house, or the nurse with the largest chest? And since Ryan was the head of the department of surgery at Rockford General Hospital, he had to make sure his balls were as big as anyone else's. So for the sake of Ryan's status, Julie woke up alone. Again. It was just like being a surgeon's wife without any of the fringe benefits. But she got to wake up each morning wondering, *Does he love me?*

She was sure he did. He said it often enough, but mostly before making love to her, and after. It would just be nice to hear those words some time when she wasn't naked. Julie looked at the alarm clock on the nightstand next to the two empty glasses of wine from the night before. Seven thirty-two. The day was just starting for most of the world. Her day would have been several hours old had she been at work this morning, but not today. Julie was enjoying the extra sleep that her leave of absence was affording her.

No more getting up at five o'clock. No more stale rolls and a cup of coffee for breakfast as she dashed out the door with her hair still wet from her shower. No. This was like a vacation. And Ryan's house was as close to a Hilton as she'd ever get on her nurse's salary. His home was gorgeous. It was state-of-the-art, but it needed a woman's touch. The bathroom was done in marble tile. A sauna and hot tub were off the master bedroom. The ground floor had a media room with wide-screen TV. The house was filled with every luxury Ryan's hefty salary could afford—except there was no room service. That's the one thing Julie would have wanted this morning. She waved her hand in the air and snapped her fingers. "Waiter!" she called out playfully. No one came. Her arm dropped onto the sheets with her realization that she'd actually have to get out of bed. Julie reached for her robe and slid into it. "Much more comfortable than scrubs," she thought. No scrubbing in. No setting out trays of equipment. No listening to the loud music of Dr. Jameson's second childhood. But mostly, she was glad that there was no one staring at her, copping a feel through her surgical gown, or making her feel uncomfortable. No one but herself.

Sure, she was enjoying her time off. Professional leave of absence, her lawyer called it. No client of Terrance Niemann was going to return to a hostile work environment now that she was suing her place of employment. Terrance—a junior partner at the law firm of Hamer, Baker and Cuda; who enjoyed power lunches and martinis with his secretary—was a clean-cut scumbag who would take the side of whomever was paying his retainer. And right now, that was Julie.

Julie knew that winning her sexual harassment suit would bring Terrance a large take. He had said so several times. The setting was perfect for a large settlement, a sexual scandal in a Catholic hospital. Terrance had told Julie that the nuns would pay a hefty sum just to make the whole thing dry up and blow away. So far they hadn't. An offer was on the table: two hundred thousand dollars, reassignment of Julie to a different section of the hospital, plus sending the offending bastard to sensitivity training. Of course, there'd be no admission of guilt on the hospital's or Dr. Jameson's part.

"Not a bad sum," Julie had said. It would take her five years to make that much. Even after Terrance took his 40 percent, that would still leave her a large chunk to drop into a mutual fund for early retirement. It was pretty easy money just for being born with a shapely bottom. She was about to accept the offer. But Ryan and Terrance quickly put a stop to that.

"I can get you ten times that amount," said Terrance.

"And ten times your own take," countered Julie.

"This isn't about the money, Julie. I'm in this for you. This is about your self-respect, about your right to work without being treated like a piece of meat."

"Yeah, hon. That's my job," Ryan added with a wink that made Julie blush.

"You two can stop that any time," said Terrance. "Or at least keep it in check. You know I don't want the news of your relationship getting out."

"Would that be so bad?" asked Julie, who wished she could hear her man shout his feelings to the world.

"A sexual relationship of your own wouldn't help your case right now," answered Terrance.

"Just trust me on this one, babe," added Ryan. He turned to Terrance, who nodded in agreement. That was all they felt that Julie needed to know.

So Julie declined the offer. Terrence told her he'd put a proper spin on their decision. She was doing this for the sake of other nurses, and to teach doctors everywhere that they couldn't treat dedicated, sacrificing caregivers like streetwalkers. A heinous act like this required a proper punishment. Terrance was willing to say anything that would get more money on the table. No matter whom it hurt.

And right now, that was starting to be Julie.

So instead of getting back to what she always wanted to do, instead of getting to work helping others and putting this event behind her, Julie was sitting on the edge of a man's bed wearing a robe that she'd never be able to afford on her own. She wondered if Ryan truly loved her or if all this romance was just a passing fling. Sure, he said that he loved her. Words can be a cheap substitute for the real thing. He showed her enough. That is, if sex is sign of love. Then her mind would yell at her: *Stop beating yourself up. You should feel lucky to have him. He's gorgeous, rich, and he fawns over you.* And he was gone most of the time.

She thought about the day they'd met while jogging on the path along the Rock River. The paved six-foot-wide trail was a beautiful addition to the waterfront that attracted joggers, bicyclers, walkers, and stroller-pushers. Weekends and after work, the path changed from a nearly deserted patch of blacktop to a gathering spot for the health conscious and those hoping to meet others with similar body builds. Julie was just out to get in a quick five miles, to clear her head, and to get out her frustrations by pounding her feet against the pavement instead of her fists against a wall.

Bad days seem to build upon themselves. And that day, Julie was a magnet for it. It started with a phone call from her mother, which eventually led to her trying to run Julie's life. Her carton of milk was spoiled. Unfortunately, she didn't find out until she had already poured it on her cereal and taken a large bite, which she tried to spit out into the sink but missed. She burned her forearm on her curling iron. Her car wouldn't start. And she forgot to bring a lunch. She certainly wasn't in the mood to deal with Greg. Not that he was all bad. He made sure that she was well taken care of by the hospital. She got all of her vacation requests. She got to leave on time at the end of the day, unlike her coworkers who often had to stay for unpaid overtime. No, he wasn't a bad sort. He just acted like a child most of the time. Like a boy who never grew up. And Julie had dealt with boys like that in college. They liked drinking and women, with little time left over for adult pursuits. She was tired of them. She was ready to be with a man. But her life was far too busy to run into anyone outside of the hospital.

So when she turned her back to retrieve the specimen tray and had to hear Greg comment on her backside, she just couldn't take it anymore. She was more hurt than offended. She was skilled, talented, and smart. She was more than just a piece of eye candy for the surgeons. Julie walked across the room to the full-length mirror. It was oval shaped and framed in solid maple. Ryan had found it at a flea market in Kenosha. She removed her robe and turned from side to side. She looked at her back, her legs, and her abs. Her shape that had been honed from hours of aerobics and miles of jogging was still holding up. She viewed herself from behind. "Damn, he's right," she said as she saw her reflection. "I do have a cute little ass."

Greg's comment seemed so insignificant now. *After all, he was only telling the truth*, she told herself. She had worked hard to look the way she did. So after work that day, after hearing Greg's ill-placed comment, she took off for the running trail to clear her head. She wanted to reach for that runner's high she had grown to crave. A tight pair of sweats, jogging bra that exposed her belly button, and a visor completed her outfit. Running along the trail she had taken notice of the other runners, silently comparing herself to them. She sneered at other women whom Julie thought she could beat in a race. She giggled at some who wore outfits that she'd never be caught dead in. Julie ogled the men she'd love to sleep with, and shuddered at those whom she wouldn't. Not in a million years. She had her eyes on everything that she should have except the trail.

A golden retriever with a much-too-long leash went to Julie's left while his owner moved to her right. The leather strap entangled her legs and brought Julie to the hard pavement before she knew that she had been caught. And caught she had been.

"Oh, crap. I'm sorry, miss. Are you hurt?" A handsome face, with deep blue eyes that seemed to look directly into Julie's, bent over her—and took Julie's breath away.

"I think I'm okay," she returned. "I guess I didn't see you."

"Here, let me help you up." He reached down with his right hand while using his left to hold off his overly affectionate dog, which was trying to lick Julie's face. "Sometimes Buster gets away from me. I'm really sorry that he knocked you down."

"It's all right. It was my fault. I wasn't watching where I was going." Julie stood up and put her weight on her feet. The pressure sent pain through her ankle, causing her to lift up her left foot and put her hand on the stranger's shoulder for support. Her ankle was sprained, but feeling a strong, muscular shoulder brought a sensation through her body that Julie much preferred to concentrate on.

"Oh, you're hurt. Let me take a look at it." The man slowly lowered Julie back to the ground.

"That's okay," Julie vainly protested. "I'm a nurse. I can manage."

"Well, I'm a doctor. I might be able to help." He stared at her again with the liquid blue eyes. "No charge."

Julie laughed and gave in to his request. She laid back and awaited her exam.

"I'm Ryan, by the way. Ryan Webber."

"Julie McMahon." She extended her hand to Ryan who grasped it with his own. "It's a pleasure."

"It won't be in a moment," said Ryan as he pressed along the outside of Julie's ankle and irritated the already strain ligaments.

"Ow, that hurts. Are you this gentle with all of your patients?"

"Don't know," said Ryan now rubbing the painful area of Julie's ankle. "They're always asleep when I'm treating them."

"Oh, great. You're a surgeon, aren't you?" Her voice reflected her hostility toward surgeons, which had been simmering all day.

"Is that bad?"

"Today it is. I'm not having a good experience with your profession today." Julie reached down and removed Ryan's hand from her ankle.

"We're not all the same, you know," said Ryan.

Julie wasn't quite sure if she agreed with him. Most of the surgeons she worked with seemed to have similar personalities as Greg's. "Is that so?" She looked at Ryan's dog, who was now busily trying to jump up on Ryan and lavish him with kisses. "Well, you certainly do have the affections of your dog."

"Man's best friend, some would say. But I prefer the company of a woman."

"Does a woman have to jump on you and kiss you all over like that?"

"I certainly wouldn't turn it down, but I think having a dog who loves me is a good sign that I'm not a totally bad guy."

Julie had to agree with him. A dog could sometimes be a better judge of character than most people. "You've certainly been nicer to me than Jameson was today."

Ryan's eyes opened up and his head tilted slightly to one side. "Jameson? Greg Jameson?"

"Yeah. You know him?"

Ryan wiped the look of interest off of his face. "Sure. We go way back. He's sort of a colleague of mine."

"Oh, that's right. You guys belong to some kind of club, don't you?" said Julie, as if those men were little boys who hung out in tree houses and talked about how much they hate girls.

"That's supposed to be a secret." Ryan tried for a laugh. He didn't get one.

"Well, don't worry. I have no interest in finding out all about your little societies or learning your secret handshakes."

"Okay, maybe it's just me, but I sense that Greg has done something to set you off. I know that I may have gotten off on the wrong foot with you, or at least hurt you with my dog leash. But I am sorry about that."

Julie tried to temper her hostility toward the male gender. She had been jogging while imagining turning Greg's scalpel onto his own male anatomy.

But at least Ryan had stopped and tried to help her. At least he made the effort of talking to her, not just starring at her spandex-covered ass or imagining her without her sports bra in place. "I'm sorry. I just have a bit of a chip on my shoulder right now. You're right. It's nothing that you've done. I forgive you and Buster for bumping into me."

"I can't let you go away angry," Ryan said. "Plus, at the way you're hobbling it'll take you a week to get back to your house. At least let me give you a ride."

"Got a car on you, do you?"

"No. Not on me. But close by. Just a couple of blocks over."

Julie's ankle was starting to swell, and each step was sure to bring pain. A ride would be a nice break. "You got air conditioning?"

"Of course."

"Deal."

Ryan helped Julie to his car. He had to let her lean on him along the way, which neither seemed to mind. "So, what happened to you today to get you upset?" Ryan asked.

"I don't want to talk about it," answered Julie. "Let's just say that sometimes men can act like pigs."

"Well, some men are, I'll admit to that. But don't you think you're being a little closed minded to group all of us together? Surely you don't think that your father was a pig or some of your teachers, or a brother, perhaps?" Ryan paused and gave Julie a smile.

Julie pondered the thought for a moment. The men in her life had been many and mostly upright, courageous, and even faithful. In the end she had to admit that it was only Greg whom she was really mad at. "Well, maybe my brother was a pain in the ass sometimes," she laughed.

"Then for the sake of all the little brothers everywhere, please give me the chance to redeem our standing with you." He took Julie's hand again. The hairs on the back of her neck stood on end as the tingle returned to her senses. "Dinner? Tonight? I promise to take a shower and be a little more presentable than I am right now," he said, motioning to his sweaty clothes.

His smile melted Julie's heart. He looked so desperate and vulnerable, like she could crush his feelings with a sour word. She liked that in a man.

"What about Buster? Will he be joining us?"

"That's up to you. Do you want him to sweep you off of your feet again?"

"No thanks," said Julie. She felt that Ryan was doing a good enough job of that himself.

Dinner that night turned out to be a catered affair at Ryan's house. He had picked her up in his BMW sedan and took her back to his three-bedroom colonial situated on the sixth fairway at Knotting Pines Country Club. Ryan had hired a chef and a waiter. The patio overlooking the fairway had been decorated in a manner fitting a summer night's gathering of young lovers. A formal dining table was placed in the center of the brick patio. A CD sound system was playing Mozart concertos. The touch of flowers set along the tabletop and the scented candles made her question his heterosexuality. But considering he hadn't been able to let go of her hand since they stepped out of his car, she chalked it all up to good taste.

"Entertain much?" she asked feeling that she was not the first woman to be brought to Ryan's house. This was not the setup prepared by a man on a first date.

"Not as much as I'd like."

The evening was beautiful. The summer's warm breeze drifted over the pair as they dined on chicken cordon bleu, asparagus with dill sauce, and twice-baked potatoes, all accompanied with an ample supply of white zinfandel. Dessert was ice cream-and-cookie smoothies from the local fast-food establishment, which was Ryan's biggest weakness and a sign to Julie that he was indeed human after all.

She talked about her life, her job, and her dreams. Ryan listened mostly as a true gentleman would. He knew that the truest way to a woman's heart was to make her the center of his attention. Hang on to every word. Listen, not just nod and grunt. His ears especially perked up when Julie described how Greg had treated her earlier in the day. The words he said still echoing in Julie's mind. Ryan was equally disgusted, and he assured her that he had never treated any of his nurses in such a way. Reaching across the table and once again taking her hand in his, Ryan promised that he'd always treat her like a lady.

Julie liked him. He was sensitive and compassionate. It was a true shift from the surgeons that she had known. He had the characteristics that she was looking for in a man, the kind that would result in his giving her a tour of the house. The tour ended in the bedroom.

Julie sat in that bedroom now and looked back on that day and smiled. Was she really that easy or cheap, she wondered. She did sleep with the man on the first date and every night since. But she loved falling asleep in his arms and waking up in the same place. It gave her a security that she had longed to feel and enjoy. It was a feeling that she didn't want to disturb. So if Ryan said that she shouldn't take the deal offered by St. John's then she wouldn't, even though she was ready to let the whole thing go and settle down. Ryan had seemed to push the lawsuit deal in the first place, as if he were trying to take care of his woman. Protect her from the evils of the world. Vindicate her.

She turned down the settlement offer. Terrance would call St. John's this morning and tell the risk management officer the news. Depositions would follow. Interrogation was a better word. But Terrance would coach her, and Ryan would be by her side. First Greg's statements would be taken, then her own. There was no turning back now.

Julie tied up the front of her robe and got up for some coffee. She could smell the aroma that indicated Ryan had left the pot on. She'd sit and sip her cup and relax for the morning. There was nothing to do but wait by the phone for Terrance's call to find out the response from St. John's. It would come by noon. It could make things get ugly. Now her job would be at risk. Regardless of the outcome of the suit, she'd lose the trust of her department. No doctor would want to work with her. She was creating waves, and doctors hated waves. She hoped that Ryan was right. She wanted to believe in him. She needed to now. There was no one else to turn to—and that's what bothered her the most.

16

The O.R. was unusually quiet. Greg spoke only when he needed an instrument, suction, or his forehead wiped. His new nurse, Glenda, was working out well. She had been specifically chosen by the sisters to work with Greg during Julie's absence. At fifty-three and weighing more than two hundred pounds, the reasons behind the nuns' choice was obvious to Greg. He wasn't in the mood to talk anyway. He had endured two weeks of backstabbing, jokes in the locker room, and stares from the nurses. He was a marked man and had been labeled a sexist pig. Greg did not intend to become their whipping boy.

Greg no longer found a need to hang around the hospital at all hours of the day and night. He had lost his former status now that he was named in the suit. Other doctors didn't want to associate with him now that the nursing staff had marked him as a pig. Greg decided that he might as well come home at night. Linda was no help to Greg there. Her newfound sobriety was making her a pain in the ass. Her shakes had started the day after she had cleared the bar of all of Greg's fine stock, even the unopened bottles that he could have used as last-minute gifts. But to top it all off, she had that new attitude. Nothing is worse than a new convert for those who prefer to stay in their sinful past. Greg was comfortable with whom he was. Especially since he'd never admit that any of his characteristics were flawed. Linda refused to let Greg keep liquor in the house. She got up early in the morning with him instead of sleeping in and giving Greg the morning to himself.

Linda fixed breakfast for him and for Paul. She kept the kitchen clean and would be dressed before 8:00 A.M. Linda would drive in to the hospital every morning to be with Will. She was becoming a mom. And Greg wasn't sure how to handle that. Having Linda at the hospital was a break in his routine. And Linda now was expecting him to break his routine even further and become more of a dad. And a husband.

Greg was trying. It wasn't that he didn't want to be a dad, but he just never seemed to find time to fill the part. Things at work always seemed to take precedence. Making a living, paying off student loans, and paying the mortgage all were more pressing than tossing a ball in the backyard. Greg figured that he would always have time for those things later on. Linda was making him see that "later on" is never guaranteed.

Paul liked to watch cartoons in the evening, which was something he did by himself after Will went into the hospital. Greg sat and watched some of the shows with Paul instead of reading the newspaper in the other room. Paul seemed to like the stories, but mutant killer warlords from distant galaxies didn't seem to be the type of subject matter that Greg wanted to relax with after a busy day of being called an ass grabber. Playing catch with a football was an option, though Paul's tiny arms could do little more than prevent the tossed ball from knocking him over or smacking him in the face. In the end they settled with reading to each other. Paul would take one of his favorite storybooks to Greg in the same way he once took them to Will. Picture books, mostly. Fifteen words to a page and a color drawing of a bug or a humanized animal character. Greg began stiffly, reading in a monotone. But after a few nights Greg began to change his voice to give the different characters their own inflections, much in the way his own father had read to him as a little boy.

Sometimes Paul would interrupt the story to ask an unrelated question about a character, or the story, or about Will. Was Will going to come home? Was he going to die? What's it like in heaven? These were questions that Greg wasn't good at answering. He'd rather take fifty questions from a patient's family than have to answer the same types of questions from his own son. It was easier to be detached and have no emotional link to a case. But that's how he had always lived his life and his career. The line between the two worlds was beginning to blur. Greg often tired of reading the same stories over and over again, but Paul seemed to enjoy their time together. It was a start, which was a place where all journeys must begin.

Greg decided to come in early—before his surgical schedule began to-day—to see Will. He realized that he hadn't seen much of Will up to now, and he wanted to fix that. He wanted to start fresh with his firstborn, but the boy was still asleep at five-thirty. Greg capitalized on his free time to review Will's medical chart, something that he knew he shouldn't do with-out Michael's permission, but he didn't care. He wanted to see how Will was doing, but he also wanted to see what Michael was up to—Greg still didn't trust him. Greg opened the chart and found Michael's note from the previ-ous day. So he hadn't made rounds yet this morning. "Late starter, huh, Mike?" Greg muttered.

Greg read the latest entry: The toxic effects of the chemotherapy seemed to be wearing off. Will wasn't having any major problems or show-ing signs of an infection. Will's exam was stable, and the blood work showed that Will's cell count had fallen as low as Michael had expected it to drop. If all went well, Michael was planning to do another bone marrow in the morning. Greg was no oncologist, but he understood that the chemo-therapy agents had wiped out most of Will's bone marrow cells, and in spite of his weakened immune system, Will hadn't acquired any opportunistic infections. Things were looking good. Greg was glad for his son, but at the same time he worried that he might now be indebted to Michael. But the good prognosis gave Greg a little lift in his walk. He could take the jokes this morning, and the stares. Even the stern looks Greg would receive from Glenda each time he asked for an instrument wouldn't be so bad.

Greg finished his last case for the morning. He took out an inflamed gallbladder from a forty-two-year-old housewife who had gotten ill from eating one too many cream-filled doughnuts. Greg finished his paperwork and settled into a soft chair in the surgeons' lounge for a cup of coffee. When he opened the paper to check the stock market, St. John's administra-tor arrived and sat down next to Greg.

"How'd your morning go?" Chuck asked.

"Great. I've got two dates for this afternoon in the clean utility room," Greg said as he flung his paper facemask into the nearest trashcan and pulled his surgical cap from his head.

"You're your own worst enemy, do you know that?"

Greg looked around at the rest of the staff who had gathered just within earshot, hoping to hear whatever the administrator had to say to Greg. Ru-mors and gossip must have a source, after all.

"It doesn't look like that to me."

Chuck glanced at the several staff members who were poised to take in their every word. "Is there someplace we can talk privately?"

"I doubt it," answered Greg. "But we can talk in the locker room."

The two men walked past the surgical nurses' station and through the double-glass doors that marked the perimeter of the surgical suites. The men's locker room was located outside the surgeons' lounge. Large sofas lined the walls, and trays of doughnuts and fruit sat uneaten, waiting to be replaced in the afternoon with trays of chocolate chip cookies and raw vegetables. A large-screen television was in the corner, perpetually tuned to a business channel that constantly ran stock prices. The room was empty except for scattered newspapers and empty food wrappers. The television was still on.

"This should do nicely," said Chuck as he escorted Greg into the room.

"I hope this is good news for a change."

"I wish. Unfortunately, that isn't the case." Chuck sat on the arm of a sofa and motioned for Greg to sit on a chair next to him. "Our offer of settlement in your suit was rejected. I got word this morning."

"Damn."

"Our lawyers are reviewing the case right now. Looking to see how winnable this would be if we went to trial."

"Did McMahon's lawyer say why they turned us down? Was it more money?"

"Oh, the usual bull crap. They threw in terms like the punishment needing to fit the offense and that they want to send a strong signal to doctors everywhere that it's time to treat nurses with respect. But I think it is a money issue. At least, we haven't found another angle."

"So, offer more. That first amount was an insult and you know it."

"It's not so simple, Greg. They didn't just reject our offer and make a counteroffer. They're insisting on trying this thing. Her lawyers are pushing for a hearing in the next two weeks. I've taken two calls this morning already asking to set up a deposition for you."

"I hate talking to lawyers."

"We can't avoid it this time. If we deny their request or delay, it'll make you look hostile and uncooperative. And right now you already have an image problem."

Greg stood up and walked around the lounge. This was his room, his turf. Surgeons were treated like kings here. And now he was feeling like he was backed into a corner. "So what's our plan? Do I meet with them?"

"I'll set up something for next week. I put them off as long as we can. But our attorneys want to meet with you today. They have some questions to go over with you and a strategy to develop."

"Find out what kind of a risk I really am, you mean."

Chuck stood up to look at Greg on an eye-to-eye level. "Yep. They're just doing their job. If we are going to try to win this thing, we have to know going into it what our chances are."

"Fine," grunted Greg.

"Come down to the risk management department at three o'clock." Chuck patted Greg on the shoulder. "And bring a better attitude than you usually do."

"I can't promise you anything."

Chuck walked out the door leaving Greg alone with his thoughts. Thoughts that raced back to his previous depositions. They had all gone well. He was a good doctor. He was the victim here, not some tight-assed bitch out to make her mark in the world. He'd get through this. No sweat. Plus, he'd get out of his afternoon clinic in order to be at the meeting.

Greg ate a light lunch in the doctors' dining room. Talk centered on problem patients, their even bigger problem families, and the incompetence of administration. The conversations were the same every day, as if they had been scripted. Greg placed his illegible signature on stacks of charts in the file room that had been waiting months for him to complete. He worked in his office to clean out the charts that remained there. He stopped up to see Will, but Michael was busy performing a magic trick for a couple of patients, and Greg didn't want to run into his former friend. He was already dealing with the bottom-feeder lawyers and didn't want a run-in with his other natural enemy.

Three o'clock came in an unusually rapid fashion, and Greg headed down to the administration offices. Greg had stayed in his scrubs all day so that he'd stand out among the suits that would be occupying the room.

"I think we all know each other," began Chuck, who was the self-appointed moderator. "Let's all have a seat."

The lush conference room had a long oak table running down the center with eight high-backed chairs arranged around it. In the corners were potted miniature palm trees. Along the near wall was a mounted dry-erase board, which looked well used. The opposite wall held posters that espoused the mission statements of the hospital and the tenets of their latest quality initiative.

Greg shook hands with the three St. John's attorneys, hoping to indicate he was a team player. Mark Brannon, the senior attorney and director of the hospital's risk management program, greeted Greg and introduced the other two members of his team.

"Greg, this is Steve Potter and Peter Koehn."

"Pleasure."

Mark Brannon had been with St. John's since leaving law school in 1964. His years of experience handling cases (and having lost only a handful) had made him somewhat of an institution. The thinning hair, expanding waistline, and thin glasses that seemed to magically hover on the end of his nose made Mark look more like a kindly grandfather than the cutthroat barrister he truly was. Working for the Catholic order seemed to give him immunity from any of the mudslinging he'd do to win a case for the sisters. He certainly didn't want to start losing them now.

"Let's get started with this, shall we?" Mark began. Mark adjusted his glasses. Peter and Steve opened their notepads and turned on their microcassette recorder. "Just to update you," began Mark, "our offer of settlement was rejected. Not unexpected."

"Who's representing McMahon?" asked Greg.

"Terrance Niemann," answered Mark.

"The Terrier?" asked Greg.

"The same."

"Why 'the Terrier'?" asked Peter.

"Because he's like one of those obnoxious barking dogs that'll nip at your feet and annoy you until you just want to stomp on him," offered Steve.

Mark and Greg laughed at the thought of the opposition being led by a small Yorkshire terrier.

"I bet he loves that nickname," said Greg.

"Hates it," said Mark. "One time in court when he was rambling on about who knows what, I pulled a muzzle out of my briefcase and placed it where only he could see it. It pissed him off something terrible."

"So we shouldn't have any problems with him then, should we?" asked Greg.

"Don't let that fool you. He's a tough one. Likes to take a bite of you and hold on for as long as it takes him to get what he wants." Mark sobered. "Typically he likes to drag cases on forever. Wear you down with depositions, discoveries, and extensions. Make you want to settle the thing just to make him go away. That's what's so strange about this case."

"How so?" asked Chuck.

"He's moving along like he needs to get this wrapped up before the summer's over. I've never seen him in a hurry before."

"Maybe he wants to buy a summer home and needs his cut of the settlement for the down payment," sneered Greg.

"Nah," Mark said, with a wave of his hand. "He's got one near mine on Lake Geneva. No, something's different about this one." Mark looked concerned momentarily; then got back to the business at hand. He read from a stack of papers and talked to Greg without ever raising his eyes. "I'm going to ask you a lot of questions about this case, Greg. So if I start to sound like I'm interrogating you, it's only because I am."

"Fine."

"Do you know this Julie McMahon, Dr. Jameson?" Mark began.

"Yep," said Greg, swiveling in his chair.

"How do you know her?"

"She's my scrub nurse. Or was, I should say."

"Did you terminate her position?"

"No, she's on leave during this lawsuit."

"Good. Whatever you do, do not get her fired or reassigned yet. We don't want to come across as uncaring. Was she in the operating room with you on the morning of July 13?"

"Yeah. I guess so."

"Just a 'yes' would be fine."

Greg let out a sigh of aggravation. "Yes, she was in the operating room with me and about five other people."

Mark looked up from the papers. "Just a 'yes' will do. Don't offer any more information than is asked of you."

"Fine."

"On the morning of July 13 did you say to Ms. McMahon, 'Move that cute little ass of yours'?"

"I might have. I don't remember."

"What if I told you that I have signed affidavits from four people attesting to the fact that you said just that? Would that clear up your memory problem?"

"Okay, yes. I said that to her."

"Did you say anything else to her?"

"Just surgical things."

"Nothing sexual in nature?"

"No."

"Did you proposition her for sexual relations?"

"No."

"Did you fondle her or touch her inappropriately?"

"No. Of course not."

"You didn't make any kind of advancement on her or make her out to be a brunt of a sexually explicit joke or comment?"

"No, dammit. I didn't do any of those things." Greg was getting tired of the accusations.

Mark looked up from his papers. "Come on, Dr. Jameson. Level with me. These people are suing us for a hell of a lot of money. And you mean to tell me it's all over a little statement about this woman's hind end? What are you covering up?"

"Nothing. I didn't touch the bitch. I never laid a hand on her. Granted, there are a lot of guys in the surgical suite who'd like to, but I never did."

Mark looked over at Chuck. Peter and Steve were still scribbling notes. "This doesn't add up. This is ridiculous. It's nothing. He makes one crude comment in an O.R. That's all they've got? This thing should have settled."

"It hasn't," chimed in Chuck. "Their side wants to go to trial on this."

Mark stared at Greg through his wire rims. "Are you rich? Have vast holdings somewhere that these people want to get their hands on?"

"I wish."

Mark looked through Greg's file. "It says here that you've had a few lawsuits in the past, but they were all medically related. There's nothing in the harassment arena before."

Greg shifted in his seat.

"Have you ever been sued for sexual harassment? Brought up on charges? Done something that these people may have on you that would indicate you'd be a windfall for them?"

Greg didn't say anything. He had hoped that all of that would have been left behind him in the past, where it should have stayed and died a lonely death.

"Come on, son. Level with me. If you've got some dirt in your drawers you better tell us. It's better that we find out now while we can still use it to our advantage. Or work to keep it out of the hands of our opponents."

Greg took a breath and looked over at Chuck, then back to Mark. Steve and Peter continued to write. "A long time ago, after I graduated from medical school, there was an incident. I got arrested for assault."

"What was it all about?" asked Mark, his level of interest growing.

Greg remembered it like it was yesterday. "Let's just say that it makes a comment about a nurse's ass seem as controversial as a member of the royal family having an affair."

"This happened where?" asked Peter.

"Hey, he speaks!" Greg scoffed. "Sorry. Chicago. Right after graduation. The charges got reduced and I got a slap on the wrist. I don't think it's important to us."

"Well, this may or may not be of significance," Mark began, "but if there is any chance that our opponents can prove you have a tendency toward this type of behavior, that would truly hamper our case. I think we'll need to find out some more about this incident."

"I'd really rather not go into it."

"I'm sorry, Dr. Jameson. But your feelings really do not matter here. Only the sanctity and integrity of this hospital are my concerns. So you'll tell us all about this."

"I'm not under a subpoena here."

"No, you're not. But you will be when the other side is questioning you." Mark's voice rose in volume. "Now tell us the name of the injured party. We may need to find her to get her side of the story."

"No."

"I didn't ask if you'd like to tell me. I said for you to tell me."

"And I said no. Look, it really isn't relevant to this case."

"It's my job to decide what is and what is not relevant to this case, Doctor. Now tell us who it is that you supposedly harmed."

Greg looked into the very determined face of Mark. His eyes never left Greg's. Chuck had an equally intense stare. Peter and Steve stopped writing.

"Fine. Her name was Lori Lange. There. Happy?"

Steve and Peter wrote down the name. Chuck looked quizzical. "Can she cause us any trouble here?"

"Possibly," answered Greg. "I don't know if she's forgotten the ordeal or not."

"Well, we'd better find her," said Mark. "Better we get a hold of her before the Terrier does."

"You certainly won't have to go far to find her, Mark." said Greg. "Lange was her maiden name. She's married now and works here." Greg paused for a moment. "She's Dr. Lori Hamilton."

17

"Now look through this tube." Michael offered his young assistant a tall, seemingly empty metallic tube with several star-shaped holes in the sides. He tried to include as many patients in his show as possible. "Do you see anything? Make sure you are using both of your eyes."

The little boy smiled. "No. It looks empty."

"Are you sure?" Michael leaned over the boy and looked through the tube from the same angle. Then he reached his arm up into the tube and stuck his hand out the other side. "I think I'm going to have to examine your eyes after the show. There is clearly a man's arm stuck in this tube." Michael waved his hand around. He got the laugh he was looking for.

In unison the captivated audience all shouted out, "You just put it there."

"Ah," said Michael with his finger pointing into the air. "You are very perceptive." He slid the tube off of his arm and handed it to the little boy in the wheelchair. "Hold this for me, all right?"

The boy took the tube while Michael turned back to his small table, which was draped with a shiny red cloth. Taking a sheet of newspaper and waving it to the crowd, showing both sides as being empty, he rolled the paper into a tube.

"Now if my assistant will give me back the tube…" The young boy slid the metal tube off of his own arm. "As you can plainly see," Michael said, "this tube is empty." He held it back up to the crowd of eager-eyed children and staff. "There also are several star-shaped holes along this side." He pointed to the small openings along one side. "These holes go all the way through the side and allow you to see into the tube as I will now demonstrate with this newspaper." Michael placed the rolled up newspaper into one end of the metal tube and began to slide it through to the other side. The star-shaped holes showed the white newspaper as it passed through the tube. "The magic cylinder is clearly empty, as is the newspaper," said Michael as he removed the newspaper tube and unrolled it. "Also, the holes along the side allow us to see right into the magic cylinder at all times." Michael set the tube upright onto his stand. "So, clearly this tube is empty." He paused. "Or is it?" Michael pulled out his magic wand and gave it a wave across the top of the tube. "Let's find out."

He reached into the top of the tube. Gently tugging, Michael began to pull out a red, silk cloth. The eyes of the children and their nurses all opened widely. Michael pulled the cloth completely out of the tube and waved it in the air. "Now how did we not see that in there?" He reached into the tube a second time. "What else might be in there?" Michael pulled out a blue cloth. Then a green one followed by a yellow one. All the time the children looked at the cylinder and could see nothing appearing in the star-shaped holes. "Maybe we need to get our eyes checked," Michael said. He reached one last time into the tube and pulled out a lollipop. "Or maybe there really is magic." He handed the lollipop to his young assistant, who eagerly grabbed the treat. The rest of the audience applauded Michael's trick. Michael's young assistant was very happy with the payment he received for his role in the trick.

Michael rolled the newspaper back up and slid it through the metal tube to show that the holes still revealed the paper through the openings. Then he held up the cylinder to prove that he hadn't placed anything into the tube, and that it was once again empty. He placed the metal tube and the newspaper back onto the stand and accepted his applause.

The children obviously loved their show. The sound of their clapping filled the lounge area and drowned out the sounds of the unit's doors opening and closing. Michael was the only one who saw that Greg had stopped in and then quickly exited the floor. Michael glanced over at Will, who was sitting at a table near the isolation rooms.

Will hadn't spotted his father. His balding head and face covered with a mask to prevent inhaling any potential pathogens made the small boy nearly unrecognizable, except to Michael. He could spot Will in a sea of cancer patients. The boy could smile with his eyes. No mask could cover that, and no chemotherapy agent could wipe away his inner love for life. He wondered if Greg ever noticed that about his own son.

"Thank you all for coming today and putting up with me. I know that you all would much rather be sitting in your rooms staring at the walls." Michael looked about the room. His young assistant was smiling with the stick of the lollipop coming through the gap in his teeth. "Next time I'll bring more treats for everyone. Now, off you go. I still have rounds to make on some of you."

A collective "Aw-w-w" filled the room as Michael started to pack his tricks into his trunk. The children all filed away to their rooms, and the nurses went back to their charting. Michael carried his trunk into the nurses' lounge for storage until taking it home, then returned to the nurses' station.

"Are my supplies ready, Sue?" he asked the nurse on duty.

"Yeah. I placed them in Will's room. Will you need any help?"

"Nah. Just make sure that I have enough lidocaine. I'd like to make sure he's anesthetized."

Michael walked into the isolation area and washed his hands. The antiseptic soap lathered quickly and always left a telltale scent. As he scrubbed his hands, dried them, and put on a gown to cover his clothes, he could overhear his two patients talking back and forth through their intercom.

"Ask him. Go on, I dare you."

"No way. He'll never tell me."

"You don't know that. I'll bet he will if you ask him. Come on, Will. I know he likes you."

"What's that got to do with it? He likes all of us."

"Nah, I think he just puts up with me. Ever since I poured ketchup on the floor after he did a bone marrow on me and I faked that I was bleeding to death, he's acted different around me."

"Can you blame him?" Will asked.

"I'm just having some fun. You can't fault a guy that's dying the right to have that."

"You're not dying," responded Will, half meaning it and half hoping it was not true.

"We all are, Will. Some are just dying faster than others."

Will gulped. What if Eddy was right? What if he really was dying and no one was letting him in on the secret?

"That's enough talk about dying, boys." Michael walked into Will's room. "No one dies on my ward. Besides, you're both doing very well."

Michael walked over to the window that separated the rooms and closed the curtain, shutting the boys off from each other. "Bye-bye, Eddy. I've got some things to do with Will. Go finish your work on your escape tunnel." He turned to Will. "You two seemed to hit it off pretty well, haven't you?"

"Yeah. He's all right." Will sat on his bed and rubbed his bald head. "There's no one else to talk to in here."

"Well, I'm here now. You can talk to me if you'd like. And don't worry. Your hair will grow back. That's more than I can say for myself." Michael pointed to his own thinning hair. "Are you ready for this?" Michael pointed to the bone marrow tray that had been brought into the room and sat on the counter.

"If I say no, will we skip it?"

Michael smiled. "Not a chance. Come on. Lie down."

Will let out a moan of disapproval, but did as he was told.

Michael opened up the tray and put on his sterile gloves. "All right, little man. Drop your pants."

Will hunched himself up and pulled his pajama bottoms down far enough for Michael to have access to his hips. Will was used to getting dressed for swim meets in locker rooms and having other people see him in various degrees of undress, but even if he wasn't, being in a hospital seemed to remove any remaining traces of self-consciousness. He'd suffered shots at all times of the day by different nurses and medical students coming and going, asking him all sorts of questions. Being examined by who knows how many different people. It was enough to make him feel more like a specimen than a kid. But Michael never made him feel that way.

"You don't have to pull them down so far. You can cover yourself with your sheet. I don't need that much room."

Will thankfully complied with Michael's directions.

Michael began to drape Will's back with paper sheets and scrub the right hip area with iodine solution to sterilize the area. Will's hip already sported the previous scars of several bone marrow biopsies along his lower back.

"So, anything you'd like to talk about today?" Michael asked. "Do you have problems at home with the wife and kids?"

Will grinned. "Yeah, they just don't understand me."

"Very funny. Where'd you hear that?"

"On TV. I get to watch a lot of that around here."

"Bet you're not used to that, are you?"

"No. Not really."

Michael drew up a syringe of lidocaine to anesthetize Will's hip. "What do you usually do in the summer?"

"I like to swim. I'm on the Rockford Dolphins swim team." With disappointment in his voice he added, "But I'm missing most of the season this year."

"Here comes a little sting." Michael injected Will's hip with the burning anesthetic solution and Will let out a little grunt. "Sorry about that."

"That's okay." Will bit his lip.

"What do you miss the most about the team? Any friends there?" Michael assembled his large bore needle in preparation for driving into Will's pelvic bone.

"Yeah. I like our coach. Don Thurston. He's really nice. He looks out for me and my brother Paul."

"It's nice to have someone like that around. Do your folks get to see many of your meets?" Michael was sure of the answer before he even asked it.

"No," Will said disappointedly. "Not as much as I'd like them to. But they're busy."

"Uh huh." How could someone be too busy for his own kid? "A little pressure now as I put in the needle." Michael broke Will's skin and began to push the needle closer and closer to Will's bone. Will closed his eyes tight.

"Anyone your own age on the team you like to hang out with?" Michael continued to try to distract Will from what he was doing.

"There is someone, but you'll laugh."

Michael stopped the forward motion of the needle for a moment. "Now why do you think I'd laugh? You know me better than that."

Will paused for a moment before he answered. "'Cause she's a girl."

Michael just smiled. "What's her name?"

"Erin," said Will softly as if the name itself was as delicate as she was.

"I'll bet she's nice," said Michael as his needle touched the surface of the bone. "I wouldn't make fun of you about that. In fact, I think it's great to have a girl who's a good friend. They can be quite nice you know."

Will agreed.

"Okay, now, this is going to hurt a little."

Will clenched his teeth and squeezed his eyes shut as the needle bore through the surface of the bone. Michael removed the stylet from the center of the needle and connected a syringe to draw out the thick, red marrow.

"Here we go, buddy. Hold on tight." Michael pulled on the syringe and created a pressure in Will's pelvis that brought tears to the little boy's eyes. The red marrow flowed slowly into the syringe until Michael had harvested 10 ccs. He released the plunger and removed the syringe from the needle. The pressure now gone, Will was able to take a deep breath.

"It's all over, Will. I got all we need."

"Good."

"Let me get you cleaned up here." Michael placed the syringe with its precious contents onto the tray. Then he removed the needle and wiped off the blood that now ran from the opening down Will's back. A couple of wipes with a gauze pad and the placement of a bandage over the hole finished the job. Michael removed the paper dressing and allowed Will to roll onto his back to put pressure on the wound to keep the bleeding down.

"That wasn't too bad, was it?"

"Maybe not for you," Will said as he gingerly lowered his back onto the mattress.

"I know that this isn't easy for you. You really are a brave man to go through all of this. But think of it this way. You might be missing one summer with your swim team and one summer with Erin. But if everything goes the way we hope it will, you'll be able to spend the rest of your summers away from this place and with all of your friends."

"This is different," Will said quietly. "I've missed a few summer days before, because I had a cold or flu. But never so many days like this."

"I understand that, Will," Michael said compassionately. He smiled at his young patient. "If your counts on this specimen look good, you just may be out of here before you know it."

"Thanks, Dr. Hamilton."

Michael picked up his specimen and equipment and headed for the door. Will stopped him before Michael could leave.

"Uh, Dr. Hamilton?"

"Yes? What is it?"

"Those magic tricks that you do," Will said hesitantly. "How do you do them?"

"That's a secret, young man. And as a magician I'm sworn to never reveal how a trick is done."

"If that's true, then how did you learn the secrets?"

Michael stopped his progress toward the door. He had been asked hundreds of times to reveal the secrets to his magic over the years. But he had never been approached with the most obvious question of all. How did magicians learn the tricks if no one is allowed to reveal the secrets? But Will had hit upon it. It was the same question Michael had posed to Bill so many years ago in the dusty corner of Bill's shop. The question that he now equally felt obligated to answer.

"A magician is only to reveal the secrets of his trade to another magician," he said.

Will looked puzzled as he tried to understand the logic behind Michael's answer.

"It's sort of like what I do with my medical students. It's my job to teach them what I know. I show them my learning methods and the procedures that I do. I let them see my way of talking to patients and understanding their diseases. Then after a while I see if they've learned any of what I've taught them. But I can't teach you how to be a doctor. You'd have to take on certain training first. It takes years of school before you're ready to learn medicine."

"Yeah, but at some point you started to learn medicine. Somewhere along the line someone started to teach you, right?"

"Yes, that's true."

"And you weren't a doctor before you started to learn how to be one, were you?"

Michael saw the support for his arguments slowly eroding away. "That's not the same thing."

"And your medical students aren't doctors yet, but you teach them about medicine."

"Well, they're actually proceeding along a continuum of their educational process as opposed to suddenly being taught a curriculum of knowledge."

"What?"

Michael's words had sailed well above Will's head, which had been part of Michael's plan. Confuse the boy and thus avoid the argument. "I teach them because they have already begun their medical career, and I'm just helping them along that path. Does that make better sense?"

Will wrinkled his forehead as he thought about Michael's perspective. "But you still haven't answered my first question. Just like someone first started to teach your students, somewhere along the line you had to learn your first trick. And from there you were a magician who could learn more and more. On that continuum thing you talked about."

Michael gave a small chuckle. He knew when he was beaten. And being beaten by a ten-year-old who somehow managed to turn Michael's own words against himself was a humbling experience for the head of St. John's oncology division. Yet not one that seemed to surprise him when it came from Will. "I think I see your point."

"So will you teach me? How to do a trick, I mean? I'm not interested in being a doctor. Not yet anyway."

"You're forgetting one thing."

"What's that?"

"I can only teach another magician how to do a trick. And you are not a magician. Sorry, little man. But those are the rules."

Michael again tried to make his way to the door before Will could stop him.

"Will you make me a deal then?"

"What's that?"

"You do a trick for me. Here in this room. If I can figure out how you do it, then I'd know a trick. That would make me a magician. Then you could teach me other tricks, because I'd be one of you."

Michael looked at his patient. A little boy who should be spending his summer at the pool holding hands with a cute girl. Swimming and playing dodgeball. Eating hot dogs and riding bikes. Instead he got to spend his time in an isolation room being injected with toxins and having needles rammed into his tender back while losing his hair. Life didn't seem fair at that moment, as it hadn't for Michael on many other occasions in his own life. And if the boy wanted to learn a few magic tricks just to keep from being bored, then where's the harm? Michael had always wanted someone to pass on his magic tricks to anyway. Like Bill had done for him. He'd never have a child of his own who could take that role. Never have someone sit on the floor of his living room and watch feats of sleight of hand. No, there'd be no one else. Will made about as much sense as any other choice.

"Deal. Let me go put these specimens away first. You don't want them to get spoiled and make us have to do your bone marrow a second time, do you?"

"Oh, no," said Will, rubbing his right hip.

"Fine. I'll be right back. But I only have a few minutes." Michael finally made his way out the door.

"You did it. You smooth operator." Eddy's voice came through the intercom. "You got him to teach you some tricks."

"You were listening to us?" Will was more angry than embarrassed. He didn't want Eddy to have been listening to his procedure and hear him talk about Erin.

"Yeah. He only closed the blinds. He didn't turn off the monitor. This is going to be great. I can't wait to see which one he's going to teach us."

"Eddy, there is no 'us' here," Will said as he walked to the intercom. "He agreed to teach me a trick only if I can figure one of his out. He didn't agree to teach us both stuff."

"I know. But I'll just sit here and listen like I just did. He'll never know."

Will thought about what Michael had said. About how he could only teach to another magician. How Michael wanted to keep his tricks a secret. It wouldn't be right to let Eddy listen in. It would be like stealing from Dr. Hamilton.

"No, he wouldn't know. But I would." Will clicked off the speaker on his wall and shut Eddy off from any future conversations. He didn't like having to do that like he was taking sides with a grown-up instead of a kid. But Will knew the difference between right and wrong. And now wasn't the time to blur the line of distinction between the two.

"All right," said Michael as he returned into the room with a deck of cards and a small, letter-sized pamphlet. "I found one in my trunk that I think should be a fair test of your abilities."

"Give me your best shot, mister." Will sat down on his bed.

Michael pulled a metal tray table over to use as a desk and sat in a chair opposite Will. "That sounds like a challenge."

"Take it however you like." Will leaned back on his arms. He had been able to figure out crossword puzzles, two-minute mysteries, and any other book of challenging puzzles that had been given to him to while away the lonely hours in his room.

"Fine," began Michael as he went into his magician's voice. "I've got a trick here that's so good. So good, mind you, that it comes with a guarantee."

Michael held up the pamphlet that he had brought along. The words across the front read "Magic Trick Insurance Policy."

"This policy states that if for any reason the magic trick I'm about to perform does not work, then the bearer of the policy will be awarded ten gold coins by the Royal Order of Magicians High Counsel."

"Who are they?"

"That's on a need-to-know basis, son," said Michael as he opened up a deck of cards and began to shuffle.

"So what's the trick?"

"Well, for a trick to be guaranteed, it has to be one that's going to work every time. And that's usually a simple one." Michael pressed and bent the cards causing them to shoot rapidly from one hand to the other. "And for us it's a card trick." Michael fanned the cards out in front of Will, showing him first the backs then the faces. Satisfied that this was a standard deck, Will nodded. Michael then held the deck up and asked Will to pick a number between one and fifteen. Will chose five. First Michael demonstrated counting into the deck for the fifth card, then had Will do the same.

"That fifth card is yours. Take it, look at it, then put it back into the deck."

Will did as instructed after memorizing his card, the eight of hearts. Michael then took the deck and shuffled four times to make sure that Will's card was well mixed with the rest.

"Now I'll find your card." Michael began dealing the cards out face down. After he had gone through several cards, he flipped one over. "There. There's your card. The nine of clubs."

"That's not it," said Will.

"Are you sure?" asked a surprised Michael.

"Yep." Will smiled.

"Hmmm." Michael opened and consulted the insurance policy. "Page three states that I actually get two more tries to get it right." He set the policy down and resumed counting out cards.

"Jack of diamonds."

"Nope."

"Ace of hearts."

"Sorry."

Michael scratched his head. "This doesn't make sense. The policy clearly states that this is supposed to work." Michael picked up the policy and opened up the pages.

"Looks like you're going to get your gold coins," said Will.

"Ah, here we are." Michael read from the paper. "If the trick fails to work after three tries, unfold the policy to reveal the guarantee."

Michael unfolded the pamphlet until it was the size of a poster. "Here's the guarantee." The policy was now in a large rectangle whose back resembled the face of a playing card. The policy had turned into a giant eight of hearts. "That, I believe is your card."

Will's mouth dropped open. "How'd you do that?"

Michael shuffled the cards in his hands. "That's your job to figure out, young man. You're the one who wants to be a magician."

Will looked at the large, paper eight of hearts and saw the challenge that it presented. It was definitely printed on the paper. It was not recently drawn as if Michael was somehow able to rapidly affix the card's identity. The eight of hearts had to have been selected prior to the trick being performed. The secret did not lie in the policy itself. It had to lie in the cards. Will turned his attention to the cards. He had selected the card. Dr. Hamilton did not force that card into his hand. Or had he?

"You somehow made me pick the eight of hearts, didn't you?" asked Will.

"Perhaps. But how would I do that?"

Will looked at the deck. "May I?" he asked as he picked up the cards.

"Of course. Knock yourself out, buddy."

Will thumbed through the cards as he recreated the scenario of his picking the card. He had selected the number for the card. He counted into the deck by himself. Dr. Hamilton didn't do it for him and slip a card off the bottom of the deck. But somehow, he had set the eight of hearts into his hand. His eyes widened as the solution hit him. "You put the card in the deck for me to find."

"You counted into the deck, not me," answered Michael.

"I know, but you put the card in there for me to get to. When you had me pick the number between one and fifteen, you showed me how to count into the deck and take the fifth card. But when you did that, you ended up putting the card that was on the top of the deck into the deck as the new fifth card. All you had to do was shuffle the eight of hearts to the top of the deck before the trick was started. You basically made me pick that card."

Michael smiled. "Very good, my young apprentice. Very good." Will had figured it out. And it took him less time than Michael had taken when he first learned it himself from Bill. "I think you have proven yourself."

"So you'll teach me some more tricks? And show me how they're done?"

Will was excited and acting not at all like a boy who had just undergone a painful procedure. Michael liked to see Will's enthusiasm. He knew that a positive outlook greatly affected a cancer patient's outcome. And as the boy's physician, it was Michael's role to do whatever he could to bolster Will's attitude. Plus, he was having fun too.

"Sure. I'll teach you some tricks, but not all of them. I'll only show you some. The ones that I think you can pull off."

"That's gonna be more than you think, mister."

Michael laughed "I'll bring you in some things tomorrow. We can start then." Michael could see that Will was disappointed in the idea of having to wait another day. So he gave Will the deck of cards and the insurance policy. "In the meantime, you can practice with these. Work on your shuffling techniques. You're going to need them." Michael turned as he reached the door. "See you in the morning?"

"I can't leave the room," Will said. "And you have to make your morning rounds anyway."

Michael returned to the nurses' station and pulled Will's chart from the rack. He still needed to write his note for the day and document that he had done the bone marrow procedure. Before Michael left the floor, he grabbed the phone book from the secretary's desk. He recalled his earlier conversation with Will and how he missed some of his friends from the swim team. Being a patient in the isolation ward can be lonely, and having visitors can make the world of difference. He opened the book to the Ts and found the name for which he was searching.

Michael picked up the phone and dialed the number for Don Thurston.

18

"Do you solemnly swear to tell the truth, the whole truth, and nothing but the truth, so help you God?"

"Is this really necessary?" asked Greg. "I'm not on trial here."

"Granted, this is just a deposition, Dr. Jameson," Terrance Niemann commented, "but your cooperation in following procedure would be appreciated." He picked up his cassette recorder from the long table in the St. John's risk management conference room. "Let the record show that the defendant is displaying hostile tendencies and behaving in an uncooperative fashion."

"Oh, give me a freaking break," Greg spat out.

"And displaying vulgar language—add that to the record as well." Terrance turned to Greg. "Anything else you'd like me to add, Dr. Jameson? Anything else you'd like to hang yourself with?"

"Time to calm down, Greg," Mark Brannon intervened. "We're here to cooperate with Mr. Niemann. We want him to get good, solid answers to his questions."

"Fine," grunted Greg, who then let out a cough that sounded suspiciously like a "woof" in reference to the Terrier. Then with the biggest fake grin he could muster, he added, "I swear."

"Gentlemen," spoke Mark, "this is, needless to say, a hostile situation. Whenever we have people with opposite views and interests there's bound to be tension. But let's settle down and begin this process. Surely none of us really wants to be here. It would be a much better world if all of these differences could be worked out in simple means. But that's obviously not the case here. So let's just go through the motions and get this out of the way, shall we?"

"Finally, a level head," said Terrance.

Mark nodded in agreement.

"Fine. Dr. Jameson, for the record if you please, do you work at St. John's hospital in the capacity of a general surgeon?"

"Yes." He gave a complete answer. No further information, just as Mark had coached.

"Do you know my client, Ms. Julie McMahon?"

"Yes."

"What kind of a nurse is she?"

"She's a surgical nurse, I believe. Also, she's a female nurse."

"What I mean is, is she a good nurse? Is she punctual, competent, cooperative?"

"Yeah, I guess so."

"Which one? Or is she all of those things?"

Greg folded his arms across his chest. "She does her job pretty well."

Terrance smiled. He got the answer he was looking for.

"Or I guess I should say that she *did*," added Greg. "She had been slacking off the last couple of weeks. Her timing was getting slow, and she was dropping things. One time her sponge count was off and we had to reexplore an old woman's belly before we found the sponge on the floor."

Terrance talked into his recorder. "Strike that last comment. It was editorial. He answered the question I asked."

"There's nothing wrong with his additions, Terry," Mark said, deliberately using the diminutive form of Terrance's name because he knew Terrance hated to be called that. "This is just an evidentiary investigation. If you want to object to his testimony and get it stricken from the record you can do that at the trial, if we ever get that far."

"Fine," said Terrance through clenched teeth. Mark leaned back in his chair and took a sip of water from his glass, reinforcing the fact that no pitchers of water were provided for the plaintiff team. "So, Dr. Jameson, you claim that Julie was slipping in her clinical skills. Did any other physician note a problem with her? Were there any other complaints? Was she written up for failure to do her duties? Placed on suspension? Lose her privileges?"

"Not that I know of," answered Greg.

Terrance turned to Mark. "Does the hospital have any records of such offenses? Is there anything to support Dr. Jameson's claims of her failure to perform her duties in a professional manner?"

Mark shook his head slowly from side to side.

"Then I guess it doesn't matter if we strike that statement from the record now or not. Bring it up at the trial and I'll embarrass you with it. Sound fair?" Terrance reached across the table and pulled Mark's pitcher of water over to his side of the table, found an unused glass, and poured himself a drink. "Now if we can get back to you, Dr. Jameson," Terrance continued. "You've established that Miss McMahon is a competent nurse who, as far as you know, has carried out her duties in a professional manner throughout her career. Is that so?"

Greg nodded as he said, "Yes."

"Fine. Can we say the same about you, sir?"

"I have not carried out any nurse's duties during my career, Mr. Niemann."

"Very funny. Remember to be a smart-ass on the stand for me. I'd love the entertainment. Allow me to redirect the question since you are having a difficult time remembering that you're a surgeon. Have you behaved in a professional manner during your career as a physician? Have you been written up for insubordination? Have a career of harassing nurses and other staff members? Put a black eye on this institution?"

"Don't answer that, Greg." Mark placed his hand on the table in front of his client.

"I'll just subpoena your records. I'm sure the distinguished Dr. Jameson has quite a file. Or you can save us all a lot of time and answer the questions now. This isn't a trial, Mark. If you don't like the information the answers give, you can always object at the trial." Terrance used Mark's own words against his opponent. It was something he loved to do. The Terrier was barking.

"If you want to subpoena our records, go ahead. I'm sure you get a bang out of serving papers. Kind of a rush for you, isn't it, Terry?"

"Are you going to answer the question or not, Jameson?"

Greg looked at Mark who ever so slowly shook his head. "I don't think that I've been written up. No. Not that I can remember."

"Fine. If that's the kind of cooperation I can expect from you, then we'll just have to let the courts settle that matter."

Terrance closed the manila folder that contained the papers and notes he had been reading. He set his briefcase on the table, opened it, and set the folder into it. Greg and Mark looked at each other surprised that the Terrier had given up so easily. "I'm really disheartened that you aren't willing to discuss your past. Or let me see your file. I thought that this was supposed to be a discovery for the exchange of evidence and information."

Terrance pulled out another file from his briefcase before setting the alligator-skinned case back onto the floor.

"Fortunately, your medical school and residency program had no problem submitting to my requests for information. Since you won't give us your current file, I'll just have to go with what I found in these."

Greg's forehead began to form beads of sweat. He felt his heart pound a few beats faster. He knew what they might find. And it wasn't something that was ever meant to be found.

"Let's see now," began Terrance as he thumbed his way through the stacks of paper. "Your residency was at the University of Wisconsin, is that right?"

Greg nodded. It was difficult to speak with a dry mouth.

"It was a five-year program. You graduated on schedule with no loss of privileges during that time. It says here that you got into a verbal fighting match with one of the nurses on the surgical floor over the handling of a patient's IV fluids. Remember that case?"

"That could be any of a number of cases. Care to be more specific?"

"She alleged that you swore at her, made unkind remarks as to her heritage, and called her incompetent."

"I really don't remember that."

"Hm. Perhaps if we found her and got her opinion on the matter that might refresh your memory?"

"Hard to say." Greg tried to stay cool. He rubbed the sweat from his face as Terrance read.

"What's this about having a New Year's Eve party? You provided alcohol on the hospital grounds. There are reports of disturbing the patients."

"There's nothing wrong with having a little fun on New Year's, is there?"

"It took place in March, Dr. Jameson."

Greg smiled with the memories that the party brought back. A room full of streamers, champagne, balloons, and inebriated nurses in various degrees of undress. Fortunately, the party had died down before they were discovered using the CEO's office. He had caught hell for that stunt. But like most of his bigger blunders, it was worth it just for the honor of having a great story to tell.

Terrance leafed through the file briefly, then moved on. He pulled another file from his case. His slow movements and patience lead Greg to feel that he either was trying to provoke anxiety, or hoped that Greg would just start talking more about his past. Greg would do neither. "You went to medical school at the University of Chicago College of Medicine." Terrance read from Greg's twenty-year-old file. "Fun time, medical school, isn't it?"

"Like you'd know, Mr. Lawyer."

"Oh, I can imagine it. Cadaver lab, study sessions, and cramming for finals. Law school wasn't too far different except for the dead bodies."

"No, you waited until after law school to start hanging around with those." Greg's remarks made Terrance drop the friendly face.

"What I mean is that you probably faced a lot of stress. Didn't you?"

Greg nodded.

"So much so that you more than likely would have to find ways to blow off steam every now and then, especially someone who was first in his class three out of the four years."

"Yeah. I guess we looked to have some fun every now and then."

"Did you have some fun after graduation, Dr. Jameson?"

Greg clammed up. He wasn't sure how much Niemann knew. And he was not about to give the cockroach any information that wasn't already known.

"Did you, you know, blow off some steam? Cause a ruckus?"

"I'm not sure what you're getting at," responded Greg.

"If you have a question, please ask it. Now isn't a time for a fishing expedition." Mark had let his opponent get away with some tangential questions, but now wanted to find out where Niemann was going.

"I have here a police report with the charges of a sexual assault and battery. What was that about?"

Greg knew, but he didn't know how much Terrance knew. "Refresh my memory, won't you. That was a long time ago."

Terrance looked over the papers. "What more is there to talk about? The charges speak for themselves."

Greg remembered the incident. He wished he couldn't. "I'd rather not talk about it."

"I'm afraid you need to."

"No, I don't think so." Greg had no intention of drumming up that issue.

"What exactly does that file accuse Dr. Jameson of doing?" asked Mark who was getting angry that his client hadn't disclosed information like this.

"I can get a copy to you if you don't think your client would be willing to give that information to you. But I'll summarize the case for you. The charges filed in Cook County state that Greg Jameson was accused of a sexual assault and battery of a Miss Lori Lange."

Greg swallowed hard and beads of sweat formed on his forehead. Mark shifted in his chair. His case just got much more difficult.

"The file doesn't say much more than that, I'm afraid," continued Terrance. "Court documents only state that the case was settled by mutual agreement in a plea bargain between the two parties. The charges were reduced to assault, and Greg Jameson received probation. Does that refresh your memory, Doctor?"

It did.

"Still don't want to talk about it?" Terrance grinned. He liked getting his way.

Greg tossed up his hands. "'Fraid not."

"That's too bad." Terrance let his eyes fall back to the pages in front of him. "I guess I'll just have to find this Lori Lange and see if she can shed any light on the incident. My team is tracking her down as we speak. It seems her name has changed since she graduated." Terrance looked into Greg's face. "But you knew that already, didn't you?"

Greg didn't say a word.

"I said, you knew that already, didn't you?"

Greg refused to answer.

"Fine. I think I got all I needed from you. Your silence tells me that I'm on the right track with this." Terrance put the remaining folders and his cassette recorder back into his briefcase and snapped it shut. Rising from the table, he turned to Mark and Greg. "It's obvious that if I'm going to get any good information I'm going to have to get it from other sources. But Dr. Lange isn't going to be hard to find. And when I find her you're going to wish that you were a little more cooperative. Good day, gentlemen." Terrance left the room and closed the door behind him.

"Well, it looks like he found her," said Mark. "This won't be good."

"Have you spoken to her?" asked Greg.

"No. I was hoping this story would have stayed in the past, and we could have kept her out of it. I guess that's no longer an option."

Greg was hoping that it would have stayed hidden as well.

Mark turned toward a now uncharacteristically silent Greg. "Dr. Jameson, I think it's time we found out exactly what you did to the young Dr. Hamilton that summer day."

19

"What are you doing?" Lori asked, half angry and half surprised to find her husband rummaging through their basement. "You're making a mess."

Michael pulled his head out of a large cardboard box that sat on the bare concrete floor of their storage room. "I'm the husband. It's my job to make the messes."

"Just as long as you know it's not my job to pick up after you."

"Yes, it is," Michael said with a grin. "You promised. Don't you remember your wedding vows? Love, honor, pick up socks, clean the bathrooms, cook, and rub various body parts at my bidding."

"There must be paint fumes in that box you've got your head stuck in if you think that's what I agreed to. I only promised to put up with you as long as your money held out."

Lori looked around the small, musty room. Years of debris had accumulated over their married years as if they were saving up for the world's largest garage sale. Old lamps and exercise equipment gathered dust. Headboards from previous bedroom sets stood next to boxes of Christmas ornaments. A corner housed a collection of tree stands that Michael kept buying—forgetting that he already owned several. The floor was now littered with stacks of books piled to various heights like tiny buildings that created a miniature skyline. "What are you looking for anyway?"

"An old book of mine." Michael sat up and looked at the stacks of books he had created. "I was sure that it was in here."

"Which one? An old textbook? Because I think those are all up in your office." Lori picked up a book from the top of the nearest stack to see what treasure had been unearthed. "*Hardy Boys*? You read those?"

"Don't talk, Miss Nancy Drew."

Lori looked through the stacks Michael was making. "These are your old books from when you were a kid. Where did you get these?"

"On one of my trips to my mom's house. I had to make those journeys worth my while."

"Don't go harping on your mom. She's not so bad. She's just lonely."

Michael stared at his lovely bride. "Who's sniffing the paint fumes now? Are you actually defending my mother to me?"

"I just know what it's like to be alone, that's all. It sucks, Mike. I just think you could cut her a little slack."

"You didn't grow up with her. I did." The smile left his face. "I'll cut her some slack when she stops treating me like I'm still her little boy."

"You do realize that you're saying that while playing in stacks of children's books."

Michael saw the irony and knew he had no defense. "Oh quiet. You know what I mean."

Lori sat down next to her man and picked through some of the books that he had already moved aside from his search. "Yes, I'm afraid that I do."

Michael sighed in frustration. "What are you talking about?"

"You want her to treat you like a man. A grown-up. But do you realize that all the time you're with her you treat her like she's the child? And you're the grown-up? Of course she's going to treat you like a kid. It's her defense. She's trying to establish a pecking order. She's still a woman and a mother."

"Don't I know it."

"Let me finish, Mr. Rude."

Michael bit his lip.

"Correct me if I'm wrong, but wasn't her identity defined by the fact that she was the wife of your father and the mother of you?"

"Well, yeah. I guess so."

"So, your father's dead. And the only other person who's around who reminds her of who she is, is a son who scolds her for wanting some independence and pushes her to do exactly as he says."

"I'm not like that."

"No? Then tell me what went on at your last visit." Lori sat back and crossed her legs. She ran her fingers through her hair to get it away from her face, then sat in silence staring at Michael waiting for him to answer.

"Fine. I showed up…"

"Were you late?"

"A few minutes. I was busy at the hospital that day."

"How late?"

"I don't know. Twenty minutes maybe."

Lori motioned for Michael to go on.

"When I got there Maggie had already left. But Mom got impatient and was trying to cook something for supper. Well, the stove was turned off, so she couldn't use that. Of course that made her angry because she had mixed up several bowls of soup and noodles. She had stuffed them in the micro-wave, spoons still sticking out of the bowls, mind you, and set the thing to run for ten minutes. So when I walk in there were sparks shooting around inside the microwave, the kitchen counter was covered with half-empty cans, the smoke alarm's going off, and she's hiding in the bathroom to get away from the noise."

Lori's face remained expressionless like she was watching a golf match on TV. "Go on."

"Then, on top of it she hadn't done any of her finger sticks for her sugar level all day. So I can't tell how much insulin she'd need for the night. Then I get to clean the whole kitchen after I heat up the supper I brought her from the hospital. And she didn't like what I brought either, did I tell you that?"

"Are you done?"

"Yeah, isn't that enough?"

"So you say she treats you like a kid, but don't you see what you're doing to her?"

"I'm trying to take care of her, that's what."

"No. You're treating her like a two-year-old. Mikey, that poor woman sits all day in her house with Maggie. It's like she's home with the babysitter. She can't walk too far unless she has a walker or a wheelchair. You might as well put her in a stroller. She has to wear diapers some of the time. Then at the end of the day you get there and act like the father scolding her and punishing her for not doing as she's told. Plus you take away the one thing that probably meant the most to her. That kitchen was hers. It was her place. She cooked in it for decades. She shooed people out of it when they got underfoot. Do you remember when she did that to me when we were first going together?"

Michael nodded and smiled at the memory of his young girlfriend being on the receiving end of his mother's cold stares.

"That room defined her. She was the cook. Now she can't even heat up a can of soup because you've cut off the power to her stove. You make her eat what you bring her, not her own cooking. She can't provide for anyone anymore. She can't cook, or straighten up a house, or even give herself a bath anymore. How exactly is that supposed to make her feel? Like the parent or the child?"

Michael tried to see things from Lori's perspective; how the years seemed to have robbed his mother of whom she was. He tried to understand why she thought he could be wrong. For once. But it just didn't register. "But you should have seen that kitchen. It's like she did it on purpose just to get my attention."

"Arrggh! You are so male." Lori threw her arms up in exasperation. "Of course she was trying to get your attention. She wants to get her life back, or at least a small piece of self-respect. Honey, I love you, but you are not a woman. I am."

"I know," Michael said as he leaned in and tried for a quick grope.

"Stop that." She smacked his hand away from her partially opened blouse. "If you think you will ever get your hand in there again, you'd better start treating me a little nicer. I'm not just a nice-looking piece of flesh put on this earth for you to get your jollies with." Her stern look told Michael that she meant business.

"I'm sorry, sweetie." Michael pulled back. "I was just—"

"I know what you were doing. You were losing the argument, so you were trying to change the subject."

"You're right." Michael felt the defeat. "I didn't mean to offend you."

"There. How'd that feel?" The corner of Lori's mouth curled into a devious smile. Michael fell for the little trap that she had set for him. She always felt that men were such easy prey to capture.

"What? How'd what feel?"

"You were trying to patronize me. Treat me like a little woman who'd do whatever her man wanted when he wanted. And when I objected and gave you a slap on the wrist, you backed down. Or cowered is more like it. That's exactly what your mother is doing."

"Excuse me, but I did not try to put the moves on my mother."

"No, that's not what I was saying. You're trying to put her in her little space. Patronize her as an old, frail woman who should just shut up and do as she's told. When she objects in the only way she knows how, you get angry with her, which only makes her push harder back at you."

"So what does that have to do with me trying to cop a feel?"

"Nothing. What I'm trying to tell you is that we women don't want to have some man telling us who we are and what we're here for. And we'll let you know that in no uncertain terms. The sooner you unclog your ears and listen to us the sooner you'll find us more pleasant to be around. Just because she's gotten older doesn't mean that your mother has stopped being a woman. Give your mother some independence and some space. Treat her like she's still a woman. Like her life matters and that the world is a better place because she's in it. Believe me, then and only then will she start treating you like a man."

Michael let Lori's words sink in, through his thick skull, as she'd say. "So you think that she's being difficult only to get me to notice her in a way other than as the old bat that she's grown into?"

Lori wrinkled her forehead. "Excuse me? What did you say? I know that she's your mother, but don't refer to her as an old bat. I'm the daughter-in-law. Thinking up nasty names for her is supposed to be my job. Don't you get onto my turf."

Michael should have known better than to tangle with Lori. Of all the arguments they had had over the years, he had only won one of them. That was over where they'd spend their honeymoon. And Lori only said that she wanted to go camping in the Smoky Mountains so that Michael would spring for a Hawaiian trip.

"So. Willing to admit that you're wrong?" Lori leaned over into Michael's personal space. Michael kept his usual silence. "That you need me and can't live without me. You're in awe of me," she continued.

"Don't push it too far, lady," countered Michael, as he brought his lips to Lori's in small kisses between his words. "I may need you and can't live without you. But how can I admit that I'm wrong when I'm so right for you?"

Lori said "You're so full of it" just as their lips pressed together and stayed for what seemed like hours. Michael brought his hand back up to Lori's breasts. This time she didn't push him away. Lori finally spoke and broke the silence. "Do you really need to be looking for this book now? Or could I interest you in moving to a different room for a while?"

"Got any particular room in mind?" said Michael, who instantly forgot about his search for his book. Reading just got moved onto the back burner in favor of a much more enjoyable pastime. "You know that I can please you in the bedroom."

"Honey, if you want to please me in the bedroom, put away your socks, bring me cookies, rub my feet, and get out. I want to be somewhere else."

"Well, I suppose I could meet you in the hot tub room."

"Sounds great. Give me a few minutes, okay? I have to pee first."

Michael grinned like a little boy on Christmas morning. Lori stood up to go upstairs.

"By the way, what book is making you turn my basement upside down?"

"My old Harry Houdini book."

"The one that you've had, like, forever?"

Michael nodded. Lori just laughed. "I can't believe you. That thing was like your prized possession. You never left it at your mother's house. You had it in your office back in Birmingham. It's probably in one of your boxes of old medical books."

Michael paused for a moment before the light came on in his mind.

"That's where it is, isn't it?" asked Lori.

Michael affirmed her suspicion and began packing his childhood books back in their cardboard homes.

"I swear. Men." Lori's voice faded as she walked back to the basement stairs. "You wouldn't be able to find your own ass in the dark without directions."

"I heard that," yelled Michael as he stacked his box on a wooden shelf and rummaged his way—through an old sound system and winter clothes hung on a pipe—to his boxes that held all of his textbooks since medical school.

The musty smell hit Michael's nose as the lid of the top box lifted off. *Gray's Anatomy. Human Physiology. Biochemistry of the Human Systems. Statistics and Probabilities in Health Care.* The titles instantly brought back memories of his many classes that seemed so hard when he took them, but held such little clinical relevance in Michael's current practice. Faded pages now nearly blended in with the aged yellow highlighter marks that a much younger version of him once made.

First year of med school was a lot of fun. Classes weren't so hard. The smell of the cadaver lab was about the worst thing. That was the year he met Lori. For all but one event, Michael remembered that year as one of his best. But he wasn't in that box to reminisce; he was looking for his magic book. And he had little time to find it. Lori and hot, bubbling water were waiting for him.

Michael heard the phone ring as he searched through the books. The sounds stopped after three rings indicating that Lori must have gotten it. Pulling back book after book, Michael finally found the object of his quest. *Harry Houdini.* The title said it all. The green cover was filled with a photograph of the master magician hanging upside down from a crane over the Boardwalk in Atlantic City. Being wrapped in a straightjacket and escaping before plunging into the icy water was one of Houdini's trademark feats and one of Michael's favorites.

Michael leafed through the pages of the first book he ever bought. Five dollars it had cost him, which was nearly a week's pay for a seventh grader with a paper route. He had wanted this book. He wanted to read about the great magician and about his life. The secrets of some of his tricks were revealed in its pages. Plus, Michael wanted to spend some of his money at Bill's shop. But more than that, this biography of Houdini was more of a milestone in Michael's life. It marked the beginning of his magic career. After spending five dollars on one book, it wasn't too difficult to drop seventy-five cents or a dollar fifty on some of the other little tricks that filled the glass case in Bill's shop. Tricks that were very simple to learn, as Bill would try his best to demonstrate each one after Michael had made his purchase. Bill's slow and fumbling hands easily revealed any secret.

But more than just the beginning of a magic career, this book signaled the beginning of a new kid. Just like the magic described in Houdini's book, Michael became something other than he once was. Michael remembered those times as well. Not so happy times. He thought about himself as a young kid who was only a ghost of a memory now. He would watch an old man on a three-wheeled bike that had a large cargo area filled with trinkets and, to anyone other than the rider, worthless junk. Michael thought about the man who peddled door to door, seeking someone to buy the objects. Slurring out his sales pitch and drooling between words. Getting doors shut in his face, or shuffling away with only a few pennies to show for his hard work.

Michael could still hear his voice as he would ride up behind the old man. Bill's weak legs could only peddle so fast, and Michael could always catch up to him no matter where Bill was riding. Shouts of "retard" echoed in Michael's mind and thoughts of summer days throwing apples at the old man and winters using snowballs for the same purpose. Days of tormenting the old man culminated in what Michael thought would be his finest act. Michael had decided not to bother the old man, but instead follow him to his house. Bill lived in the basement apartment of an old house not too far from the main business district. The family that lived upstairs kept up the yard. A small terrier was tied to a rope in the middle of the yard. The always-barking dog ran around in a small, dirt circle, which showed the limited radius of the length of rope.

The family seemed to take care of the old man as they helped him get his bike into the detached garage and safely settled into the apartment. *What a bunch of jerks*, thought the young Michael. *Taking care of a worthless cripple like that.*

But Michael would make them see what a man like that was worth. Later that night, Michael sneaked out of his house, and made his way back to the old man's apartment. The garage door was easily lifted up, and Bill's bike slid out into the night. Michael rode Bill's bike all over town. No one seemed to notice him. No one seemed to care. That justified his actions. Why should he care if no one else in town did? Michael made his way to the edge of town. Henderson's woods would be the perfect place. No one would find the bike there. Michael rode off the road and pushed the bike through the pines. The heavy bike was a lot easier to ride than push. But a determined boy can do a lot when destruction is on his mind.

He found a secluded area far from the road. Michael pulled open the cargo compartment. *What a bunch of junk*, he thought as he pulled out the plastic items. The sounds of breaking plastic and glass echoed off the trees. Some of the items flew and smashed against the sturdy pine trunks. Snow globes became baseballs and were thrown at any rock Michael could find. Once the compartment was emptied and Bill's entire inventory was reduced to scrap, Michael turned his attention to the bike. Spokes were kicked out of place. Michael twisted his foot on one spoke, which only made him kick harder on the next one. The handlebar twisted to the side. The bike seat was slashed with a trusty Scout knife. When he was done, Michael pushed the bike under a dense tree and onto its side. Never again would he have to look at that stupid bike coming down his street or that ugly old man. It seemed like a small price to pay for getting his street back.

Michael looked at the book. The price tag of five dollars didn't seem like nearly enough for what he had done. Replacing that bike would have cost him a lot more if he had ever been caught. His dad would have made him pay more than just in a dollar amount. But no one ever found out what he had done. Michael wasn't the only one who tormented Bill. Sheriff Wilson just assumed it was one of the Hunt brothers who had stolen the bike.

The streets seemed emptier after that day. People who never seemed to care started to talk about Bill. "Where is he?" "Why don't we see him anymore?" A man who was invisible when he was always around now became greatly missed.

The town seemed to rally behind the disappearing bike. Small towns need causes to fight for. There often is little else for them to do. Fundraisers were organized. Businesses banded together. New bikes were donated. People brought the man casseroles. It was like Bill was the town's favorite son. But the biggest idea to emerge was to get Bill off the streets and away from the vandals who seemed to torment him. "But how?" was the question.

A small, unused former butcher shop in an out-of-the-way location became the answer. With donated items and a workday provided by the local church youth group, what was once an empty building became Bill's new store—the What-Not Shop.

The grand opening was spectacular. Everyone who was anyone in the town of Marengo turned out for the gala event. Mayor Gould showed up and helped Bill cut the long yellow ribbon that spanned the front of the store. Bill's crooked frame and awkward stance required the assistance. Door prizes were given out. Candy, cookies, cakes, and cotton candy were being handed out along with popcorn from an old-fashioned cart. Michael felt a little odd being there, but as the son of one of the town doctors he had an obligation to show up. Michael walked along the shelves looking at replicas of the very items he had destroyed. The sight of them made his young stomach turn. The only place to hide in the store was an area far away from the rest of the plastic junk.

A counter on the far end of the store had a small crowd gathered around it. Bill was behind the counter smiling with his lopsided grin. Next to him was a portly fellow whom Michael had never seen: Tom Mansfield. Tom was a local magician. He performed mostly at birthday parties and at the local nursing home when he wasn't involved in his main career as a tire salesman at the Farm and Fleet. Tom was busily demonstrating sleight of hand and card tricks to his captive audience. He wasn't much of a magician. More of a showman who liked to hear the sound of his own voice. But he could hold an audience in the palm of his hand. And that's just what he was doing.

One by one, Tom showed off many of the tricks that he had personally donated to Bill's new magician's corner. Canes that turned into silk scarves, levitating glasses, rings that could slide through ropes, and dozens of other tricks that were guaranteed to amaze your friends and were easy to learn. Tom even had Bill do a couple. Bill's fumbling hands couldn't pull them off, but Tom covered for him.

It was then that Michael noticed that Bill was not some old discarded piece of skin. Someone who could get a whole town together must be more than that. Michael watched the old man. How he delighted in the smallest of things. How he gave away candy to little children without a thought of making a profit. How hard he tried to fit in, and be like everyone else.

Michael left the grand opening early. Mostly out of shame and partly out of hunger. He just couldn't bring himself to take any of the free food offered at the shop. He had taken enough from the old man. Not just his bike, but also some of his dignity. The bike had been replaced hundreds of times over with the opening of the shop. But the dignity for Bill would be harder to return. That was going to take a little longer.

Michael rubbed the cover of his book. The image of Houdini looked a little blurry due to the misting of Michael's eyes. Tears that had been brought on by sadness that Michael still had not found a way to erase. Up to now. Somewhere there was a little boy who felt a loneliness that Bill had learned to live with. Will was surrounded by people but often left alone. Will also thought that magic tricks were fun. Will enjoyed finding out the secrets and showing tricks to others. The book was for him. The book was for Will.

Michael had spent the last few afternoons in Will's lonely room— showing the boy tricks and teaching sleight-of-hand techniques—all the while wondering why he was the boy's only visitor. Will let it slip more than once that he missed having friends around and a dad. Seeing the little boy's face at the idea of knowing his own father seemed too busy to visit made the childless Michael even sadder. He wanted to do something about that. He needed to show Will that someone cared, and if he had to step on Greg's toes in the process, all the better.

That was enough self-pity, he thought, rubbing away the tears. Lori was waiting for him, hopefully naked and pouring a glass of wine. It was just the prescription that he needed to be filled. Michael closed up the box and returned the remaining books to their place of rest. He dried his eyes one more time before heading upstairs. Michael shut the door to the basement as he reached the kitchen. The large room, with more counter space than a couple needed, was spotless. Off to one side was the doorway to the sunroom, which overlooked the backyard. That's where Michael had installed their hot tub. But the lid was still on. No bubbling water. No wine glasses filled with his favorite merlot. But more disturbingly, there was no sign of Lori. Michael felt his erection ease down a bit at this new development. He walked around the house and found Lori in their bedroom. It was neatly decorated in colonial style with lots of frilly stuff that Michael didn't like, but he knew better than to argue with Lori. The bed had a maple headboard. Its king-sized mattress seemed to make the sitting figure of Lori seem small. But that's not what Michael noticed. He saw her face covered with her hands. Her shoulders were trembling. Michael's girl was crying.

"What's the matter, hon?"

Lori removed her hands, revealing her inflamed eyes and tear-soaked face. "Oh, nothing," she lied.

"Was it the phone call? What's happened?"

"This is stupid. I shouldn't be so upset." She wiped her eyes and stood up to walk around the room.

"Well, if you'll tell me what's wrong, maybe I can help."

"You can't fix this. I have to deal with this myself."

"You never have to deal with anything by yourself. I'm here."

Lori reached out and took Michael's hand. A wadded up tissue fell from her grip. "I know," she blurted before breaking out in tears again.

"Did you take your medicine today? You know how it affects you if you don't."

"Yes, I took it. And no, this isn't about that. I'm not getting hormonal. I'm just reliving something."

"Who called? What's this about?"

"It was some lawyer. Terrance Niemann. He said that he was going to subpoena me for testimony against Greg."

Michael sat down on the bed as the news hit his own memory bank. "They must have tracked you down. I do assume that this has something to do with that stunt he pulled."

"Really? Do you think?" Lori shot back sarcastically.

"Well, what'd you tell him?"

"I didn't say anything. Do you think that I want to relive those days? But he said I had to comply. So I called Mark Brannon over at the hospital real quick. He said that they knew something was going on, but Greg wouldn't talk to them about it."

"Go figure."

"They want to talk to me too. Mike, I don't want to do this. It took a long time to get over that stunt. And even longer for everyone else to forget about it."

"I'll take care of it." He pulled Lori into his arms and rubbed her back in a way that always seemed to calm her down. "I won't let them hurt you."

"They said if I don't come in for a deposition that they can drag me into court. I don't want to tell that story in front of a courtroom."

"You won't have to. I'll figure something out." Michael held his girl in his arms and tried to think of a solution to this new snag. He had kept their secret for years. No one in town or at the hospital knew. And no one was going to know.

20

"Hey, buddy."

"Don!" Will's eyes lit up as his swim coach stuck his head in the door. "What are you doing here?"

"One of my swimmers has been absent from practice for a couple of weeks. I had to come and find out why you're blowing us off." Wrapped in a yellow hospital gown and with a mask covering his face, Don entered the room.

"I've been trying to get out of here, but they won't let me."

"I know, Will." Don pulled a chair over toward Will's bed. "Looks like you've gotten a permanent swim cap there, my man."

Will grinned. He had come to accept his new look even if it was only temporary. He hoped. "Yeah. I think it will take a few seconds off my time. Don't you?"

"It should. Not that you'd need it though." Don looked around the room. It reminded him a little of his freshman-year dorm room: sparse and small. Aside from the large entertainment center there wasn't much worth staying there for. "Does this place drive you nuts? Being cooped up in here all the time?"

It did. Will had never spent so much time stuck in a room in all his life. "Yeah. You can only play Mario Brothers so many times before the music gets stuck in your head. Thanks for coming to see me. You're the first person from the team to stop by."

"Yeah, your doctor called me. He said that it might do you some good to see a friendly face."

"And that's the face you brought? I can still see your ugly puss under that mask."

"Yeah, what's with all the gown stuff? Some nurse nearly tackled me out there when I tried to come into your room. Granted, she was something that I wouldn't mind being tackled by."

"You must mean my nurse, Cynthia. She's pretty."

Don thought about Cynthia and fantasies about nurses with tight, white uniforms flashed through his mind. "That's one word for her."

"Be nice or I'll tell Rachel on you."

"Don't do that. I get in enough trouble with her on my own. I don't need any help from you."

Will smiled. He liked having his friend in the room with him. Having a chance to talk about anything except how he felt was a refreshing return to the fun things of summer.

"I won't tell."

"Thanks, man. So what's with all the masks and gowns?"

"If I get an infection I could die. So, until my immune system is back up to where I'm safe, everyone has to keep really clean and avoid spreading any germs."

"They wouldn't even let me bring you in the cookies that Erin made for you."

Will's eyes lit up with the mention of his own girlfriend, although he'd never admit that to anyone. "Erin made me cookies?"

"Yup."

"The kind with both chocolate chips and M&Ms in them?"

"They were so good. I had to eat them all myself since I couldn't bring them in here."

"You did not. Did you? You better not or I'll have to pound on you."

Don had had enough fun. "Nah. I'll stick them in the freezer at home and give them to you when you get out. Maybe next weekend?"

"I don't know if I'll be out of here by then, but Dr. Hamilton said I'm getting pretty close to being back to full strength."

"Well, you better hurry up. I may need you next weekend. We've got our district swim meet then."

"There's no way I could swim at that, Don. I haven't done a lap in weeks. Look at my arms. I've gotten flabby." Will pointed to his now out-of-shape physique. His face was puffy and arms were scrawny, courtesy of the high-dose steroids that had been pumped through his veins. Will's skin was pocked with discolored spots from bruising.

"It doesn't matter. You've put in the time before you came in the hospital."

Will hadn't thought about what he was going to do once he got out of the hospital. Sure, he had thoughts that extended more into the realm of living than just to the see the age of twelve. But now the notion that life was going on outside his four walls hit him. Time hadn't stood still. Kids were still swimming and playing. And somewhere a little red-headed girl was baking him cookies.

"Do you think I'd do any good?"

"Hey, who's your coach?"

"Rachel," said Will, who quickly laughed and ducked from the playful arm punch that he was sure to receive from Don.

"Watch it, little man. Don't forget that I still make the lineups for the meets. Be nice or I'll put you in the relays with Smitty."

"Smitty the snail? No way. I can move faster with weights tied to my ankles."

The two laughed, talked, then laughed some more. Their times together over the past four years seemed to erase the nearly ten year difference in their ages. They were more than coach and athlete. They were the kind of friends who are there for each other. Someone who'd hold you when your dog dies and wouldn't tell anyone you cried. Or come over to be with you just because you might be lonely. Or someone to just be in the same room when you knew you'd be getting some bad news.

"I'm glad that you're doing okay, buddy."

"Me too."

"I'll tell you, I was pretty worried about you when I first heard that you had cancer." Don leaned back on his hands and stretched his back. "We all were."

"Who? The team?"

"Sure."

"I had never even heard of this cancer before this summer. Now I've seen lots of kids with it."

"You seem to be holding up pretty well though."

"I think I am, at least for now. My doctor said that so far the cancer is in remission. That means that it's not growing anymore. He said that I have a pretty good chance of being cured."

"So this might be the only time you have to be in the hospital for this?"

"I hope so. I can still get sick, or get an infection that would be pretty bad. My friend Eddy, who was in the room next door, has been in the hospital a whole bunch of times. I'd hate that."

"What happened to him. Did he get to go home?"

"No. He's in the intensive care unit. After he got a bone marrow transplant he got really sick. He has pneumonia and has to have a machine do his breathing for him."

"Is he going to be okay?"

"I hope so. It was really scary when it happened. I was asleep one night when I heard some alarms going off. I got out of bed and walked over to our window." Will pointed to the large window on the near wall. "The room was full of people. Someone had a mask over Eddy's face and was squeezing a bag that pushed air into Eddy's face. Someone else was pushing on his chest really hard. I thought they were gonna break his ribs or something. Then they stuck a plastic tube down his throat and hooked him up to the breathing machine. The strangest thing about it was that Eddy's eyes were open the whole time. But he never looked around at anything."

"Were you scared?"

"His parents were there. His mom just cried a lot. I couldn't get back to sleep after that. The night nurse came in and told me to get back to bed. She told me that Eddy was going to be fine, but she wouldn't answer any of my questions. She treated me like some dumb kid or something."

"You miss him, don't you?"

"With him gone, I don't have anyone to talk to. It gets kind of lonely in here."

"This hasn't been much of a fun summer for you, has it?"

Will just looked off into the window and watched the breeze blowing in the trees. "Did you ever have someone who you really hated and wished that they'd get sick and go away?"

"Yeah."

"Well, I'd never wish for that again. I'd never want to see anyone go through this. Having cancer really sucks."

Don had to agree with Will. "Hey, little man, I've got to get going." Don stood up and went to shake Will's hand. "I need to let you get some rest. Plus, I've got to get some work done today."

"You've got a date, don't you?"

Don shook his head with a grin. "Guilty as charged. But it was great seeing you. Think about what I said about the district meet. We sure could use you."

"I'll try." Will looked toward the ground as Don made his way to the door.

"Hey, cheer up. I'll be back. And you'll be out of here in no time." Don came back and gave his favorite swimmer a hug. Don pulled away from Will to find the imprint of tears on his shirt. "You're crying. What's the matter, Will?"

Will tried his best to keep the tears inside, but they had only one direction to go. "I'm scared. I'm so scared." He sat back down on the bed and held his small face in his hands. "I can't sleep at night. Ever since Eddy got sick, I stay up and listen to the sounds in the hospital. Kids are crying and phones are always ringing. I hear sounds and beeps going off all night. It's an awful place.

"Then I remember that I'm not at home in my bed and that my mom and dad aren't just down the hall. I get frightened at night. Then during the day all I see are the faces of other sick kids. Kids like me or Eddy. I wonder if I'm next. If I'm going to get sick and have people jump on me, pound on my chest, and shove tubes in my throat. I know that I have cancer. I know that I can die from this. But I still get scared."

"Do you talk to anyone about this? About how you feel?"

"Yeah. I talk to my nurse and my doctor. He's pretty good about that. I guess it comes from taking care of so many sick kids."

"He's the one who called me, you know. He told me you might need someone to talk to."

"He does do a lot of that. And not just doctor stuff. He talks about me. Things I'd like to do when I get out of here."

"See, he even knows that you're going to get well and go home."

"I know." Will drew small circles on the blanket with his finger as he spoke. "He's the one who's been teaching me magic tricks. Sometimes two a day."

"Sounds like a neat guy."

"He is. I like him. He's been more of a dad to me than my real dad."

Don was well aware of Greg's obvious absences in his son's life. A fact that now in the present situation was made even more depressing. "Talk to your dad about it. Let him know how you feel."

"I can't. I'd have to make an appointment."

"So it hurts to have him not be around?"

"Not really. That's the sad part. I'd love it if he did. If he'd come here and hold me and tell me that everything was going to be okay. But sometimes when you hope for things that you know will never come true you'll only get hurt."

Don nodded in agreement.

"I'm not that scared for myself about all of this. I mean, I don't want to die or anything. But if I did die, that'd be okay. I'm not afraid of that. I'm more afraid for Paul."

"Pipsqueak? Why are you afraid for him? Are you worried that he might get this too?"

"No. That's not it. It's just that I'm all he's got, Don. If I were to die, what would happen to him?"

"Hey, let's not even talk about you leaving us. You yourself just said that you're getting better. I'll bet your doctor's going to dismiss you home in a day or two."

"Do you think so?"

"Sure." Don had no idea if the words he spoke were true. But he was a coach, and motivation was something he was good at. "By this time next week you'll be with Paul at the pool making sure that he's got enough sunscreen on."

Will grinned. The idea of making it to the next meet seemed more and more like fun. And fun was becoming a scarce commodity. "I'd like that."

"Then I have your word on it? If you are home by next weekend you're coming to the meet?"

"Deal." Will extended his hand for a confirming handshake. Don gripped Will's hand firmly enough to make the gesture manly.

And as they shook their hands and softly started the Dolphin's poolside chant, Will began to think about the things of summer. His spirits were lifted. His mind was carried far away from the smell of anesthetic and vomit basins. His day-to-day routine was interrupted. His calendar now had an entry and he finally had something to look forward to.

21

"Let's see if you've learned anything." Michael sat down in the chair next to Will's bed. Michael had taken the techniques he used to teach residents and applied them to his magician relationship with his young apprentice.

"All right." Will stood in front of the small table Michael used when he performed his magic shows. His small hands struggled to hold the entire deck of cards. "Watch and be amazed."

"Expand your delivery. Say, 'Watch and be amazed as I make these cards move on their own right before your very eyes.' Sounds better, doesn't it?"

Will nodded as he repeated his doctor's words. Then he continued, "I have removed the four jacks from this deck." Will fanned out the four cards and held them up to his one-man audience. "I shall make these cards move through the deck all by themselves."

"Add some style. Make your audience believe that something extraordinary is about to unfold."

"Like what?"

"Something more along the lines of, 'Jacks are known for being the troublemakers in a deck of cards.'" Michael waved his arms and moved his eyebrows up and down to emphasize his words. "They are always misbehaving and causing trouble. Running around when they should be holding still. I even saw one make an ace of hearts cry. But one little-known fact about these cards is that they hate to be alone. They travel in packs, like wolves. So today I'm going to separate them and allow you to watch them find their way back together.' See? Something like that. Add a story. Make the cards seem to be alive."

"But they're not," argued Will.

"The idea is to get your audience in the mood to believe that your sleight of hand is really something more mystical. It's all about your presentation. It's the show of it all."

"Okay." Will tried to mimic Michael's speech. "Watch now as I let these cards wander through the deck and make their way back together." He looked at Michael who nodded approval. "Now what do I do?"

"Go ahead with the trick just like I showed you."

Will held up the cards for one last inspection before folding them together. He placed the jacks onto the top of the rest of the deck face down. "I shall now take the first jack and place him near the bottom of the deck." Will pulled the top card off and placed it lower in the deck. "I shall now do likewise with the other jacks." Will took the remaining cards and placed them at various spots in the deck. "Now I'm sure that you can hear the cries of the jacks as they realize that they are no longer all together."

"Nice touch."

"Thanks. But as you are aware, the jacks will try their hardest to overcome this separation and bring themselves back together. So I'll tap the deck four times and bring all four jacks back to the top."

Will took the small magic wand that Michael had given him and tapped the deck. "One, two, three, four. All the jacks have returned once more." Will put down his wand and began turning over the top cards on the deck. All four jacks were on top.

"And how do you finish?"

Will wrinkled his forehead in thought. "Just say ta-da?"

Michael shook his head. "No. Make it seem more fanciful. Add some words of warning or a short story. How you leave the audience is just as important as the trick itself." He leaned over the table and picked up the four jacks that lay face up. "So if you ever hear a sound in the night coming from your toy chest, if you ever wonder how some of your game pieces have wound up in a place that you didn't put them, look at your deck of cards and see if your jacks are smiling. They've probably been up to something." He winked at Will. "See? Like that."

"Won't that scare some of the kids, hearing a story like that?"

"I guess you're right. Maybe we should change that a little for our younger audiences."

"Yeah. I don't want to end my show biz career before it even starts."

"I think that you're off to a pretty good start." Michael pointed to the number of other tricks that lay on Will's bed that the two had been working on over the past few days. "And I've got something for you here that will help you to continue." Michael reached into his briefcase and pulled out his book on Houdini. "Here. I want you to have this."

Will reached for the book with a wide-eyed expression. "Another present for me? Thanks. You didn't have to do this, you know."

"I know. But I wanted to." Michael saw the look of joy on Will's face. It was a sight that he'd never get to see in his own house so he enjoyed the moment for what it could bring him. "That's not just any book on the great magician. It's my very own book. The one I had when I first started out in this many years ago."

"How long was that?"

"Never mind about that. Let's just say I was about your age."

Will thumbed open the book to see sections of old photographs of Harry Houdini performing some of his tricks and drawings of the many handcuffs and other escape devices he had used.

"This is really cool. Thanks."

"Thought it'd give you something to read when you're not too busy teaching yourself new tricks." Michael picked up his briefcase and made his way to the door. "I've got to get going. I have a few more patients to see."

"Speaking of that, how's Eddy doing? Is he going to be okay?"

Michael was impressed with Will's level of compassion. Will never asked about himself and how he was doing; his concern was always for his friends. "He's going to pull through," Michael said. "He's pretty sick still, but we've got him off the ventilator. With any luck he'll be back down here bothering you in a couple days."

"Great. I've got a lot of tricks I want to show him." Will smiled at his doctor, and Michael gave a wave good-bye before leaving the room.

Michael was washing his hands outside Will's room when he noticed Greg standing next to him.

"You spent a lot of time in there this morning," Greg said. "How's he doing?"

"You've got one tough son. He's going to pull through this round."

"That's great news." Greg paused for a moment as he tried to form words of gratitude. "I appreciate all that you're doing for him. Especially after what we've been through in the past."

"I'm not about to punish your son for things you're guilty of."

"If you remember, the judge said I wasn't guilty of anything."

"That's your version of it, Greg, not mine." Michael wiped his hands on a paper towel and tossed it into the trash. "Besides, what good could possibly come of my not giving the best to your son? From the sound of it, he's needed someone to give him attention for a long time. You've been so busy building a practice and covering your own ass for so long that you've failed to discover what a great boy you have."

"Am I going to get a lecture on child-rearing from you?" Greg asked. "At least I'm able to have kids. That much of your past I'm able to remember, and I'm sure my version of that is the same as yours."

"You haven't changed one bit, have you? No wonder I still can't stand the sight of you." He turned to walk away but saw the door to Will's room was still open. The little boy stood in the doorway. "Hi, Will," said Michael gently. "I didn't see you standing there."

"I just came to close the door. It's too noisy out there."

"Don't close it," said Greg. "I was just coming in for a visit." Greg glared at Michael. "I was done talking out here anyway."

Michael turned his attention to the nurses' station, where he picked up Will's chart and began writing his note for the day.

After only a few minutes, Greg emerged from Will's room and left the floor before Michael had even finished his note.

Quality time, thought Michael, his lip curling in disgust. Evidently Greg thought that was all his son needed. Michael replaced Will's chart in the rack. Will was getting better. His bone marrow showed no evidence of recurrence. His cell counts were returning to normal. Soon he'd be able to go home. Home to Greg. He'd be out of Michael's life and that bothered Michael—he was getting attached to the little boy. Something that Lori had warned him not to do. He did it anyway, knowing the price he'd eventually have to pay. It was worth it. He'd pay it again if he had to.

Michael walked off the floor. His clinic wouldn't start for twenty minutes so he had enough time to stop in the cafeteria for a cup of coffee before heading over to Mark Brannon's office.

He sipped the hot fluid through the hole in the plastic lid of his cup as he walked through the wooden doors leading to the hospital administration wing. The carpet was thicker and the wallpaper was nicer. St. John's had no issue with showing where the real money of the organization was located. Mark's office in the risk management division looked more like a lawyer's office with its high-back leather chairs and shelves filled with books of various thicknesses. Live plants were potted in the corners. Everything a lawyer would need, except a wet bar.

"Is Mark in?" Michael asked the secretary.

"He's on the phone, Dr. Hamilton. Is he expecting you?"

"No. I just needed to talk to him about something."

"Shall I have him call you when he's free?"

"Nah, I've got few minutes. I'll wait."

Michael sat in one of the chairs and picked up a copy of *Newsweek* from the coffee table. He didn't like having to wait. It made him feel like a patient. He checked his watch three times before Mark came out of his office.

"Mike, how are you?"

"Fine. Got a second?"

The two walked into Mark's office and closed the door.

"So what's on your plate today? Difficult patient threatening to sue?" asked Mark as they approached his desk.

"No, nothing like that. I need to talk to you about Lori."

Mark picked up a pen and ran it between his fingers. He leaned back in his chair. "She got subpoenaed, didn't she?"

"You knew?"

"I know she got a call from Niemann this morning. It seems he's been a busy little asshole."

"What's this all about?"

"You know about Dr. Jameson getting sued for sexual harassment."

Michael nodded.

"Well, Niemann is trying to find anyone who can prove that Jameson's had a track record in this area. We've had a few complaints about him in the past, as you well know, but nothing that ever needed to go for disciplinary action. So they dug deeper into his past. Residency, medical school, stuff like that. Then they found out about a complaint that was lodged against him by your lovely wife."

"But that case against him was settled. It should be irrelevant."

"It doesn't matter. This isn't a criminal trial we're talking about. It's about reputation. And if Niemann can defame Jameson in any way it'll help him get a bigger settlement."

Michael sighed heavily. "Isn't there any way you can block this? I really don't want Lori to have to go through this ordeal a second time. It was pretty rough on her the first go round."

"Wish I could, Mike. But the little bastard's got the law on his side. If Lori doesn't give her statement, she can be held in contempt. And not talking would make it seem as if we have something to hide. We'd lose either way."

The conversation wasn't going the way Michael had hoped. He wanted Mark to say, "No problem. Take Lori out of town for a few weeks. Hit the beach somewhere and let this whole thing blow over while you're getting a tan and a little sex on the sand."

"So who'll be there?" Michael asked. "For the deposition, I mean?"

"You want to keep it small and confidential, I take it."

"As best as we can."

"Was it pretty bad? What Jameson did?"

"Allegedly did. We couldn't prove it."

"Fine. I'll clear it. It'll be a small group. Just Lori, me, and Niemann will be there. No one else, unless you want to be there."

"Yeah. I do. She may have trouble talking about it, and I want to be there for her."

"I understand."

Mark reassured Michael. "I'll keep everything in the strictest confidence. No records of the conversation will ever leave my office. Though I have to tell you that this will be another matter if the case against Greg ever goes to trial. Confidentiality can only go so far when the justice system is involved."

"When do we have to do this?"

"I'll put them off as long as I can. I can delay a bit. That might help Lori get mentally prepared. I'll say she's a busy doctor, patient care issues, full schedule. I'll feed him a line. It'll have to be by next week though. I can't work miracles like you doctors can."

"I'll leave the miracles to God and the lawyers to you."

"Sounds like a reasonable plan. I'll get a hold of you and Lori when I have a date for the deposition."

Michael shook Mark's hand and left the posh office. He felt disappointed in himself for not being able to make Lori's problem disappear. But he was realistic. This problem had been dormant long enough. And no amount of avoiding Greg would make it go away. Maybe this would be a good thing. Maybe it was time to get this all out in the open and let people see who the esteemed Dr. Jameson really was. It amazed Michael what a person could do to justify to himself an unchangeable situation. "Right. And maybe mother will behave, never get sick, and move far away." A guy can dream too.

Michael would have to tell Lori. She'd expected him to take care of the problem, but he wasn't able to. Nervously twisting his wedding ring, he realized he'd let her down, something he swore he'd never do. He ached inside at the thought of Lori's being disappointed. But the hand that she had slid that ring onto was the same hand that Michael had used to break Greg's jaw. With one clean shot he brought the cocky Jameson down and made him spit blood. Greg never saw it coming. Michael was sure that Greg would've pressed charges against him, but he never did. That was just more proof, to Michael at least, that Greg was guilty.

Michael tightly clenched his left hand. He hoped that things wouldn't come to the throwing of fists a second time. But if it did, he'd be ready. A man will fight for his woman. No matter what anyone else says about her.

22

The sounds of coffee dripping through the natural filter and into the glass carafe filled the otherwise silent kitchen. Michael leaned against the counter, waiting for his morning brew to finish coming to life. Next to him were two mugs. Each one had the right amount of sugar and creamer already added, ready for the pouring of the main event. His had sugar and plain creamer. Lori liked amaretto and lots of it. She'd pour in a quantity of the flavor that only seemed to hide the true taste of the beans. For years Michael had teased Lori, asking why she even bothered to add the coffee if all she wanted was a warm cup of flavored cream.

"I need the caffeine," she'd say as the two played out their daily argument over their choices of morning beverages. It was as if they needed something to argue about because there weren't any real problems in their relationship.

But there'd be no such "arguments" this morning. Lori had enough on her mind. She needed silence and time to herself. Michael was going to give her just that. Lori needed time to get dressed and do her hair, put on makeup and other girl things. They were things that Michael didn't need to be present for, but still had to be around in case a man was needed for his opinion.

Impatiently, Michael poured himself his cup—before the carafe was completely filled—and sat at the kitchen table. It was a sturdy oak table, made with the finest craftsmanship the local Amish community could produce. Its sturdiness had been tested out shortly after moving into their new house. The memory brought a smile to Michael's face.

"Come on. Help me put the tablecloth on," Lori had said after adjusting the position of the table for the fifth time to make sure that it was centered under the ceiling light.

"Why do we need a tablecloth? Can't you see the tons of boxes that still need to be unpacked?"

"It'll make the room look better. Don't you think?"

"I gotta be honest with you, sweetie. The first thing a guy thinks when he walks into a kitchen isn't 'You know, this room could use a little color.'"

"Don't be like that. I want to brighten up the place." She spread the cloth on the table herself, then turned to Michael, unzipped her pants and slid them to the floor. "Besides, I need a little cushion for my boom-boom." Lori pulled Michael toward her and planted a long kiss on his surprised face.

"What are you doing? We don't have any curtains yet. Someone might see us."

"The movers are gone. It's the middle of the afternoon with no one around. Besides, I want to. Come on, we have to break in the new house." She raised her eyebrows in a way that let Michael know he wasn't going to get away.

Michael dropped his own pants and climbed on top of the table with Lori. "I can just picture us being in the middle of this and the electrician will walk in."

"Well, if he does, we'll just tell him that everything is plugged in just fine."

"You're so crude."

"What, little ol' me?" she drawled, emphasizing her own accent. "But I know you love me anyway."

The spontaneity and the risk of suddenly being discovered didn't allow for a prolonged lovemaking session. But the desired effect was achieved for both of them, and the tablecloth didn't get ruined.

Michael smiled at Lori. "Wow, that was fun."

"Has it ever not been fun?"

"Can't say that it has. It sure didn't take us long to break in the house." Michael stood up from the table and pulled up his pants.

"House, nothing." Lori sat up and took off her T-shirt and bra, leaving on only a pair of short, white sweat socks before standing up. "That was the kitchen. One room down, nine to go." She patted Michael's butt before walking away. "I'll meet you in the den, stud."

The memory warmed Michael's heart as the coffee warmed his mouth. All of their time together was like that. Things to look back on that allowed a smile to grow all on its own. But Michael knew that today wouldn't be one of those days. He wasn't afraid of letting St. John's hear what a jerk Greg was. Most people knew that already. But after today, they'd all know about Lori. No matter who was in that deposition room, the information was sure to leak out. No conference room ever had all its gossip leaks sealed.

"What are you thinking about?" Lori walked in the room, her auburn hair flowing above her shoulders. She looked ravishing. She always did.

"I poured you some coffee."

"Thanks." Lori grabbed her mug and pulled up a chair next to Michael. "You didn't answer me."

"I know. Just about today. About us moving here. And how when you found out that Greg worked at St. John's we sat at this table and I promised you that I'd protect you from him."

"Yeah, you did a lot of things on this table when we first moved in."

"I don't think that I'll be able to protect you from him today," Michael said sadly.

"You don't have to worry about that, hon." She slid her hand across the table and took Michael's hand in hers. "I knew that sooner or later what he did would come out and then everyone would know about me. I'm not ashamed of who I am. Nor would the comments of Greg or anyone else change that. I've got nothing to hide."

"You're a stronger person than I am. I'd want to bust Greg's skull."

"I think you already did that once. Don't do it again. You could have got ten arrested the last time. The stupid bastard would probably sue you this time."

"You're right."

"I usually am." Lori released her husband's hand and picked up her coffee mug. "Come on. There's no reason to delay this. Let's get going."

Their trip was more silent than usual. No discussions of difficult cases or complaints about problem patients they were likely to see that day. Instead, they just listened to the radio.

They arrived at St. John's and parked among the other doctors' cars. But Michael and Lori didn't head into the main hospital entrance like the rest of the doctors did that morning. Their morning rounds were with Mark Brannon and Terrance Niemann. And, they hoped, no one else.

The conference room had been appointed with two carafes of coffee. A tray of doughnuts sat next to a bowl of fresh fruit in the center of the table as a goodwill offering to appease the plaintiffs and make them feel less hostile by filling their bellies. It rarely worked.

"Good morning, Dr. Hamilton," Mark greeted Michael. "And Dr. Hamilton." He shook Lori's hand. Mark was dressed in his trademark three-piece suit, which always distinguished him from the nonlegal professionals who filled the hallways. "Mr. Niemann has arrived, but he's using my office to make some calls before we begin. Have a seat." The three took places on one side of the long wooden table. "Have something to eat. Who knows how long he'll be."

"No, thank you," responded Lori, polite as always. "I'm fine."

Mark looked intently at Lori. "This morning, Mr. Niemann is going to ask you some questions about an incident that supposedly occurred the week after you graduated from medical school. No need to worry. You aren't on trial here, so just answer the questions the best you can. I'm sure you'll do fine."

"I know," she began. "You don't have anything to worry about. I've been in depositions before and there's nothing this Mr. Niemann can do to rattle my cage."

Michael put his arm protectively across the back of Lori's chair as he muttered, "Speak of the devil."

Terrence Niemann closed his cell phone as he entered the room, closing the door behind him. "Sorry to keep you waiting. I had to turn down a settlement offer. It was way too low for what they did to another client of mine."

"I just hope that justice will prevail," said Mark. "As I'm sure it will in this case."

"Shall we just begin?" asked Terrance. He opened his briefcase and took out a pad of legal paper and his microcassette recorder. He turned on the recorder and spoke into the microphone. "July 28 deposition with Dr. Lori Hamilton of St. John's hospital. Also present are Dr. Michael Hamilton and defense attorney Mark Brannon." He set the recorder in the center of the table, then sat back in his chair. "For the record, Dr. Hamilton, would you state your name?"

"Dr. Lori Hamilton."

Terrance began flipping through his legal pad of scribbled notes. "But that's not your maiden name, is it?"

"No," Lori said. "It was Lange."

"And that's the name you used during medical school, is that correct?"

She nodded.

"Please answer the question. My recorder has trouble picking up head gestures."

"Yes, that's the name I used during medical school."

"And you went to medical school where?"

"The University of Chicago."

"That's quite a distance from Birmingham, Alabama, isn't it?"

"Yes. It is."

"Why'd you pick the U. Chicago?"

"I wanted to see snow. I didn't have any growing up."

"I'm sure that Chicago gave you plenty to see."

"I've had enough of winters up here, that's true."

Terrance continued to jot down words as he spoke. "Did you know the defendant during medical school?"

"Do you mean Greg Jameson? Yes, I knew him."

"And how did you meet him?"

"He was a classmate."

"Did you get along well?"

"What do you mean?"

"Were you friendly or just acquaintances?"

"I started dating his roommate." Lori turned toward Michael and gave him a wink, as if she wanted to break in the conference room table.

"And that would be Dr. Hamilton."

"Yes. He and Greg lived together."

"And the three of you got along fine? He didn't act like a third wheel. Didn't get in the way of your romance? Act rude to you? Leave underwear all over the apartment?"

"Greg was fine. He even studied with Mike and me from time to time. Greg started dating my roommate, Linda, who's now his wife. We were sort of a group, the four of us."

"Sounds cozy."

"It was."

"Was it like that all through your years at school?"

"For the most part."

"That's nice. Are you still friends with him now?"

Lori looked straight ahead. "No. No, we're not."

"Does your falling out have anything to do with the night of June 5 shortly after the three of you finished school?"

"Now, Mr. Niemann, of course it does. Why else are all of us here this morning?"

Terrance cleared his throat. "Very true." He looked down at his notes and began again. "I have a copy of a police report dated that June 5 stating that you pressed charges against Dr. Greg Jameson for sexual assault and battery. Is that true?"

Lori thought about that night. The kind nurse in the emergency room had held Lori's hand as she signed the statement Lori had given to the policeman. "Yes, it's true."

"Charges that were later reduced in a plea bargain?"

"If that's what the court papers show."

Terrance pulled out another packet of papers from his briefcase. "This is a copy of the court findings. Only the charge of misdemeanor assault was entered as the final verdict. Jameson pleaded no contest."

"That's what I recall happening."

"I want to know what else happened that night. The court records are sealed, you see, and I feel that my client needs to know what kind of a man she's really working for."

"That's not her job, Niemann," Mark said. "She's here to answer your questions, not do your job for you. If you don't have anything concrete to ask her let's just call this session over."

Michael nodded in agreement. He didn't want this to go on any further anyway.

"It either comes out now or in the courtroom," Niemann said smugly. "I'm not about to let this drop."

"Face it, Niemann, you have no case here. You're looking for any kind of information that'll give you an edge. Set up Jameson as some sort of sex pervert in order to win over a jury. But you've got nothing. This is a dead end and you should just stop it right now."

Both Niemann and Brannon were escalating their voices as if that would somehow make the other back down. The testosterone level in the room was rising as insults were hurled at each other along with threats of reporting each other to the Illinois Bar Association.

Lori listened to the tirade long enough and decided that a more feminine, level head was needed to break the tension in the room and calm down the men. "Mr. Niemann, Mr. Brannon, there's no need to get your dander up." The lilt in her soft voice filled the room with an air of peace. The men sat back down in their chairs like little boys who knew they were about to be scolded by their mothers. "I certainly don't want to bring on any further stress in this situation. No one's intention is to harm the other. It's the truth that we all want to get out into the open. After all, isn't that what the law's all about? Finding the truth? Not seeking your own personal agenda even at the expense of another, innocent party? So if y'all would take a seat, I'd be happy to tell what really happened that spring in the fine Yankee town of Chicago.

"We were best friends, the four of us. Michael and I, and Greg and Linda. Linda and I were roommates. We hit it off right from the start. She was working at a department store and was able to get me a discount on designer clothes. And I was in school with a bunch of eligible future doctors. We became very close.

"After I began dating Michael, I decided that I'd try to match up Linda. I was spending a lot of time with Michael at his apartment, and I had gotten to know Greg fairly well. I thought he and Linda would hit it off. We started double-dating and took turns cooking for each other. It was a lot like playing house. We felt like we were old married couples. Those were happy times."

"What happened to that friendship?" asked Terrance.

"It grew for a while. Linda and Greg got engaged. I was real happy for her. She asked me to be her maid of honor, and Greg asked Michael to be his best man. We started planning the wedding partway through senior year. Previewing bands and addressing invitations took a lot of time away from my studying, but I didn't care. After graduation, Michael had to move down to Birmingham to get started on his residency and to find us a place to live. I stayed behind to help Linda with the final preparations. But a week before the wedding, she moved back to her home in Monroe, Wisconsin. She was a hopeless romantic and didn't want Greg to see her until the rehearsal dinner. That left me and Greg in Chicago by ourselves."

Lori took a deep breath and continued. "One night, Greg wanted to go out, just the two of us. He said he wanted to thank me for all that I did for Linda and for introducing them. So we went out. It was a nice dinner, though I think he had a little too much to drink. I had to help him back to his apartment.

"When we got there, he started in on me. He said things like he wasn't sure about getting married. That he might want to play the field a little longer. I just thought he was getting cold feet, so I sat down with him and tried to talk up Linda to him.

"The next thing I knew, he was on top of me. He was grabbing me and holding me down. He said that he always liked me and thought Michael was a lucky guy for having such a hot girlfriend. I tried to push him away, but he was strong and drunk. He ripped my shirt and pulled off my bra. All the while he kept trying to kiss me and tell me that I needed to give him one last night of fun before he got married. He was halfway to getting my pants off before Linda walked in." Lori cleared her throat. "She had driven back to spend the night with Greg. So much for staying away from him and being the romantic. Linda saw us and started shouting. She said some things to Greg that made me feel like I wasn't the first girl she saw him with. Greg climbed off of me and started shouting at Linda. He said things like she didn't trust him and that I was the one who came on to him.

"She stormed out of the apartment and Greg pulled up his pants and ran after her. I tried to piece my clothes back together to get out of there as fast as I could. I could hear the two of them fighting out in the hallway, but I couldn't understand what they were saying. But when Greg stormed back into the room and began yelling at me, I knew what Linda must have said to him."

"And what was that?" asked Terrance.

Lori wiped her nose. "She told him about me. About what I am. You see, gentlemen, I'm not exactly a woman." Lori looked at Michael. Tears were welling in her eyes as the words began to fall from her lips. Michael sat up straight and nodded to let her know that he was there. That she wouldn't go through this alone. She took a deep breath and continued. "I was born with an X and a Y chromosome. Genetically male. Only I didn't know it. I have a condition known as testicular feminization. When I was born I looked female. Had the right parts and was missing the obvious male parts. Daddy was so proud to have a little girl. Everything seemed normal for quite some time.

"I grew up with all the trappings that the daughter of a lumber tycoon in the south could afford. Frilly dresses. Coming out parties. Social events at the country club. I was raised to be a true southern belle. I loved my life and who I was. As I hit my teen years, all my friends began to get their periods. Well, I didn't get mine. I was assured that it was only a matter of time. But as I turned fifteen, Momma decided that we had waited long enough. She didn't want her little girl to have some kind of strange condition that would limit her ability to become a grandma. So off to the gynecologist we went.

"After a careful exam he was able to find some very small testicles in my external genitalia. I hadn't noticed them before and certainly he was the only man to get his hands in that particular portion of my anatomy up until that time. Anyway, poor old Dr. Humphrey had to break the news to Daddy. That his little girl, the apple of his eye, his future Miss Alabama, was really a boy. I cried for a week. So did he, I think. Having me be surgically turned into a male was out of the question. I wouldn't be able to have a functional penis. My testicles had to be removed in order to prevent the testicular cancer that is a strong possibility in my condition. So the only option was to remain a woman. I looked like one. I felt like one. In my mind I was a woman. The only difference was my cells had a different genetic code. But aside from being unable to compete in the Olympics as a female, my life would be just as normal as it was before.

"I was started on estrogen and my body continued to develop along the lines as a woman. My breasts grew. My life continued along its way with only our immediate family knowing the actual truth. When Michael and I became serious, I told him the truth. I could tell that it was a shock to him, but as a medical person he understood the genetics and the true nature of the condition. He accepted me for who I was. It meant that we'd never be able to have children, but we'd have each other. That seemed to be enough for us.

"Michael took the news in stride. And he's never told another soul the truth. I had hoped that Linda would have been the same, so one night I told her what I've just told to you. And I can tell you that she took the news about as well as y'all are taking it now." Lori motioned to the two attorneys who were seated with their mouths held slightly open. Terrance hadn't taken a single note with his pencil. Mark was slowly running his eyes up and down Lori as if he could somehow see her genetic makeup under her female form.

"So this secret was just between you and Michael?" asked Terrance.

"Yes, at first. I mean, it certainly isn't something that I want to put on a billboard or anything. But I confided in Linda. One night, Linda was packing up some of her things to go over to Greg's for the night. She filled an overnight bag that was the size of a large suitcase. I think she was intending to stay there longer than one night. As she was putting her eyeliner and curling iron into her bag, she noticed that she had run out of her birth control pills. So she asked if she could use some of mine. I had a large bottle of hormones in my drawer that she knew I took every day, so she wanted to just take a few to tide her over until she could get a new prescription filled. But the doses I take are far too high for her, or any woman for that matter. I couldn't let her take them. It wouldn't be safe. Well, she started in on me about how I wouldn't share with her. How we were friends but how things had changed. That she wasn't sure how we could ever have been friends what with me being so selfish. I guess I broke down. I didn't want to lose her as a friend. I thought that she was someone who I could trust, so I decided to tell her the real reason why she couldn't use my estrogen.

"It kind of shocked her. She wasn't sure what to make of me. But after a while she got over the strange feelings. She had seen me naked in the shower and we certainly acted like women around each other. After a while it really wasn't an issue. But that night, she must have said something to Greg about it. Something like he was trying to have sex with a man. Something to hurt his masculine pride, because when he came in he shouted 'You're a guy?' He must have been sickened by the thought that he had tried to make out with me, because he took out his hostility on me.

"First he slapped me across the face, then he tore open my shirt again. He grabbed my breasts and asked if they were implants. He kept slapping me and shouting, 'You're a man' over and over. I grabbed my clothes and ran out the door, but not before he tried to kick me. I fell and hit my head against the wall and opened up a cut on my forehead. I made it back to my apartment and tried to stop the bleeding, but the cut was deep. So I changed my clothes and went to the nearest E.R. While I was getting seven stitches in my forehead I told the nurse what happened. She told me that I had been sexually assaulted and that I needed some protection.

"I guess I hadn't realized that fact up until she said those words, because I just started bawling my eyes out. She called the police, who took my statement. They took some pictures of my head, but I didn't have any other marks on me. Greg got stopped before he got too far to leave any DNA evidence, and my breasts weren't bruised enough to notice. I didn't even have any of the original clothes on, so there wasn't that evidence either.

"After a few days, I spoke with the district attorney, who said the best we could get was assault. There just wasn't enough evidence of a sexual attack. My word against his was how he put it. Linda begged me not to push it any further. Greg had somehow talked her into believing that he was just drunk and that it would never happen again. That and the fact that she really wanted to go through with the wedding must have been her biggest motivators."

"So you plea-bargained the charges?"

"Yes. I didn't want a drawn-out case that I wasn't likely to win. My best friend wanted me to drop the charges against her soon-to-be-wealthy husband. I was moving away in a week or so. I thought it best."

Lori had finished. There was nothing more to say. Terrance was looking down at his blank piece of paper. He hung on every word that Lori had spoken, but didn't jot down a single one. He didn't need to. He knew that he'd never be able to forget what he just heard.

Mark looked at Lori, then at Michael, then up at the ceiling. His case just got a lot tougher. This kind of story would not help his case. Greg would come across not just as a sexual harasser, but as a predator as well. He had visions of headlines accusing St. John's of hiring a cross-dressing neurologist. No newspaper journalist would be able to pass up the truth about the nature of a testicular feminization syndrome in favor of a sensational lie.

Lori and Michael just looked at each other. Neither had to speak a word. Lori was more of a woman than Michael could have ever hoped to have married. And her strength to do what she just did proved it all over again to him. Michael's strength and loyalty—during not just her statement but their whole lives together—made her feel truly loved in a way only a man can love his woman.

The silence remained until Lori decided that it needed to be broken. "Now, Mr. Niemann, is that what you needed to hear, or was there another story that you had in mind?"

A stunned Terrance snapped himself back to where he was. Things had definitely changed for him and his case. A story like this would certainly want to be silenced by St. John's. A silence that would come with a large price tag. "No. That's all I think I needed to hear today. If I need to get any further information, I know where to find you."

"So may I go now?"

Terrance and Mark both nodded in agreement.

"Not a word of this leaves this room." Michael stood up and spoke to the two other witnesses of the morning's unfolding. "Not a word. I know all about this attorney-client privilege. You breathe one word of this to anyone not involved in this case, I'll sue you both and have your licenses taken away."

"Don't go getting all upset, Michael," said Mark. "No one is going to say a word. This will stay in complete confidence. Right, Terrance?"

Terrance nodded.

"I didn't hear you. I have trouble picking up head gestures."

"I'll share this with my client, but no one else."

"Fine." Michael put his arm around Lori and escorted her from the room. He'd take the rest of the morning off to be with her. She would protest, but in vain.

The exodus of the doctors left Terrence alone with Mark.

"Quite a turn of events, huh, Mark?"

"Doesn't change much. You have a case of assault. There isn't any document proving my client is guilty of sexual assault. There won't be one man on the jury who didn't take a swing at someone in his younger days. In the end, all you've got is something circumstantial that I can easily get the judge to disallow."

"Oh no, Mark," Terrance said smugly. "Dr. Hamilton wouldn't want his name or his wife's dragged through the mud. Innocent people are often the ones who most want to protect their reputations. As I'm sure you'll want to protect the reputation your organization will receive from a sex scandal." Terrance saw the amount of his settlement offer start to rise like the price of gasoline. "This changes everything."

23

Michael unfolded his handkerchief and offered it to Lori. "You were very brave in there."

Lori shrugged as she dried her eyes. The adrenaline was wearing off, and her emotions were close to the surface. Still, her fears of confronting her past were over—she had done it. The worries of how she'd handle herself were relieved—she'd performed admirably. There was nothing now but waiting for the tremendous aftermath. And there *would* be an aftermath. She was sure of it. It wouldn't be long before her story broke into the open. Confidentiality only lasts until the words reach someone's ears—if that long.

"I got a little emotional," Lori said softly.

"That's only natural." Michael wrapped his arms around Lori and pulled her in tightly so there was no space left between them. "You know how women can be."

Lori freed one hand long enough to smack her husband on the back of his head. "Sexist pig," she teased. "Thanks. I needed to know that you still thought of me in that way."

"I always have, baby. I always have."

As they held each other in a warm embrace, the conference door opened and Terrance Niemann walked out.

His smug smile made Lori's skin crawl. "Thanks again for your time this morning, Dr. Hamilton," he said as he extended his hand. "And yours too, Dr. Hamilton," he added, nodding at Michael. "I'll see you both in court," he said as he walked away.

Lori audibly gasped. "Court? You mean I'll…I'll have to tell this whole story over again in a courtroom?"

"That's exactly what he meant." Mark emerged from the conference room, looking defeated. "That little bastard thinks he has us by the short hairs. He feels he can parlay your story and an old police report into a pattern of behavior for Dr. Jameson. It might be enough to convince a gullible jury. But if not, then he's banking on our being willing to pay off on Jameson's case just to keep the story about Greg's roaming hands and your DNA out of the papers."

"What a prick," Lori said evenly.

"Pricks make the best lawyers, Lori," Mark said. "I should know. I'd do the same thing with this information if I were in his shoes."

"Well, then I guess I have nothing further to say to you, Mark."

"Standard procedure, Lori," Mark said matter-of-factly. "Doesn't make it easy for us, but it's the name of the game." He turned to Michael. "I'll call Niemann and threaten to get Lori's testimony listed as inadmissible. It's hearsay and totally irrelevant to the case."

"You do what you need to do," Michael said firmly. "I don't care what it is. You could get Jameson fired and reassigned to performing rectal exams in a men's prison for all I care. Just keep him away from my wife." He turned to Lori. "Come on, sweetie. Let's go get some breakfast." Michael took Lori's arm protectively, and as they turned to walk away they saw Greg.

"Speak of the devil," Lori muttered.

"I see you two met the Terrier," Greg said pleasantly. "Did you have as much fun as I did?" Michael tried to push past Greg without responding, but Greg grabbed him by the arm. "I'm not enjoying this, you know," he said. "If you think this lawsuit is fun and games, you're wrong."

Michael shook off Greg's hand and glared at his old roommate. "And what about Lori? You think she wants to relive this?"

Greg took a step closer to Lori and spat out his words. "Is that what you told those shysters in there? That I attacked you years ago?"

"We told them the truth, Greg," said Michael, drawing Lori closer to him. "Or do I have to refresh your memory of that night?" Michael pounded his fist into his hand. "And what happened afterward."

"Your version of it," Greg said angrily.

"There's only one truth, Greg," Michael said, trying to control his anger. "And that's what I told them. Does that make you nervous? That your co-workers will find out what kind of a person you are?"

Greg laughed. "I don't care what people think of me. Or what stories you make up about me."

Michael eyed Greg with disgust. "Spoken like a true sociopath."

"You've got nothing on me. You never did," Greg said with his usual bravado. He walked away but not before calling over his shoulder, "Don't you have some little tricks or games to play while we grown-ups go to work?"

Michael stared after Greg with clenched teeth. He would not let Greg bait him any further.

"Come on," Lori coaxed. "Forget about him. He's not worth the trouble." She tugged on Michael's coat collar. "Let's get out of here. You promised me breakfast."

Michael nodded. "Good idea. But I have someone to see this morning before we go. I'll meet you in the doctor's lounge in a few minutes."

Lori smiled at her husband and gently patted his arm. "Don't be late," she whispered playfully. "I don't like to be kept waiting."

Michael waved over his shoulder as he headed off to the elevators. He rode to the pediatric floor and stepped into the nurses' station. He had several patients to see this morning, but only one was on his mind. Michael was thinking only about a little boy who finally got to go home. As Michael arrived on the floor he was greeted with several questions from the nursing staff—labs to be checked, results to be analyzed, calls to return, and nurses with vomiting patients who needed medication. He waved off the nurses with an "I'll deal with that later" look on his determined face before grabbing Will's chart and heading into the isolation area. He didn't gown up or wash his hands. Neither was needed for this visit.

Will's room had been tidied up. A suitcase was next to the door. Will was sitting in front of the television, watching a game show.

"Not watching a talk show today?" Michael asked.

"Nah," Will answered without looking up. "There's too much yelling on those shows."

"If you're bored around this place, why don't we get you out of here? Feel like going home today?"

Will didn't need to be asked a second time. He had been asking Michael every day what his cell counts were. When would they be high enough? Was the cancer coming back? And every day Michael had to say, "Maybe tomorrow we'll know."

"So it's good enough today? I'm not sick anymore?" His wide eyes and open mouth accented Will's questions.

"There's no sign of your leukemia yet. Your immune system seems to be back to where you can fight off most things. I think it'd be safe enough to let you go today. Unless," Michael continued with a twinkle in his eye, "you want to stay."

"Not a chance!" Will jumped from his bed and wrapped his arms around Michael in a hug that Michael wished would last forever. Will wiped the tears from his eyes. "Thanks a lot, Doc."

"My pleasure. I'm just glad you've responded so well to the treatments. Now, of course, this doesn't mean that I'm done with you. You still may have many more treatments to go."

"But I still get to go home, right?" Will's arms remained tightly wrapped around Michael, and Michael imagined for just a moment that Will was his own son. He held on to the small boy for a moment longer before pulling back and continuing

"Is your mom coming to get you this morning?"

"Yeah. I called her this morning to see if she was coming for a visit. She's been doing that about every day now. At first I was afraid that I'd called her too early, but she was already up. She was in the kitchen cooking Paul's breakfast. French toast today. That lucky kid. All I got was oatmeal."

"Hospital food just isn't the same as home, is it?"

"Not anymore. Mom's really started to do stuff like that. Paul calls to brag about what he's had for lunch, supper, even bedtime snacks after she's tucked him into bed and reads him a story. I can't wait to get home."

Michael realized Linda must have changed while going through her son's ordeal. He only hoped that it wasn't a temporary thing.

"So she'll be here later?" he asked.

Will nodded.

"How about your dad?"

"I don't know. I know he's here today."

"He's here every day, Will," Michael reminded him. "That's the life of a doctor."

"Yeah. I guess so. But if you guys are both doctors, why aren't you friends?"

Michael looked uncomfortable. "What do you mean? We're friends."

"You don't seem like friends," Will insisted. "I heard you arguing outside my room one day. You said you didn't like my dad 'cause he did something once that hurt you."

"Well, I suppose that's the case," Michael admitted. "We were arguing, but sometimes grown-ups disagree."

"I know," Will said sadly. "I asked my dad what you two were arguing about, but he wouldn't tell me."

No doubt, thought Michael. He rubbed Will's bald head and said offhandedly, "I'm sure he just didn't want you to worry about anything. Your job is to work to get better."

Will wouldn't be deterred. "Mom makes me and Paul say we're sorry and makes us forgive each other when we fight. Even if I didn't do anything wrong."

"Sounds like she's making you learn to get along with each other."

Will nodded. "Maybe someone should make you and my dad do the same thing."

Michael chuckled with nervous laughter. "Maybe so," he said. "Now…what do you say we get you out of here?"

Will nodded and started to pick up his things.

"I see you have all your magic stuff packed away."

Will nodded.

"You left your book I gave you." Michael found the Houdini book sitting on the nightstand. "Aren't you taking that with you?"

"I thought I'd give that back to you. I thought it was something important of yours."

"It is very special to me. But so are you. That's why I wanted you to have it. Don't you want it?"

Will moved over to the nightstand and retrieved the book. He leafed through the pages until he found the spot that he was looking for. "I found this," he began. "After I saw it, I didn't think that I should keep it." He held the book up to Michael. On the bottom of a page, at the end of the chapter about Houdini's work to uncover frauds in the psychic medium, was a black-and-white photograph.

Michael looked at the picture. He remembered well the day it had been snapped. The memory brought a smile to his face that greatly resembled the one of the little boy in the picture. It was a picture of Michael standing next to Bill Collins behind the magic counter in the What-Not Shop.

"I must have been only thirteen in this picture," Michael said with a grin. "That's the little Dr. Hamilton." Michael sat back on his chair and let the image soak into his mind and into his heart.

"I could tell that it was you," Will said. "You have the same face. I just couldn't figure out who that man was who was standing next to you." Will pointed at Bill. "Who is he?"

Michael looked at the kindly face in the faded photograph. "He was my friend," Michael whispered. "He was a very nice man. He owned the magic shop where I learned all of my tricks when I was a kid."

Will arched his neck to get a better view of the picture. "Why was his smile so crooked?"

"He had cerebral palsy. It's a brain condition. His brain was injured when he was born. He couldn't talk very well. Or walk that well. He was slightly retarded as well. Cerebral palsy slows your thinking and makes the ordinary things that you and I can do very difficult."

"And he was your friend? Wasn't he kind of old to be your friend?"

"Nah. Bill was the kind of guy who would have been friends with anybody. Besides, I've found that age really has little to do with who your friends are. We're friends, aren't we?"

Will nodded.

"We really got along well. You'd have liked him."

"How can you tell?"

"Because you like magic, just like he did. In fact, if it weren't for Bill, I wouldn't have learned any of the magic tricks that I do."

"Wow." Will bent over to take another look at the man who was responsible for teaching magic to Michael. "So he was a magician too?"

"Yep. That's what we were celebrating that day when the picture was taken. That was the day Bill told me I had become a magician. He was so proud of me, and of himself for having been able to teach something to someone. A customer in the store took that picture of us and made a copy for each of us. Bill hung up his in the store behind the counter, and I taped that one into my book. He was a real special guy."

"Did he teach you a lot of tricks?"

"He did, Will. He did." Michael closed the book and stared at the cover. "He taught me a lot of things. Not just magic, but things that aren't tricks. Things that are a little more important."

"Like what?"

"Sit down and I'll tell you." Michael took a deep breath and then began. "When I was younger, I had a paper route. It was a fun job for the most part. It was pretty easy money, and I only had to work about an hour after school. I made about six dollars a week."

"That doesn't seem like much."

"Not compared to today. But in those days it was a lot. And it was all mine. I could spend it on anything I wanted.

Will nodded. He got a hefty allowance every week with which he could do anything.

"My route was in our downtown area. I had both sides of the main street. There were lots of businesses. Restaurants, a hardware store, dry cleaners. Stuff like that. But around a corner, far away from the rest of the main strip was this little old shop. The What-Not Shop."

"What's a 'what not'?" asked Will.

"It's a trinket. An ornament. You know, little junky things that you have around the house."

"Yeah, we have a lot of those things."

"I'll bet you do. Bill's store was full of them too. But his store wasn't big and nice like your house probably is. It wasn't too flashy or fancy. There wasn't anything about it that would draw your attention to it. I don't think most people would have even known it was there unless they went looking for it. Bill was the owner. He sold little plastic things. Toys and bumper stickers. But it was his place, and he was proud of it. I didn't think too much of the man when I first started delivering his paper. He drooled when he talked and his words were drawn out so far that I had a hard time under-standing him most of the time. He'd walk around his store very slowly as if one leg just didn't want to keep up with the other one.

"I used to just drop his paper off on the sidewalk in front of his shop, just like everyone else's, until I noticed how hard it was for him to reach down to pick it up. So I started to get off my bike and walk into his store to hand him his paper every day. The place was kind of odd and had a strange odor, like it hadn't been cleaned in a while. But I eventually got used to it.

"Once a week I had to collect my paper route money from all of my customers. Friday night. We'd get the money from our customers on Friday, then on Saturday morning we'd turn it in at the newspaper office. I'd run from store to store and hold out my hand." Michael put out his hand as if Will were a paying customer. "I usually got pretty good tips from most of my customers. The paper was only seventy-five cents a week, so most people would hand me a buck and have me keep the change. When I got to the What-Not Shop, somehow it just didn't seem right to take the man's money. I don't know why I felt that way. I delivered his paper just like I did to everyone else on my route. But all of the other stores I went into had lots of people in them and paying customers. Those stores could afford to pay me. I rarely saw anyone in Bill's shop.

"But each week he'd go behind the counter and pull out his metal coin box. He'd fumble with the coins and carefully count out the nickels and dimes. Sometimes he'd stop and comment on how some of the coins were particularly shiny. He'd give those ones to me. It would take him a while to get to seventy-five, especially if he'd drop a coin on the floor and have to start over again. But I'd get my seventy-five cents every week.

"One week he didn't have enough coins to pay me. He searched through that box as if new coins were just going to appear. I tried to get him to forget it. I told him that I'd cover his payment for the week. I had made four dollars in tips that week anyway, and it would have been no problem. But he wouldn't hear of it. He went into the back room and searched his coat pockets. He eventually found enough. Eighty cents. I can still hear his slow speech mumbling for me to keep the change as he let out a laugh like he was a big spender. Well, I'll tell you, that money in my little hand just about made me sick. I couldn't keep it. Who knows? Maybe that was his food money."

"I don't think I could have kept it either."

"Right, so I decided that I was going to buy something. You know, to give it back to him somehow. So I asked him to show me his store because I was in the market for something fun. Well, you should have seen his face light up at the prospect of having a genuine customer. He showed me around the whole store and demonstrated each item. He'd put on the silly hats and wear the masks. He tried to make the yo-yos work, but he couldn't. Nothing seemed worth buying until he went to the magic counter."

Will leaned forward in his chair. Hearing an adult open up and discuss something of a personal nature was alien to him. But his wrinkled brow and probing eyes went unnoticed by Michael, who was reliving his own youth.

"He pulled out box after box of one trick or another. They were simple tricks, like disappearing balls or coins that seemed to float in the air. They were tricks that Bill could do, though not very well. But I was bound and determined to buy something. Then he brought out a trick of multiplying rabbits. The trick basically was a sleight of hand, passing small sponge rabbits from one hand to the other. With each pass you'd add a rabbit to give the appearance that the rabbit family was growing. Bill tried, but his hands weren't very nimble. He'd get a rabbit stuck between his fingers or drop them to the floor. It wasn't too hard to see the secret. The poor guy was getting frustrated. Not just at the trick, but at himself. So I acted as if he had showed it so well that I understood the trick. I took the rabbits from him. I put Mommy and Daddy rabbit in one hand, then started to move them back and forth. Each time I opened my hand, another baby rabbit would be there." Michael moved his hands demonstrating his technique.

"That made Bill smile more than I had ever seen before. He was pleased as punch that he had taught me a trick. And I didn't dare let him think otherwise. So for one dollar, I bought that trick. Who'd have thought that selling one little cardboard box filled with seven tiny sponge rabbits would have brought so much pleasure into that man's life? But as I thought about it, it wasn't the fact that he had made a sale; it was that he had been able to pass something on to me. Something of himself."

"Like you're doing to me by teaching me magic?"

"Right. So after that, each week I'd go into his shop to collect my money, then without even needing to say a word, we'd walk over to the magic counter. Whatever money I made from my route I'd end up spending. And whenever he'd get a new shipment in, he'd take the time to show me each and every new trick. As time went on, I was better able to understand him. We'd talk about stuff. Mostly we'd talk about me and my family. But eventually he told me about his life. He told me about where he lived, his pet dog, what he liked to do for fun. I started to help out around the shop for him. Sweep or dust. Open a box or move heavy stuff. Sometimes he'd try to pay me for the extra work I'd do, but I wouldn't take it. It just didn't seem right taking money from a friend."

Will opened up the book and found the picture. Bill seemed to look more important now. "So he's the one who taught you how to be a magician. That's pretty neat."

"Yep. But he taught me something much more important than that, Will." Michael looked intently at Will. "He taught me about people; that just because someone is a little different than you are, looks funny, acts strange, or isn't exactly what you think a person should be, that doesn't give you any right to treat him badly. No one deserves that.

"You should love and accept people for who they are. No one is a mistake. Each one of us is special. Each one of us has something to give. Because sometimes, Will, in the least likely place, hidden or tucked away from everyone's eyes, virtually unnoticed, you just may find someone who can change your life. Make you a better person. Open you up to a whole new world that you can bring with you wherever you go and share with someone else.

"If I hadn't spent time in a shop that most people wouldn't have stepped foot in, or if I'd ignored an old man who others only made fun of, I wouldn't have found that treasure inside of him. I wouldn't have learned the magic that makes you and other kids around here happy. You just never know who or what you'll find if you're willing to look past what your eyes see."

Will seemed saddened by the story. "You mean people ignored that old man just because he was different? They stayed away from his store just because it was out of the way? Or ugly like it was invisible?"

"Yeah. Sad, isn't it?"

Will paused for a moment and kept his eyes glued to the floor. "Sometimes I feel like that. Like I'm a little shop that's out of the way and no one wants to go into."

Michael seemed surprised by Will's take on the story. "What do you mean? Do you feel ignored?"

"Dr. Hamilton?" Will said quietly. "Could I have caused my cancer? Could all of this be my fault?"

Michael had heard that question from many patients over the years. People who had spent their lives smoking the wrong things, eating too much, drinking for decades. People who were most likely to blame for their own health problems. But not from a child. Not someone who couldn't have possibly caused a leukemia. "Of course you didn't cause this. Why would you think that?"

"Because I think I did. I asked for this. I prayed to get sick."

Michael reached over and took the young man's hand. Something was hurting Will. Michael stayed silent and waited to let Will release his worries.

"For a long time I felt like I was invisible. Like no one noticed or cared about me. I would go for days without my parents even noticing that I was around. My dad, especially. He's gone a lot, you see. I mean, you're a doctor. You know what it's like. He's not home much. And even when he is, he's always on the phone and too busy to do anything. He stays late at the hospital to take care of sick people. Someone's always sick. Sometimes I hear him get up in the middle of the night to go to the emergency room just because someone's sick. He's missed my birthday parties. My swim meets. He never pays any attention to me or Paul. He only seems to have time for people who are sick. So I thought that, you know, if I got sick, I mean really sick, then he might pay some attention to me. I hoped for some disease to happen. A broken bone. Something. Anything to get him to notice me. For him to say, 'Hey, that's my son.' But I didn't mean to get cancer. I didn't think that it would go this far. But still he has hardly come to see me. I can't even get sick good enough for him."

Will's words tore at Michael's heart. Such a fragile young life begging to be noticed. It made Michael hate Greg even more. He reached over and put his arms around the crying boy.

"I'm sorry that your dad is like that. But you didn't cause your cancer. You didn't do this. Don't blame yourself. And don't blame yourself for the way your dad treats you."

The morning sun streamed through the windows, the mini-blinds casting small shadows across the floor. Michael held Will in his arms and gently rocked back and forth.

"But I can understand what you mean; how you feel like you're that little shop that no one notices. In a way you are like that, Will. We all are." He straightened his arms so he could look directly into Will's eyes. "You may not be perfect. You may not be what someone else wants you to look like or be like. But inside you there are some wonderful treasures just waiting for anyone who ventures into your life."

Will sniffled and wiped his nose on his sleeve. "What do you mean?" he asked, his voice quavering.

"It's like a pearl hidden inside of an oyster," Michael explained. "No one can see the treasure that lies within the rough shell, but once you can see past that shell, you can find something amazing. You have things inside you that only you can give to someone. And once people see those treasures, they can take them along into their own lives and share them with the world. Like the magic from the What-Not Shop—you have that inside of you." Michael smiled as he gazed at this boy who had become so dear to him. "Does that make sense, my little friend?"

"I…I guess so," Will said slowly.

"You are a terrific kid," Michael said. "I can see how wonderful you are." He pulled Will close again and said huskily, "And I know that my life and my world are better because of knowing you."

Will's tears spilled over Michael's arms, but this time they were tears of joy. He was worth something! His life mattered to someone! Michael tightened his grip on the little boy. It was what Will needed and what Michael could offer. Staying with Will would cause Michael to be late for his breakfast date with Lori, but Lori would understand. That was just another one of *her* many special treasures.

24

Michael's pager went off.

"Damn it."

"Language, please," corrected Lori.

"Sorry," said Michael. "I gotta take this page. It's the hospital."

"Go ahead; my eggs won't get cold." Lori blew on her steaming cup of coffee before taking a sip.

Michael pulled his cell phone from his pocket and dialed. The other customers at the Country Kitchen restaurant didn't seem to notice. The plaid tablecloths and farm-implement décor couldn't detract from the fact that the clientele of the country-style breakfast restaurant consisted mainly of fast-paced businessmen and women who lived in the world of fax machines and teleconferences.

"When did it happen? This morning? How is she?" Michael let out a sigh as he covered his forehead with his free hand. Lori put down her fork and silently waited to hear what bad news her husband was about to deal with. His problems often became hers. "Fine. No, I'll be there later this morning. I'm in a meeting with a very important client." He winked at Lori who blew a small kiss in return. "I'll see her by noon. Thanks for the head's up." He clicked his phone closed and set it by his coffee cup.

"Who's hurt?" asked Lori.

"Mom. She fell again."

"That's, like, what, her fifth time?"

"I don't know at this point. At any rate, this time she's done it right. Her left hip is broken. Maggie found her on the floor this morning. She had fallen in the bathroom, but somehow managed to crawl back to her bedroom. She must have been on the floor all night."

"Poor thing."

"Poor nothing. Too stubborn to push her medical alert button and get some help."

"Just where does she get that stubbornness?" Lori asked pointedly.

"I am not that stubborn. You may think I am, but I'm not."

"Your argument causes me to rest my case." Lori put a bite of ham into her mouth.

Michael let out a soft grunt. "Anyway, it really freaked Maggie out. Mom was hollering and carrying on until the ambulance showed up and gave her a shot of morphine. She called Maggie nearly every name in the book for not being there when it all happened. And you know how Mom treats Maggie when she is there. She yells at her for being around so much. I think I may have lost another caregiver this morning."

"So how's your mother after all of this?"

"She's going to need surgery. They'd like to just pin her hip, but I think they may have to replace the whole joint."

"Who's the surgeon?"

"Richardson."

Lori nodded in agreement. "He's good. I wouldn't worry about her."

Michael took a bite of this three-cheese omelet and washed it down with a glass of orange juice, which had a thick layer of pulp floating on the surface. "Oh, I'm not worried about her. She's too ornery to die. She wouldn't give me the satisfaction of doing that. My problem is that there's no way I can let her live alone anymore."

"You knew something like this was going to happen at some point. That she'd have to go into a home eventually. This has just speeded things up a bit."

"I know. It still doesn't make it any easier."

"Is she doing all right?"

"Oh, yeah. Busy telling the nurses how to do their jobs, seeing as she's the expert on nearly everything."

"Again, I fail to see any familial tendencies. Come on, let's finish up and go see her. I'll go with you."

Michael nearly choked on a bite of biscuit. "Why would you want to go with? You know how she feels about you."

Lori had endured many insulting remarks from Cheryl over the years; comments that were dropped in casual conversation about choosing career over children, as if Lori had a say in the matter. But mostly the rude comments were made because Lori had the audacity to marry Cheryl's only son.

"I know. But that can't stop me from treating her well. After all, she did give birth to you. I am indebted to her for that."

Michael reached across the table to take Lori's hand. It was soft and warm.

They hastily finished their breakfasts and paid on the way out of the restaurant, and they drove back to the hospital that they had left only forty-five minutes earlier. They parked and walked into the doctors' entrance. Security waved them in and they stopped off in the doctors' lounge long enough to grab their coats and name badges. They rode the elevator to the orthopedics floor. Several other staff members were in the crowded car. Lori looked around and wondered if any of them had heard the news of her story that she had told earlier in the day. If they had, what were they thinking? No one spoke. The silence only worried her more.

The elevator doors opened to reveal a noisy and congested surgical floor. No evil stares. It was business as usual. Lori took a deep breath and stepped off the elevator.

Nurses were flowing in and out of the rooms, taking vitals on their patients. Nursing techs and volunteers were giving baths. Nurse practitioners were performing pre-op physicals on the cases for the day. The large dry-erase board on the wall across from the secretary's desk was full with patient names and room assignments, indicating that all the beds were occupied. The place was busy. Michael looked on the board to find his mother's name, and then proceeded to that room.

"Old people falling down must be big business," Michael said to the nurse coming out of his mother's room.

"Tell me about it. I've got four cases myself today," she muttered as she passed by.

Lori walked into Cheryl's room first with Michael on her heels. Cheryl was lying in a bed with her left leg straightened by a traction device. An IV pole was next to her bed. Fluids and pain medications were running into Cheryl's right arm, and oxygen tubing ran under her nose blowing a gentle stream of air to her nostrils. Her matted hair and pale complexion made her look much older than Michael recalled.

"Hey, Mom. If you wanted to see me you didn't have to get admitted."

Cheryl opened her eyes briefly to see who was in her room before closing them again. "I'm sorry I'm such a burden to you. You can go back to your more important things."

"You're not a burden, Mom." Michael hid his true feelings. In a way he was glad that she was here. He wouldn't have to drive to her house tonight or lose sleep worrying about her being alone. "If you were, would I be here?"

"You do work here. It's not like you had to go out of your way."

"We don't need to be here at all, you know." Michael went on the defensive.

"Then go. I've got people here to look after me."

"Stop it, you two. I swear you're worse than little children," Lori interrupted. She truly believed herself to be the peacemaker in the family. No one else ever volunteered for the job. "Now, Mom, how are you feeling? Are you in much pain?"

Cheryl held up her hand, which held an electric cord with a button. "I push this thing and I get a shot of morphine. Gotta get me one of these for the house."

"I doubt Medicare will pay for one," said Michael.

"Damn bureaucrats."

"Did they tell you what time your surgery will be?" asked Michael.

"Sometime after three thirty. They're going to make me starve until then."

"They have to, Mom."

"All part of the joys of getting older. Starve you, cut you open, and then pack you off to a nursing home when they're done. That's what they're planning for me, aren't they?"

"We'll see about that. For now let's concentrate on your surgery. We'll worry about where you'll go after that." Michael decided to put off the inevitable for one more moment. Why not? He had put it off for nearly a year anyway.

The three chatted for a few more minutes. Who was going to watch the house, water the plants, take in the paper, and check the mail? They were jobs that seemed of minimal importance to Michael, but were so significant to one with little else in her life. Michael agreed to take care of it all, which seemed to give his mother some sense of peace.

A nurse came in to do a pre-op check, which ended the visit. Before they left the room, Michael and Lori agreed to be there when she came out of surgery. Upon leaving the room, Michael was greeted by a hospital case-worker.

"Dr. Hamilton, I'm Michelle Simpson. I'm the case manager for this floor. I was alerted by a social worker about your mother's case. I need to talk to you about your mother's safety. There are some issues that we must address before your mother is discharged from the hospital. Do you have a moment to talk?"

Michael recalled seeing Michelle around the hospital. She and her co-horts had been valuable in helping some of Michael's other patients get set up with visiting home nurses, home infusion services, and nursing home placement. He had worked with them on many cases, but handling a familial situation was always more difficult.

Lori listened to that introduction and politely excused herself to go back to her office for some paperwork. The unpleasantness of planning a discharge was not what she had in mind this morning.

Michael and Michelle went to a meeting room, off of the nurses' station, that had been set up for such family conferences. Michelle had a large notebook, a laptop, and a three-ring binder filled with the names of care agencies, nursing homes, and government-assistance programs. Hers was a job that Michael didn't envy. Sending a loved one to a nursing home usually was the one thing that many family members swear they never will do. "I'd die before I'd send Mom to a nursing home" should have been tattooed on Michelle's forehead for all the times she had heard the phrase. But life is full of unpleasantness. And human mortality and frailty are just such things.

Michelle relayed the findings from the social worker and the floor nurses: Cheryl's multiple bruises from recent falls, her uncontrolled diabetes, several emergency room visits in the last few months, her living situation. They were things that Michael already knew and that all pointed in one direction. He didn't need some second-hand nurse pointing out the obvious to him. He knew where the conversation was heading.

"So, Dr. Hamilton, I think that at least in the short term we should consider placing your mother at an extended care facility."

"A nursing home."

"We prefer to use the other term. It more correctly describes the nature of the care."

"Call it what you want. People of my mother's generation call it a nursing home, and it's where you go to die."

"You know that's not true. Many people go to extended care facilities for short-term rehab, or to complete a course of antibiotics."

"I know that, miss. I'm saying that my mother doesn't. I'm sorry. I know you're only trying to help. I've known that my mother's needed to go to a nursing home. I should have sent her to one a long time ago. But she's stubborn and really wanted to try to make it at home."

Michael described the home care agencies that he had contracted. The private caregivers employed. The safety features added to the home. And the promises Michael had made to his father. Michelle understood. Michael's story was not a new one to her.

"So you've thought about this a lot, have you?" she asked Michael after hearing his detailed attempts at keeping Cheryl in her home.

"Does every day count?"

"Have you thought of any places that you'd like to have her placed in?"

Michael had made up his mind. He had looked at all the options. The issues of therapy services, access to medical care, food palatability, odors in the hallway, and response time to call lights were weighed in his mind. But he boiled his decision down to one that would actually please his mother the most: location.

"Yeah. Sunset Manor. It's in Marengo."

"I know that one. Any particular reason for that choice?"

"It's close to home for her. Her friends can visit. Hell, most of her friends live in that home already."

"Sounds like a good choice. Do you need me to make a referral for you?"

"Sure. I'll drive over there this morning and make it official. I'm sure that they'll have papers for me to sign."

"Only a stack. And bring your checkbook. They'll need one month's deposit for the costs that Medicare won't cover."

"Great." Michael shook the young nurse's hand and went in to say good-bye to his mother before leaving the floor. She was asleep.

He headed up to Lori's office to tell her that he'd be gone for a while. She had immersed herself in work and decided to see her list of patients for the day. Her morning testimony was becoming a fading memory with her return to her calling.

Michael walked out to his car. On his way, he saw Will getting into Linda's car. Paul was hugging Will as if he'd never let go. Linda was grinning ear to ear. Greg was nowhere in sight. Michael swore at him under his breath.

Michael drove out of the lot and out to State Highway 20. The trip to his hometown was quick as he drove the familiar route. He never turned the radio on. For a minute or two he'd enjoy some silence with his thoughts.

Sunset Manor came into view as he pulled into town. Built in the 1930s to help with the indigent population caused by the depression, the nursing home had grown from its original one building to four wings and three floors. Administration now filled the original section that had somehow managed to maintain its original charm of the early twentieth century.

The grounds were accented with a pond and a surrounding walking path for those who could handle the distance. A cabana overlooked the pond for those who couldn't. Bushes lined the circular drive that led up to the main entrance. A large overhang designed to keep the rain and snow off the patrons arriving by car was in the front. An ambulance bay of similar design was off to one side. Large trees and flower beds added to the tranquility that Michael knew only hid what the reality of the setting truly entailed, once one set foot inside the doors.

John Kline, the administrator, greeted Michael. "I'm really glad that you've selected Sunset Manor for your mother's ongoing care, Dr. Hamilton." Kline was a thin man in his early sixties and not far from needing the services of the facility himself. His large Adam's apple was dwarfed only by his oversized bow tie. Thinning hair covered a balding scalp, and wire-rim glasses perched on a pointed nose.

"You're welcome. I just hope she'll like it here."

"I'm sure she will. A broken hip can be a dangerous thing, but after she completes her rehabilitation, we can move her over to our residential wing. She'll like that much more. More homey, if I may say. We have plenty of activities to keep her busy. I like to have my people busy. You know what they say about idle hands and all that lot. We offer weekend passes so she can get out and about. No restless legs allowed."

"I'm sure she'll like that." Michael hated being there. A musty smell of urine still seemed to permeate the clean floors. Michael knew what placing her there would do to her. She'd feel abandoned. Tossed out like yesterday's newspaper.

Michael began to sign the papers that John had placed in front of him. There were forms allowing the nursing home to bill Medicare and Cheryl's supplemental insurer, agreements to conform to the rules of the institution, and a release of medical information. Michael wondered if he ever made any of his patients sign so many papers. The thought of that made him shake his head in disbelief.

"Yes, it will be quite an honor to have your mother staying with us. I knew your father. Did you know that?"

"No, I didn't." But then, everyone in town had known his father.

"Yes, quite the pillar of the community, he was. I'm so sorry to hear of his death."

"Thanks. I miss him too." He signed a form ensuring that Cheryl had no food allergies.

"But he was nothing compared to your mother." Michael stopped signing and looked up at John with disbelief. Surely he must have misspoken.

"My mother? A pillar?"

"Oh, yes." John leaned back on his chair and folded his hands behind his head. "Very civic minded, she was. Always right there behind your father. I don't think he'd have had the career he did without her. Fund-raisers for the community health center. Woman's Guild. Founder's Day Society. I think she was even responsible for the additions they made to the Memorial Hospital during the seventies. If there was ever anyone who was out to make this town a better place, it was Cheryl Hamilton."

Michael was dumbfounded at the thought of his mother doing anything for anyone other than for herself.

"She did those things?"

"Oh, yes. I would have thought that you would have heard about all of them."

"No." Michael went quiet. "She kept all of that to herself."

"Well, you must have heard about what she did for that old retarded fellow. Everybody knew about that. I think you knew him. Bill something. Funny guy, he was."

"Collins," Michael said, putting down his pen.

"Yeah, Collins. His bike was stolen. Or he lost it. Who knows for sure? Anyway, she took that poor fellow's case to heart. Made it a personal quest, if you will, like she had something at stake in it for herself. She got the whole chamber of commerce behind her. She must have made a hundred phone calls. In the end she got the guy set up in his own shop and got the town to pay for the damn thing too. Like we all were responsible to look out for our own. Quite a gal, your mom is. She was always trying to take care of those who couldn't look out for themselves."

Michael was speechless at the idea that his own mother was responsible for Bill's store.

Michael froze in time. He journeyed back to seventh grade. To a time when he rode a gold Stingray bike with a basket for his newspapers. To a time when he stole Bill's bike and vandalized the poor man's inventory. The idea that his mother was the one responsible for the creation of the What-Not Shop was unsettling. He wondered if she knew that he was responsible for the bike's disappearance and destruction. Was she trying to cover for her own son's acts of terrorism or was it all just a coincidental act of a woman who was out to show her benevolence to the whole town?

Michael felt ashamed that a complete stranger knew more about Cheryl than he did.

"Quite a woman, your mother. You must be proud of her," John had continued to ramble. Michael only heard every other word; they were drowned by Michael's thoughts.

"Yeah," he lied. "She is." Michael looked down at the papers set before him that would commit his mother to a life of wheelchairs and living in someplace that wasn't her home. Days of boredom highlighted only by a bingo game at three o'clock. He pictured her lying in a bed and forgotten. Like Will had been. Like Bill had been.

"I've got the room all picked out for her. It's a bit small, what with her roommate having all of her rehab equipment and restraining devices for when she climbs out of bed at night, but I'm sure she'll grow to love it here." John talked as though he was the only one in the room. He was the only one listening anyway.

Michael pulled himself out from his downward spiral of depressing thoughts and returned to the matter at hand. "Restraining devices?"

"Yes. Emma tends to wander a bit at night. She likes to climb into other people's beds. But don't you worry. We stop her. Her bed alarm goes off whenever she moves too much. Bit of a noise that thing can make. But I'm sure you're familiar with things like that."

Michael nodded. He knew all too well what a night on a nursing home floor could be like.

John continued to spew forth his diatribe. Having a physician as a captive audience made John want to bring up every aspect of elder care that he was aware of. And he had an opinion on every issue of government involvement in health care, long-term care insurance, pharmaceutical costs, and staffing shortages. No subject was too dry or short on relevance that it couldn't be used to suck some life out of Michael. Finally, he had had enough of John.

"You know, this is a fascinating discussion, but I just realized that I really haven't gotten my mother's consent for this transfer."

Lack of consent caught John's attention. No consent meant no billing. No revenue. "You don't?"

"No." Michael turned on the charm. "And I know how busy you are. I must apologize for dropping the ball like this. I didn't mean to waste your time."

"Oh, no, that shouldn't be a problem. Just give her a call. You can use my phone." John reached forward and turned his phone around for Michael to use. "Hit nine to get an outside line."

Michael sat back in his chair and moved the stack of papers away from him. "I really think this is something that I should do in person. I think that she'd be more accepting of the move that way."

John liked things happy. "That would be for the best. Tell you what, I'll reserve the room for her. I won't fill it with anyone else until I hear from you. Hopefully, we'll have her out here in a few days."

Michael lied. "That sounds good. I'm sure I'll have no problem convincing her of this." Convincing himself would be another matter. But he may have been selling his mother short. Maybe she would like to be there. Some of her friends already were residents. Granted, most of them were demented and also thought that Roosevelt was a personal friend.

"I'll give you a call after I speak with her." Michael reassured John that this was all but a done deal. But Michael was having second thoughts. Thoughts about who his mother was. The notion that a mother could have possibly been a woman in her own right outside of being a mom was a concept that Michael was having trouble accepting. Michael rose and shook John's hand. John took the papers, tapped them into alignment, and set them on the front corner of his desk.

"I'll walk you out, Dr. Hamilton. I'd love to hear your opinion on end-of-life issues."

Michael wanted nothing further to do with any more of John's views. "I can find my own way. I've taken up enough of your time."

Michael began his return trip to St. John's. Visions ran through his mind of a much younger version of his mother leading a rallying cry to build a shop for Bill Collins. He pictured her marching from store to store, getting pledges for financial backing, shelving units, and cleaning supplies. Not taking "no" for an answer from any would-be contributor. She'd have been fighting with banks for low or no-interest rate loans. In other words, being herself. He could picture it. He could see her in that role. With all the fight and stamina she carried before age and disease stole it away.

He wondered how much she had truly influenced the town. How much had she done to change the life of one lonely, poor man? How much had she helped others that Michael didn't know about? How many others had she helped over the years? How many other Bills were there? He didn't know. Ashamed, he didn't even know the possibility as someone she could have been. His own words to Will earlier in the day came back to hit him right between the eyes; words about how some people may not fit the mold, but may have more to offer others than ever realized.

He pulled into the parking lot of St. John's. He hoped that his mother either had gone to surgery and was out, or hadn't left yet. He had questions to ask that couldn't wait for long. They had waited long enough.

25

"Here." Terrance tossed two slips of paper onto the kitchen table. "I got you a present." In his humble opinion, if he ever had one, his morning's session with Lori Hamilton couldn't have gone more his way. Watching Mark Brannon squirm and busily take notes at a discovery session with one of his own clinic's physicians was a very favorable sign.

Julie picked up one of the small colored cards. "Lottery tickets? What are these for?"

"'Cause today is your lucky day. The luckiest day of your damn life, that's why."

Ryan pulled up a chair and sat down with his two co-conspirators. "I take it the discovery session went well this morning."

Terrance grew a devilish grin. "That's putting it mildly. Never in my dreams would we have stumbled onto a witness who would so seal our victory." Terrance reached across the table and grabbed the cup of coffee that Ryan had brought for Julie. He never stopped to assume that it might not have been for him.

Julie knew the cup was meant for her, but she kept silent, which was something that she was noticing to be more of her usual response when potential conflict arose. Biting her tongue was her response to Greg for years. It was how she reacted to her obnoxious brothers when she was growing up. Her classmates in college, her lovers, anyone whom she should have stood up to turned into another person who could take advantage of her. She had hoped that filing the lawsuit against Greg would have been the starting point to a new behavior.

Standing up for herself and speaking her mind was what she wanted to do. Letting others know that she just plain existed was her dream. But that didn't seem to be what she was allowing to happen. For now she resigned herself to sit in silence. Julie rationalized that Ryan and Terrance seemed to know what they were doing. They were handling her case pretty well, which was better than she thought she could do on her own. After all, what did she know about legal things like this?

"Hey, Julie. How's about some cream for this?" asked Terrance as he took a sip of the hot brew.

"Yeah, sure." Julie stood up from the table and walked away from the conversation as she was once again being turned into a scrub nurse. Only this time she wasn't fetching scalpels and specimen trays; it was cream and sugar. Today she was more like a waitress bringing drinks for the table. Other days she was the office clerk finding pens and paper for Terrance and Ryan. Often she was asked to be a runner, going out for doughnuts or pizzas. After a planning session, she always was the maid, cleaning up after the two had so meticulously worked out Julie's case for her. *They must be doing a good job*, she always thought. They didn't seem to need her very much, though, except they didn't have much of a case without her name there as the plaintiff. At least she was being included in some small aspect.

She brought the cream and a bowl of sugar to the table. She laid out spoons for the two men, then returned to the counter to pour herself a cup. After nearly emptying the pot, she made a mental note to herself to wash out the pot later. Better than having to be reminded by Ryan.

"So what's the good news?" she asked as she sat down across the table from Terrance.

"Don't interrupt, honey," snapped Ryan. "Terry was just telling me." He patted the back of Julie's hand briefly, telling her to just sit there and be a good girl.

Julie bit the inside of her lower lip, then retrieved her hand to wrap around her warm mug, which was the only warmth she was feeling in the room that had once again grown suddenly chilled.

"As I was telling Ryan," continued Terrance, "our discovery interview went very favorably in our direction. It seems the fine Dr. Jameson does, in fact, have a history of behavior that would call into question his treatment of women."

Julie felt that she could add two more names to that list of men.

"Back when he just finished medical school he committed a crime that, in my legal opinion, caused serious deleterious emotional harm to another physician. Bet I could have signed her up as a client after this case is finalized and gotten a fair settlement if the statute of limitations hadn't expired already. And I think I pissed her off."

"Imagine that," muttered Julie, as she brought her cup to her lips.

"Anyhoo, this stunt of Jameson's was a deliberate attack on a woman."

"What did he do? With the way sexual remarks flew around my school, he'd have to have done more than just fondle her in the cadaver lab to get charges brought up against him," chimed in Ryan.

"Oh, it was worse. And he did get charges brought against him, even though they were eventually reduced."

"Reduced. Won't that hurt our case? I mean, if the charges were dropped then it's just going to be anecdotal evidence."

"Hearsay," Julie quietly stated. Terrance and Ryan glanced in her direction letting her know that her assistance was not needed.

"Right." Terrance drew the word out nice and slow. It was his show and he wanted to do the talking. "Normally, I would agree with you. The charges of sexual misconduct against the younger Dr. Jameson were eventually dismissed. And as far as I know, he only received probation."

"As far as you know?" Ryan was surprised that his highly paid attorney wasn't more up on his facts. "You mean you don't know what happened in the case?"

"Oh, I know what happened in the case. And I'll tell you about it if you give me a chance. Julie, honey," he said, turning to his waitress, "would you get me something to eat? I didn't get any lunch today."

"Sure," she replied as she once again left the table.

"Anything would be fine."

"Nothing for me, sweetie," said Ryan to Julie's back as she walked to the counter. She hadn't thought about getting him anything. She wouldn't.

"Even though the charges of sexual misconduct were dismissed, and the record would be pretty much our witness's word against his, it's still pretty damaging stuff. Remember, we don't have to prove that he did anything, we just have to convince twelve relatively stupid people that he did. And that he should pay heavily for it."

"So what you're telling me is that all you have is some story about Greg wreaking havoc on some young chick. That's it."

"Yes. And normally, that'd be enough to establish his having a pattern of this type of behavior. That he's some sort of sexual pervert out prowling for any young woman to sink his hands into. I could use this to paint any story about him I wanted to. Convince the jury that none of their daughters would be safe if this guy lived anywhere near them."

"But it's just our word against his without some sort of conviction or records of the matter."

"I know that. I know the law. But even if I can't prove he has a history, even if the judge disallows the whole story—labels it inadmissible evidence—the story I tell will still be in the minds of the jury. They'll still hear my words. The judge may strike the story from the record, but he can't erase the minds of the jury."

"That's what you're counting on, isn't it? Just plant the seed of his past into their minds and let it grow."

"Actually, I'm not planning on letting it go that far." Terrance paused for a bite of his sandwich that Julie had placed in front of him. Ham on whole wheat with Dijon mustard and sharp cheddar. He chewed slowly to let his last words sink in.

"Not let it go that far? What do you mean? Surely, you're intending on using the information. Or are you not planning on taking this to trial? We need a trial, Terry. I told you that. I need a public statement of his guilt," argued Ryan.

Terrance swallowed his bite and washed it down with a sip of his coffee. He motioned to Julie that his cup could use a little warming up. She rose from the table before her chair even had a chance to get warm.

"Take it easy. I'm going to get you your results just as soon as I can. But I think this story might be more useful to us if we don't bring it out into the open. At least not right away. This is something that is better off being treated like the trump card that it is."

"Well, are you going to tell us what he did?" asked Julie as she brought back a full cup for Terrance. She had fought off the urge to spit in it. "You've certainly beaten around the bush long enough."

"Yeah. Spill the dirt on this guy."

"Okay." Terrance's words were muffled by his mouthful of bread and meat.

"Back after graduation, Greg Jameson attempted to rape one of his fellow students. And I do mean fellow. Turns out that the lovely Lori Hamilton is really a guy."

Julie and Ryan both gasped.

"What do you mean, a guy?" Ryan asked.

"She's a he. But not like you and me. I mean, he's not a cross-dresser or anything. Technically, he's only male genetically. On the outside he looks and acts like a woman. She's physically a female. She has the genitalia and breasts of a woman, only she has the male chromosomes."

"I don't get it," Julie said. "I've seen her around the hospital. She looks and acts like a woman."

"I don't understand all the science behind it, but according to her, she was born looking like a girl. Apparently, she was born with testicles, but somehow the hormones didn't have any effect on her. She developed like a girl, both physically and socially. That is, until she hit puberty. When the plumbing didn't start working the way it should, her parents took her for tests and they found out her true gender."

"Testicular feminization," said Ryan. "I've heard about that."

"Maybe you can fill us in on what it's all about."

"Oh, I don't know too much. Never seen a case myself, but there have been a few over at General. Some of the members of my department have been asked to do some reconstructive surgery on some little girls. Reduce the size of the penis and make them more female in appearance."

"That's how Lori explained it," said Terrance.

"Yep," said Ryan. "I've seen it tear families apart. A little girl is found out to be a boy. The dad wants a son, and the mom wants the girl. The kid ends up not knowing who or what he or she is. If they turn her into a boy, the penis never functions right, and she has to get hormone shots all the time."

"What about if she stays a girl?" asked Julie

"Well, it is not as much of a problem. The girl already was raised as a girl. Thought like one, acted like one. They get put on estrogen and get the testicles removed. Cancer risk. Then it's life as usual, or as usual as it can be. I know that they can't have children, which is the biggest emotional hurdle to overcome. Otherwise, they look just like any other women," finished Ryan.

Terrance agreed. "I know. I have to tell you, here I was sitting across from this stunning woman. I was watching her every movement. She was every bit of the southern belle that she makes herself out to be. If I had met her at another place or time, I'd have made a play for her myself. I think that's the most incredible part of this story. That she's been nothing but a lady all these years. That no one even suspects that there's anything amiss about her.

"Except there is, which is what Jameson found out. Only he didn't find out until after he felt she looked so much like a woman that he attempted to rape her."

"He did?" asked Julie.

"Yup. He got her back to his apartment and tried to have his way with her. He grabbed her, pulled her down, and ripped her clothes off of her. He did everything except what he was trying to do."

"How awful," said Julie. "That poor thing."

"What stopped him?" asked Ryan.

"Jameson's wife walked in on them. Well, she was his fiancée at the time. She was shocked at what she saw, and trying to get back at Greg, she blurted out that her manly husband-to-be was trying to seduce another male."

"Bet that spoiled the mood," joked Ryan.

"It did more than that. Jameson flew off the handle and attacked Lori. He tried to beat her up. She escaped with a few bruises and a cut on the forehead. It was when she was at a hospital getting stitches that she filed charges against him."

"This is sweet," said Ryan.

"This is horrible," said Julie.

"This is a gold mine," said Terrance.

"So what finally happened?" asked Julie, who was more concerned about Lori than her own lawsuit.

"Lori eventually dropped the sexual attack charges. She figured that she didn't have enough actual evidence to support those charges. She didn't want her genetic makeup being dragged out into the open either."

"But that's what you're thinking of doing, isn't it?" asked Ryan.

Terrance smiled. "Only if they aren't willing to pay to keep us quiet."

"Well, that's a rotten outlook," Julie said.

"Do you want to win or not?" asked Terrance.

Julie thought about that. That maybe the price to win can sometimes be a little high. That other lives were being dragged into her case. Lives that had a right to their own privacy. Lori Hamilton had chosen to keep her life private. If she had wanted others to know about her genetic makeup she would have told them. But she didn't. And Julie wondered if she had the right to reveal that information.

"I thought I did."

"Well, you better get with the program if you do, because we've got a gold mine right here."

"And how does this affect us?" asked Ryan.

"Because the pure ones always make the loudest noise when they fall," Terrance said cruelly. "Think about it. No one cares if a wino goes to a hooker. But if the head of a church or a government official does, that's big news. Take someone who's clean and dirty him up. That's news, my friends. And this stuff is news."

Julie didn't like the sound of that. She didn't approve of the tone of Terrance's voice. "You don't plan on dragging that poor lady into this, do you? This case is not about her."

"Of course I do. Anything I can do to make that organization look corrupt or pass it off as a place no one would want to go to, the better off we are."

"But she shouldn't have to expose herself like this. She has the right to her privacy."

"Nothing is private in this case or in this world. This is a piece of evidence that can really help us and turn the tide of the case to bring a decision in our favor."

"It isn't right," said Julie in a much quieter tone than she had been using.

"I'm not talking about what's right. I'm talking about the law."

Julie didn't like that final comment, nor did she care for the way Terrance was starting to handle the case. Slowly, she had noticed that her issue with Greg had taken on a life of its own. A life that now was being run by Terrance and Ryan, who were two people she wasn't so sure she trusted anymore.

"I thought you said that you might not let this story get out. That you want to hold this as a trump card," said Ryan.

"This is the kind of stuff that just may work that way. Think about it. The story on Lori Hamilton is one that St. John's just may want to keep quiet. The wife of a prominent oncologist, who they paid dearly to get to join their ranks, is married to a genetic male who almost gets raped by one of their surgeons. If you were the administration of that hospital, would you want to deal with the publicity that would come from that? I don't think so."

"So they may pay handsomely to keep the whole thing silent."

"Right. Both Hamiltons may put enough pressure on St. John's that Jameson will be forced to settle this thing for a much higher figure than we originally asked for."

"And if they don't settle?" asked Julie.

"Then I call my buddies down at the *Rockford Register* and accidentally leak the story."

Terrance and Ryan gave each other a high five as if they were watching a football game. Julie just became more disgusted with the male egos that seemed to have little care for the lives around them. She didn't want to remain in the room with them. She needed to go running. She needed to be off by herself pounding the pavement. She knew that they wouldn't miss her.

"Well, it seems like you two have this worked out pretty well. I feel like getting some air, if that's okay."

"That's fine, honey. We're just going to stay here for a while."

Julie rose and went up to Ryan's bedroom. The room that she had spent so much time in that she had been starting to call it her own. She had been feeling welcome and wanted there, but she never felt fully at ease. As she changed into her running shorts and a tank top, she could still hear the voices of the men in the room at the bottom of the stairs. She was growing tired of their sounds, so she stood up, intending to close the bedroom door. But she paused to listen to what other damage they intended to inflict.

"This is great stuff you got," continued Ryan. "I can't believe that that fox is really a guy and that Jameson tried to rape her."

"I was pretty startled too. I had to work hard in order to keep a straight face."

"Sounds like you've got this case all sewn up."

"You bet I do. You'll get the result you're after."

Ryan grinned. "I'd better. He's been after my university appointment for a year now. I'm not going to let anyone take that away."

"I'm moving as fast as I can on this," stated Terrance.

"I know. I hope that this information will speed things up. The board of governors of the U. of I. is meeting next week to decide on who gets the medical school clerkships. I'm two years away from being named a full professor, Terry. If Jameson succeeds in getting the surgical students pulled away from me and Rockford General, that'll blow my whole plan."

"I'm well aware of your ambitions, Ryan. Trust me, with the black eye we put on Jameson, no one will put any medical students under him, especially the female ones." He laughed at his own joke.

"I'm serious, Terry. You have to make something happen soon. I'm going to need something hard against him. A mere pending lawsuit isn't enough these days to discredit a surgeon. Why do you think I worked so hard to get this suit filed? I need something bad to come out. I need admission of misconduct. I need a confession of improper behavior. I need something that will make the governors tear up every single one of his requests to take over as director of the surgical program. And I need it by next week. If you don't make this happen, I'm sure I'll have trouble getting my clinic administration to hire your firm to handle all of our legal work. A deal's a deal."

"I can only go so fast. But with this new edge I suppose I can make some calls. I'll send off another settlement offer. Only this time I'll insist on getting an admission of guilt on Jameson's part as a formal requirement of the settlement."

"Just make it happen. I didn't hire you to drag this thing out for years like your usual litigation cases."

Julie had heard every word. She now knew Ryan had been playing her for a fool. He had been caressing her body as well as her ego, but all the while he was only out to advance his own career. She returned to the bed and sat down. Betrayal is a feeling that always arrives unannounced and never by itself. Betrayal stops off to bring along guilt. She felt guilty for not being able to see it coming. She was ashamed for knowing that someone was taking advantage of her.

Julie felt all the emotions. She thought Ryan loved her. He certainly had made the physical effort to prove that. He showered her with romantic evenings, nights in the hot tub, and mornings in the shower. He had given her all the pampering that she had longed to receive. But the other signs were there, too, though she had chosen to overlook them. Ryan continually asked her questions about work. Who she worked for? What was Greg like? How did he treat his staff? It was all there. He pried into her life and focused on her job. She just didn't see it. Or did she just want to believe the fairy tale that was unfolding in front of her? Whatever the truth was, she didn't like how it left her feeling. Dirty and used, like one of Ryan's surgical sponges that would be tossed to the floor after it had done its job.

She laced up her new shoes. Cross-trainers that Ryan had bought for her, which was just one of the many payments she had received for services rendered. They looked so clean, but were filthy in her mind. She couldn't wear them. She took them off and tossed them into the corner. She looked around the room and felt more like she didn't belong. She had to get out, so she packed up the clothes she had been wearing into her sports bag. She'd go home and change into her own clothes. The room felt stuffy and the walls felt like they were closing in on her. The pavement was calling her. Running was the one thing that never let her down.

She walked around the room and thought up an excuse for her to leave for the night. She needed some time alone to figure out what she was going to do. She didn't trust Ryan any more, and never did like who he had picked as her attorney. But she knew something they didn't. She knew that the men were using her, and she wasn't going to let that happen. That information she'd keep to herself. As Terrance himself had said, sometimes it's good to have a trump card.

26

The evening sun had begun its descent beyond the horizon. Streaks of red and orange swept across the summer sky as the sun set. Clouds were gathering, promising the possibility of a late-evening shower. Michael gazed at the sky through the window of the waiting room on the second floor. Most of the other families already had left the area. Surgeons had completed successful appendectomies, gall bladder removals, and hernia repairs. Loved ones were now sitting in hospital rooms holding hands, glad that the surgeries had all gone well and were over. Michael remained by himself.

Delays and emergencies bumped Cheryl's minor hip repair onto the latter part of the schedule. Being the mother of one of the groups' physicians didn't seem to carry the weight that Michael had hoped it would. More urgent cases came first, as they should.

But she was finally in the O.R. And her fractured hip was being replaced. He had seen the X-ray. Dr. Richardson had shown it to him. There was a clean break of the femur without any penetration into the skin. It should heal well, barring any complications. But Cheryl was a diabetic, which almost guaranteed complications.

Worry filled Michael's mind as he paced from the window to his chair and back again. She could have a heart attack on the table, or throw a blood clot into her lung. Michael wiped the sweat from his forehead as he pictured an anesthetic error that would leave her in a coma and prevent him from getting to ask his questions. Questions he should have known the answers to a long time ago. Questions he wanted answered about her life and about

Bill. He wondered about himself and what she knew. Michael was kicking himself over the number of times he had spent with his mother and missed the opportunity to find out who she really was.

"Is she out yet?" asked Lori. She came into the room carrying two cups of coffee from the bistro across the street. Michael wouldn't drink the local stuff.

"Nope. Not yet."

The two sat, holding hands, on a couch. He told Lori about his visit to Sunset Manor and about his meeting with the administrator, which gave her a laugh. About his discovery of Cheryl's involvement with the What-Not Shop, which didn't bring on the same laugh. Then, after being married to Lori for fifteen years, he told her about the night he stole Bill's bike. How he had smashed everything the man had owned and ruined his livelihood.

Tears filled Michael's eyes as he spoke about his hatred of a man who walked with a limp. Who spoke with a slur and smelled of mothballs. Michael could have blamed his youth for his lack of judgment. He was only a stupid kid doing what kids did, but the defense of being young carried little weight with him. He knew better, or at least he should have. Michael continued to talk about how he had grown to love the disheveled man, and how he had even defended him against groups of kids who were no different than himself. She listened and held him in a comforting way that only a lover could. There'd be no accusations. No storing away this information to be used against him in a later fight. It wasn't time to tear down, but to build him up.

"You're not that little boy anymore, Michael," Lori said. "Look at you. You're a man who takes care of others. Think about all the patients you take care of. What about them, and Will? You come to the aid of those who are weak and in need. You don't attack them or knock others down just to make yourself look good."

"I know that I'm not the same little boy who did those things to that poor man. I realize that I've grown up and started to fight for the underdog. But sometimes I wonder if I became a doctor and take care of the sick just to ease my conscience about it."

"I think you became a doctor because that caring person is who you really are. You're not paying some penance for a past sin."

"It's just that I never told anyone about it before. I'm tired of holding it all in. Being here with my mom in surgery just made me think about how short our lives are. Despite how my mother never supported me in my decision to be a doctor and how she treats you, I just can't bring myself to kick her out of her house and put her in a nursing home. It's like, how can I not forgive her for what she's done to me and us when here I am, guilty of doing that horrible thing to Bill so long ago?"

Lori pulled Michael's tearful face onto her shoulder. "You have to let it go, honey. It's all in the past. Like what Greg did to me all those years ago. I could either let it eat me up inside or let it go. Forgive yourself. I'm sure Bill did, whether or not he knew you were to blame for those things."

"Dr. Hamilton?" a nurse entered the room. "Your mother is out of surgery."

Michael sat up straight and wiped his eyes on his shirt sleeve. He cleared the drainage from his throat to return his voice to its normal pitch. "Already? That was quick."

"It went well. She'll be in recovery for about an hour. Dr. Richardson will be in shortly to talk to you." She was gone before her last syllable reached Michael's ear.

"Sounds like things went all right," Lori said.

Michael nodded and took a cleansing breath. His mother had survived her surgery. Michael and Lori followed the nurse to recovery. Cheryl still had an oxygen mask covering her face as she was wheeled into the room. The large bed bounced off the door and the nearby wall as the nurse tried to navigate a corner. The jarring made Cheryl moan, which upset Michael.

"Can't you be more careful?"

"Sorry," said the nurse. "These beds are kind of hard to steer. I'll give her some of her pain medicine when I get her all settled."

Michael knew about the mechanics of taking care of patients, but having a personal connection turned him from a doctor into a patient's family member.

"I know. Thanks for your help."

Cheryl lay still as her bed was pushed up against the wall and her IV poles were positioned. Her arms were bruised from the frequent blood draws, and a large Styrofoam wedge was between her legs, keeping her new hip in the proper position.

The nurse finished her assessment of Cheryl and wrote down the vital signs in the bedside chart. "She's doing fine, Dr. Hamilton, but she'll probably sleep for a while. Do you want me to have you paged when she wakes up?"

Michael looked at his mother, who was now snoring. She was the quietest she had been in Michael's presence in years. "No. I'll wait." He pulled up a chair next to the bed and took his mother's hand in his.

"Is the surgery over?" Cheryl's voice was groggy and she cleared her throat between words.

"Yeah, Mom. It's over. The doctor said you did just fine."

"Well, I'd hope so."

"Are you in much pain? The nurse said to call her if you needed a shot."

"No, honey. I'm fine for now. I'm just a little sleepy."

"You just had surgery, Mom. You go ahead and get some rest."

Lori looked at her watch. It was nearing seven o'clock. "Michael, do you want to go grab a bite to eat?"

Michael nodded to Lori and then turned to his mother. "Mom, get some rest. I'm going to go for a bit. I'll be back in a while."

Cheryl's light snoring let Michael know that he wasn't going to get any arguments from his mother for once.

Michael and Lori went down to the hospital cafeteria and enjoyed two plates of the daily special. They held hands as they said grace and ate their dinner and acted like they were on a date again. Michael carried their trays to the conveyor belt when they were finished.

"I'm going to go on home," said Lori. "I'm sure you'll want to talk to your mother alone when she wakes up."

"Thanks."

Michael kissed Lori good-bye, and he headed back up to his mother's room.

"Don't you have any place better to be than sitting here with an old woman?" Cheryl greeted Michael as he walked into her room.

"Hey, you woke up."

"Of course I did. No sense lounging around all day." She began to rub the outside of her left hip. "My word, what did they do to me? Feels like I've been hit by a truck."

"They put in a new hip, Mother. It's not like they took off a mole."

"Well, maybe they should have. I've got enough of them. They could've done it while I was asleep and thrown it in for free."

"Still a bargain hunter, I see."

"Well, you try to make it on a fixed income. It's not like I'm loaded or anything."

"Pop left you well off. Don't try to kid me."

"Yes, he did," she agreed. "He did see to that. His family came first, that's for sure, followed closely by his patients and the community. The whole town came out for his funeral, you know."

"I know, Mom. I was there too." Michael interrupted in order to prevent Cheryl from telling the same story for the fiftieth time. He wouldn't be successful. Her memories were too much a part of her.

"The whole town came out like he was a hero or something. Well, he was to me. And they had better come out for him, after all he did for that place. Up most every night to deliver a baby or fix a broken arm. I swear I don't know how he lived on as little sleep as he did."

"Especially with you waking up everyone so early in the morning."

"Oh, hush. That was my job."

"You know, Mom," Michael said as he began his investigation, "I found out today that you were quite the town hero too."

"Me? What on God's green earth are you talking about?"

"That you seemed to have a bit to do with helping people out about as much as Dad did."

"Oh, I did not neither. My job was to be a good wife for your father and raise you," she protested.

"So you weren't on any hospital guild or women's league? You had nothing to do with taking care of those less fortunate than us?"

"Not any more than any of the other doctors' wives did." Cheryl folded her arms across her chest and thusly assumed her defensive posture.

"Modesty isn't something you're very good at, Mother."

"Oh, and I suppose sticking my nose into other people's business is."

"Yes," resounded Michael. "You excel in it. But I'm not talking about that. I merely asked you about your activities with the town. I grew up thinking you were nothing more than a mom, and today I find out that you were some sort of civic leader—the Mother Teresa of Marengo."

"I was no such thing," she huffed. "I might have helped out when I was asked to. Take meals to shut-ins or help out with the Christmas clothing drive down at church."

"Why is it so hard for you to just admit that you've done some good things in your life? What is with your humble attitude?" Michael hated her stubbornness as much as Lori hated it in him.

"Because it isn't right, that's why." She raised her voice and pointed her finger as if lecturing her young son. "Tooting your own horn is egotistical. It shouldn't be done. I help out because that's what you're supposed to do.

Serve others. Help them. It's my Christian duty. I don't need any public recognition. My rewards will come later."

"So you admit it? You were the civic leader that I had been told about."

"Depends on what you've heard, but, yes, if it makes you so happy, I'll admit it. I was very active in our town. There were lots of things that needed getting done. Someone had to pick up the ball and run with it. Why the sudden interest in this? You never cared about such things before."

"Because I didn't know about them before. About how you helped the hospital, or built that senior day care center." Michael took a swallow. "Or helped that old man get his trinket shop up and running."

Cheryl smacked her lips and looked down at the powder-blue blanket that covered her from her waist down. "Heard about that, did ya?"

"Yes. I did. I heard that you practically did everything except hang the drywall for that place. Why did you take such an interest in that?"

"The man needed some help, that's all."

"No, Mom, you're not telling me everything."

"Son," she said, looking into Michael's eyes and lowering her voice, "he needed someone to look out for him. That's all. Now let it lie."

"You're the one who's lying. I know that you did a lot for that town, but no one takes a man under his wing the way you did with old Bill. What gives?"

Cheryl pulled herself back into her bed and pushed the button to raise her head up. "Guess you're not going to let this drop are you?"

Michael shook his head. "I'm not leaving here. And you can't get up and walk out. At least not until your leg mends."

"Fine." She took a breath and blew the air out of her nostrils. "I helped him. Sure I did. Seemed like the right thing to do. But I wasn't out to give him a livelihood or make him a prominent figure. I had a wrong to right. And I had a child who needed to be raised the right way. Who had some hard lessons to learn."

Beads of sweat formed under Michael's nose and he felt his antiperspirant lose its effect.

"I know what you did to that man, Michael. I always knew." She looked up at the ceiling as if the scene were playing out in front of her. She was a much younger woman in her thoughts, with less gray hair and a slimmer figure. Michael's face was smaller, but still had the same dimples and freckles. "You know, a mother can learn a lot about her children from doing laundry. I used to find all kinds of things in your pockets. Used to play a game to figure out where you had been and whom you had been with. Grass-stained knees usually meant you had been playing football with your friend Keith. Gum wrappers and sucker sticks meant you had been downtown all day.

"I usually had fun with it until that one morning. You had been out pretty late, later than usual. Next morning your pants had such dirt stains on them. More than you'd get at the ball field. Your shirt had pine tar and needles stuck to the back. I went and looked at your shoes that you so smartly took off before stepping foot on my carpeting. There was just as much mud and pine needles on them. I thought maybe you had fallen down or been hurt, but you never said anything about that. Then the people in town started to talk about old Bill Collins. How no one saw him riding his bike around town the next few days."

Michael began to get nervous in the way he would as a ten-year-old about to get chewed out.

"His neighbors reported that his bike had been stolen. Sure enough, Sheriff Wilson found it out in the woods someplace. Pine woods, he said it was. Then I knew what had happened." She looked over at her son whose head was hanging down so as to avoid any eye contact. "I knew, Michael, what you had done. I had seen how you treated that poor man over the years. I heard your insults. Saw you throwing things at him. I was ashamed, ashamed that my own son would do that to another man. Or anyone for that matter."

Cheryl cleared her throat. "So I had a choice to make. I could confront you and make you pay for the man's bike out of your paper route money. But I figured that would have only made you resent that man even more."

Michael nodded in agreement. He probably would have gone out of his way to torment Bill even more if he had to use some of his own hard-earned money to buy something for a cripple.

"No, I needed to do something more. I needed to pay restitution to that man, but I also had to see to it that you would see your own bigotry. Make you see others as something important, simply because they are human beings. I had to rid you of that evil that would have made you grow into the kind of man who'd take pleasure in harming others with differences, instead of cherishing them because of their differences."

She took a long-needed breath after her litany. Michael sat confused. He knew that he had been awful. Most kids are, and some make a career of it.

But he thought he had been careful enough to hide that fact from his mother.

"So you knew I stole his bike? You knew all along?"

"Well, actually I only just found out for sure this second. Thank you for your confession. But yes, I can put two and two together. You would rant about that man and hurl insults at him from our own front yard. Then after the bike was taken, you clammed up. I never heard a peep, as if the guilt was keeping your mouth shut tighter than a drum.

"I hoped you'd confess or something. Own up to your actions. But you never did. And I wasn't about to sit by and let you think you could get away with it. I knew that if you started to see him as something other than a crippled old man you'd start to become more of what I wanted you to be. So I started working to get him off the streets and away from you young hooligans. Set him up someplace safe and out of the elements. That was the easy part. Then I had to talk to your boss down at the paper."

"Mr. Miller?"

"That's him. I told him that it would mean the world to me and your father if you could get your route reassigned to cover the downtown district. Get you over to be the delivery boy for that man. I thought that making you serve him and treat him like any other customer would open your eyes. Well, you'd have thought that I had asked that man for the moon. Seems nearly every kid in town wanted that section of the paper. Did you know that there was a waiting list for that route?"

Michael nodded in agreement, but he was dumbfounded at his mother's ingenuity and tenacity.

"Told me that there was no way he could give that route to you. So I made him a deal. Or I should say, your father did. By the way, he just wanted to whup you for what you did, but I stopped him. I told him I had a plan. Anyway, your father agreed to take care of Mr. Miller's mother over at the nursing home and give free medical care for a year if he'd give you that route. Bribery works. Or it did in that case. So you got transferred to the business district and got thrown in with that old man."

"Mr. Miller told me that I had earned that spot. That my time had paid off."

"That's what we wanted you to think. You seemed so happy to have that section of town until you found out about Bill Collins being on it. You used to fuss about him. How he never gave you a tip. How you hated the smell of the store. But over time, you started to change. You softened up and actually started to take an interest in him. I remember when you started to learn magic from him. How you'd bring home new tricks that he had shown you. You'd practice them every night after supper. You started to do little magic shows for us in the kitchen. You even wanted to start inviting him over for dinner and a show. I knew that you had started to shed those awful tendencies. You were becoming the man that I'd hoped you'd be."

"Why didn't you tell me any of this before?"

"Because, Son. Because if you ever want someone to learn anything you can't just tell him what you want him to know. You have to let him experience it for himself. To see what life feels like. Isn't that what you do to your students? You don't just lecture them, do you?"

"No. I don't." Michael thought about how he would pull his students in and force them to experience medicine. He would make the students interact with patients and families and make the experiences of their patients their own. He just didn't think that his own mother would be able to teach him in the same way.

"See? I had to get you to learn something."

Michael chuckled at hearing his mother use the same line that he threw at his own students.

"I had to get you to learn to accept others despite their differences. For who they are. Because you never know when you might have to work with someone like that, or live next door to someone who's different." She took Michael's hand. "Or find yourself falling in love with someone who's different."

Michael's jaw fell open.

"I know about Lori, Son. I know she's not your typical woman."

"What are you talking about, Mom?" Michael had never uttered a word to his mother about Lori's genetic makeup. Neither had Lori, as far as he knew.

"Don't go sounding like me. As long as we're spilling our guts out like this you can come clean with me. I know she can't have kids, and I know why. I may not understand all of the science behind it, but I do know that she's sterile."

"Who told you this?"

"Then you admit it's true?"

Michael wondered if he had just opened up his mouth and let out another secret. "Yes, Mom. It's true."

"Don't worry; I always did know. Mothers of the bride and groom do spend time together and share information about their children before a big wedding."

Michael thought about how poorly his mother had treated Lori over the years. How she'd dig in about having grandchildren and how any other normal woman would want to have a family. "If you always knew, then why did you rip at her all the time? Why did you insult her and give her such a cold shoulder?"

"I hoped, Son, that you would have been able to tell me the truth. That you wouldn't feel a need to hide who Lori is from me. I tried to give you chances to tell me. I even tried to pull the truth from your own mouth. Prod you, push you, poke you, and even insult you. But you wouldn't."

"I wasn't so sure how you'd handle the truth."

"Telling the truth is always the right thing to do. You should do it, if for no other reason."

Michael felt as if he had received lectures for the past twenty years. And he had deserved them all. His mother was right, which is a tough thing for any child to have to admit. Especially if that means you are wrong.

"You're right, Mom. I should have told you about Lori, and about Bill. About lots of things, I guess."

"Don't tell me you have more things to confess. I've just gotten out of surgery and am a little tired."

"No. Nothing more." Michael laughed.

"Good. Now where is that lovely daughter-in-law of mine? I thought the two of you were attached at the hip."

"I sent her home. It was getting late."

"Well, why don't you go on home yourself. Besides, I want to take a nap."

Michael stood from his chair and started to walk toward the door.

"Michael, one more thing."

He turned to listen.

"Do you think that if you hadn't gotten to know Bill and learned to accept him that you would have ever been able to marry such a beautiful and caring woman as Lori?"

Michael thought about it. Would he have been a bigot all his life? Would he have only seen the deformities and not her inner beauty? Could he spend his life with someone who wasn't just like everyone else? He knew the answer, and it shamed him. And he wasn't going to lie to his mother about it anymore. "Probably not."

Cheryl laid her head back onto the bed and closed her eyes. "You're welcome."

27

Linda looked around at her kitchen. The calm of the evening now had replaced the earlier chaos that somehow had kept her from seeing the mess. And what a sight she was seeing. This was different from the state in which she usually left the kitchen. Gone were the empty vodka bottles lining the countertops, the crumpled remains of tortilla chip bags along with the crumbs from their contents, bottles of aspirin, and cardboard pizza boxes with stale crusts tossed about like unwanted children. The sights that she'd usually face when she'd wake up just before noon the next morning weren't there today.

It was not the next morning and the empty bottles were from soda and chocolate syrup. Her usual headache and cotton mouth weren't there. Neither was the nausea or the smell of her own vomit lingering in her nostrils. Instead, she wore a smile. Warmth was in her heart and she liked that feeling.

Linda looked at the mess she and her children had created. It was supposed to have been a quiet evening; the three of them together again after such a long time apart. Paul had wanted to make sugar cookies. Will wanted ice cream sundaes. Linda tried to make them both happy. And why not? She had just brought her son home from the hospital. He had faced cancer and won, this round anyway. She knew he wasn't out of the woods. Michael had told her so. But for now they were together and they were all alive. That was worth celebrating. If her kids wanted two types of desserts, then she was going to provide them. She would have driven to Gudemann's bakery for their éclairs if that's what they had wanted to pig out on.

She left the dinner dishes to sit while she brought out the ice cream and toppings. Paul pulled out flour and sugar canisters. Eggs and butter were placed near the oven. Bowls, spoons, cookie sheets, and mixers occupied the previously empty counter. Linda mixed the butter and eggs in the electric mixer, then filled bowls with generous scoops of vanilla ice cream. But she turned her backs to her boys, and that's a mistake every mother realizes when it's too late.

"This scoop of ice cream looks just like your bald head," Paul announced as he picked up his bowl and showed it to Will.

"Fine. Then let's put some hair on it." Will picked up the bottle of chocolate sauce and squeezed a large amount onto Paul's dessert.

"Hey, not so much." Paul's screams were mixed with Will's laughter. Paul put his bowl on the table and sought revenge. "Then I might as well make you look like it." He picked up the chocolate sauce and squeezed the topping onto Will's head.

Will didn't move as the sticky syrup dripped down his neck and off the tip of his nose. Paul finished by placing a cherry on top of Will's head.

"There—a brother sundae." Paul stood back with his short arms crossed over his chest to admire his handiwork before bursting into laughter.

Will broke out in laughter. He had missed getting into trouble with his brother. Linda looked at her sugar-coated son dripping sticky sauce onto her previously clean floor. She had felt anger at her younger son for creating a mess, but his giggles were infectious. She began to scold Paul for ruining Will's shirt and spilling syrup on the floor. But then she saw his chubby face begin to lose its shine and return to the look that she had seen far too often—disappointment. And usually because of what she had done to him.

"Paul, I'm really surprised at you." She reached for a tall can on the counter. "You know a sundae isn't finished without some whipped cream." Linda proceeded to squirt a white ring of cream around the top of Will's head before shooting some into her own and Paul's open mouths.

"This means war," announced Will who couldn't possibly have looked threatening with a dessert melting off the top of his head.

But war was just what he intended to wage as he reached into the container of flour. One quick toss and Paul became a ghost with large, blue eyes sticking through a mask of white powder. The rest became a blur to Linda as sugar, flour, chocolate sprinkles, and eggs were thrown about the room. Cookie dough was pressed into faces. Orange juice was poured over heads. Peanut butter became hair gel. After the floor became coated in liquids it became difficult for sure footing to be attained.

In only a matter of minutes, cupboards were emptied and the refrigerator was depleted. Linda, Will, and Paul were left sitting on the floor coated with various shades of color. After a good laugh, Linda carried the boys upstairs for a much-needed bath.

Warm water and soap rinsed away their hard work. Along with the dairy products, sugar, and baking goods, Linda felt that many other things were rinsed down the drain. Bitterness, empty promises, abandonment, and things that Linda had done to her children over the years washed away from her mind. The guilt of many of the things that she hadn't done left her, too, like not acting like a mom.

Bonding can take place in the oddest of places. It can be unexpected and unplanned. But the strongest of connections come from sharing something. And these three did that. They shared themselves and became a family again.

She tucked the boys into bed and read them one story after another. She planted kisses on the boys' foreheads before turning out the lights. Paul and Will fell asleep before Linda could make it back downstairs. Sleep comes easy to those who feel safe and loved. Paul and Will felt that now, as did Linda.

The sight of the kitchen in its current state would have brought many emotions to Linda a few weeks earlier. Love would not have been one of them. But tonight she didn't mind the mess. It would take her a while to clean it up, but she didn't mind.

"What the hell happened in here?" Greg chuckled as he walked into the kitchen.

"Our welcome-home party for Will got a little out of hand," said Linda as she began to fill the sink with hot water.

"I'll say. It must have been some party."

"It was." She wanted to tell him how wonderful it really was. How Will and Paul laughed the whole time, and that they had a blast. That for one hour Will wasn't a boy with cancer, but a boy in his home. But Greg wouldn't hear that. He could only see a mess that he wouldn't have to clean up, but would somehow mess up his world. "You should have been here. You missed out on having some fun with your kids."

Greg picked up the remains of an ice cream carton. "Well, someone has to earn the money to pay for all of this."

Linda waited to hear the rage and the lashing out. The words of anger being spoken through clenched teeth and his pronouncement that she wasn't fit to take care of children. That she was wasting his money by throwing food around the house. She stood facing the sink with her hands gripping the counter as she braced herself for the attack. But it never came.

"Are they asleep? I'd like to see them."

Linda turned around to look at Greg. His face showed the countenance of a beaten, worried man. "I think so. They were pretty tired."

"I think I'll go check on them anyway."

Greg walked out of the kitchen and up the stairs. He peered into their rooms. Will's bed was empty; Paul's had two occupants. Linda walked up quietly behind Greg and put her hand on his shoulder.

"Looks like they decided to spend the night together," Greg whispered. "Remember when they'd do that years ago? Paul would come into Will's room in the middle of the night and snuggle up to him? Or vice versa? They hated to sleep alone."

Linda nodded. She remembered those times too.

"But they'd never come into our room. I wonder why that was?" remarked Greg.

"Because you insisted on locking our door," answered Linda, with the truth that can oftentimes hurt. "You didn't want to be disturbed by them."

"Please tell me it was because we were messing around."

"I wish I could." Linda patted Greg on the back. "But the truth is you were on the phone and I was probably passed out."

Greg let out a sigh. "Quite a pair, huh?"

"What's bothering you?" Linda could sense something different about Greg; a sort of compassion and a touch of humanity that seldom rose to the surface. "I've never seen you act like this before. It's like you care or something."

"Is that so wrong?" Greg turned to Linda and looked into her eyes. "Did you ever think for a minute that maybe I do?"

Greg walked away and headed into Will's unoccupied room. Linda followed, waiting to see what he was going to surprise her with next. He turned on the light in Will's room and looked around to acclimate himself to the room that he rarely had entered. The floor was tidy. The bed still made. An unopened suitcase sat on top of the bed. Greg stepped into his son's realm and made his way over to his shelves. He found a picture of Will from the first grade, and he picked it up. "Man, he really has grown up quickly, hasn't he? Is this really our little boy?"

Linda stepped into the room, stood by her husband, and took the picture into her own hands. "Hard to believe, isn't it? I remember that day. His hair just wouldn't lie flat. See the tuft sticking up in the back?"

"Yeah." Greg took the picture back. "You remember that day?"

Linda nodded. It was one of the few, but she remembered it.

"I don't." Greg put the picture back up onto the shelf, then turned to the other objects that kept the portrait company. Trophies, medals, model cars that Will had assembled and painted. Witnesses to Will's life and reminders to Greg that he had not been part of it. "Look at all of this stuff. All the things he's done. Places he's been." Greg picked up the stack of swimming ribbons that Will had won but not yet placed onto his bulletin board. "I've missed all of it. It's like I didn't exist during all of this."

Linda narrowed her eyes and placed her hands on her hips. "All right," she said evenly, her hands resting on her hips. "Who are you? And what have you done with my husband?"

"Very funny." Greg put down the ribbons and sat down on Will's bed. "He's what, ten now?"

Linda nodded as she sat beside him.

"He's halfway to being out that front door. Off to college. Probably as far away from me as he can get. Only coming back for holidays and when he needs money. I've missed out on his childhood, Linda."

Linda put her arm around Greg, still not sure where he was going with this line of speech or where it was coming from. But she had only seen him like this once before—when his mother died. It made her wonder what bad news he was about to tell her.

"He doesn't hate you, you know."

"How could he? You can only hate someone if you know him. No, it's worse than hate. He doesn't know me. And I don't know him. And it's getting to the point when it'll be too late to do anything about it."

"If you wanted to spend time with him you could have visited him when he was in the hospital. That really hurt him—that you didn't come around."

"I know. I tried to see him. I really did. But every time I'd go there, that Hamilton was there. Talking to him. Showing off. Teaching him magic tricks."

"He was giving Will attention. Will needed that."

"He was doing more than giving Will attention," Greg said wearily. "He was being a father to him."

"Don't be silly. He was just rounding on his patient."

"I was there, Linda. I heard every word they spoke to each other. He was much more than a doctor to Will."

Linda leaned back to take a longer look at Greg. "You eavesdropped on them?"

"I didn't mean to. It sort of happened accidentally. Well, the first time anyway." He shifted in his seat and cleared his throat. "I finished my rounds early and thought I'd show up. See how his first round of chemo went. When I got there, Hamilton was in the room. I didn't want to go in. You know how he feels about me."

Linda knew. And why.

"So I sat at the nurses' desk for a few minutes hoping the ass would leave before I had to go to clinic. Well, the nurse called into the room on an intercom, and after she was done talking I could hear Will and Hamilton's voices. Clear as day.

"I was pretty much alone at the desk, so I held down the button and listened for a while. I don't know why. To hear what he might say about me to my son. I figured he always was out to discredit me after what I had done to Lori."

Linda nodded in agreement that what Greg had done was wrong.

"But he never bad-mouthed me. Not once. And he had chances too. Will asked about me. Where was I? When would I come by? Every time, Hamilton would stand up for me. Say that I was a busy guy and would come when I could.

"I started making my rounds in such a way as to make sure I could catch the two of them together. Hear what they'd talk about. Swimming. School. Girls. Did you know that Will has a girl that he's sweet on?"

Linda smiled. "Yes. Erin."

"Hamilton got to hear all of that. The important stuff. Stuff a father should know. So after a while I stopped listening to find out what Hamilton was saying about me, and I started to listen to hear about my son. Listen to him. Find out what he's like. I started to get jealous of Hamilton. Mad at him too.

"I mean, why should he get to hear all of that stuff? Why was he getting to sit there and find out about Will's desires to swim for Northwestern? He wants to be a marine biologist when he grows up. That's the kind of stuff that I should get to hear. Not him."

"Well, he was there for him during this time," Linda said.

"It should have been me," Greg said forcefully.

Linda couldn't argue with him. She knew that they both had not been ideal parents. But Greg's behavior had never been held up to such self-scrutiny before. He wasn't looking for Linda to make himself feel better. He wasn't looking for someone to come to his defense.

"It hurts when you realize what you've been missing out on," she said. "But why now? What brought this on today? Did you have a case go bad? Or is your lawsuit not going very well?"

"No. My O.R. schedule was fine today. In fact, I had some free time this morning." He took a deep breath and exhaled slowly. "Today they questioned Lori."

"Lori? What about?"

"What do you think? They were trying to see if I had a pattern of behavior that would fit the profile of a sexual predator. Someone must have tracked down Lori and brought up what happened that night."

Linda remembered it well. It was one of the last times she had spoken to her once-best friend. "I had hoped that was buried." Linda walked to the window and looked at nothing in particular. "I hated you that night."

"I know," mumbled Greg. "I was surprised that you even went through with the wedding."

"What was I supposed to do? Cancel, with all my relatives coming into town in three days? My poor parents had taken out a loan to pay for the whole thing. I would have been totally embarrassed."

"So instead, you thought you'd just take your anger out on me."

"Anger doesn't begin to describe how I felt. My own maid of honor backs out on the wedding. Your best man breaks your jaw and then refuses to come to the wedding. Then you tell all your friends that I had uninvited my maid of honor just to try and embarrass Lori even further."

"You know, you could have talked to me about this before the wedding. Or maybe you could have at least spoken to me on the honeymoon instead of hanging out in the bar of the resort."

"Hey, the drinks were free at that all-inclusive place, and they were a lot more pleasant company than a two-timing husband. Is it any wonder that I got hooked on the stuff?"

"No," Greg said softly. "I can't say I blame you. After this week I can see that a lot of what went wrong was my fault."

Linda turned from the window to look at her husband. "Are you accepting blame? Are you finally admitting that you made the mistakes that caused our problems?"

"Sure looks that way."

"My word. What happened today?" Linda knew that to get Greg to see his own fallibility meant he must have heard some very bad news. "What did Lori say at the meeting?"

"Hell if I know. I wasn't allowed into the room. Hamilton made it a closed session. But whatever it was must have been a major kick in the balls because later this afternoon I was informed of a meeting this Saturday morning that I have to show up for. Terrance Niemann, the other side's attorney, is pushing for a settlement. He wants to have the whole thing wrapped up before next week for some damn reason. So if I value my job, guess where I'll be that day."

"I can see why that got you so upset."

"That's not the worst of it. Not by a long shot." Greg rubbed his eyes like they were heavy from a lack of sleep. "Right after that session Hamilton went to see Will. I thought for sure that this would be the time that he would spill the beans on what kind of a man Will had for a father. Really rip into me. Make me out as the asshole that I am."

"Do you think he'd really talk about that to Will?"

"Oh, I don't know. But I wouldn't be surprised. Even I hear what people say about me, I just act like I don't care. But he didn't say a thing. He never let Will think that his father was anything but a decent man. It blew my mind. And I heard what Will had said about me. Like I didn't even know he existed. That my patients and anyone else came first in my life. And he's right. I've ignored him for ten years. Then to make matters worse, I ran into Michael afterward. He summed it all up for me. That all Will wanted in the world was to have a father. Unfortunately, what he got was me."

Greg focused on Will's words. He had heard Michael talk about people who quickly pass judgment on those who are different. He felt the words could have easily applied to his own treatment of Lori years ago. Greg started to cry. He had turned into his own father, who was a successful surgeon in his own right but had no time for his son. "Here I am with the possibility of losing my job. But instead of having a family to go home to like almost everyone else, all I have are strangers who share an address."

Linda agreed. She had been part of his neglected family. Vodka on the rocks could only go so far to take the place of a man, and Will and Paul found each other for companionship. But she knew that Greg was right. That it had gone on far too long. That having a family was what she really wanted. It seemed that Greg finally wanted it too.

"Well, I know how you can change all of that."

"How?"

"This weekend is Will's conference swim meet. It's all he's talked about today. He really wants to swim in it, and I called Don Thurston to clear it. I know it would mean the world to Will if you were there."

"This weekend? You mean Saturday morning, don't you?"

"Yeah. That's when these things usually take place."

"Weren't you listening? I have to be at the hospital this Saturday for my defense on the lawsuit. I can't risk my job for his swim meet."

Linda shook her head. Greg's enthusiasm for having a family seemed to mean only if nothing else got in the way. "Sometimes you have to make sacrifices if you want to have what's really important."

Greg just grunted. Linda didn't seem to understand just what his job meant to him. For twenty years it was all that drove him. All he planned for. All he was. He just couldn't walk away from that.

"I'll make it up to him. I will. This time I mean it."

Linda got up from the bed. "I know you will, Greg," she said, trying to believe his words. "I'm going to go check on the boys."

28

"Where's Dad?" Will asked as he bounded into the kitchen. The smell of bacon and waffles had coaxed him out of bed earlier than Linda had expected.

"He had to leave early this morning, honey. He has an important meeting today. But he said he'd try to get over to the club when he can."

"Oh." Will slumped into a chair at the kitchen table. He could translate his mother's words. Morning meetings and morning rounds became afternoon rounds, then evening rounds. Seeing his father today was not likely.

"I made breakfast," Linda said. She called upstairs to Paul, who stumbled downstairs dragging his blanket behind him.

Linda enjoyed cooking breakfast for her boys. She knew she couldn't change what she had done to them in the past, but she was comfortable with her penance.

Paul gobbled his food, syrup dripping from the corners of his mouth as he asked for more.

But Will just poked at his food with a fork. Linda's heart went out to him. How disappointed he must be.

Will liked being home, but he also missed the hospital. There, the people cared about him. The nurses would talk to him. Dr. Hamilton would spend time in the room showing new tricks. He missed the special attention. He thought about the swim meet that he'd be going to this morning. He hadn't swum a lap in weeks. Would he be able to race? Would the other kids remember him? Would they tease him about his bald head and steroid-induced chubby face? Would Erin?

His daydreaming was interrupted when Paul tossed a piece of waffle onto Will's head. The syrup made the waffle stick to his face.

"Oh, no, we're not starting that again," Linda said, trying to appear stern. She quickly dropped her spatula and stepped between the boys. "We have to get to the pool in thirty minutes, and we don't have time to hose off your breakfasts and clean the kitchen."

They finished their breakfasts and loaded their swim bags into the car. Linda lathered up the boys with sunscreen. Will coated the top of his head and put on a large canvas hat.

Linda added three folding chairs and a cooler of drinks and snacks to the trunk before slamming the lid down. A refill for her travel mug and the three set out for the Alpine Valley club after setting the house alarm. Saturday morning traffic in Rockford is fueled by families with sporting activities. Soccer leagues, baseball, football, cheerleading camps, and basketball leagues were only a few of the programs offered by the park district to keep children busy. Minivans and overloaded SUVs filled the streets from Perryville Road to Alpine, all filled with excited children and sleepy parents on their way to one sporting event or another.

The parking lot at the Alpine Valley club had already started to fill by the time the Jameson family pulled in. Vans from all over northern Illinois had staked out their claims, with the choicest spots under the shade-providing trees all but taken.

Linda found a spot for her Mercedes. Paul jumped from the car and ran to the entrance, carrying his bag off one shoulder. Linda and Will took the remaining luggage and toted it across the hot asphalt.

"You sure you're up to this today?" Linda asked as they made their way through the open gate to the pool area.

"Yeah. I want to be here."

"You'll do fine," she reassured him.

The concession area consisted of three tables set along the sidewalk leading to the bull pen. Homemade cookies, popcorn, bags of brownies, candy bars, and snow cones filled the tables. Coffee and doughnuts for the adults were complemented with bagels and varieties of spreads. Paul briefly stopped at the candy counter before seeing Will coming up behind him. The little boy then dashed off again.

"Come back here, Paul. Carry some of your own junk."

But Paul continued on toward the Dolphin's tent. The large canvas awning covered the plot of ground staked out by the Dolphins. A large banner with the Dolphin's name and club was stretched across the opening. Other clubs from the surrounding areas had similar tents with their names embossed on the doorways.

Teams from all over the northern district were present; Sterling, Woodstock, McHenry, and Freeport among them. In and out of the tents ran children of all ages, from little kids who barely filled their suits to young men and women who seemed to enjoy seeing the other gender in theirs.

For Will it was a time to see if he was still one of them. He lugged his bags and the cooler toward the tent that Paul had just ducked into. The morning was still cool, but the distance he had to walk was beginning to make him feel a little short of breath. He had become tired by the time he reached the tent.

"Thanks for helping me carry this stuff, Paul," he shouted as he entered the tent. Then Will's eyes opened wide as he looked at the scene before him.

"Surprise!" shouted his teammates in unison.

Will's team stood in several rows facing toward him. A large paper banner was held across the front row. It read:

WELCOME BACK, WILL. WE MISSED YOU.

Will was speechless. He hadn't known if he had been missed, but this seemed to put his mind at ease. The group smiled and waved. They shouted his name and began the Dolphin cheer. Will looked on in amazement. He had never had a surprise party before. He looked around the tent at all the familiar faces. It was his team, all right. But they looked different. His team members, every one of them, including Erin, were completely bald.

Will stood motionless as the kids started to crowd around him. Don stepped forward rubbing his own shining scalp.

"You made not having any hair look so good I thought we'd all give it a try." He crouched down to be at eye level with his young swimmer. "Besides, I hear women love bald heads. I couldn't let you get all the attention."

Don pointed in the direction of the far wall of the tent. Rachel was coming toward the two, her head just as bare.

Rachel had tears in her eyes as she bent over to hug Will. "I'm so glad you're here today. I don't care what your head looks like. Hair or no hair, you're still our Willy." She leaned over and kissed Will on the top of the head.

Will blushed.

"Save some of that for me, woman," interrupted Don. "I've got a smooth top too." He rubbed his scalp as if making a spot clean for Rachel to place her lips.

"Yeah, but you're not as cute," sassed Rachel.

Don rolled his eyes, then patted Will on the back before moving out of the way for the rest of the well-wishers.

Will stood still as the whole team came up to him, patting him on his head, back, and bottom. He heard them say "welcome back," "cool head," and "not the same place without you" over and over again. He also endured questions like "How much did you puke?" "Are you still sick?" and "Will your hair grow back?" All the while Paul was tugging on his shirt, asking Will if they had surprised him.

Will answered each question as best he could in the few seconds he had between each inquiry. He repeated the same answers as if no one heard his earlier responses. But Will didn't mind. It made him feel welcome. It made him feel like he belonged.

As the line thinned, a smaller figure approached Will. Erin held herself back. She didn't want to have to say a few words to Will, then walk away.

"Do you like what I've done to my hair?" she asked as she motioned to pat long locks that were no long there. A thin layer of red fuzz was all that remained of the hair that previously had spilled down her back.

"I can't believe you cut it all off," Will told her. "Didn't your mom have a fit?"

"Nah. It was Daddy who freaked. He likes his girls to have long hair. But when I told him it was for you, he finally agreed." She reached over and held Will's hand. She escorted Will over to her blanket and sat down.

"I baked you some cookies." Erin pulled out a plastic container filled with chocolate chip M&M cookies. "I wanted to bring you some at the hospital, but Mom thought I should wait until you were out. I guess she didn't want me to see you when you were so sick."

"I was quite a sight. You missed out."

She opened up the container and Will took out two cookies and offered one to Erin.

"So, are you still sick? I mean, do you still have the cancer?"

Will nodded. "Yeah. They gave me my first round of chemo. That's the medicine that fights the cancer. What it was supposed to do was wipe out all the cancer cells. Now I have to go back every couple of weeks for blood tests. They're going to watch to see if any grow back. But whether they do or not, I'm going to have to go another round of the stuff, just to try and keep the cancer away."

"That sucks."

Will nodded in agreement.

"Will your hair grow back?"

"Probably not before yours does." He reached over and felt the top of Erin's head. Will's head had been rubbed by everyone in the tent, but he had never touched anyone else's. He saved that for her. "Feel's smooth."

Erin felt a chill go down her back. Then she smiled. "It doesn't bother you, does it?" she asked.

"What do you mean?"

"My hair. It doesn't make me look ugly or anything, does it?"

"I don't think you could ever look ugly."

Will's words made Erin smile. It was what she wanted to hear. It was what he wanted to say. They both knew that they didn't have to say anything more about it.

"So who's idea was this?" Will asked. "The shaving of heads, I mean."

"Don's. He found out that you'd be coming, and he wanted to make sure that you didn't feel out of place; that you'd know you will always be one of us. He really likes you, you know. So after practice he had Rachel shave his head. Right there in front of everyone. Then he cut Rachel's hair. You should have heard the screams from the rest of the girls. The boys all lined up for it after that. They all thought it'd be cool. The rest of us had to ask permission first."

"That's always a good idea."

"But everyone did it. Being so close to the district meet probably didn't hurt since a lot of the kids were going to shave anyway, but I still think it's neat."

Will grinned. It was neat. His friends cared about him. They thought of his feelings instead of their follicles. He was more than just a swimmer who could bring in fast times. He was a member of their group.

"Then they got Paul there to let us know when you were coming so we could all line up."

"So that's why he ditched and made me carry all the stuff. I thought he was just trying to get out of work."

"Well, with Paul you never know."

Erin and Will sat together in a sea of sleeping bags and coolers, waiting for the meet to start.

"All right, everyone," announced Don with his hands cupped over his mouth to create a small megaphone. "Warm ups. Warm ups now. We've got lanes one through five. And we've only got them for fifteen minutes, so move it or lose it."

Like race horses out of the gates, kids dropped Game Boys and snack bars, leaving the floor of the tent looking like most of their bedrooms, and headed for the pool. Goggles were placed over heads. Swim caps were left behind. There was no need for those today. Don walked down to the poolside with his team and lined the kids up by ages into the different lanes. He shouted commands that were followed to the letter. Each child found his or her assigned lane and jumped into the cool, clear water.

Arms flailed out of the water as the swimmers began their strokes. Each packed lane slowly filled from one end of the pool to the other. Will stood on the edge of the pool waiting his turn to jump in. He hadn't been in the water in weeks, but like a duck with instinct, he hopped in and began his stroke.

Pulling the water past him, Will felt his muscles stretch in a way they hadn't in a long time. The water felt cold as it flowed past his hairless chest and belly. Every other stroke brought him to the surface for a refreshing gulp of air. His lungs burned by the end of his second lap.

The other swimmers had begun to back up behind Will as his slower pace became more evident. He finally stopped and held onto the lane lines to let the other swimmers pass him by. Gasping for air, Will decided that he had had enough warming up. He would need to keep a little of his strength for his events. He walked slowly through the water to the side of the pool and pulled himself to the deck.

"You're really dogging it today, man," said Don as he pulled the tired Will from the water.

"I guess I'm a little more out of shape than I thought," Will said between gasps, as he bent down and rested his hands on his knees.

"You sure you want to race today? I could pull you and just let you rest."

"No." Will straightened up, his strength seemingly restored by the prospect of being benched. "I can do this. I'll be fine." Will didn't want to let anyone down. It would not have been right for him to have everyone shave their heads only to watch Will keep stats on the poolside.

Don was uneasy. He didn't want Will to hurt himself. He didn't understand Will's illness or its effects on the little boy's body. He wasn't sure if he wanted to put that kind of pressure on himself or Will. "How about if we ask your mom if it's okay?"

"How about if you ask his doctor?" Michael approached the side of the pool. His running shorts, tropical T-shirt, and sun glasses made him look just like any other middle-aged parent.

"Dr. Mike. What are you doing here?" asked Will.

"This was all you were talking about for the last week. Don't you remember?"

Will nodded. He still had air to catch.

"I couldn't let you make your big comeback and me not be here for it. That's all right, isn't it?"

"You bet."

"So what do you think, Doc?" asked Don. "Can we let this guy swim today?"

Michael looked at Will who had assumed a face like a child pleading for a new puppy. "How'd he do out there?"

"He seemed to tucker out after about one hundred meters."

Michael looked into Will's pleading eyes. He knew that Will was healthy enough to be out of the hospital. He also knew that something like swimming one event would be a real boost to Will's self-esteem and wouldn't really cause any harm to his patient.

"Maybe one event, something that wouldn't be more than fifty meters."

Don thought for a moment. He had a line-up all set for the day, but nothing is set in stone until the kids actually hit the water. "I think you'd do fine in a relay. I can put you in the medley. If you can't keep up the pace, the rest of the team might be able to make up some time."

Will liked the idea. He could do fifty meters. And because the event was the medley relay, he could pick which of the four basic strokes he'd have to perform.

"How about backstroke? That way I'd be on my back and could breathe the whole time."

Don liked the idea and quickly flipped through his clipboard to find whom he had listed on his relay team.

"I'd have to move a few people around, but since I'd be bumping you from some of the other events I don't think they'd mind." Don pulled his pen from behind his ear and began changing the lineup. "I'll go tell the judges about this. You go and find your other team members. The medley is in the first series of events."

Don walked away leaving Michael and Will alone.

"This is a pretty impressive sight," said Michael, who was looking around the pool and at the large grassy area that was now filled with tents, lawn chairs, blankets, and kids.

"Yeah. It's pretty neat. I always have fun at these."

"Just don't wear yourself out too much."

"I won't."

"Say, are your folks here?" Michael wouldn't mind seeing Linda, but really didn't want to run into Greg.

"Mom is. Dad's got some important meeting he had to be at."

Typical, thought Michael. The most important day in his son's life and Greg was at the office. "That's too bad. But I'm sure he'd be here if he could."

Will just nodded. He didn't want to dwell on the subject any longer. "Come on. I want to show you our spot."

Will grabbed Michael by the hand and led him over to the tent area. Will liked having his doctor on his own turf instead of the other way around. Michael was introduced to Erin, who was a perfect lady. Michael met dozens of people. He felt like he was at a family reunion being introduced to every obscure cousin. But Will was having a ball being the host, and Michael wasn't going to spoil it. They finally met up with Linda who was equally glad to see her old friend there to cheer on her boys.

"Thanks for coming, Michael."

"I wouldn't miss it."

"You always were someone to count on."

"Still am. That's one neat kid you've got there. I can see a lot of you in him, Linda."

"The good stuff, I hope."

"He's got to get that from someone."

Don walked into the tent and started calling for his swimmers to make their way to the bull pen. Will said his good-byes and headed off with the other three members of his relay team. Michael and Linda made their way down to the poolside to get a better seat for Will's event. The two were able to find a spot where Will would be able to see them.

"This is great to have you back, Will," said Blake Richards. Blake was one of the fastest swimmers and planned to be in four events that day.

"Yeah, I'm sure you're going to do fine," said Howard Hill, another tough competitor.

Chapter Twenty-Eight

"I hope so. I don't want to let you guys down," said Will.

Blake leaned over to Will while he swung his goggles on his index finger. "Don't worry. We've made a pact. No matter how you do. You could even come in a minute behind the other teams. We're going to pick up the slack. We're not going to lose this race, Will. We'll get you a medal today."

The other boys nodded in unison. They had been given their instructions from Don. They were in full agreement. Their goal today was to give Will a win. They hadn't all shaved their heads for nothing.

Will sat looking at his friends. Their streamlined, muscle-toned bodies made his pudgy, steroid-altered one stand out. They were tanned. He was pale. But they were one unit. They were a team. And their physical differences didn't matter one bit.

The boys heard their event called, and they stood to walk to the blocks. The other teams filed along as the crowd of ten-year-olds made their way to the far side of the pool. Will walked to the fourth lane and stood next to the starting block awaiting his instructions from the starter. Will stood at the edge of the pool as the event was about to start. Will's pulse was picking up. He felt a nervous twinge in his stomach. He hoped he hadn't forgotten how to race.

Will looked around the crowd. He was able to find his mother and Michael waving. He gave a small wave back as not to be noticed. His final ritual commenced. Will looked around the deck for one more person. One more face. The same one he always looked for but never found. Today was no different. Will pulled his goggles over his head, once again grateful that they were waterproof.

Joe, the coach who was running today's events, picked up his clipboard and looked at the next race. He put his megaphone to his mouth and spoke. "Two hundred meters, boys ten and under medley relay. Get into the water, boys."

The first swimmer of each team jumped into the water to position himself for the start. The sounds of feet hitting water echoed across the pool. Joe was ready to start the event. But there was one problem.

"Swimmer number four," he called on his speaker. "Lane four. You need to get into the water, son."

Will stood still. Motionless. Howard moved forward and tapped him. "Will. Come on, man. Get in the water. You want to get us disqualified?"

But Will didn't move. His eyes were fixed across the pool as if he were held in a trance. But he wasn't looking at the water. He wasn't afraid to get in. He wasn't nervous. Will's eyes were focused on a figure moving through the wrought-iron gate. He wasn't hard to spot in his three-piece suit, Pierre Cardin tie, and penny loafers.

The man moved through the crowd and made his way down toward the pool. Will began to smile. Greg Jameson had come to watch his son swim.

29

Julie's feet pounded the pavement. She had put three miles behind her and had two more to go. She pulled her water bottle from its Velcro strap and took a mouthful of water. The pathway along the Rock River was nearly deserted; the morning crowd had cleared out and the afternoon group still was several hours away from showing up. Having the asphalt to herself had become part of her routine since she no longer needed to be at work during the day.

She missed her friends from work. She missed the challenge of the O.R. She missed her work. Running, alone with her thoughts, was starting to get a little lonely for her.

"Am I doing the right thing?" she asked herself. "Sure, Jameson is a creep, but at least I know where I stand with him. That's more than I can say for Ryan and Terrance." She rounded a corner and squinted her eyes from the glare of the sun. "Why couldn't things just go back to the way they were? The money from the lawsuit would be nice, but it's not like I need it. It won't get me back with my friends or make me have more to my day than running out here by myself. But I can't back out now. All the other nurses would be disappointed in me. They all want to see something happen around that place. They'd love to see some respect get thrown our way. I just hate having this whole thing put on my shoulders."

Julie ran past the spot where she had first met Ryan. It was a spot that she had loved, but now she held it with some disgust. It had become another place where she had relinquished control of her life to another man.

"It's not fair. All I want is to be a nurse, not a champion for a cause. But I guess it's too late for that." Julie ran along with a pace that would have gotten her into the top finishers of a 10K. She marveled at her endurance. What she needed was some strength. "I guess I just have to decide what to do with myself. I either get to run my own race, or have someone else do it for me."

Julie took another drink from her bottle, then picked up the pace and kicked for the final distance.

30

"Where the hell is he?" Terrance asked. He didn't like to be kept waiting. Time was money. But he wasn't charging an hourly fee with this case. Having a case on contingency did have its drawbacks. There was no one to whom he could send a bill for the extra time spent waiting. His impatience followed a pattern. He'd sit for a while. Look at his watch. Get up and pace around his side of the table. Walk to the window. Poke his finger through the blinds and look outside. Then he'd loudly ask, "Where the hell is he?"

"I told you, Terrance. I don't know where Dr. Jameson is." Mark was equally angry at Greg for not showing up for their meeting.

"He's over an hour late." Terrance looked at his watch. "No, make that an hour and fifteen minutes. See? This is the type of disregard that man has for others. This is very evident in his insensitivity, callousness, and utter contempt for others."

"Relax, Terry." Mark twirled his pen in his left hand without lifting his eyes to Niemann. "You're not testifying. None of your remarks can be submitted."

"The hell they can't." Terrance pounded his fist on the table. "My time is valuable." Terrance paced back to the window and poked his bony finger through the slats once more.

"Maybe he's stuck in a case, or rounding with patients. He is a busy doctor, you know," Mark added.

"He was supposed to clean his schedule this morning and hand off all his hospital patients to the doctor on call." Mark looked at his watch. He had other things to do this morning as well. Being stuck in a boardroom on a Saturday wasn't tops on his list. "Why don't I have him paged again?"

"Yeah, why don't you." Terrance was making his laps around the table again.

"I saw his car this morning," said Mark. "It's hard to miss that thing. It was in the parking lot this morning when I drove in. He must be here somewhere."

"He better be." Terrance decided to take a break and sit down. "In fact, I just may go after that car of his that you saw. Maybe I'll take his house too."

"Cool heads, gentlemen," Mark said. He stood up from the table, walked to the door, and stuck his head out into the foyer.

"Susan, would you mind having Dr. Jameson paged for us again?" Mark's secretary nodded and picked up her phone. "Have the message marked urgent, okay?"

Mark closed the door and returned to his seat at the table. The papers in front of him were neatly stacked after having been shuffled several times already that morning. It wasn't like Greg to walk away from a situation like this. He had a lot to lose if the hospital had a large judgment made against it. Greg always had seemed to look at a fight with a personal edge. It wasn't his technical skills that were being questioned with this lawsuit. But Greg acted as if he were being called a bad person. Like he was a child on a playground being picked on. He needed to stand his ground. Not get bullied. So then where was he?

"Perhaps you'd like to take the time that we have while we're waiting to go over the parts of your offer that don't pertain to Dr. Jameson?" Mark suggested.

Terrance paced one more time to the window. He liked to make things more dramatic than they really were. "I had hoped to cover everything with full attendance, but since that doesn't look possible, I guess we'll just have to proceed. But trust me, Jameson's absence will be properly noted in my brief to the judge."

Mark waved him off. "Whatever."

Terrance opened up his briefcase and removed a legal notepad and his microcassette recorder.

"August 9," he said, speaking into the microphone. "Meeting with Mark Brannon et al. in *McMahon v. St. John's*, tape one." He set the recorder on the table and leaned back into his chair. "I've had several meetings with my client, and we feel that your last offer doesn't begin to meet our needs."

"Not enough money? Is that it?" Mark asked.

Terrance pulled himself upright and cleared his throat. "You can believe what you want, Brannon." Terrance's interests in the case had little to do with Julie and her work environment, but instead he thought about his own deal with Ryan that would have brought most of Rockford General Hospital's legal work his way, providing, of course, that Ryan was able to secure his position with the university.

"I'm sure that you do, Terry. So why don't you tell us what you think would be a fair arrangement."

"Fine." Terrance flipped open his notepad and scanned down his long list of items. "One concern is the area of your facility having a policy directly addressing the issue of physician misconduct. I had a chance to review your impaired physician and sexual harassment protocols. The policies seemed to be in order. But they obviously lack any true power."

"I don't follow."

"Your policies do no good if they sit in the filing cabinet of some administrator. Why wasn't the issue of Dr. Jameson addressed according to your own government-sanctioned policies? Why did he get away with several obvious infractions over the years with little or no reprimand?" Terrance pulled out sheet after sheet of paper from his stack and one by one handed them to Mark. "I've interviewed several nurses here at your institution. Each one gave a statement that sounded awfully similar to another. Inappropriate speech, sexual references, crude remarks, unwanted physical contact; all statements that, according to the nurses, were filed with their supervisors. But I don't see any evidence that these complaints were followed up on. Where's the documentation of compliance with your own policies? The meetings that should have taken place between Dr. Jameson and the vice president of medical affairs, and the plans of action to remedy the situations? The follow-up to make sure the nurses in question weren't continuing to be subjected to the continual harassment of Dr. Jameson? Why didn't you follow your own policies? It seems that in addition to Dr. Jameson being at fault here, we're going to seek punitive damages against the hospital for failure to provide a safe working environment for my client. And of course, if there is evidence that your legal office tried to subvert some of these cases in the interests of the hospital, I'm sure the Illinois Bar Association would like to hear about it."

Mark leafed through the papers that Terrance had handed him. He glanced at the names on each of the statements and logged them away in his memory along with Terrance's idle threats. "Where did you get these statements?"

"I do my homework, Mark. I don't do yours."

"I don't seem to recall seeing any complaints against Dr. Jameson made by any of these people. And according to the dates on some of these statements, these nurses are discussing events that took place years ago."

"Are you saying that if something happened long ago it shouldn't matter?"

"Not at all." Mark straightened the stack of papers and handed them to Steve. "Go make copies of these, will you?" He turned to Terrance. "You don't mind if I keep a set of these, do you?"

"No, go ahead." He waved his hand in the air as if he couldn't care less what Mark did with the documents. "In fact, just keep those. I've got plenty of copies."

Mark filed the copies in his briefcase. "What I'm saying is that if these events truly occurred as long ago as they indicate, then we most certainly would have the original complaints on file. I agree with you, Terry, that if these nurses had in fact filed formal charges against Dr. Jameson and we didn't follow through on the complaints in accordance with our policies to such occurrences, then you would have an argument against the hospital for failure to comply with said regulations.

"If these reports are coming to light only now, however, in the background of a lawsuit against Dr. Jameson, then they can only be used to try to establish a pattern of conduct against the defendant. And I'm not saying that these statements do establish a pattern. But until we do verify that these are valid complaints and not just recent revelations, I'm not willing to add them to the mix of our current conversation."

Terry wiped the bead of sweat from under his nose. His play had been trumped. He had indeed spent the last three weeks seeking out and interviewing every nurse who had ever heard the name Jameson, looking for anyone who had listened to a dirty joke, had a hand pressed on a butt or back, heard a wolf whistle, or even saw him looking at her in the wrong way. He found a few and had helped develop small stories into potential dollar-winning arguments. But none of the nurses had ever bothered to actually submit a written complaint against the man. *Bitches*, he'd thought. *There goes money out the window.*

"Fine. You review your records, providing that they're accurate, and get back to me. But I do intend to call these women as witnesses during the trial."

"I thought we were here to try and avoid a trial, Terry."

"Yes, I'd like to avoid a long, drawn out and costly trial, but we'll just have to see how much headway we can make here this morning." Terrance pulled out his next stack of papers. He had a lot of items to go over, each with a dollar amount attached. But he wanted to see the reaction on Greg's face as he revealed them to find out their level of importance.

Terrance was taking Jameson's absence in a personal way. Anyone or anything that delayed him with his own schedule quickly became a personal enemy. He cleared his throat and looked at his watch again. "What's keeping that man?"

A knock on the door caused all the heads in the room to turn. Mark's secretary opened the door and stuck her head inside.

"Mr. Brannon, there's someone here for the meeting."

"About damn time," shouted Terrance. His prey had arrived. An hour of frustration had built up and was about to be heaped upon Greg Jameson's head.

"Send him in," Mark calmly replied. He, too, was looking forward to talking to Greg. Several days of unanswered e-mails and unreturned phone calls had left Mark wondering where his client had been.

The door opened wider. The men's eyes opened as they saw who had entered the room. It wasn't Greg Jameson. "Julie. What are you doing here?" asked Terrance as he saw his client.

"Ms. McMahon," said Mark, who rose to shake her hand. "It's a pleasure to see you. This is certainly an unexpected surprise."

"Thanks for seeing me, Mr. Brannon." She turned to Terrance who still had not risen from his seat. "Good morning, Terry. Are things going okay?"

Julie walked around the table to an unoccupied seat. Gone were the sweats and tank tops. An Anne Klein skirt and sports coat had taken their place and gave her a very professional look. Her head was held high. She had stamina and poise. She was there to do business. And everyone else there knew it.

"I hope you don't mind my intrusion at your meeting, but I thought it best that I hear exactly what kinds of deals are being made. I know how sometimes cases can drift away from their original intent."

"I've got things well in hand, Julie." Terrance motioned to rise briefly now that Julie was seated. "You don't need to be here. Things can get kind of heated. I'll fill you in later this afternoon."

"I like heat, Terry." Julie leaned forward and rested her arms on the table. "Heat has the tendency to burn away the impurities." She had grown tired of listening to Terry and Ryan decide the fate of her case. That was about to end. Greg Jameson, pig that he was, wasn't her enemy anymore. And she was here to make that switch. "So tell me, Mr. Brannon. What sorts of things has Mr. Niemann been saying I wanted?"

Terry tried to interrupt. "We really haven't settled on any of the details, Julie. We've only just begun some of the preliminary discussions. It's sort of difficult without the defendant being present."

"I didn't ask you, Terry. I asked Mr. Brannon." Julie turned to the man who represented her hospital. It was the hospital that had been her home since she had graduated from nursing school. She had missed this place since she went on her leave of absence.

"In fact, Julie, we have only begun some of the early discussions. Settlement amounts, terms of Dr. Jameson's reeducation and or punitive actions, and your employment situation are still up in the air."

"Good. Then it's not too late for me to make my own suggestions, is it, gentlemen?" Mark and Terry both shook their heads. "Mr. Brannon," she began. "Do you know Dr. Jameson? I mean, really know him?"

Mark nodded. "A little. Mostly from what I've heard around the hospital."

"You?" she looked at Terry, Steve, and Peter.

No one added to the conversation.

"Well, I do. I can say I know him pretty well. Probably better than anyone in this room. And I can tell you that he is a chauvinist."

Terrance sat up straighter to listen to his client chew out the opponents.

"A chauvinist. A frat boy. A spoiled child. All of the above. But that's not all. He's also a gifted surgeon. He's probably the best surgeon I've ever worked with. And I've seen quite a few come through this place. If push came to shove, he's probably the only one I'd let operate on me. But there's one more thing that he is. He's honest about who he is. You ask him for what he thinks, and he'll tell you. He'll tell you that he's crude. That he tells dirty jokes and flirts with all the new nurses as well as the old ones. He listens to rock music in the O.R. because he likes it. I've heard him tell off the nuns in a way that we all would like to."

Mark nodded in agreement with that last statement.

"He's a hot shot, but he's up front about it." She turned to Terry as if her next words were chosen specifically for his ears. "He's honest about who he is. He doesn't tell you one thing while he's off doing something else." She knew all about Terry and Ryan's arrangement. Her last desire was to see that it came into being. "And I have to tell you that I kind of admire that in a man. There are enough phony people in the world. I don't think we should try to squash the few honest ones that remain."

Mark saw his options being thrown wide open. And he wasn't about to let them slip away. "What exactly are you trying to say? Do you want to drop the case?"

"Not exactly."

Mark took a deep breath. He had been holding it since Julie had begun her short speech.

"I think what we need to do is handle this in a way that sees to it that all the parties get exactly what they deserve. I think the hospital definitely benefits from having Dr. Jameson working here. I know the patients benefit from his skills. Most of the nurses have learned to put up with him, except for a few. What I want is to make sure that he stops doing his little boy act around those of us who find it offensive. Some of the younger people may not be able to stand up to him or tell him to shove his head where his mind is. Earlier you mentioned some sort of sensitivity training sessions."

Mark acknowledged her. "Yes. I believe that was in one of our original offers."

"How about extending that session for all the physicians?"

"The entire hospital staff?"

"Yes. I know that Dr. Jameson isn't the only man here who misbehaves from time to time. Let's say I want to make this place better for all of my nurses."

"No harm in that. Might be a good idea," agreed Mark.

"And perhaps once he completes the program, you could get Dr. Jameson to lead the class each year to all the new incoming physicians as part of their orientation program."

Mark nodded. Both of those demands would cost only pennies for the hospital.

"Just think about it. In a couple of years Dr. Jameson will be known as the most ethical physician on staff and the resource person for discrepancies between nurses and physicians."

The irony made Mark chuckle. "I like it. Very fitting. I'm sure the sisters would go for it."

"Good. Then that's item number one."

"What's two?" asked Mark, who was still jotting down notes from Julie's statement.

"My job here. I miss it. I want to come back, but not on its current terms."

"Fire away."

"I want to return with all of my vacation days intact. I want a five percent raise that is not considered to be part of any settlement cost. And I want a new nurses' lounge to be made that is of equal standing to the one the hospital built for the surgeons, down to the last television, refrigerator, and doughnut."

Mark knew the rough costs for remodeling. Costs that could easily be built into the next year's budget. "Sounds like you're doing some good things here."

"Finally, let's address the price of my pain and suffering."

Terry heard his language being spoken. "We were just coming to that when you came in, Julie."

"I'm talking about *my* pain and suffering, not yours and Ryan's."

"Who's Ryan?" asked Mark. "You don't have a partner on this case, do you?"

"One might say that he does, Mr. Brannon," said Julie. "And that's mostly what brought me here today. You see, Mr. Niemann and Ryan Webber were helping me with this case. Or I should say, running things. They'd tell me how I didn't understand legal terms or how to negotiate very well."

"I think you're doing just fine today," argued Mark.

"Thank you." She smiled like any true lady who had received a genuine compliment. "But what I later found out was that Mr. Niemann had different ideas about what this case was truly about. While I was trying to make this a better place for us women to work, Mr. Niemann and Dr. Webber were working on contracts for legal representation with Rockford General and tenure positions with the University of Illinois."

Mark looked at Terry who had pulled himself back from the table and crossed his arms over his chest. Mark was aware of lawyers who had turned cases around for their own benefit and the consequences of such action.

"As it seemed that they were straying from the original design of this case, I felt it was my constitutional duty to come here today and straighten everything out. So I am happy to say that I have no intention of letting either of those deals that they made come to fruition. I want to settle things today with you, gentlemen. And doing so ensures me that neither Terry nor Ryan will get what they want, though they may just get what's coming to them. And knowing that is more than ample compensation for my pain and suffering."

Mark never took his eyes off of Terry. "You manipulated a case for personal gain?"

"These are allegations. The woman feels jilted by a lover." A nervous Terrance pointed at Julie like she was on the witness stand. He saw his case falling apart. He saw his settlement reward dwindling to nothing. He saw a career-interrupting allegation being thrown at him. "I have no idea what she's talking about. I've worked very hard for her to represent her best wishes all through this case."

"I'm sure that you think you have, Terry," said Julie. "That's what's saddest about all of this."

"And don't think you can get away with settling for no monetary amount on this matter, missy. We have a contract that entitles me to 40 percent of any settled amounts. If there is no settled amount, I get to charge you for my hourly work. And right now that's a hefty number."

"You want a monetary settlement, Terry?" she asked.

"Damn straight I do."

"Fine." Julie turned her attention to Mark. "Mr. Brannon. In addition to the above listed items, I would like to receive from St. John's Hospital a financial award in the amount of one dollar."

Mark and Terry both dropped their jaws.

"One dollar? That's all you want?" asked Mark. He knew that if she made an official offer and he accepted, it was an oral contract that was legally binding.

"That's it. One dollar." Julie turned toward her counsel. "I believe you said you get 40 percent of my settlement in lieu of an hourly rate. Is that correct, Mr. Niemann?"

Terry nodded. He had been had.

Julie reached into her purse, pulled out two quarters, and tossed them across the table at Terry. "Here's fifty cents. You can keep the change."

The tinkling of the coins was the only sound coming from Terry's side of the table.

"Now, gentlemen," Julie said as she stood up from her seat. "If you'd be so kind as to write all of this up and have it ready for me to sign, I'll take care of that on Monday morning when I come back to work."

"It'll be on my desk by seven o'clock in the morning," said the joyful Mark.

"That'll be fine." She walked toward the door. "Now if you'll excuse me, it's a lovely day outside and I intend to enjoy it. Have a lovely weekend. Gentlemen. And Terry."

And with that, Julie left the room, leaving only a lingering hint of her perfume and devastation for Terry.

"That went well, don't you think?" Mark said, biting his cheek to keep from laughing.

"Shut up, Brannon. This isn't over yet."

"I should say not." Mark reached across the table and picked up Terry's cassette recorder. "It seems that I have in my possession a record of allegation of misconduct." He popped the cassette from the recorder and put the small plastic gold mine of evidence into his own briefcase. "Manipulating clients. Collusion. Breaching of attorney-client confidentiality. These are serious things, Terry."

"Give me that. That's mine."

"I don't think so. But I tell you what I will do. I think I'll go along with you and your earlier request. Perhaps it is time that we bring this matter before the state bar association."

31

Will held his breath and dove his head under the water. The submersion momentarily muffled the screams of the crowd. He flipped his feet over his head and planted them squarely on the far wall of the pool. Twenty-five meters down, twenty-five to go.

He pushed off the wall with all his might. His arms were sore from pulling his body through the water of his first lap. His legs were quivering from all the kicking. But he had to continue. His team was counting on him. He needed to finish for his own sake. And for once, his dad was watching.

Will kicked his legs until his head broke through the surface of the water. The cries from the crowd returned, along with the whistles, shouts, and the blowing of horns. Will started to pull arm over arm in a rhythmic motion. Will had dropped into fourth place by the midway point, and so he pulled. His arms ached each time he lifted them out of the water. He stretched them over his head as far as he could reach before plunging his hands back into the water. Time and time again. Until his lungs and his shoulders felt like they were on fire.

Finally, the flags appeared overhead signaling Will's final five meters. Three more strokes. He could do it, he told himself. He pulled using all the crowd noise as a personal cheering section. One final thrust was given as Will threw his head back and reached for the wall ending his ordeal. Will sank into the water as he saw Howard's legs sail overhead. The exchange had been made. Will was done. The cheers from the crowd were now meant for others' ears.

Will pulled off his goggles and hung onto the side of the pool. He was too exhausted to climb out. Don reached his hand down into the water and helped pull Will to the surface.

"Fantastic job, little man." Don rubbed Will's back and hugged his young swimmer. "I knew you could do it. You were third to finish. The rest of the team can make up that distance."

Will just nodded, wiping the water from his face. He turned back to the crowd. There was one face he had to find, but the sea of spectators made that difficult. People were standing and jumping, shouting and waving. Will began to wander away from the starting blocks.

Howard touched the wall sending Evan into the water for his fifty of butterfly. Don was shouting for his team while Will's eyes were searching for the brown suit that was nowhere to be seen.

Will was breathing easier now, but Will's heart was starting to pound. He saw his mother standing next to Michael. They were waving to Will, but they were alone. But before he knew what was happening, Will felt himself being picked up. "Dad!"

"Hey, you're quite a swimmer," Greg said, wrapping his son in his arms. "Are you hiding an outboard motor in your suit?"

"You came. You came to watch me swim."

"I wouldn't miss it. I hear this is the biggest swim meet of the year."

"But what about your meeting?"

"It's just going to have to start without me."

Will threw his arms around his father's neck. "Did you see me? Did you see me swim?"

"Every stroke. I tried to find you after you climbed out of the pool."

"I was looking for you."

"And I was looking for you."

"Guess we found each other."

Greg smiled and rubbed his son's head. "I guess we did."

The crowd erupted as Blake touched the wall one stroke ahead of the boy in the next lane.

"Looks like you won," Greg said. "You'll get a medal."

"I already won what I wanted to have," said Will as he buried his face on his father's shoulder.

Greg felt his son's wet swimsuit begin to soak through his own suit. But he didn't care. He wasn't concerned about how he'd look. Or what the people at the hospital would think about him being there. Or that his business suit stood out in a sea of T-shirts. He was making his son happy. Not because he made a lot of money or had a big house, but in a way that mattered to his son. He was there.

"I'm sorry. I'm getting your clothes wet." Will pulled himself away from his dad.

"That's okay. It's wool. Sheep are used to getting rained on." Greg put Will back onto the concrete deck as Linda and Michael approached.

"You did just great, sweetheart." Linda bent over and kissed her son on the top of his head. "I'm so proud of you." She looked up at Greg. "Of you both." Greg knew the words were directed at him. He had finally taken a step to put his children and his family first. "I thought you weren't coming." she said.

"So did I." Greg looked into Linda's eyes. Two nights ago she had seen him at his weakest. Now, they had a chance to build something together.

"So what happened?"

"I got to the hospital parking lot and just sat there in my car. I watched as dozens of people got out of their cars and walked into a building. And I thought about how many of them had families, who at that point were without that person who donned a white coat and headed off to take care of strangers. Then I thought about our two kids and how much they needed me. Not because I was someone who could removed their appendix or fix a laceration, but because I was their dad. I realized that I needed to be here. So I started my car and drove straight here." Greg patted Will on the back. "And just in time it seems. I would have hated to miss that race."

"So you missed your meeting? What'll happen to you?"

"I don't have the faintest idea," Greg said, smiling. "If they were going to nail me, they were going to do it whether I was there or not. I figure I'll find out on Monday when I show up."

Will had had enough of grown-up conversation. "Come on, you guys, I don't want to hang around here and talk. Let's go back to the tent." He began to pull on his father and mother's hands.

"Yeah, show me where you hang out with all of your friends."

"I want you to come with too," Will said to Michael, who had been keeping a safe distance from Greg and Linda's conversation.

"Are you sure?"

Greg looked at Michael for a brief moment before motioning with his head that Michael could tag along if he was so inclined.

The four headed off across the compound to the Dolphin's tent. Will showed his proud father around the tent. "This is Blake and this is Howard. That's Andy over there." Greg was eating it up.

Michael backed away from the group, as he felt a little out of place. Will was Greg's son, and Michael was back to having the role of physician. He didn't belong, and now that Will was done swimming he wondered if he should just leave.

"Okay, Will," Linda said. "Get your relay team together. I want to get a picture of you."

"Okay, come on, guys." Will grabbed his friends and headed out of the tent.

Michael saw his old best friend standing alone. He had seen so much of Greg in Will, much more than Michael was willing to admit. Facing death, Will had shown the same strength that Greg used to have. Michael reluctantly approached Greg. It was time. "So, you blew off your meeting this morning with your legal team? That doesn't sound like you."

Greg shrugged. "Maybe I'm not who you thought I was."

Michael nodded. "Fair enough."

Greg stared off toward the swimmers, unable to look Michael in the eye as he spoke. "I'm not the same guy you used to room with. Sometimes people aren't what they seem on the surface. You shouldn't be so quick to judge someone without finding out who he really is."

"I can't argue with that."

"Didn't think you could," said Greg. "I heard it from someone who is pretty knowledgeable on things like that. Someone who seems to know what he's talking about."

"Who's that? Your shrink?" asked Michael.

"No. You." The two stood in silence, both aware this was a turning point yet neither knowing quite what to say. Greg shuffled uncomfortably as he struggled to find the right words. "I want to thank you, Mike," he said at last, "for what you did for my son."

"All part of my job."

"I'm not talking about treating his cancer, although I am very grateful for that."

"What then?"

"All those days while he was in the hospital," Greg went on. "All those times when I never seemed to be around. Well, I was."

Michael seemed confused. "You were…where?"

"I was there. Mostly, it was when you were there too. I hated that you were Will's doctor and that his life was in your hands." Greg sighed. "Not that I ever did much for the boy, but to have you in control was a nightmare for me."

"Your show of appreciation could use a little work," Michael joked.

"Let me finish, Mike. I'm serious." Greg focused his gaze on his sons as he spoke to Michael. "I would come by to keep an eye on you. To see what you were telling my son. I listened in on your conversations from time to time. By the way, you should probably get that intercom system fixed or you'll have all sorts of breaches of confidentiality."

"You listened in on us?"

"I didn't say I was proud of it. Just that I did it. I've done a lot of things in my life that I'm not very proud of. You of all people should know that. But you certainly didn't give me what I was expecting to hear. I never once heard you bad-mouth me. Not once. And you, of all people, certainly have a good reason to do that."

"Bad-mouthing isn't my style."

"I'm finding that out. But it wasn't just what I didn't hear that impressed me; it was what you did say to him. The stories you told. The things you showed him. The magic tricks." Greg took a deep breath as he struggled to keep his voice from quavering. "You were like a father to him. You taught him lessons he should have learned from me, if I hadn't been so self-involved." He smiled as he watched his two sons. "It's amazing—the treasures that are right under my nose if I just take the time to see them." Greg extended his hand to his old friend. "It's funny how much you may find out about yourself in the least likely of places."

Michael grinned as he warmly accepted Greg's outstretched hand.

"I'm sorry, Mike," Greg said, "about what I did to you and Lori back in the old days. I was pretty smashed that night—"

"You don't have to do this, Greg."

"Yes, I do. I've been carrying this around long enough."

Michael had wanted to hear an apology for a long time, but seeing Greg so downcast at that moment seemed to make an admission of guilt unnecessary.

"I could easily blame the beer for my making a move on Lori. Let's face it, she's quite a looker."

"For a man, you mean?"

"I guess I just freaked out," Greg admitted. "It was quite a shock finding that out."

"I guess I understand that," Michael admitted. "But why did it bother you so much?"

"It was the fact that I made a move on her. It made me feel like I was gay or something. I didn't know what else to do, so I just attacked her."

"Does it still make you 'freak out'?"

"No. Lori's always been so adult about it all. I've been the jackass, time and time again, but she's been very proper." Greg exhaled loudly, as if admitting his faults left him short of breath. "I thought I was such hot stuff," he said, "but lately I've been shown that I'm not." He smiled at Michael. "I enjoyed the stories you told Will about your old friend Bill. It opened up my eyes."

"How so?"

"Oh, lots of ways. I realized how blind I've been to my own faults while being a critic of others' imperfections."

"You're a doctor, Greg. You should know that flesh is imperfect."

"I know. I see enough of the bodies that are broken down. How often the flesh fails."

"It's just a covering, Greg. Male or female, shapely or not. What matters is what's underneath."

"You'd have thought I'd have realized that before now."

"You always did pick up things a little slower in school than I did."

This time Michael offered his hand and they shook hands once more. The years of hostility had come to an end. They were ready to move forward, and both were relieved.

"So," Michael began, "do you think you'll have a job come Monday morning?"

Greg shrugged. "Don't know. But if I don't that wouldn't necessarily be a bad thing. I could use some time off to get to know those kids again." Greg pointed to his sons who had finished their photo session and had now returned to the tent. Will sat on his sleeping bag and pulled out a deck of cards. Paul joined him. The two doctors walked toward the tent.

"Hey, I'm sorry to hear your mom was injured," Greg said sincerely. "Anything serious?"

"Broken hip."

"Too bad."

"She's tough. She'll get well, if only so she can torment me again."

Chapter Thirty-One

Greg laughed. "So what nursing home did you choose for her?"

Michael paused for a moment. "I didn't." And in that instant, his decision was crystal clear. "I'm taking her home to live with us."

Greg looked surprised. "What does Lori have to say about that?"

"Actually," Michael said, smiling at the memory, "it was her idea."

"Man, I don't think I could have my mother-in-law living with me. That'd be too difficult of a house."

"That's what I thought at first, but Lori said it'd be good for me. And you know what? She's right. I do need to get to know my mom better."

"That Lori, she's quite a lady, Mike."

Michael nodded in agreement at the words he had so longed to hear. "She certainly is."

The two turned their attention to Will, who now had a small gathering of children seated around him. Will handed the deck of cards he had been using to Paul and began to instruct him.

"Let's see if you've learned anything of what I've shown you," he said to his younger brother.

Paul tried to hold the cards in his small hands, and Will gently helped his brother hold the deck of cards and start to shuffle.

Michael and Greg stood silently as the scene played out in front of them. Their Will was once again enjoying being a boy. The tent filled with laughter and applause. It was a good day. A time to laugh. A time to share. A time to pass something along.

Acknowledgments

No novel can be written in a vacuum. This novel is no exception. So many people, whom I feel deserve special recognition, were involved in this production.

I am forever in debt to my parents, Kenneth and Sharon Schuh, who instilled in me at a young age the importance of reading. They took me to the library several times a week as a child, and they served as fine examples of people who lived a well-read life.

I'd like to thank my kindergarten teacher, Mrs. Walkington, who told me that I had a good imagination.

My editor and friend, Marna Poole, worked tirelessly to shape my words and characters into the fine story that is now in your hands. It isn't easy to put up with the ego of an author, but Marna put the story first. The polishing of this story is greatly due to her, and I thank her very much.

I would like to thank C. Lee Nunn and all the fine individuals at American Book Publishing for believing in my work and taking me on as a client.

I am forever grateful for the love and support I have received from my wife, Kim, and my children, Jonathon, Daniel, and Sarah. They stood behind me all through the writing of this novel and several more that will soon grace the shelves of bookstores. They are my inspiration and have put magic in my life.

Finally, I need to express my gratitude to God and my Lord, Jesus Christ. Not only has He given me life, now and eternally, but He also has given me a reason to be alive.

About the Author

William Schuh, M.D., is a practicing physician who also holds a Ph.D. in biochemistry and a master's degree in business administration. Additionally, he is a second-degree black belt in Tae Kwan Do. He has been writing since 1998, in between seeing patients.

Dr. Schuh lives in Illinois with his wife, Kim, and children, Jonathon, Daniel, and Sarah. For more information about him and his books, visit his Web site at www.parablesoftoday.com.